Praise for *The Taken Ones*

"Setting the standard for top-notch thrillers, *The Taken Ones* is smart, compelling, and filled with utterly real characters. Lourey brings her formidable storytelling talent to the game and, on top of that, wows us with a deft stylistic touch. This is a one-sitting read!"

—Jeffery Deaver, author of *The Bone Collector* and *The Watchmaker's Hand*

"*The Taken Ones* has Jess Lourey's trademark of suspense all the way. A damaged and brave heroine, an equally damaged evildoer, and missing girls from long ago all combine to keep the reader rushing through to the explosive ending."

—Charlaine Harris, *New York Times* bestselling author

"Lourey is at the top of her game with *The Taken Ones*. A master of building tension while maintaining a riveting pace, Lourey is a hell of a writer on all fronts, but her greatest talent may be her characters. Evangeline Reed, an agent with the Minnesota Bureau of Criminal Apprehension, is a woman with a devastating past and the haunting ability to know the darkest crimes happening around her. She is also exactly the kind of character I would happily follow through a dozen books or more. In awe of her bravery, I also identified with her pain and wanted desperately to protect her. Along with an incredible cast of support characters, *The Taken Ones* will break your heart wide open and stay with you long after you've turned the final page. This is a 2023 must read."

—Danielle Girard, *USA Today* and Amazon #1 bestselling author of *Up Close*

Praise for *The Quarry Girls*

"Few authors can blend the genuine fear generated by a sordid tale of true crime with evocative, three-dimensional characters and mesmerizing prose like Jess Lourey. Her fictional stories feel rooted in a world we all know but also fear. *The Quarry Girls* is a story of secrets gone to seed, and Lourey gives readers her best novel yet—which is quite the accomplishment. Calling it: *The Quarry Girls* will be one of the best books of the year."

—Alex Segura, acclaimed author of *Secret Identity*, *Star Wars Poe Dameron: Free Fall*, and *Miami Midnight*

"Jess Lourey once more taps deep into her Midwest roots and childhood fears with *The Quarry Girls*, an absorbing, true crime–informed thriller narrated in the compelling voice of young drummer Heather Cash as she and her bandmates navigate the treacherous and confusing ground between girlhood and womanhood one simmering and deadly summer. Lourey conveys the edgy, hungry restlessness of teen girls with a touch of Megan Abbott while steadily intensifying the claustrophobic atmosphere of a small 1977 Minnesota town where darkness snakes below the surface."

—Loreth Anne White, *Washington Post* and Amazon Charts bestselling author of *The Patient's Secret*

"Jess Lourey is a master of the coming-of-age thriller, and *The Quarry Girls* may be her best yet—as dark, twisty, and full of secrets as the tunnels that lurk beneath Pantown's deceptively idyllic streets."

—Chris Holm, Anthony Award–winning author of *The Killing Kind*

PRAISE FOR *BLOODLINE*

Winner of the 2022 Anthony Award for Best
Paperback Original

Winner of the 2022 ITW Thriller Award for Best
Paperback Original

Short-listed for the 2021 Goodreads Choice Awards

"Fans of *Rosemary's Baby* will relish this."

—*Publishers Weekly*

"Based on a true story, this is a sinister, suspenseful thriller full of
creeping horror."

—*Kirkus Reviews*

"Lourey ratchets up the fear in a novel that verges on horror."

—*Library Journal*

"In *Bloodline*, Jess Lourey blends elements of mystery, suspense, and
horror to stunning effect."

—*BOLO Books*

"Inspired by a true story, it's a creepy page-turner that has me eager to
read more of Ms. Lourey's works, especially if they're all as incisive as
this thought-provoking novel."

—Criminal Element

"*Bloodline* by Jess Lourey is a psychological thriller that grabbed me from the beginning and didn't let go."

—*Mystery & Suspense Magazine*

"*Bloodline* blends page-turning storytelling with clever homages to such horror classics as *Rosemary's Baby*, *The Stepford Wives*, and *Harvest Home*."

—*Toronto Star*

"*Bloodline* is a terrific, creepy thriller, and Jess Lourey clearly knows how to get under your skin."

—Bookreporter

"[A] tightly coiled domestic thriller that slowly but persuasively builds the suspense."

—*South Florida Sun Sentinel*

"I should know better than to pick up a new Jess Lourey book thinking I'll just peek at the first few pages and then get back to the book I was reading. Six hours later, it's three in the morning and I'm racing through the last few chapters, unable to sleep until I know how it all ends. Set in an idyllic small town rooted in family history and horrific secrets, *Bloodline* is *Pleasantville* meets *Rosemary's Baby*. A deeply unsettling, darkly unnerving, and utterly compelling novel, this book chilled me to the core, and I loved every bit of it."

—Jennifer Hillier, author of *Little Secrets* and the award-winning *Jar of Hearts*

"Jess Lourey writes small-town Minnesota like Stephen King writes small-town Maine. *Bloodline* is a tremendous book with a heart and a hacksaw . . . and I loved every second of it."

—Rachel Howzell Hall, author of the critically acclaimed novels *And Now She's Gone* and *They All Fall Down*

Praise For *Unspeakable Things*

Winner of the 2021 Anthony Award for Best
Paperback Original

Short-listed for the 2021 Edgar Awards and 2020
Goodreads Choice Awards

"The suspense never wavers in this page-turner."

—*Publishers Weekly*

"The atmospheric suspense novel is haunting because it's narrated from the point of view of a thirteen-year-old, an age that should be more innocent but often isn't. Even more chilling, it's based on real-life incidents. Lourey may be known for comic capers (*March of Crimes*), but this tense novel combines the best of a coming-of-age story with suspense and an unforgettable young narrator."

—*Library Journal* (starred review)

"Part suspense, part coming-of-age, Jess Lourey's *Unspeakable Things* is a story of creeping dread, about childhood when you know the monster under your bed is real. A novel that clings to you long after the last page."

—Lori Rader-Day, Edgar Award–nominated author of
Under a Dark Sky

"A noose of a novel that tightens by inches. The squirming tension comes from every direction—including the ones that are supposed to be safe. I felt complicit as I read, as if at any moment I stopped I would be abandoning Cassie, alone, in the dark, straining to listen and fearing to hear."

—Marcus Sakey, bestselling author of *Brilliance*

Praise for
The Catalain Book of Secrets

"Life-affirming, thought-provoking, heartwarming, it's one of those books which—if you happen to read it exactly when you need to—will heal your wounds as you turn the pages."
—Catriona McPherson, Agatha, Anthony, Macavity, and Bruce Alexander Award–winning author

"Prolific mystery writer Lourey tells of a matriarchal clan of witches joining forces against age-old evil . . . The novel is tightly plotted, and Lourey shines when depicting relationships—romantic ones as well as tangled links between Catalains . . . Lourey emphasizes the ties that bind in spite of secrets and resentment."
—*Kirkus Reviews*

"Lourey expertly concocts a Gothic fusion of long-held secrets, melancholy, and resolve . . . Exquisitely written in naturally flowing, expressive language, the book delves into the special relationships between sisters, and mothers and daughters."
—*Publishers Weekly*

Praise for *Salem's Cipher*

"A fast-paced, sometimes brutal thriller reminiscent of Dan Brown's *The Da Vinci Code*."
—*Booklist* (starred review)

"A hair-raising thrill ride."
—*Library Journal* (starred review)

"The fascinating historical information combined with a story line ripped from the headlines will hook conspiracy theorists and action addicts alike."

—Kirkus Reviews

"Fans of *The Da Vinci Code* are going to love this book . . . One of my favorite reads of 2016."

—Crimespree Magazine

"This suspenseful tale has something for absolutely everyone to enjoy."

—Suspense Magazine

PRAISE FOR *MERCY'S CHASE*

"An immersive voice, an intriguing story, a wonderful character—highly recommended!"

—Lee Child, #1 *New York Times* bestselling author

"Both a sweeping adventure and race-against-time thriller, *Mercy's Chase* is fascinating, fierce, and brimming with heart—just like its heroine, Salem Wiley."

—Meg Gardiner, author of *Into the Black Nowhere*

"Action-packed, great writing taut with suspense, an appealing main character to root for—who could ask for anything more?"

—Buried Under Books

PRAISE FOR *MAY DAY*

"Jess Lourey writes about a small-town assistant librarian, but this is no genteel traditional mystery. Mira James likes guys in a big way, likes booze, and isn't afraid of motorcycles. She flees a dead-end job and a dead-end boyfriend in Minneapolis and ends up in Battle Lake, a little town with plenty of dirty secrets. The first-person narrative in *May Day* is fresh, the characters quirky. Minnesota has many fine crime writers, and Jess Lourey has just entered their ranks!"

—Ellen Hart, award-winning author of the Jane Lawless and Sophie Greenway series

"This trade paperback packed a punch . . . I loved it from the get-go!"

—*Tulsa World*

"What a romp this is! I found myself laughing out loud."

—*Crimespree Magazine*

"Mira digs up a closetful of dirty secrets, including sex parties, cross-dressing, and blackmail, on her way to exposing the killer. Lourey's debut has a likable heroine and surfeit of sass."

—*Kirkus Reviews*

PRAISE FOR *REWRITE YOUR LIFE: DISCOVER YOUR TRUTH THROUGH THE HEALING POWER OF FICTION*

"Interweaving practical advice with stories and insights garnered in her own writing journey, Jessica Lourey offers a step-by-step guide for writers struggling to create fiction from their life experiences. But this book isn't just about writing. It's also about the power of stories to transform those who write them. I know of no other guide that delivers on its promise with such honesty, simplicity, and beauty."
—William Kent Krueger, *New York Times* bestselling author of the Cork O'Connor series and *Ordinary Grace*

THE
TAKEN
ONES

NONFICTION

THE
TAKEN
ONES

A STEINBECK AND REED THRILLER

JESS LOUREY

THOMAS & MERCER

Published by Thomas & Mercer, Seattle

www.apub.com

Amazon, the Amazon logo, and Thomas & Mercer are trademarks of Amazon.com, Inc., or its affiliates.

ISBN-13: 9781662507618 (paperback)
ISBN-13: 9781662507601 (digital)

Cover design by Caroline Teagle Johnson
Cover image: © Nana Kakraba / Shutterstock; © DEEPOL by plainpicture / Dirk Wüstenhagen / plainpicture

Printed in the United States of America

This book is dedicated to the brilliant, warm, and funny Jessica Tribble Wells, who said, "Hey, want to write a short story?" and thus invited Van and Harry into the world.

PROLOGUE

July 1980
Leech Lake, Minnesota

The sun smiled violently overhead, causing the tar beneath Rue's blue-striped Adidas to glisten and pulse. She swiped at the sweat dripping down her cheek and wondered how much longer until they reached the icy coolness of the creek.

Amber, seemingly unaffected by the heat, began skipping.

"One, two, hop to my Lou," she sang, tossing her butterscotch curls. She wore a bubble gum–pink gingham summer set that Rue thought was the prettiest outfit she'd ever seen. "Three, four, bonked into a door!"

All three girls busted into giggles.

Those weren't the real words, but they were close enough. Or maybe they were *better* than the real words. Mr. Ellingson, Amber and Rue's third-grade gym teacher, had made them square-dance to the song the last day of school. They'd been making fun of it ever since. Lily didn't know exactly what the two older girls were talking about, but she liked being included.

"Can I eat my sandwich now?" she asked, when the laughter settled into purrs.

Rue sneaked a glance at Amber to see if Lily's question bugged her. Rue hadn't wanted to invite her baby sister, but her mom had insisted.

Said she needed some rest, and wouldn't Rue be a dear and look after Lily for a few hours? Their mom had been tired a bunch since their dad ran out. She said she was still getting the best part of him—a check every other week—but the raw purple around her eyes told a different story.

So Rue had said *okay*, said it in a put-upon way so her mom knew what it cost her to drag a five-year-old on an adventure with Amber Marie Kind, the prettiest and most popular girl in third-going-on-fourth grade. Then Rue set out Lily's favorite plum-colored romper and packed a double lunch so her mom wouldn't have to get out of bed. Two olive-loaf sandwiches on white bread (mustard and lettuce on hers, Miracle Whip on Lily's), two snack-size bags of Fritos, a can of Hi-C Fruit Punch for each of them, and two red apples in case her mom asked to look inside the paper sack.

Lily had been begging for her sandwich since they'd left, asking for it nearly every minute she wasn't scratching around the bright-yellow Band-Aid on her knee. The bandage covered two mosquito bites, side by side and swollen with itch juice. Rue didn't think it would stay on in the water, but you never knew. She still couldn't believe she was finally getting to swim in Ghost Creek, and with *Amber*.

Amber's parents were the richest folks in Leech Lake, her dad a heart surgeon up the road in Minneapolis and her mom a real estate agent right in town. Despite their wealth, Rue's mom marveled, the Dr. and Mrs. Kind were *so down to earth*.

Just like regular folks.

Her mom had said that at the beginning of the summer, after Mrs. Kind dropped off Amber for their first hang-out. Rue had no idea what godly miracle had compelled Amber, with her milky skin and golden curls, to want to spend time with her, but she hoped it lasted until school started back up so the other kids could see. Even if it didn't, even if it was only a summer friendship, Rue would still have the necklace Amber had surprised her with. She touched the metal, warm against her skin. The front was half a red enameled heart, two glass chips that glittered like diamonds embedded in its plumpest corner. On the back, "Best" was engraved below Rue's initials. Amber's half was identical, except hers said "friend" and beneath, "AK."

"You can't have your sandwich now, but you may eat your apple," Rue said primly.

When Lily held out her hand, Rue reached into the paper sack she'd been carrying, its top wrinkled and dark from her sweat. The inside smelled like hot lettuce.

I bet Amber's Strawberry Shortcake lunch box doesn't stink.

I bet there's even a thermos inside to keep her drink cool.

Amber's wooden Dr. Scholl's sandals slapping against the sticky pavement provided the beat to those thoughts.

Click clap. Click clap.

Rue located the apple and handed it to her sister. Lily accepted the warm fruit, but she screwed up her nose before taking a bite, swiping the back of her hand across her mouth as she chewed. Her ruby Ring Pop sparkled in the sun before it snagged her hair, a hunk of which had escaped from her pigtails even though Rue had twisted in the marble hair bands herself.

Rue untangled the ring as they walked, sneaking a glance at Amber to make sure she didn't notice. Lily got on Rue's nerves sometimes, but she wasn't bad for a kindergartner, and anyhow, like their mom kept saying, it was the three of them against the world now.

"How much longer?" Lily asked, squirming under her sister's attention.

"We're almost there," Rue said. She let her sister go and tugged at the edge of her creeping swimsuit bottoms. They were giving her a wedgie beneath her shorts. Lily'd asked whether they should wear their swimsuits or pack them in another bag. Rue had said wear them. She hoped she'd guessed right. "It's through those trees, I think."

"Yep," Amber confirmed, nodding happily, still skipping.

Click clap. Click clap.

The creek—or "crick" as Amber called it, before giggling—was on Amber's end of winding Elm Street. Rue, Lily, and their mom lived on the whole other end. This side felt like a different planet, the houses huge and clean looking, the lawns golf-course-neat. Rue and Lily's section wasn't bad, but the houses didn't look new down there, only big. Rue's grandpa had built theirs, and he'd left it to her mom in his will. There hadn't been any money to go along with it, but staying in the fat ol' house and paying upkeep was *the same price as renting a shitty little apartment in town.*

At least that's what Rue's mom said.

"The swimming hole is through there." Amber pointed ahead as she led them off the swampy tar and into the ditch that marked the very end of Elm Street. Or the beginning. Rue supposed it depended where you stood.

The three of them stepped into the dusty grass, took a few strides forward, and without uttering a word, came to a dead stop at the forest edge. The dark-green leaves of the canopy tangled with each other, promising cool shade, and Rue thought she heard the music of water ahead. Still, something pushed back at her.

Despite melting in the heat, she didn't want to enter those gloomy woods.

She swiveled. Behind them was a scene so perfect it looked plucked out of a movie: one huge, glamorous house after another; a few shiny vehicles parked in driveways, all of them free of dents and rust; a line of new brown telephone poles like a row of guards with wires looped between them, getting smaller and smaller in the distance until Rue thought she could pinch their tops with her fingers.

Somewhere, a dog barked.

She turned back to face the forest's hungry mouth. A path curved through its center, narrow like a tongue. The three of them were teetering on a sharp edge, the world overbright and familiar behind, an unknown fairy tale ahead. Rue shivered despite the heat, thinking about the stories of the Bendy Man twisting and humping his way through those woods, stories her mom said were silly but felt really, really *real* as she stood here, on the lip of the forest.

Amber must have felt it, too, because she hadn't moved from the ditch, either, just stood there staring into the thick forest. The path was enticing them to step out of the blazing sun and into the coolness; still, Amber and Rue didn't budge. It was Lily who finally pulled them in, tossing her apple so she could grab each of their hands.

"Last one to the creek is a rotten egg!"

Her excitement broke the spell. Amber and Rue smiled at each other over her head, and they crossed the forest boundary. The drop in temperature was delicious against Rue's bare skin, like they'd opened a giant fridge door. She had overheard kids, mostly boys, talking about the swimming hole at Ghost Creek, how there was an old tire swing hung over the widest spot, how you could do cannonballs so deep into the crystal water that you'd send the fish flying. But nobody had ever invited Rue before, and she wasn't exactly sure where the creek was.

Amber was, though.

At least she'd said she was, and she was marching forward like she knew just where they were headed.

It was difficult to walk three in a row down the hard-packed path, its narrowness forcing Rue to release Lily when the trees crowded too close. Rue would drop behind until the path widened, and then she'd hurry back alongside Lily and clutch her hand again, grateful she'd worn sneakers rather than sandals so the fallen branches didn't scrape at her feet's tender edges. It would have been easier for her to simply remain in the rear, trailing Amber and Lily, but she found she didn't want them out front alone. It had something to do with the temperature of the woods, she thought, such a troubling coolness after the burning sun.

Or maybe it was the absolute silence, like they'd stepped into an empty church rather than a living forest. Shouldn't they hear the happy yells of other kids playing in the creek? Kids like Jacob Peters? He'd asked her to square-dance on the last day of third grade. Everyone had made oohing sounds when he did, then kissy noises. She'd hated the teasing, but she'd liked do-si-doing with him. She thought she'd enjoy swimming with him, too, maybe demonstrating how good she was at jumping off a tire swing.

She was holding Lily's sweaty little hand and wishing her traffic-cone-orange one-piece wasn't stretched out and secondhand from Goodwill when yet another tree loomed in front of her, its trunk thick and rough. She'd almost barreled straight into it. She'd just released Lily to step behind her when she noticed Amber frozen like a statue, staring ahead, her skin gone the color of cottage cheese. Rue leaned over her sister to shake Amber, that's how terrible her expression was, but then she noticed Lily's face, too.

It had closed in on itself, tight as a puncture wound.

The enormous tree blocking Rue's view meant that she couldn't see what awful thing they were staring at, not without stepping around the trunk. She didn't want to look, but how could she not? How could she let them be paralyzed, wearing those awful, scared masks, and not see what they were seeing? What person could have?

So she leaned around the tree.

Distantly, she felt the warmth of pee trickling down her leg.

"I'll get another one prettier than you," Amber groaned, but it wasn't her voice.

Rue would later remember Amber saying that. She would remember thinking it was a real line from "Skip to My Lou," not one of their silly made-up ones.

And that was the last thing she would remember about that day.

CHAPTER 1

Present
Van

"They don't remember the past, you know."

I twitched, moving away from the industrial broom I'd been leaning on as I stared into the dog's pen. He was a huge, slobbery mutt, part Saint Bernard, part woolly mammoth. The laminated sign on his cage said his name was MacGuffin, that he was good with cats, and that he was being surrendered by a couple who was about to have a baby.

"When animals are adopted, they forget the *before*," the volunteer continued. I put her in her twenties, her grape-colored tracksuit expensive and immaculate, her face radiant with purpose. She was speaking in that "helpful" tone a certain kind of woman uses when talking to people she believes are beneath her. They never tried it on me when I had a gun and badge clipped to my belt, but given my height and schlubby clothes, my white-blonde hair twisted into a ponytail, I looked much younger—and softer—than I was.

She'd mistaken me for someone she could play with.

"I read it online," she said. "It can take dogs a while to forget, of course, but once they're adopted, thoughts of their old family are eventually erased. They learn to love whoever takes them home."

"*If* someone adopts them," I said, staring at the grizzled pooch.

The Minneapolis Animal Haven was a no-kill shelter, so MacGuffin would live here for as long as it took. It wouldn't be easy on him, though. He'd get food and water plus his pen cleaned once a day, and if there were enough of us volunteers, he'd get walked, but the cries of scared animals never ceased. The smell must be bad, too. It was rough on humans, and we could only detect the urine and feces. For a dog or cat, an animal that could discern the messages in those scents? It must be torture.

"Oh, he'll get adopted!" the woman said, pinning on her smile. Her professionally colored auburn hair was piled so thickly atop her head that it must have included extensions. Something like that would really mess up a crime scene. "Won't you, MacGuffin? Won't you get adopted?"

The enormous dog's tail gave a thump, and he blinked his rheumy eyes.

"It looks like he was just walked," she continued, tapping a fingernail on the placard. "Maybe you should pick a different dog."

"Maybe you should mind your own goddamned business," I said, keeping my tone light, as if I were offering her directions in an unfamiliar neighborhood. I'd reached the end of my short rope. The only thing worse than a stranger telling me what to do was discovering that I shared a life philosophy with someone wearing $200 yoga pants.

Forgetting is the best thing.

It was like she'd read my mind.

She sniffed and walked away, looking for someone else to quarterback. I watched her go. I'd signed up for a four-hour evening shift. How I spent that time was up to me. Some days I scooped turds in the cat room before dragging a string across the floor so the kittens could burn off their hunting energy. Other times, I replaced cedar-scented bedding in hamster, mouse, rabbit, and guinea pig cages. One afternoon I'd even exercised an albino hedgehog.

But most days?

Most days I played with the big dogs after making sure their cages were immaculate.

Growing up, I'd had my own pup—at least I'd thought of him as mine—at the Farm, a beagle-colored, mastiff-shaped beast I called Honeybear. When the feds marched us out, he was taken away in a caged truck, yowling for me. *So.* You didn't need a psychology degree to figure out why I gravitated toward the big dogs. I whispered to them as I cleaned. Cooed silly words of love. Promised that if they were mine, I'd never give them up just because things got hard.

"Come on, MacGuffin," I said, unhooking the leash from his pen. "Let's get you some fresh air."

He lumbered to his feet, shuffling toward me. He was eight years old, close to the end of the line for a big dog. He had the tail of a puppy, though.

"That's a good boy." I entered the cage, patting his head while I clipped the leash to his jangly blue collar. He probably wouldn't need the restraint, but it was protocol. "Want to go for a walk? Yeah? A walk?"

His tail speed doubled. If there'd been a vase within three feet, he'd have knocked it into next week.

"That's what I thought." I checked to make sure the dog brush was still tucked in my back jeans pocket. It'd be satisfying to comb that matted fur off him, to wipe the gunk from his eyes, to walk him around the exercise yard so he could work out the cricks and knots from his old joints.

We were finishing our second loop around the yard, the sun descending into a violet haze but the July air still humid and close, when my phone buzzed in my pocket. I tugged it out.

Kyle K, the screen said. My mentee. He was only five years younger than me and a few months behind my tenure at the Bureau of Criminal Apprehension, but the deputy superintendent had counted my time at the Minneapolis Police Department when assigning mentors. I hit the answer button as a siren grew close, red lights strobing the exercise field from the highway running parallel.

"What's the word?"

"Hey, Evangeline," Kyle said. He was using my full name, and his voice was higher than usual. Those were my first two warnings. "You up?"

"I'm talking to you, aren't I?" The cherries disappeared, the keening siren with them.

"I meant, did I wake you? I know you've been working overtime. Maybe you went to bed early tonight."

I sighed. Kyle was a good agent, green and a little too excitable, but time would cure both. "No, I'm at the animal shelter. What d'you need?"

He paused. His silence was my third warning, trailing like ghost fingers down my spine. MacGuffin whined and tugged at his leash, pulling toward the shelter door.

"There's a homicide on the north edge of the Warehouse District," Kyle said. "Minneapolis PD wants us to come take a look."

I massaged my neck. Out of all the BCA agents to be sent out, I'd bet good money they were hoping it wasn't me. And it shouldn't be, not unless the homicide was connected to a cold case or the BCA's Death Investigations team was overloaded. "It's an odd one?"

He made a sound like a cough. "You don't know the half of it."

In that moment, a cold sliver of memory broke through my defenses. Last evening's nightmare. A child's weeping coming from a basement. A woman in a crimson pantsuit descending, carrying a ring of keys, her face in shadows. She stops in front of a door. Inserts a key. When the door swings open, the weeping turns into terrified sobs.

Goose bumps exploded across my skin, the recollection hitting me like an ice truck.

"I can be there in twenty."

CHAPTER 2

Van

I made it in fifteen.

The address Kyle gave led to an undeveloped lot north of the Salvation Army where I sometimes shopped for clothes. The warehouse's top floor held a regular thrift shop, all used stuff, but the basement carried new-with-tags department store donations. I'd nabbed some steals, all in my signature black, and the parking was good.

The entire neighborhood—originally called the Warehouse District but rebranded to the North Loop—had been a Midwest commerce hub in the early 1900s. Wholesalers and warehousers set up shop where the railroad met the river, peddling the farm machinery that settlers needed to homestead. By the 1920s, the area expanded to selling and shipping everything from mouthwash to nuts. The North Loop had witnessed the birth of famous labels, including Creamette pasta and the Milky Way candy bar, before mutating from industrial to largely residential. Most of the old warehouses had been transformed into sleek, masculine housing. A handful of holdouts—the Salvation Army, for instance—squatted like skin tags among the high-end haunts.

I loved the ugly old holdouts.

The fancy developments dropped off abruptly as I neared the crime scene, giving way to an area that wasn't sure what it wanted to be. It held a mix of abandoned factories, a scattering of upscale apartments bleeding over from the North Loop, and scrubby lots. Three police cars and an ambulance clustered on the lip where city met wild. Minneapolis had a lot of blurry thresholds like that, stately brick mansions next to the overrun brambles of a native creek, a bike path that took you from a busy shopping district to lush emerald woods in under a minute, sparkling lakes in the shadows of skyscrapers. I'd lived here for half my life and still wasn't used to the disconnect. Made everything feel borrowed.

When I stepped out of my car, the summer night was like silk on my skin. Kyle stood on the edge of the police tape waiting for me, a good twenty feet from the responding officers and the ambulance, nervously shifting his weight from one foot to the other. The single flickering streetlight found his scalp below clipped-close hair. His white button-down shirt and dark-brown slacks were rumpled from a day of sitting, his gold-and-navy tie cinched so tight his skin mushroomed out above his collar. It was a terrible invention, the necktie. Provided nothing but discomfort for the wearer and a handy tool for the violent. I can't tell you the number of murder victims who were strangled with their own tie.

Reason 478 I was glad to be a woman.

I swallowed a gluey, salt-edged wad of emotion as I approached Kyle, a blend of dread and anticipation that I felt walking onto any new crime scene. The trio of Minneapolis PD standing near the ambulance were already tossing me suspicious glances and whispering among themselves. I tipped my head in their direction.

It was only going to get worse when they realized who I was.

"What do you know?" I asked Kyle when I reached his side.

"I'm glad you're here, that's what." He blinked rapidly, his chiseled face washed with relief. He'd been a patrolman in Plymouth, a calm northwestern suburb, before accepting a job at the BCA. This might have been his first homicide.

He was about to continue when I held up a hand. "I want to write this down." I tugged my notebook out of my back pocket but couldn't locate my favorite pen, the one that wrote like a dream. It must have fallen out at the shelter. I felt a pulse of guilt. It'd been a gift from Detective Bart Lively, my old partner at the MPD. I'd go back later to look for it.

"You have an extra pen?"

Kyle offered me a disposable ballpoint.

"Thanks," I said. One of these days, I'd teach him the pleasures of a good pen. "You were saying?"

He started up again. "A bum was—"

I cleared my throat.

"Sorry. A guy without a place to stay was walking down to the river, he said."

"For what?"

I studied the man Kyle was referring to. He was leaning against the ambulance's rear fender, his clothes too layered for the humid night. His hair was mostly tucked beneath a mud-colored cap, two or three locs peeking out, his cheeks sunken. He either didn't have teeth or had very few. A black backpack covered in buttons and patches lay nearby, likely his. I thought at first that his hands were dirty, but when he moved, the streetlight glinted off them, revealing they were red.

Fresh blood.

"Sex, drugs, or a place to sleep," Kyle said, shrugging. "Hey, why don't they clean him up?"

One EMT was talking to the officers, the other standing near the injured man, holding bandages but not touching him. I'd beaten the crime lab folks. "Our witness might have evidence on his hands."

Kyle grimaced. "Sucks to be that guy."

My eyes moved to the crime scene at the far edge of the cordoned-off lot, maybe fifty feet away. A single man in a charcoal suit stood next to a hole, his back to me. Even from behind, I recognized him. That awareness made my blood sting.

"Yeah," I said, drilling holes into the man's back. "So our witness was walking down to the Mississippi, and then what?"

"Said he heard someone crying."

The man in the charcoal suit turned. My stomach kicked even though I'd guessed right: Detective David Comstock. I became acutely aware of my appearance. I'd cleaned up as best I could on the race over, yanking off my crusty sweatshirt and replacing it with the clean black T-shirt and blazer I kept in my back seat. There'd been nothing to do about my ripped jeans and vintage Doc Martens, though, both of them coated in shelter filth.

"Man, woman, or child doing the crying?" I asked.

Kyle's brow furrowed. "The witness said he thought it was a little kid at first, and so he hollered for them. But he couldn't locate anyone. So he started a grid pattern—"

"Grid pattern?" My glance shot back to the thin man perched on the rear of the ambulance. His hand shook as he brought the water bottle to his mouth. He spilled more than he drank. Forensics better hurry. "Former law enforcement or former military?"

"Military," Kyle said, smiling. He wiped the expression off his face when he saw mine. "Sorry. Anyhow, he's walking the grid, thinking he must be hearing the crying coming from the woods over by the river. But he starts to realize that's not where it's coming from at all. It's coming from there."

He pointed at the hole in the center of the crime scene, the one Detective Comstock hovered over, dirt flung from it in every direction like a pack of dogs had tried digging up a dinosaur bone. I swallowed even though I knew what was coming.

Kyle continued. "That's when the bu—the guy without a place to stay—realized that some of the dirt in that spot was softer than the rest. He said he could smell it, a smell like worms. He didn't have any tools with him, he said, not even a knife."

I felt the shock of realization, my eyes widening.

"Yeah," Kyle said. "He started digging with his hands. You only have to look at them to see how hard he went at it. He said he didn't know whether to run off and find a phone or to keep drilling at that dirt, but he couldn't leave her, he said. Not once he realized it was a woman down there. Buried alive."

I felt myself go distant from the story. It was the only way to survive the job.

Kyle rubbed his hand across his face. It made a scratching sound against the stubble. "He said that at some point the lady understood he was there, too, and screamed even louder. But he was digging at the wrong end. He was tunneling toward her feet, and by the time he figured that out, she'd gone quiet."

Forgetting is the best thing.

"He said she was still warm when he found her," Kyle finished. "But it was too late. Too, too late."

I barely heard the last part. I was already under the police tape, donning latex gloves and disposable shoe covers as I strode toward the crime scene, careful to follow the print path from the ambulance to the hole.

CHAPTER 3

Van

When I worked homicide with Bart Lively at the Minneapolis Police Department, they called us the dream team. Our legendary clearance rate was attributed to Bart's methodical, almost obsessive investigative techniques and my solid-gold hunches. At least that's what they said to our face. Behind my back, they called me a witch. As soon as Bart was in the ground, the second his reputation was no longer shielding me, they started making my life miserable.

You'd think when you grew up that it wouldn't matter anymore, the bullying. The exclusion. But it did. Punched me right back to my childhood. There I was again, a knock-kneed girl sporting hand-sewn clothes and a church cult haircut. When I couldn't take the Homicide Department's harassment anymore, the heartaches it caused, I quit.

That'd been nearly two years ago. I'd had no plan, just an animal need to escape.

What happened next was some "leap and the net will appear" crap that you'd find loopily embroidered on a pillow in a store that sold overpriced candles and "it's wine o'clock somewhere" tumblers: a job in the Minnesota Bureau of Criminal Apprehension Cold Case Unit opened up.

I was hired to fill it.

I'd almost exclusively run analytics since, which was the BCA equivalent of a desk job: researching on phone and computer, corroborating, writing reports. Quite a change from homicide, and I didn't mind one bit.

After Bart died, I'd needed the recovery time.

But in an illustration of "you pay the devil now or later," my months spent in the chair meant tonight was my first time in the field for the BCA. What stupidly bad luck that the scene belonged to Detective Dave Comstock, the ringleader of the mob that had driven me out of the MPD. The idea of facing him soured my stomach, but I'd lick shit before I'd let him see it.

Unclipping my flashlight from my waistband, I scanned the area as I crunched gravel toward the crime scene. The ambulance must have driven right to the edge of the burial site before retreating to its current location. The tire tracks it'd left were thick, potentially erasing important trace evidence, but that couldn't have been helped. If there was any chance the victim was alive, the EMTs needed to use speed.

As I neared the site, I imagined I could smell the muddiness of the Mississippi, part funk and part fish, though the river was five or six blocks away. I flashed my light to the opposite side of the lot and noted that someone had also driven in from there in the past twenty-four hours, the last time it had rained. The killer? Nearer the hole, loose dirt—dusty surface gravel, finer sand, and then deep black earth—was piled in every direction, its layout frantic. The soil had covered up a lot, but it hadn't concealed everything. I made out what looked like one pair of male footprints plus a smaller set coming out from where the unidentified vehicle had stopped. A pile of sawed-off two-by-fours was tossed haphazardly between that vehicle's parking spot and the grave.

I felt the weight of Comstock's stare as I approached, but I hadn't yet given him the courtesy of eye contact. I knew what I'd see. Caucasian, early sixties. Sparse hair that always looked wet, a face defined by Richard Nixon jowls. A suit that would be shiny at the contact points but neat, covering a body that still held the shape of a younger man.

Comstock had buddied up to me when Bart was alive, would slap my back at the bar like I was one of the guys, even put my name in for a commendation once. He'd traveled up the ranks with Bart, and any partner of Bart's was going to be a friend of Dave Comstock's. But the second Bart keeled over from a heart attack while watching *Dateline* with an honest-to-God TV dinner perched on his lap, Comstock turned on me.

Him being the responding detective on this scene was going to make tonight about as interesting as a jagged fingernail to the eye. My only hope lay in the fact that, like Bart, Comstock had a reputation as being a stickler for procedure. He didn't need to like me to work with me. It was promising that he'd so far managed to keep the uniforms at the perimeter. This was the sort of crime scene that most cops would fight for a front-row peek at. Get you two, maybe three, free rounds at the bar, depending on how long you dragged out the story.

Overhead, a nearly full moon beat down, soaking everything in an eerie liquid glow. Careful to keep my feet inside Comstock's prints, I did a three-sixty, expanding my survey from the immediate crime scene to the surrounding area. To the east lay the last ten feet of the gravel lot, then a pitted blacktop road. Beyond the road was the beginning of woods thick with shushing leaves leading down to the Mississippi. West was the road we'd all driven in on, utility poles alongside it auguring the development inevitably leeching this way. Behind those, railroad tracks. To the north lay a row of abandoned lots and then at the very end, maybe half a mile up, jutted a dark office building.

Five feet to my right, going south, was the crime scene epicenter. The lot rolled out eighty feet beyond that, followed by another empty tract edged by two abandoned factories, a sliver of space dividing them. Their brick was gray and crumbling, their wide third-story windows cracked. I gave it a year, two tops, before both time-eaten buildings were converted to million-dollar lofts with the downtown Minneapolis skyline as their backdrop.

"Detective Comstock," I said, my eyes finally migrating to him.

18

He was staring into the hole. He grunted in my general direction.

I couldn't put it off any longer. I stepped forward and followed his gaze.

I stopped myself—just—from gasping.

Very often the dead look at peace, so serene you'd think they were sleeping. I had a colleague back at the MPD, a creeper named Derek who everyone gave a wide berth to. Derek collected original negatives of mobsters who'd been killed in gunfights. Said he loved how even a man who died violently could look peaceful at death.

Not this victim.

She looked like she'd gone shrieking.

She lay in a rough hole approximately four feet deep, dug just wide and long enough to hold her. I dropped to my haunches for a closer look. A strip of duct tape dangled alongside her mouth, covered in what appeared to be blood and mucus. The victim's eyes protruded half an inch outside of the sockets. Her hair was blonde or light brown streaked with gray, not the expensive-looking silver dye job that was all the rage but rather the natural hair color of a woman in her early fifties. She wore navy-blue slacks and a tangerine-colored sweatshirt with a yellow puff-paint sun on the front. Her arms were taped to her sides just above the elbows. Her knees were also trussed together.

The pungent smell of human waste was strong.

I stood and flashed my light back at the two sets of footprints to the east. "Yours?"

"What do you think?" Comstock asked, his voice sharp.

"I think you stuck to the EMT trail." It's what any homicide detective worth their salt would have done. I brought my beam to the woman's bound knees, then back again to the smaller set of footprints to the east. Either the victim hadn't been tied up until she was dropped into the hole—which seemed unlikely—or there'd been another woman or a child on the scene.

"Do you think she was alert when she was buried?" I asked.

Comstock's shoulder twitched. "Above my pay grade. He sure as hell planned for her to wake up if she wasn't already, though."

He pointed his flashlight at the pile of boards near the grave, then down to a ridge dug a few inches above the victim's body. It was a six-inch ledge that ran the perimeter of her upper torso, outlining her head and shoulders.

It took me a moment to realize what that second level was for.

Whoever had buried her alive had rested the boards on the ridge to create a small container within the grave, presumably to provide enough air for her to suffocate slowly, aware of her impending death, able to cry out but certain she wouldn't be heard.

Something fluid and hot settled into my chest. I tilted my head toward the boards. "Who dug her out the rest of the way? Your guys or the EMTs?"

"Him," Comstock said, jabbing his thumb behind him. "The homeless guy."

My forehead creased. I glanced back toward the man leaning against the ambulance. "The *whole* grave?"

"Yeah. We were as surprised as you. Nothing left for the EMTs to do but check for her pulse. Dead on scene."

"Think he's the one who buried her?" It was a question that needed to be asked.

Comstock was quiet for a moment. "I don't," he finally said, his voice a rumble. "And I think it about killed him that he couldn't save her. Said if he'd started digging at her head rather than her feet, he'd have gotten to her in time. You see his mitts? Him and the victim got a matched set."

Comstock shined his light on the victim's hands to illustrate. They were frozen in claws, palms up near her shoulders, the tape just above her elbows preventing them from reaching any higher. Her fingers were unusually short, their ends blunted and blackish red.

"She dug right down to the bone trying to get out of there." Comstock was professional enough to mute his shudder. "Good luck getting fingerprints."

I stared off into the distance. Then I looked straight at Comstock.

"Are your crime scene techs coming, or are ours?" I asked.

He returned my gaze, looking me square in the eye for the first time since I'd shown up. He'd been the worst of them at Bart's funeral, taunting me, blocking my way when I ran to the bathroom to find some privacy before I lost control and wept for my friend.

I wondered if Comstock was remembering the same thing, because his eyes dropped first, like he felt bad. Well, let him. That's what feeling bad was for.

"Yours," he said, his gaze back on the victim.

That's what I'd figured, which begged the Big Question.

"So why'd you call the BCA?"

CHAPTER 4

Van

In the 1920s, Chicagoland mobsters John Dillinger, Al Capone, and Baby Face Nelson used the Minnesota landscape from Saint Paul north like their own private resort. Local officers were ill-equipped to capture them or to address the crime sprees they introduced, so the state legislature proposed creating a separate agency. It would have no jurisdiction of its own. Its sole purpose would be to assist law enforcement across the state at their request.

The Minnesota Bureau of Criminal Apprehension, or BCA, was born.

The Bureau started small, basically a mobile backup team. In the '30s, it grew to include a statistics division to track and better respond to crime and criminal patterns. In 1947, the BCA built the first forensic science laboratory in the region. It had since become one of the finest labs in the nation, renowned for its crime scene processing and evidence analysis. Since then, the BCA had not only added more agents and field offices, but it'd also initiated multiple task forces and founded one of the first dedicated cold case departments in the country, small as it was.

"I'll do my best to keep you in Cold Case," Ed Chandler, the deputy superintendent of investigative services, told me when he offered me the job. "Just keep your head down, and remember to stay friends with local law enforcement. BCA agents are like vampires: we have to be invited in."

Detective Dave Comstock *had* invited us. As he was employed by the best-equipped police department in the state, the burning question was why.

By way of answer, he leaned over and delicately grabbed a plastic bag from the ground with all the daintiness of a man choosing a cucumber sandwich at a tea party. That he didn't carry the bag on his body told me it contained liquid evidence, likely blood or tissue, that he didn't want warmed and smudged. His flashlight illuminated the bag from below.

I leaned forward.

The evidence bag held a piece of jewelry. A brass chain, the cheap kind, gone greenish brown with age. At the end, a charm. I blinked. It was half an enamel heart, its middle an artificially jagged edge. In the US, every generation of kids claimed a similar bauble, popular for a month or two in middle school. You gave your friend one half and kept the other. If you were sentimental, you hung on to yours into adulthood, and it ended up in some keepsake box full of valentines and ticket stubs that your kids had to throw out when you died.

This necklace had a unique detail, though: two glittering chips embedded in its top right. Rhinestones, for sure. The rest of the half-a-heart charm was red, the cherry-tomato color it'd started with accented by drying blood. Comstock flipped the bag to reveal the back of the necklace. Something was engraved on it, what looked like initials above a word, but it was too thick with gore to read.

"What's it say?" I asked.

"I don't know." He cat-eyed me. "You don't recognize it?"

I shook my head.

"You *really* don't know where this necklace is from?" he asked, using the mock-incredulous tone he'd mastered at the end of my MPD tenure.

I felt the sudden urge to punch him. Instead, I held my silence.

He stared at me so long I wondered if his disbelief was genuine. "The Taken Ones? Most famous abduction in Minnesota after the Lindbergh baby?" He rolled his eyes. "Don't tell me you've never heard of it."

If he noticed my hands hitch into fists, he didn't comment.

"Happened in 1980 in Leech Lake, about fifteen miles northwest of here." He was still holding up the bag with the flashlight trained on it. The blood caking the heart charm was black or ruby colored, depending how the light caught it. "I was a patrolman one town over at the time. Three little girls skipped into the woods, a pair of sisters and a friend. Only one comes out. I get you weren't born yet, but you haven't even seen the cold case?"

I didn't owe him an explanation, but if I'd given him one, I'd have told him that the BCA files contained more than three hundred cold cases. I hadn't been on the team long enough to pick and lead my own. Running analytics meant I worked second on whatever Chandler assigned me to, which mostly involved building out time lines and scouring old files with a fine-toothed comb, searching for something the original investigators had missed. As Chandler was fond of saying, "The answer's almost always in the file." That's why Cold Case made cops defensive, even though they were the ones who called us in. Everyone craves justice; few of us want it at our own expense.

Comstock took my silence for whatever he took it for. "The girl who came out of the woods?" he continued. "She was as mute as a monk for weeks. Her only injury she got leaving the forest. She walked across pavement so hot they had to cut it out of her feet. Woman who found her said the girl smelled like slow-roasted pork. Said the child was oblivious to it. Said she kept staring straight ahead like she'd had the soul scared out of her."

Disconnecting from your body was a common reaction to trauma, but to do it so thoroughly that you didn't notice your feet were cooking? My heart squeezed to imagine what that poor child had seen.

"Back in 1980, you better believe everyone in the state knew what those three girls looked like and exactly what they'd been wearing that day. It was front page in all the newspapers and on every channel for weeks. Two of the girls, the one who walked out of the woods and her friend who went missing, were each wearing a necklace exactly like this one." He gave the evidence bag a shake. "Identical down to the stones in front and the two levels of engraving on the back."

"Which girl did this one belong to?"

We both turned toward the rumble of a car approaching, a black sedan belonging to Agent Harry Steinbeck, legendary forensic scientist and a man so tightly wound I was shocked when the chair didn't go with him when he stood. I'd considered the possibility that he'd be the scientist on this case. I hadn't prepared for the uncomfortable heat in my chest that would come with confirming it.

"That's what I'm hoping your guy can tell us," Comstock said, tipping his head toward the car.

CHAPTER 5

Van

Harry emerged from his vehicle looking like he'd dropped by a 1950s dinner party on the way home from his fast-paced job at the ad agency. His brown wing-tip oxfords were shined, his slacks creased, his dressy linen shirt the perfect material for the muggy air. A straw fedora was perched on his head, and he carried a doctor's bag of the same color leather as his shoes and his belt.

He'd once told me he kept an outfit and a field kit by his door—work and home—for after-hours calls like this one. He said it was terrible, the scenes we were summoned to, the horrors men, women, and sometimes even children inflicted on one another. He couldn't undo the damage, but out of respect to the victims and their families, he'd show up looking his best. Often, they would never know about the care he'd put into his appearance, but *he* would, and so would the other officers on the scene.

He and I met up by the ambulance, where Kyle joined us.

"An apparent vivisepulture?" Harry asked me.

My eyebrows lifted. Harry was only seven or eight years older than me, but he talked like he was ancient. "If you mean buried alive, then yes. Victim presents as female, appears to be in her early fifties."

Harry was struggling to maintain eye contact, his gaze clearly dying to drop down and confirm the rips in my black jeans. I squashed the urge to tell him where I'd been when I received the call, to let him know that I hadn't shown up like this by choice. I'd worked hard to starve the part of me that cared what people thought of my appearance. I wouldn't feed it around Harry.

"Any identifying information?" he asked.

I shook my head and indicated the witness a few feet behind us still perched on the edge of the ambulance, a sour smell emanating from him. He'd lifted his head when we approached but then let it drop.

"This is Mr. Shaw. He discovered the victim." I cleared my throat. "He did his best to save her life."

Mr. Shaw's chin quivered, his eyes as bright as gemstones in the cracked landscape of his face. His layers of shirts—I counted four—had likely started out as all different colors but had blurred to shades of brown over time.

"Weren't enough, was it?" he asked.

"I'm Agent Steinbeck," Harry said, removing his hat and stepping forward. He offered a handshake but gently retracted it when he noticed Mr. Shaw's raw, bloody fingers. "You need medical attention."

"Don't want it," Mr. Shaw said. His age was difficult to gauge, bowed as he was by pain. Sixty? Seventy?

Harry glanced toward the center of the lot. "How many people have been on the scene?"

"Detective Comstock," I said, wondering how he and Harry would get along. "He's the guy standing by the hole. Swears his three responding officers stayed off scene, so that leaves the EMTs to confirm death and Mr. Shaw here."

A BCA crime scene van rumbled into view. Harry's team. He kept his focus on me as they parked. "You've seen the victim?"

It was a courtesy question. He'd watched me walk back from the crime scene.

"I have," I said, massaging my forehead. Last evening's nightmare had robbed me of deep sleep, and the horror of the woman buried alive was a weight strapped to my neck. Still, there was comfort in seeing

Harry. He and I had worked one case together, the Sweet Tea Killer mission that took us to Costa Rica.

I knew Harry was a good agent. The best.

"Excellent," he said as his team stepped from the van and began hauling out equipment. "You can give us the lay of the land." He turned his attention to Kyle. "Agent Kaminski, please ask the MPD officers to help my team set up perimeter lights. I'm treating the area for one hundred and fifty feet in each direction from the burial spot as the main crime scene."

"You got it," Kyle said, stepping away.

I got the sense that Kyle wanted to yell out the orders, but to his credit, he strode over to the trio of cops just on the other side of the ambulance, speaking quietly and pointing to me and Harry. The two female officers were eyeing Harry with open admiration, and I couldn't blame them. He was a good-looking guy.

He glanced approvingly at the gloves and foot covers I'd donned. "Before we visit the scene, can you assist me in gathering evidence from Mr. Shaw so his wounds can be dressed?"

I nodded, pressing my lips into a tight line.

CHAPTER 6

Van

"We don't need to wait for a search warrant?" Harry asked as he studied the distance separating us from the crime scene. Mr. Shaw had taken some convincing to allow the EMTs to drive him to the hospital. He didn't think he deserved care, not after he'd "let her die." It wasn't until I said we'd be better able to gather evidence if we didn't have to worry about him that he finally agreed to go.

I shook my head. "No search warrant. Comstock says it's city property."

"You know Detective Comstock."

He worded it as a statement. Given my time at the Minneapolis PD, it was a safe bet. I also knew what he was really after: he wanted to know what he was walking into.

"I worked with him in homicide," I said. "He was good friends with my former partner."

Harry's eyebrow raised. "He happy to see you?"

"Nope."

Harry's lip twitched.

"He thinks this homicide is connected to the Taken Ones," I said. "You've heard of the case?"

"I have," Harry said, any sign of humor gone. "What makes him think they're connected?"

I filled him in on the heart charm necklace as well as the state of the scene, finishing just as the arc lamps were switched on. They lit up the lot like a movie set. The perimeter established, BCA agents Deepty Singh and Johnna Lewis walked over to join us, Kyle just behind them. All the BCA crime scene collectors were trained forensic scientists, but Deepty and Johnna were the ones Harry always requested in the field, Deepty a gifted photographer and Johnna a genius at locating trace evidence.

"What's the plan?" Deepty asked, her black hair showing up nearly blue in the light. She was surveying the area, no doubt planning all the angles for her recordings. She'd come to the BCA after graduating from the University of Minnesota five years earlier, and she kept current on all the digital field technology.

"We follow the path," Harry said, pointing toward the track I'd used.

"We're positive it isn't a body dump?" Johnna asked. She was a brunette in her fifties with a famously strong stomach. The other Cold Case agents told me she'd handled a weeks-old corpse discovered floating in a swamp in the heat of summer without so much as wrinkling her nose. For this scene, she'd donned white protective gear, opting for a hairnet instead of the full hood.

"As certain as we can be," I said. "Mr. Shaw said she was screaming as he tried to dig her out. He couldn't find a pulse, but she was still warm when he finally reached her. We'll have to wait for the autopsy to confirm time of death, but I'm comfortable calling this the murder scene."

Deepty shuddered as she slid on two layers of gloves. She wore tailored denim coveralls. "Buried alive. You think you've seen everything."

"We'll stick with the usual," Harry said. He'd donned a Tyvek suit, exchanging his fedora for its hood. "I'd like video first, and after you've gathered that, start on photos. Johnna and I will scan for visible and latent evidence. Once you have all the photos, we'll collect any evidence that could be lost in transporting the victim and bag her hands."

He held himself straight as he continued. "Agent Kaminski, I'd like you to work with the officers to scour the area beyond the police tape. Evangeline, will you please introduce me to Detective Comstock?"

I didn't care for the use of my full name, but I'd given up on getting him to call me Van. What I *did* like was him requesting I make the intro. It'd signal to the Minneapolis PD that he was deferring to me as the first BCA agent on scene. That subtle passing of authority would go a long way if this became an activated cold case.

The walk to the burial site was slow, both Harry and I methodically placing our feet into preexisting prints, as delicate as dancers.

Comstock hadn't moved from where I'd left him.

"Detective Comstock," I said when we reached the scene, "this is Agent Steinbeck. Steinbeck, Comstock."

They both nodded at each other before Harry crouched next to the grave. It was my second time seeing the victim, but the chill hadn't lessened. Over a decade on the job, and I'd never seen terror stamped so vividly on another human's face. I wondered what her last twenty-four hours had been like. Had she lived a carefree life, working a nine-to-five job, raising her kids, paying her bills, until one day she was snatched from a grocery store parking lot by a maniac? Or had she lived a life of suffering, a captive in her own home, her brutal death a miserable crescendo?

"EMTs found no ID in her accessible pockets," I said, reviewing what Comstock had told me. "The footprints I mentioned are over there, just beyond the ones left by the paramedics." I flashed my light to the spot, the beam eaten by the arc lights.

"What are those?" Harry asked, standing.

"What?" Detective Comstock said, lurching away from the grave.

Harry winced. "Please don't move to any new ground," he said. "Not until we've had a chance to scan the area."

Detective Comstock scowled but stayed put.

"And I was referring to those indentations," Harry said, pointing.

I inched toward the spot he was referring to, pausing to study the ground before putting down a foot. Harry followed. We were five feet from the circles when the EMT prints ran out, meaning the paramedics hadn't come this far. We couldn't take another step without polluting the crime scene. Still we were close enough to see there were four circles total, each the size of a fifty-cent piece, equidistant from one another.

My stomach plummeted. "A chair," I said.

"Why the hell would there have been a chair out here?" Comstock called from the graveside.

Harry and I exchanged a look.

"He made her watch him dig the hole he would bury her in," I said.

CHAPTER 7

Van

On our first case together, Harry and I had been sent to Costa Rica to keep an eye on the supposed Sweet Tea Killer, a woman accused of poisoning three pedophiles, one of them her husband. The press gave her the name because all three men had drunk ethylene glycol in what police initially thought were three unrelated suicides, though only her husband's had been cut with sweet tea. Harry and I had been assigned to make sure she and her daughter didn't vanish into the jungles before all the evidence was processed. We were glorified babysitters, in other words. We ended up letting her go because in the end, despite the men all swallowing the same poison and the fact that all three were missing a lock of hair above their right ear, there hadn't been enough evidence to move the deaths from the suicide column over to murder.

The cases were closed.

Except Harry couldn't get over those chunks of hair missing from each man; the cuts were too precise to have been coincidence. Me, I knew it was a triple homicide and was equally sure the world was a better place without those creeps. If Bart were alive, the case never would have gone down the way it had. He and I would've caught the pedophiles and put them behind bars.

But there was no Bart. Harry was the closest thing I had to a partner, and we were worlds apart, and not only in how we went at cases.

Harry was *dapper*. He was a dead ringer for Michael Fassbender in *X-Men*, except Harry was leaner and perpetually clean-shaven. Honestly, I wasn't sure his skin would allow anything as unruly as facial hair. That's how buttoned-down he was. I guessed he was in his early forties, but he didn't have a wrinkle on his face, not a single worry line between his ice-blue eyes.

It was unsettling.

I'd heard of him even before I was hired by the BCA. His crime scene processing was legendary. Rumor was he also managed his field team like a master conductor leading an orchestra. Most forensic agents at his skill level stayed out of the field. The hours were crazy—we'd be working this empty lot until at least sunrise—and the conditions were uncertain. But Harry must have thrived on it because here he was, and I was happy to observe that all the glowing stories I'd heard about his forensic wizardry were true.

He quickly ascertained that the shoe, tire, and what we assumed were chair prints were plastic—meaning visible and three-dimensional—and so impressions could be made of all of them. Soil samples were collected in case any of the dirt on scene was from a different location. Johnna gathered four loose hairs from the scene, three that appeared to be the victim's long, gray-blonde hair and a fourth that was short and brown. It was when Harry was gently bagging the victim's hands that he thought to ask Detective Comstock where he'd discovered the necklace.

Comstock had been taking notes of his own, recording the forensic team's preliminary findings, presumably writing down his own thoughts about the case, and generally staying out of the BCA team's way.

Until Harry's question.

"By her shoulder," Comstock said, pointing near where her bloody right hand lay fixed in its eternal claw.

I'd been studying the duct tape binding her arms, searching for a hint of the age or brand or a story in the way it had been applied, but the caginess in Comstock's voice caught my attention. It had also alarmed Harry, I could tell by the set of his shoulders.

"Was she *wearing* the necklace?" Harry asked, sitting back on his heels, the bagging temporarily forgotten.

Comstock rubbed both hands across his face like he was soaping up. Dawn was bruising the sky. Every one of us was dragging, and it was only a matter of time until the press showed up. Kaminski and the other officers would keep them at bay, but a murder this lurid, potentially connected to an infamous child abduction? The story would burn like oil through the city.

"No," Comstock said. "It was lying there. Like I said, by her shoulder."

Harry blinked. I wondered if this was what he looked like when he was pissed. He must have been wondering, as I was, why in the sweet hell Comstock had moved evidence.

"Did it appear as though she'd pulled it off herself, pulled it off someone else, or," Harry asked, "that it had been dropped in there with her?"

Why'd you move evidence before it was photographed?

That's what I heard, and Comstock seemed to catch the same drift. "She'd *clearly* been holding it," he said, his tone reading annoyed. "It was beneath her hand."

Harry raised an eyebrow, but he let it slide.

Not me. I stored the information in the mental file I'd opened for Comstock. *Not moving evidence was Homicide 101, yet he'd plucked a key piece right off the scene.* I put that detail alongside tonight's other entry: *he was a patrolman one town over from Leech Lake when the Taken Ones disappeared.*

I was about to ask Comstock some follow-up questions when something flashed behind him, appearing in the crack between the two abandoned factories to the south. I stood, my knees protesting. My first reaction was that it had been a camera flash, but I quickly discarded that notion. The space between the buildings was six inches wide, tops. No human could squeeze in there. My second thought was that I'd spotted a light reflecting off evidence, maybe a shovel quickly stashed, except the flash had been at waist level. Besides, what light source would have caused the reflection? I must have imagined it.

Still. My nerves were buzzing.

"Be right back."

I started toward the buildings, tucking my notebook and pen into my blazer pocket and flexing my fingers. I'd taken so many notes that my hands were cramping. For the first time since I'd arrived, I became acutely aware I wasn't wearing my firearm. What was it about the space between those buildings that had made me think of my weapon? I stretched my shoulder blades, trying to shake the uneasy feeling that'd settled between them. I was within sight of three cops, one detective, and four agents.

I was safe.

I reached the edge of the crime scene lot. A second empty tract separated me and the factories, maybe one hundred yards across. A quick jog and I could check out whatever it was I'd seen, but suddenly I didn't want to step even an inch closer.

"Van!" Kyle yelled. "They're coming."

I turned, heart thudding, grateful to be pulled away. "Who?" I called back, ignoring the look Harry threw me. He didn't care for loud voices.

"Press," Kyle said.

I was surprised it'd taken them this long.

Harry made hand gestures that resulted in protective screens immediately being set up to shield the victim's dignity. We'd almost cleared the scene. All that was left was to request photos of the on-scene officers' shoes to add to those Harry had taken of the EMTs' to rule out any of their prints gathered. The MPD would close up, Harry and I would head over to the BCA to file preliminary paperwork, and after returning their company vehicles, Agents Kaminski, Singh, and Lewis would head home for much-deserved rest.

I stared toward the narrow alley between the buildings, then glanced back at the well-lit scene. I knew where my job lay. I returned to the hum of activity, kneading the rock of tension at the base of my neck.

I didn't see anything between the buildings, nothing but the fairy lights of a tired mind.

Yet . . .

Hiss.

bad so close to busted
shouldn't be here

He jerked farther into his hidey-hole. She couldn't have seen him. The white-haired woman in ripped jeans, her car so full of garbage that a wrapper spilled out when she opened her door.

Impossible.

She was too far away, he too deep in the crevice. His skin still burned where the brick had scraped it.

He'd seen it in *Tales from the Crypt.* Burying someone alive, that was.

He'd stolen the comic book—#28 in the series—from Ollie Lietz back in sixth grade, pinched it out of Ollie's locker when no one was looking. Stuffed it into his own book bag.

He'd done it because Ollie loved that comic book and he hated Ollie.

It'd burned hot in his bag all day long. He assumed everyone could see that he'd taken it. Figured it shone as bright as kryptonite. But somehow, impossibly, no one said a thing.

It was a miracle that continued outside of school.

When he got home, his mother was sitting in front of the TV watching *The Virginian.* She loved Westerns.

"Keep it quiet," she said without even looking at him, accordioning her cigarette into the tin tray left behind from her lunchtime TV dinner. Same thing she always said when he came home.

"All right," he said happily, warm with a sudden joy.

She couldn't tell her son was a thief.

Ha HA!

He scurried to his room. Tore open that comic book, delighted by the transformation of fear to power, nay, *dominance*. He'd fooled everyone. That headiness mixed right in with the comic book's brightly colored images, the drawings and words making him laugh out loud, making him feel like he wasn't such a freak. There was the story of the man with the murderous head growing out of his wrist in "The Ventriloquist's Dummy." Reverse-aging voodoo magic in "A-Corny Story." Sex and zombies in "Ants in Her Trance." But the crowning tale was the cover story, "Bargain in Death!" It featured a man in a suit, a man who looked a lot like Ollie Lietz all grown up, buried six feet below the surface, yelling with no one to hear him, hands scraping uselessly at the inside of his coffin.

That story had really stuck with him.

He'd pored over it so many times that the pages turned soft as suede.

And now he'd witnessed it in real life. He'd seen the bum try to dig her out, too, then the ambulance followed by the cop cars. Then the sloppy one drove up. She looked so young, her hair so pretty. Like an angel.

Like his first girl, Lottie.

Made his heart push against his rib bones to look at her.

Once they were all on the scene, they got down to brass tacks, those officers. They worked the ground like busy insects. It was fascinating. He never lost sight of the messy one, though. How could he, with that hair?

Then, out of the blue as if she could suddenly hear his thoughts, she'd stared in his direction. The whole team had been there for hours and hours, and not once had someone glanced between the two abandoned factories. Why would they? But when she began walking toward him, he actually gasped. He unlocked his shoulders to crawl even deeper into the six-inch crevice, but it was a tight fit. If he moved any farther back, he might not be able to get out. He'd die there, leaving behind a very confusing skeleton.

As she strode nearer, his cramped heart began to force blood to his ears, which were squeezed by brick on each side, amplifying the sound. For a moment he had the ludicrous notion that he could close his eyes and she wouldn't see him. There was no exit behind him, even if he could jam himself deeper. Still, it was instinct to try. One arm spasmed, making a scraping noise against the unforgiving wall. His breath grew hitched. He thought he tasted blood.

He'd read about a man who'd gone spelunking in Utah's narrow, twisting Nutty Putty cave system. That man had taken a wrong turn and gotten trapped upside down. For over twenty-four hours, rescuers had tried to save him, even got so far as tying a rope around his feet. But he was stuck good. They'd finally had to give up.

He'd felt righteous reading that story. Who couldn't free themselves from a spot they'd willingly entered? But in this moment he understood, and the panic was suffocating. He was raising his eyes, searching for an escape route up, when the Black man yelled for the white-haired woman, calling her Van.

She gave the crack he was hiding in one last look—like a sassy girl, like Lottie—before returning to the crime scene.

He *loved* sassy girls.

CHAPTER 8

Van

I startled awake at my desk, drenched in sweat, gasping. Acid lemon sunlight cut through the blinds. I forced myself to take deep breaths, to ground myself to reality. I was in a chair that squeaked, seated at a metal desk that was two inches too high. The office was small, ten by ten feet, and *it was mine*. My things—blazers I could pull on, notes, wrappers I'd yet to throw away—were piled on the threadbare couch and the plastic chair opposite me, reassuring me that I wasn't in the dormitory at the Farm any longer.

What I could see belonged to me.

The digitized files from the disappearance of Lily Larsen and Amber Kind—the so-called Taken Ones—sat open on my computer, the paper reports fanned across my desk. The moment I'd returned to the BCA, I'd scratched out a summary of the burial crime scene before collecting all the cold case data I could get my hands on.

The 1980 police report was lean, but hundreds of tips—possible sightings of the girls, accusations against a relative or a friend believed to have been involved, theories about alien abduction and government-sponsored sex trafficking—had come in since. Despite all the information added to the case file, a time line of the girls' disappearance had been created only once: during the initial investigation.

Technique and technology had changed dramatically since then.

I was hungry for the Taken Ones cold case, and it wasn't only that I'd been senior investigative agent on last night's potentially related homicide. It wasn't that I'd spent the last year hiding behind this desk and it was time to step out. It wasn't even that it involved children, three innocent girls who'd had their childhood cleaved from them.

I needed this case because of the photos of Rue Larsen's—the girl who walked out of the forest that day—feet.

I'd discovered them in the original Leech Lake police report, four horrific Polaroids. Her soles looked like they'd been barbecued, the skin crisped and the flesh underneath gone opaque from heat. Looking at them, I became so enraged that I'd had to close my eyes and count backward from fifty.

I will find the person who did that to her.

I will make them pay.

But first I needed the case.

Because I'd been on scene last night, I stood a good chance of Chandler giving it to me, but no way was I leaving this up to luck. I was going to write the best cold case petition the DS had ever read. I'd gathered all the info and had been about to rough out an updated summary when the blades of sleep found me. I'd hoped to work through the day but was jelly-bone exhausted. I'd last seen my bed some thirty-plus hours earlier. Sometimes, when I got that tired, I could sleep uninterrupted, swim in the sweetness of pure rest, avoid the lucid dreams that'd plagued me since my childhood on Frank's Farm.

This had not been one of those times.

The moment my head plopped onto my desk, there it was. The same nightmare I'd had the last time I'd slept, the one I'd been thinking of last night when I was outside with MacGuffin at the animal shelter, except this time, I saw the eyes of the woman wearing the crimson pantsuit. They were deep and black, like two traps in her otherwise featureless face. She descended into that same basement in that same two-story rambler as before, only now it was thick with the stink of urine and fear. The lucid dream was ramping up.

This time, I saw three doors, hands beating at the inside of one of them, little fingernails making not even a mark as they scratched fruitlessly at the wood. The woman paused in front of the first door. The noises—mewling, pleading—stopped, waiting. She took out the plate-size brass key ring and opened the door.

I stood just behind her, unable to look away, pulled along against my will. I tried screaming, but I made no noise. If not for the people laughing outside my office just now, I would have seen things I'd kill to make go away.

I took a deep, shuddery breath, once again pinging off the familiarity of my office: couch, chair, file cabinets, desk. While I hadn't grown used to the lucid dreams, at least I no longer thought I was going crazy. I'd decided they came from my animal instincts. A heightened version of the sixth sense we've all experienced. That flash of someone's name across the back of your eyelids right before they called. Dreaming about a guy you met at a party a decade ago before bumping into him the next day. A buzzing in your skull that told you to drive a different route to the reunion only to find out later that there'd been a terrible pileup on the road you almost took.

Survival instincts, all of it.

The only difference was mine had been sharpened by my uniquely dangerous childhood growing up on Frank's Farm.

If you're from Minnesota, you've heard of Frank. His organic jams, jellies, pickles, and homemade bread were sold at farmers' markets, before they were the bougie draw they are today. His smiling face was plastered on every label, his eyes deceptively kind beneath the straw hat. Frank had been good at many things, but he'd *excelled* at marketing. Soon, a local grocery store carried our famous plum jelly, the one that glittered like a violet jewel when you held it up to the sun. Next, a major chain picked it up, and Frank's commercials were broadcast across the Midwest.

Until Frank was led away in handcuffs.

He had a very uncompromising way of leading his life, and unfortunately for him, it didn't involve paying taxes. That's what he was eventually jailed for. The rumors of what he did to the women and children who worked his Farm? Never rose to the same level of scrutiny as cheating the government out of its share.

I shook my head with such force that my chair yelped.

Forgetting is the best thing.

I rubbed my face and got back to work.

❖

"Hey, I thought women were supposed to be multitaskers," Kyle said, poking his head into my office. He looked well rested.

"What?"

It'd taken three hours after my midday nightmare to complete the necessary forms for Chandler, including a rough but thorough time line of the 1980 abduction as part of my request to lead the cold case. According to the original file, Amber Kind, eight years old, and sisters Rue and Lily Larsen, aged eight and five, had departed from Amber's house at 11:30 a.m. on the twenty-third of July 1980. Their destination had been the swimming hole at Ghost Creek. They'd never made it.

Rue was discovered by a woman named Carol Johnson. Mrs. Johnson lived three houses down from the Kind family and was walking to her mailbox when she spotted the girl standing stock-still in the middle of the street holding a crumpled brown sack. She would later learn that the bag held a picnic lunch that Rue had packed for her and her little sister: two sandwiches, two bags of chips, two cans of fruit punch, and a single red apple.

Mrs. Johnson said she asked the girl if she was hurt.

When the police later asked her what made her think Rue was injured, Mrs. Johnson struggled to answer. She said that at first, she'd figured Rue was a neighborhood kid out to meet some friends. Sure, it was odd she wasn't moving, but other than that, she appeared normal.

Long brown hair held back with a headband. A Dr Pepper T-shirt with a bright-orange swimsuit peeking out at the collar. White terry cloth shorts. One skinned knee.

Barefoot.

Mrs. Johnson said it was that last detail that made her heart start knocking like a salesman. The sun was roasting the ground, turning the tar so sticky you'd lose a kickstand to it, and here the girl wasn't even wearing flip-flops.

"Are you okay?" Mrs. Johnson had asked, jogging toward the child.

Mrs. Johnson told the police that when she finally saw Rue's face up close, she relieved herself a little. Said she couldn't help it. She'd never seen eyes so empty. She shook Rue out of instinct. When the girl didn't respond, Mrs. Johnson raced back inside her house. Dialed 911. Told the operator that there was a hurt girl out front, Caucasian, brown hair and eyes, eight or nine years old. (When the police asked her why she offered those details, she informed them that she watched *Starsky & Hutch*. She knew what information they'd want.)

When the operator asked what the child's injuries were, Mrs. Johnson had paused.

"Just send someone," she'd finally said.

Then she slammed down the phone, grabbed a blanket and a glass of water, and raced back outside. She bundled the child up, careful to avoid her eyes, and led her to the curb. Said it was like moving a mannequin. She offered the girl water and was still offering it to her when the police car howled down Elm Street.

Rue was sent home from the hospital three days later, her feet bandaged. She was mute for twenty-seven days. Wouldn't draw, wouldn't write, wouldn't speak. Sat in front of the television, according to her mom, and didn't care if it was on or off. Her mother fed and bathed her like her daughter was an infant again. It was not until the twenty-eighth day after Carol Johnson discovered Rue Larsen in the middle of Elm Street, her tender flesh baking into the pavement, that the girl finally spoke.

She'd whispered two heartbreaking words: *Where's Lily?*

Her mother and the police gently and then more forcefully questioned Rue, even sent her to a psychiatrist, but she could say no more about what had happened in the forest. The psychiatrist's notes confirmed that the girl had no recollection of the day, that she looked believably confused when asked what had happened to her sister, and ultimately declared that Rue Larsen was suffering from dissociative amnesia. When the police tried to bring her back to the location, she turned feral. Growling. Twisting. Spitting. Anything to get away.

As far as the files indicated, she'd never entered those woods again, though she and her mother stayed in the same house a mile away. She started fourth grade in the fall, gradually returning to—according to her mother—a shell of her former self.

I'd had to pause when I read that. *Of-damn-course* she was a shell of her former self. When I thought of what the girl had lived through, the trauma and then the aftermath, my gut twisted. I knew what it was like to pretend to be normal. Her school years must have been torture. I'd located a current photo of her from her job as a psych nurse at the Ridgeline Medical Center. She was smiling, but she looked sharp at her edges, uncomfortable, wearing her scrubs like a costume. Her career choice made a mountain of sense.

Most of us try to heal our wounds by operating on others.

In my summary for Chandler, along with the time line, I'd highlighted the lead suspects from the 1980 case. Both sets of parents. A classmate of the two older girls. A convicted pedophile who lived in Leech Lake. The elementary school band teacher with a troubling reputation. All had confirmed alibis except Rue and Lily's father, Mr. Rolf Larsen, a railroad worker who'd claimed he was out of state when his daughter went missing, but the police had been unable to verify it. He earned the top spot on my list, but I would leave room for suspects who hadn't yet been named but should be.

The only unusual—unusual for a cold case file, that was—thing I'd discovered in going over what we had was a faded yellow Post-it stuck on the top of the paperwork inside the file, a single instruction written in loopy handwriting:

Talk to Erin Mason/accounting

I'd checked the internal staff directory. Erin Mason was still employed by the BCA.

"I said I thought women were supposed to be multitaskers," Kyle repeated, gesturing at the chaos of paperwork, jackets, shoes, and empty potato chip bags as he stepped all the way into my office. He offered me an extra-large cup of brew from Magnolia's, the coffee shop next door. "You know. Like ladies are super detail-oriented and organized and all that. Able to do many things at once."

I took the cup, inhaling deeply of the rich, dirty smell of the best mocha on the planet. "Why do people only say that about women when they're referring to thankless jobs, like cleaning or raising kids, and never when they're talking about who they'd vote for as president?"

Kyle smiled. He might be green, but he was smart enough to leave that one where it dropped. "How's the coffee?"

I took a sip and felt it buzz like electricity through my veins. "Heaven. Thanks."

He nodded. "You haven't gone home at all?"

"Too much to do." I glanced at the wall clock. It read 5:02. I'd been here for nearly twelve hours and still had a 6:00 p.m. meeting with Chandler to get through. "You ready to run if Chandler gives me the go-ahead?"

"Ready as rice," Kyle said, glancing at his notebook. I'd always thought of him as solid, but he looked leaner today. Focused. "I stopped by to tell you that they've completed the autopsy on last night's victim."

My eyebrows shot up. "Already?"

It was rare for the ME to conduct an autopsy so quickly, but I imagined everyone wanted to get ahead of the press on this one. If the victim was connected to the Taken Ones—or if she *was* one of the

Taken Ones—the BCA, Minneapolis PD, and medical examiner's office would want to share that news before speculation began.

"Yup," Kyle confirmed.

"Was Harry on-site for it?" I asked.

Kyle nodded. "And he's in his lab right now."

CHAPTER 9

Van

The BCA moved to its present Saint Paul location on Maryland Avenue in 2003. Over half its space was dedicated to forensics. There were DNA labs, crime scene analysis labs, toxicology labs, drug chemistry labs. Harry preferred to work in the smallest of them, a catch-all space that was a carryover from the way the BCA used to conduct analyses. Next to the updated rooms available, many of them flooded with warm natural light, Harry's workshop looked like a grade school chemistry classroom. Its overhead fluorescents shone bleakly onto glass-fronted cupboards, which were mounted above counters neatly lined with beakers, hand pipettes, and the stainless-steel equipment he needed to do his job.

It smelled of disinfectant.

"So, this is where the magic happens," I said, glancing around. I knew what wing his lab was located in, but this was the first time I'd visited.

Harry leaned away from the blue-fronted machine he'd been working with, QIAGILITY stamped on its side. An expression I couldn't read rolled across his face. Annoyance? Defensiveness?

"Gets the job done," he said mildly.

He looked so well put together, so capable. While I was still wearing the clothes from last night's crime scene, Harry had managed to change into pressed slacks and a clean white shirt accented with a green-and-blue plaid tie.

"You went home to change?" I asked, tilting my head.

"No," he said.

We stared at each other for a couple seconds. I broke first. "Another one of your 'just in case' outfits you keep on-site, then?"

His eyes narrowed like he didn't know whether I was making fun of him. Truth was, I wasn't sure myself.

"Yes," he finally said. "You're here because you've heard I came from the autopsy." He stretched his shoulders like he'd been leaning over for a while. "The victim died of asphyxiation between six and eight p.m. last night, which squares with Mr. Shaw's testimony."

I nodded, relieved. I'd hoped Shaw was telling the truth.

"There was no sign of sexual assault immediately preceding her death. She's estimated to be between forty-five and fifty-five years old, and while she appears to have been healthy previous to her premature burial, her bone density and pattern scarring show evidence of malnourishment in her formative years as well as periodic physical abuse. Her larger right humerus suggests she was right-handed, and markings inside her pelvic bone indicate she's been pregnant at least once."

I felt my skin go tight. "How long ago?"

"No way to tell," he said. "Her wisdom teeth were still intact. She had a single silver filling in her upper left second molar. A dental impression has been taken. Her DNA has been collected; I'll have it processed within the next forty-eight hours."

"What do you know about those?" I asked, indicating the evidence lined up in front of him: the bag holding the half-a-heart necklace and four vials.

Harry paused. "The necklace has the initials 'AK' engraved on the back. It fits the description of the jewelry last seen on Amber Kind when she went missing."

We'd all been expecting that, but hearing it said out loud felt like a stomach punch. "Do you think she was last night's victim?"

Kept alive for decades? Abused? Forced to bear a child?

"Impossible to know without DNA," Harry said.

I knew from working with him in Costa Rica that he would not speculate on something he couldn't prove. I'd bet good money that he had zero expectation that last night's crime was in any way connected to the Taken Ones case.

It wasn't that it was unlikely.

It was that—according to Harry Steinbeck—certainty was the death of truth. I respected but did not share his self-discipline.

"The victim's last meal was cherry tomatoes and green beans eaten approximately four hours before she died," Harry said, moving the conversation back to the autopsy.

I closed one eye in thought. "Such a simple meal. That's something a woman with a big garden would eat."

"Or a person who's just visited the farmers' market."

"Maybe," I said, musing. The clothes she'd been buried in didn't suggest to me she was someone who visited farmers' markets, though. "According to the files, we have dental records from one of the Taken Ones. I'll have to double-check my notes, but I'm pretty sure it was Amber Kind."

"I'll take those to compare with our victim," he said. "Any DNA?"

I grimaced. "Limited. We have some from Rue Larsen, the girl who walked out of the woods. We also have the jewelry, clothes, and shoes she was wearing that day."

Harry sat up straighter. "On-site?"

"That's what the roster says, though I haven't had a chance to locate it yet. My focus has been on gathering the written files. But as far as I've been able to tell, other than what was taken off Rue, no evidence was gathered at the 1980 crime scene."

Harry appeared disappointed but not surprised. Crime scene collection forty years ago had been a different world.

"Amber's parents are alive," I continued, mentally running through my notes, "though divorced. Mrs. Kind still lives in Leech Lake, and

Dr. Kind moved to the West Bank neighborhood in Minneapolis. Rue lives across the river, near the airport. Married twice, divorced twice, kept her maiden name."

"Have you spoken to her yet?"

"I'm hoping to talk to her tonight or tomorrow. Schedule a meeting to show her a photo of the necklace, ask her what she remembers." The room swayed for a moment, and I had to grip the counter, hoping Harry didn't notice.

"Shouldn't you—" Harry managed to catch himself, but it was too late.

I smiled. "Get some sleep?"

He looked away. Did I have something in my teeth?

"If it were me, I'd want to wait to rest until I had final approval as team lead," he said, his eyes on the necklace.

I instantly felt defensive. "You think it won't happen?"

"It's unlikely you'll be denied." He was still staring at the bloody jewelry.

It was true. I'd been first on scene. I was qualified. When a case was this big, however, things could get political. And ugly. As the on-scene forensics team leader, he'd automatically be working with whoever the DS put in charge.

Harry cleared his throat. "If it ends up being your case, I'd like to go with you when you speak with Ms. Larsen."

His request surprised me. Mostly, other than crime scene collections, forensics stayed in the lab. He must have had his reasons. Anyhow, I liked his company.

"Sure. I'll let you know when it is. In the meanwhile, I'll have Kyle send over the dental records."

CHAPTER 10

Van

Deputy Superintendent Ed Chandler's office was located on the top floor of the BCA. It had a view of Magnolia Street with an oak tree sprawling outside its south-facing window. His massive desk took up the east side of the office, dusty plastic ficuses standing guard on each side. Diplomas decorated the wall behind him.

Harry and I stood across from Chandler's desk. Harry was wearing the clothes I'd last seen him in plus a matching suit coat. I'd beelined straight out of his lab to Target for a clean pair of slacks, which did little to blunt the tang of the last twenty-four hours clinging to my blazer and T-shirt. I handed a copy of my summaries—one of last night's homicide, the other of the Taken Ones case—to Harry and another to Chandler.

"Van," Agent Chandler said, accepting the papers. "Harry. Please take a seat."

We did. When Chandler finished scanning his documents, he leaned back in his chair, eyes squinched in an expression that implied thoughtfulness. He was a bald man who favored dark suits, which gave his head the appearance of a floating egg. "We've got a real opportunity here," he said.

I winced. A thick manila folder containing any information I might be called on to produce at this meeting lay on my lap, but I hadn't prepared for the gruesome death of a woman to be considered an "opportunity."

"Press will be on us like white on snow with this one," Chandler continued. "Doesn't matter if it ends up being one of the Taken Ones who died or not. If there's a leak and the press gets wind of that necklace, everyone will be riding us. No room for a cock-up."

Ed Chandler may have been born in Rice, Minnesota, a dot of a town located in the central part of the state, but he made sure that people knew he'd studied abroad in England his junior year of college. Phrases that I assumed were British often worked themselves into his conversation, delivered with a faint Minnesota accent. Chandler was an intelligent man. He wouldn't be deputy superintendent otherwise. His talents were more political than investigative, however.

"No there isn't, sir," I said. "That's why I'm requesting lead. After my ten years there, I know the Minneapolis Homicide Department inside and out. I've worked assist in Cold Case for over a year, so I know what's required and who to ask for help. Finally, I was first on scene last night. I have the lay of the land." I closed my mouth with a snap. Why was my heart beating so fast?

Chandler was studying me. "You know why most cases fail originally, right? Why law enforcement can't solve them, and they end up in Cold Case?"

I tensed but managed to hold my tongue.

"There are four reasons," Chandler said, not waiting for a response. He held up his pointer finger. "The first is that whoever's handling the original case thinks they know who did the crime before they even start investigating. This gives them tunnel vision, and they incorrectly eliminate ripe suspects to follow dead ends."

He gave this a few seconds to settle in, then raised his middle and ring fingers. "Second, they don't ask for assistance when they realize they're in over their head, and third, they're geared toward a short-term focus. That's true of most cops. They're overloaded. They don't have the budget—time or money—for forever cases."

Chandler laced his hands behind his head, warming up to his topic so much that he forgot about the fingers. "Fourth and most common, they either didn't canvass the area or did a bloody poor job of it."

Chandler knew I was well versed in this. It was standard training in Cold Case, literally part of our manual.

"Understood, sir," I said, my voice overbright.

"And there's three things we use to solve cold cases," Chandler went on, forging ahead with stating the obvious. "New leads, new technology, and new eyes."

No offense to Harry, but it was almost always the last one that broke open old cases.

Chandler suddenly sat forward, his chair squeaking in protest. "Interagency cooperation is crucial. You swear you're good with the Minneapolis PD?"

I stiffened, and then nodded. "Right as rain, sir." Here I glanced at Harry, waiting for him to contradict me. He said nothing.

"And you're positive you want this?" Chandler asked.

That's when I realized what Chandler was up to. He was nervous about this one, more than he was willing to let on, maybe even to himself. The showboating was an attempt to cover that up. I'd seen the behavior in bosses before. I had no choice but to swallow it.

"Yes, sir," I said. "I'll give everything to this case. I think my clearance rate at the MPD speaks for itself."

"All right. Two investigators, total." Chandler was all business now, his previous paternalism gone in a poof. "You pick the second."

"I'd like Kyle Kaminski."

Chandler's eyebrows met above his nose. "Your mentee?"

"Yes, sir. He's a good agent."

I had specifics ready if he asked. He didn't.

"Fine, but if I catch one whiff of this going south, you're off it. This case is your only focus until it's solved. Harry here will be your go-to in forensics. Is there anything else?"

"No, sir," I said.

I could feel excitement radiating off me, but I did my best to keep my face straight.

I was going to find out what happened to Amber and Lily.

CHAPTER 11

Rue

Rue Larsen sat in her car studying her bungalow. Like most houses in her pocket of southeast Nokomis, hers was a single-story box, a style popular in the 1950s. Some of her neighbors had expanded on theirs, building up or out, but she'd kept her home in the exact same starter shape it had been when she'd bought it straight out of college, hanging on to it through two divorces with men who'd asked only that she go through the motions of being a wife for them, nothing more.

Cooking. Cleaning. Sex.

She'd managed to maintain the performance for one year with the first guy, twelve with the second. She'd been single for the past ten years. She could now afford a nicer home and neighborhood, one not immediately abutting the airport, but the sound of airplanes soothed her.

It reminded her that she could escape.

Whenever she wanted to, she could grab her passport and her credit card and flee.

She'd never left the country. She hadn't even traveled outside of Minnesota, but it was important to know that she *could*.

When she confirmed there was no movement inside her house, she exited her car and locked its doors. She owned a garage, but men could hide in garages. Even in the savage cold of winter, she left the vehicle parked in her driveway so she could peek under and inside of it before getting in.

Two blocks away, a truck rumbled onto her street. She watched it motor toward her and then pull past. Only then did she leave the side of her car and hurry onto her porch. She wore special shoes, their inner padding molded to what was left of the soles of her feet. They nearly erased her limp.

The front door was the only way in or out of her house. She'd had the back door sealed before she'd moved in. She'd also installed motion sensors throughout, including at the windows, which hadn't been opened since she'd purchased the home. Husband number two had complained viciously about that.

It had ultimately ended their marriage. The last straw, he said.

Because she opened every curtain before leaving, she was able to peer through the front window and see into her kitchen, living room, and dining room. She could also eyeball the basement door off the kitchen, the stack of colored blocks in front of it arranged in exactly the pattern she'd left. It'd cost her over $8,000 to have the inner walls knocked down. Worth every penny. The only two rooms she couldn't peer into were the bedroom and the bathroom, which was why she gripped the Taser as she unlocked the front door. The alarm system beeped when she glided inside. She closed the door behind her, turned the alarm off, then checked its records.

No disruptions.

She set her purse on the table before stepping into the bedroom and the bathroom to make sure they were as she'd left them. Once she'd cleared the house, she went out to gather the mail. She grabbed the newspaper off her front porch on the way back and reset the alarm once she had the door locked behind her.

Then she leaned against the door, breathing deeply.

Her lower back ached. She'd twisted a muscle trying to restrain a patient twice her size. It happened a lot on the psych floor. She didn't know how much longer her body could take it. Part of her wanted to order a deep-dish pizza as consolation for her day, the top dripping with gooey cheese, but she'd been so good about sticking to WeightWatchers. She padded to the kitchen and opened her silver fridge, peering at the questionable contents.

"Hey, lettuce, thanks for hanging on," she said, holding the bag up to the light. Only a little bit of brown. "You too, peppers."

Amy from the WeightWatchers meetings had turned Rue on to the trick of buying three or four Costco rotisserie chickens, tossing the skin and the bones, and freezing big bags of the meat. The way WW was set up these days, you could eat a whole bird without racking up points, something she'd tried. It hadn't taken long to discover that some foods you didn't want that much of. Salt-and-vinegar potato chips? A boatful, please. Skinless rotisserie chicken? Tasted and chewed like wet cardboard, if she was honest. Still, it was protein, so she tugged her last bag out of the freezer, ran it under warm water until she could transfer it from the bag to a glass bowl, and set it to defrost in the microwave while she rinsed the lettuce and chopped the peppers. She tossed it all in a big bowl along with a small serving of ranch dressing, so small it was more of a suggestion than a flavor.

She brought the salad to her kitchen table and considered watching TV on her smartphone. She didn't own an actual television. It would be too immersive; she couldn't allow herself to be that distracted. The newspaper was right there, though.

She flipped it open.

Jane Doe found buried alive in north loop of Minneapolis

Her body gave out as if she'd taken a fist to the solar plexus. She dropped to the floor, on her hands and knees, panting like a dog, her heartbeat cutting through her chest.

She was a psych nurse. She knew how trauma memory worked. Or rather, how it *didn't*. How it distorted the past or erased it altogether. Still, those words reached out like a live wire through the fog of time.

buried alive buried alive buried alive

She wasn't surprised when her landline rang.

58

CHAPTER 12

Van

"Shower and hours," Chandler ordered as I walked out of his office.

We'd used the same shorthand at the MPD. It meant, *You've been here too long. Go home, clean up, and get some rest.*

I'd nodded in agreement but waited until Harry and I were halfway down the hall to sniff my armpit. "I really do smell, don't I?"

"It's been a long day," Harry said.

He was trying not to curl up his nose, which ended up making him look like he was fighting a sneeze. It took everything in me not to laugh. I was surprised at the sudden urge to convince him I wasn't as stupid as Chandler had made me out to be back there. I clamped down on that impulse. All that mattered was how I did my job. "It's been a long one for you, too."

Except Harry looked like he'd just returned from a spa experience. That was how he always looked. When I'd sat next to him on the plane from Costa Rica, I'd poked him to see if he felt real. I fought the urge to do it again.

"I'm going home as soon as I check in with the medical examiner," Harry said. "Agent Kaminski sent over Amber Kind's dental records, and I forwarded them on. I want to make sure they were received."

What's home look like for you, Harry Steinbeck?

Probably had plastic covers on his furniture.

"I'll see you tomorrow," I said.

Harry nodded, something curious in his blue eyes. I didn't have the energy to figure out what.

❖

There were a lot of good reasons to drive straight home, starting with the fact that I was going on forty hours without real sleep. But there was at least one compelling argument to be made for stopping off at the First Precinct cop shop first: I needed to get on Comstock's good side. I didn't know if it was possible, but for the sake of the case, I needed to try.

Comstock wouldn't openly freeze me out. He couldn't without risking his own reputation now that I was the official BCA team lead. But in law enforcement, there were a million small ways to undermine someone you didn't like. I couldn't let Comstock's disdain for me get in the way of learning what happened to those girls. So as much as I was going to choke swallowing my pride in front of my past colleagues at my old precinct, I saw no choice.

I parked in front of the two-story brick building, studying it, fear and anger racing like rats across my skin. I'd loved my job here. Loved working with Bart. I'd given it ten years of my life, and they'd run me out like a thief. I hadn't returned since the day I'd left, clutching a sad little cardboard box of stuff from my desk, mostly trinkets Bart had bought me.

Here, kid, I got you a snow globe, he'd say, after returning from one of his solo vacations. Or, *I thought you'd like this coconut candy. Everyone in Hawaii eats it.*

But I'd marched out with head held high and my back straight because screw them. If they didn't want me, I didn't want them.

At least that's what I told myself.

I rubbed at my burning eyes and stepped out of my car, striding toward the building before I lost my nerve. It occurred to me that I should have taken a full shower, not just the trucker's bath I'd done before the meeting with Chandler, but it was too late now. Besides, if memory served, the precinct reeked like a locker room on its best day.

"Agent Reed here to see Detective Comstock," I told the guy at the front desk, flashing my badge. I didn't recognize him, thank all that was holy.

"He expecting you?"

The guy was early twenties, buzzed hair, cocky expression. His name tag told the world he was a Lentz. The lie came easy. "We have an eight thirty meeting on the books."

Lentz clacked on his keyboard. "I don't see it."

I silently thanked him for confirming that Comstock was still around and then flashed him a "tell me why that's my problem" face. He scowled but waved me back.

"Office 217," he said.

And just like that, I tumbled from the top of the hill down into the ditch. Two-one-seven was Bart's old office, the best one in the precinct. Lentz could have punched my teeth and hurt me less.

"Thanks," I said, walking toward the stairs. The place smelled like I remembered, and it sounded so much like home it made me ache. It'd been my heartbeat for a decade—the ding of the elevator, the howl of outrage when you discovered someone had finished off the coffee and hadn't made a fresh pot, the nicknames, the in-jokes.

I was striding with my head down, eyes on my feet, when I realized that was how I'd walked around the precinct after Bart had died. I lifted my eyes and aimed them like lasers. To my surprise, not a single person on the first floor even glanced my way. Same was true on the second—there were some familiar, curious looks, but none that made me feel small. Turnover was high in the city, officers moving within the five Minneapolis precincts to chase a promotion, and so there were a lot of new faces, but that was only part of it.

The other part was that I'd just discovered what the cops here thought of me didn't matter as much as it once had.

Face your fears and make them disappear.

Another saying you'd find embroidered on a pillow in a shop that sold fifty-dollar candles that smelled like ten-cent dryer sheets.

I rapped on Comstock's door.

"Yeah?" He sounded grumpy.

I opened his door and stepped in.

The desk was the same. Bart's. For a moment the floor tilted, but I kept steady.

"Detective Comstock. Just wanted to let you know we've reactivated the Taken Ones cold case over at the BCA. I'm team lead."

He tore his face away from his computer. At first, I thought its reflection was making him gray, but it was his pallor. The man was wearing his job. He removed his bifocals to rub the bridge of his nose. "Not my lucky day, is it?"

I stayed still, no easy feat with my stomach twisting. A naive part of me had considered he might choose to be respectful. It would've cost him nothing.

He shoved his glasses back on his face. "Let's be clear on one thing. The hot case is mine. Minneapolis PD. Cold case is you. You stay in your lane, and we don't have a problem. Yeah?"

I refused to *yessir* him. It wasn't ego. Well, it was only a speck of ego. More, I knew what worked with Comstock, and he'd never appreciated blatant ass-kissing. At least not the surface kind, the batted eyelashes, the formalities.

He liked the stuff that left a mark.

So I bared my throat. "This is my first time as lead," I said, staring at his hands rather than his face. "I can't mess it up. That's all I care about. If making sure you get the credit for the hot-case collar helps me with mine, then you've got it." I cleared my throat. "I hear it with my left ear, and I tell it to you before it reaches my right."

His voice was low, dangerous. "That doesn't sound like you."

"Bart dying changed me."

I despised Comstock right then, hated him for making me say the truest thing I knew. But I thought of those three little girls in the woods, and I kept my expression neutral. "Your lane is the homicide. Mine is to get you any information that can help you as I time travel to 1980. That's what I came here in person to tell you. Fresh start."

I leaned forward and offered my hand.

Comstock stared at it for a beat before turning back toward his computer. "Glad we understand each other. Close the door on your way out."

I ground my fingertips across my palm, wishing I could smack those bifocals off his saggy gray face. Instead, I turned toward the door.

To my back, he muttered, "You never belonged."

It made my eyes hot. Worst fear spoken and all that. Turns out I'd been lying to myself. What people thought of me still mattered. A lot. I hadn't fit in at Frank's Farm, and I hadn't fit in at my job.

My hand shut his door and my legs walked me forward thanks to years of practice. I wanted to get out of there, but rather than head to the stairs, I strode over to the photograph wall, ignoring the way the bullpen grew quiet as I threaded my way through it. I didn't look at anyone because if I made eye contact with someone I'd known, it would make Comstock's words permanent, a fact tattooed on my bones. *You never belonged.* If I kept it on the surface, though, didn't see the truth reflected back in the eyes of people I'd thought of as colleagues if not friends, well, then maybe I could forget about what he'd said.

The photograph wall contained the five-by-seven-inch headshots of the homicide detectives who'd graced—and sometimes, *dis*graced—the First Precinct, lined up chronologically by the year they'd been hired. My photo had hung somewhere to the right, likely vandalized if it hadn't been taken down. I didn't care to confirm which. Instead, I stood in front of Bart's black and white. He'd been an angel-cheeked kid back when he was hired.

It was the Dark Ages, kid, so long ago that an honest-to-God dinosaur took that photo, he'd said when I'd teased him about all the hair he had in the picture, thick and dark and slicked back, his gray eyes bright, his smile wide.

When Bart was alive, he'd helped me to carry the weight of my heightened intuition. My occasional "hunches," as he called them, sparks of insight that would have had most officers calling Internal Affairs? Bart accepted them as fact, methodically working backward from what I told him so he could then move forward, providing cover for my lucid dreams with his by-the-books groundwork. Our first case together was the bludgeoning of a woman and her three children. I kept seeing the crime on repeat, the mother trying to shield her babies, her hands bloodied, her screams raw. Then one night, the nightmare moved from playing the murder to showing the killer tossing the tire iron he'd used over the Third Avenue Bridge. He'd clearly meant for it to hit the Mississippi and wash down to the Gulf of Mexico, but it hadn't made it.

We'd already scoured the surrounding neighborhood for the murder weapon, but when I told Bart about this hunch, he ordered a second search, starting with the crime scene as the epicenter and then working outward until we reached the bridge. The tire iron was found, viable prints still on it. That located our perpetrator in the system, and straightforward police work nailed him on the rest.

Next came the serial rapist who'd been terrorizing Minneapolis's Longfellow neighborhood. I woke up one morning with an image of his face as clear as my own in a mirror. It was the same face I'd recently seen on a billboard for the downtown law firm of Coelo, Schneider, and Calhoun. I told Bart, who went by the book to gather enough evidence to justify a DNA sample, definitively ID'ing the lawyer as the perp.

The last insight I'd shared with Bart led to the identification of a Jane Doe whose body was discovered by a cross-country skier in Theodore Wirth Park. My visions brought us the woman's name. Dental records confirmed.

Bart never asked questions when I brought him a premonition packaged as a hunch. He simply furrowed his brow and buckled down, his investigation as slow as molasses and completely aboveboard. We'd formed a well-oiled machine until his death.

Until I'd been run out of the PD. Turns out the other officers didn't have Bart's equanimity. My solves had been making them uneasy for a while, and with my partner out of the way, there was nothing to keep them from letting me know how they really felt.

Staring at Bart's old photo made the pain as real as an axe to the neck.

I slid my phone out of my back pocket and held it up, opening the camera function.

Because as much as I missed him, I hadn't come to this wall to look at Bart.

Anyone who recognized me, any snitch who was gawping at me now and would whisper what they'd seen to Comstock later, would only be able to say I'd been mooning over my old partner's picture like a brokenhearted girl.

I pretended to wipe away a tear to grease the story.

Then I snapped a pic of the headshot next to Bart's. It was a photo of Dave Comstock back when he was a new hire. The year was 1980, shortly after the Taken Ones had disappeared from Leech Lake.

When he'd been working as a patrolman one town over.

Photos of him from that time were conspicuously absent from the World Wide Web. I'd figured this might do the trick, which was the second reason I'd had to drop by the First Precinct. A homicide detective with Comstock's years wouldn't have moved evidence without a reason.

I intended to find out what it was.

CHAPTER 13

Van

I'd planned to dash into the shelter, find the pen Bart had given me, and run out, but when I couldn't locate it in lost and found or by my locker, I realized I'd have to search the exercise yard. And if I was heading to the exercise yard, I might as well take MacGuffin for a quick stretch.

He was tail-thumping thrilled to see me.

"That's a good boy," I said, letting him lick my face while I clipped on the leash. "I only have a minute, though, so don't get your hopes up. Two times around the yard, tops."

I located my pen on the first circuit, right where I'd been standing when I took Kyle's call about the woman buried alive. It seemed like a lifetime ago. I shoved the pen in my back pocket and was leading MacGuffin in a slow jog when the shelter door opened. The bossy volunteer who'd tried to school me yesterday was being led outside by a full-size poodle. Poodles didn't last long at the shelter, especially purebreds like this one appeared to be. I glanced down at MacGuffin to see how he'd handle the new dog in the open area. He merely blinked.

"Gentrification, am I right?" I reached down to scratch the sweet spot behind his ear. "All these fancy pooches are gonna raise the rent."

I didn't feel his growl until my hand was dug deep into his thick neck hair. The primal rumbling made me shiver. The poodle was pulling the volunteer toward a tennis ball. MacGuffin wasn't upset with either of them. He was growling at the person who was joining them, a white woman in her late forties wearing the uniform of the suburbanite: a loose, gray ombré short-sleeved shirt over skinny jeans and strappy brown sandals. Her back was to me as she watched the poodle exercise the volunteer. It was common for potential adopters to take dogs out into the playfield. They could interact with them free from the echoing chaos of the cement-floored shelter. There was something off about this woman, though.

"Know her from somewhere, boy?" I asked, scratching MacGuffin's neck. "Maybe a Mary Kay saleswoman who did you wrong?"

The woman turned toward the door as two children walked out of the shelter, their ages eight and ten if I had to guess. They were as well dressed as her but kept their shadowed eyes pointed toward the ground, holding themselves despite the heat, huddling close to one another. The girl jumped when the door closed behind her.

My chest grew tight. I recognized the posture. Those were scared kids. I willed the woman to turn around so I could see her face, but she obstinately kept her back to me.

"You smell it, don't you, MacGuffin?"

The woman raised her hand—it looked like to push the hair out of the girl's face—but MacGuffin wasn't having it. His growling intensified and he lunged forward. For the first time since I'd leashed him, I was glad for the restraint. I stepped in front of him to break the sight line. As soon as he could no longer see the woman, his tail began wagging again.

The volunteer had been right about animals being better off forgetting.

It'd certainly served me well in my lifetime.

There were lots of reasons for those children to carry themselves like they'd just escaped jail. They could have recently been in a car accident. Maybe they'd just lost a beloved grandparent and their mom was getting them a dog to distract them.

Or maybe they were being abused.

The earth tipped beneath me, and I felt myself sliding toward the past. I tried to focus on Bart's admonition that because of my background, I saw child abuse everywhere, that I needed to be careful when children were part of the case because it sent me out of my skull. I tried to latch on to the memory of his voice, his support, to keep me in the moment. When that didn't work, I used the corner of my blazer to wipe the goop out of MacGuffin's eyes.

"Help," I whispered to him.

His eyes told me he wanted to.

It wasn't enough.

CHAPTER 14

August 2000
Evangeline

"Evangeline, come with me."

My face prickles with shame. Frank—he doesn't want us to call him Father—doesn't talk to us kids very much. If he wants us to do something, or to do something differently, he tells one of the Mothers. Direct attention from him is rare and either very good or very bad.

"Yes, sir," I say.

The other girls toss me worried glances as I follow him out of the kitchen, where we've been preparing Sunday dinner. Does he know about the abandoned barn kitten that I've been feeding with table scraps? Or that moments ago I sneaked a pinch of sugar from the pantry and let it sparkle-melt on my tongue? Worry grows like a weed inside me as we step into the sunlight.

Frank's Farm is a mix of rolling hills thick with hardwood trees and flat fields with the richest black dirt you've ever seen. We even have a swimming pond on one corner of the property. The land surrounds the compound—two pretty red barns and five sheds, plus our living quarters. There are thirteen of us kids here now, ten girls in the female dormitory, three boys left in the male.

The only adults allowed other than Frank are women, and they live in a third dormitory with the infants, unless they're called to be Frank's

One, in which case they join him in the main house until he grows tired of them and selects another. We have dogs and cats we're not allowed to feed—Frank says it'll make 'em soft—plus three dozen chickens. One barn houses three horses and a cow, and the other stores hay.

Frank stops dead in the center of the compound. I halt a few feet behind him. A Mother is standing in the doorway of their dormitory, a couple others peeking through the window. They look scared. My belly fills with ice.

Frank turns to face me. He's so tall that he blocks the sun, but then he drops into a squat and our noses are almost touching. He smells like tobacco. He's smiling a tiny, sad smile. I don't believe I've ever been this close to him before.

"You're happy here, aren't you, Evangeline?"

It's a funny question, and a giggle leaks out like a burp. Happy? I'm ten years old. "Yes, sir," I say.

He nods. Cocks his head. Frank keeps his hair short, but his face is all beard and mustache, bristly and bushy. "Do you think Cordelia was happy here?"

The ice is back. Cordelia is older than me, old enough that she looks more like a Mother than a girl. She sleeps in the bed next to mine, or she did before she ran away two nights ago.

I do *not* think she was happy.

I also know that Frank doesn't want to hear that.

"She never should have left," I say. I don't consider whether it's true or not, any more than I think about whether the sky is blue or water is wet. It's just a thing I know.

Frank nods. "What did she say to you before she abandoned us?"

My eyes slide to the girls' dormitory before I can stop myself.

"She *did* say something," he says, anger sharpening his words.

I swallow dust. We are not supposed to talk at night after the electricity is turned off, but sometimes we do. I don't know Cordelia well. She wasn't born here, like most of us. She showed up with a Mother a few years ago. She always kept to herself until she ran away. That night, she tiptoed over to my bed after lights-out and told me that Frank wanted her to become a Mother.

"You're so lucky!" I'd said, gripping her hand as I pushed down the buzz of jealousy. All male children must leave the Farm when they turn eighteen. Most females do, too, except those not related to Frank, the ones he chooses as Mothers. It is a glory to be allowed to stay.

"I don't want to be a Mother," she said. Her face was shadowed, but she sounded small, scared.

I patted her hand. "Sleep on it," I said. "The sun will bring answers."

It was something the Mothers taught us. It felt good to say it to a girl older than me.

The next day, she was gone.

I still haven't answered Frank. I'm not sure why not.

"You're trying my patience, child," Frank says tightly. "What did she tell you?"

Something is bubbling in my belly, something new and upsetting. It takes me a moment to realize what it is: Frank, our Father and Savior, is *worried*. I've only seen him angry, or happy, or serious.

"She didn't say anything," I say. It's a lie, and I can tell by the way his eyes spit fire that he knows it. I pray he'll only hit me. He's yet to strike me, but I've seen him do it to others. It looks like it hurts, but it's over quick.

"Take your dress off," he barks instead.

My skin lifts from my bones in horror. This isn't going to be quick. This is going to be the other option. Why didn't I just tell on Cordelia? She's no longer here. It wouldn't have hurt her at all.

I undo the single button at my neck. My shapeless cotton shift falls to the ground.

"And your underpants."

My Sisters and Brothers have joined us outside. I can't imagine being naked in front of them. Not where everyone can *see*. There is no more shameful state for a girl on Frank's Farm. The bathroom is the only place we're allowed to fully expose our bodies, and only when the door is locked and only for as long as is required to bathe. I glance down at my hands, pink and shaking. At my belly button, which is an outie. Then up at Frank, who has stood to his full height.

His head is between me and the sun. He looks faceless, holy.

I pull down my underpants—heavy cotton drawers we sew and wear until they are nearly ragged.

I stand naked to the world.

My shame crushes me. It feels like forever loneliness, but I know better than to try to cover myself with my hands.

"Clean the kitchen as you are," Frank commands, his voice gone soft. "I will come by with a white handkerchief later. You will not get your clothes back until that handkerchief shows me you've done a good job. It must remain white no matter what it touches. Understand?"

Through sheets of tears, I watch him pick up my dress and my drawers. *At least I haven't earned a baptism,* I think, desperate to comfort myself.

We'll do anything not to get baptized by Frank.

I am on my knees on the wood floor of the kitchen when Sister Veronica runs in to tell me Frank found Cordelia and he's ordered us all to gather in the compound. Veronica has a gap between her two front teeth, and when she's excited, like she is now, it makes a whistling noise when she speaks. I follow her outside. Cordelia cowers next to Frank, a loose circle of Brothers, Sisters, and Mothers surrounding her. She spots my nakedness and begins crying, her shoulders shaking.

"I want to apologize," she says. Her voice is quiet, but I hear it. "I want to apologize to you all. I am lucky to be betrothed to Frank. When I turn eighteen, I will become a Mother. I will move into their building immediately so I can better prepare."

The girl speaking looks like Cordelia, but it doesn't sound like her.

Frank orders everyone back to their tasks. That night, I have a terrible nightmare of a man stabbing a woman, over and over again. I wake up screaming, shivering on my bed, naked, exposed, knees raw from scrubbing.

I hadn't done a good enough job on the kitchen floor.

CHAPTER 15

Van

By the time the Cordelia flashback passed, the woman and her terrified children who had triggered it were gone. The exercise yard was empty except for me and a very worried MacGuffin. I kissed his white muzzle as thanks for getting me through the worst of it, walked us both until we'd calmed—I intended to put the whole incident into the "forget" file with the rest of my Farm memories—and returned him to his kennel before picking up dinner.

Minneapolis offers a lot of great pie, but for my money, nothing beat Pizzeria Lola's Sunnyside. The crust was chewy with a light char, the occasional burnt bubble sweetening the pizza with its contrast. The Sunnyside was slathered with cream rather than red sauce. On top of that rested guanciale, which my research told me was essentially Italian for "bacon of the gods." Then came a sharp pecorino followed by leeks so thinly sliced they gave the pizza body rather than flavor. And the pièce de résistance? Two sunny-side up eggs, their yolks like liquid velvet as they rolled over the chewy, salty guanciale.

Served with a crisp, cold IPA and you had yourself a slice of heaven.

I carried my bounty up to my studio apartment on the seventh floor of a gray block of a building off Loring Park, the no-man's-land between Uptown and Downtown Minneapolis. The kitchen, living room, and bedroom were all the same large space, my bathroom and two closets the only closed-off areas. The walls were the bland Band-Aid color they'd been when I moved in, and other than a Yellowstone National Park poster Bart had bought me on one of his vacations, they were bare.

Every other surface was covered.

It was how I claimed it as mine. Separate from Frank, from the Farm. *Mine.*

I did the slalom of the sloppy from the front door to the kitchen table, sniffing at the sour smell. There was messy and then there was hazardous, and I'd always managed to stay on the razor's edge between the two. Right then and there I vowed to bring two full bags of things I no longer needed out to the garbage chute.

But first, my reward for surviving the Cordelia flashback at the shelter.

I stood as I chewed, making *mmmm* noises as I polished off the pizza, trying to remember the last hot meal I'd eaten. My plan for the night was to pick up my apartment, shower, and hit my bed so I could get up early and dive headfirst into the case. My first stop would be to visit Erin Mason in Accounting, whose name had appeared on a Post-it Note in the Taken Ones files. Next, I'd start conducting interviews with all the original suspects.

I knew the statistics. Most abducted children were taken by family members, which was why I was hot for Lily and Rue's father, Rolf Larsen, the one parent without a confirmed alibi. I'd also look for suspects not previously considered. Fewer than 1 percent of abductions were committed by strangers, but I would leave no stone unturned. I intended to build my life around finding out what happened to Amber and Lily, no matter how long it took. I refused to let those poor little girls be reduced to an evidence locker and a file, a faint memory to all but their closest family.

Pizza finished, I made my way to the bathroom. I had to put my back in it to pull the door open against the tide of clothes stacked in front of it, but I stepped inside a six-by-six room so clean that you could eat off the floor. There wasn't even a garbage can to empty.

What was usually the dirtiest room was the one I kept religiously clean.

Frank's voice came as clear as if he were standing next to me: *a woman's work is to keep home and heart pure.*

I gripped the clean bathroom sink so hard that my fingers cramped. Before the exercise yard today, I hadn't thought of Frank in so long that I could hardly even picture him anymore, and here he was visiting me twice in one evening. Frank was the only adult male I'd known the first eighteen years of my life, and he'd nearly broken me. It wasn't until I was partnered with Bart that I began to believe there was a different kind of man. A steady one.

Then I lost Bart, and the Sweet Tea Killer was born.

Me.

My visions were how I first knew all three of the men had been pedophiles, their crimes escalating. I'd made them drink the poisoned cocktails at gunpoint.

I glanced at the thin drawer on the front of my vanity, the one that looked like a decorative front but hid a shallow lip for a toothbrush and toothpaste. My sight grew blurry as I opened it, studying the three tiny bags I'd tucked inside. The hair that had alerted Harry to the possibility that one person may have murdered all three men. I knew how close I'd come to being caught. I'd closed that chapter, but I couldn't get rid of the hair. I'd snipped it to remind me of what I'd done. That it'd been real men I'd killed. I knew how my brain was inclined to erase the past, and I had to make sure I could never forget my crime.

But I wasn't sorry they were dead. It meant they were no longer preying on children.

I shoved the bags back in the drawer.

Forgetting is the best thing.

I folded my clothes over the closed toilet seat and stepped into a scalding shower.

My phone was ringing when I came out.

CHAPTER 16

Van

The bar resembled a wooden houseboat that had been added to, then added to some more, then washed ashore and baked in the unforgiving sun. The green awning over the door asserted that the Spot had been established in 1885. When Kyle called, he swore that it was low-key, a relaxed place where the clientele wouldn't mind if we smelled like narcs walking in.

But I wasn't sure that I *wanted* to walk in.

Investigations at the BCA, volunteer work at the shelter. Those two provided the tent poles of my life, and I liked it just fine. Back at the MPD, I'd drop by the bar after work when Bart was there. He showed me how to be with people. I'd stopped going when he passed, and I'd never picked it back up.

And look at how that worked out for you.

That's what pushed me over the tipping point, the thought that they'd start crowding me out at the BCA just like they had at the MPD if I didn't show up with my game face.

You never belonged.

Fear of exclusion, driving my social life since 2022.

Kyle had claimed "Hot Harry"—Harry had that effect on people, making women sigh and men go quiet—as well as Deepty and Johnna would be at the Spot tonight, too. That meant it was also good for the case for me to join them. Still. I sat in my car for another ten minutes, watching a mainly blue-collar crowd peppered with hipsters enter and leave. I'd dressed like I always did—black T-shirt, black jeans, black boots—though I'd taken the time to twist my hair into a braid. Would I stand out?

When the devil on my shoulder who was insisting this was a terrible idea began winning, I lurched out of my car. If I didn't go in tonight, it would only grow harder each time I was asked until they stopped asking. Besides, I'd taken out those two bags of garbage, just like I'd promised myself I would. Tonight would be a night of healthy firsts.

My car beeped as I clicked my key fob and strode toward the front door, which swung open as I reached for the handle.

"Sorry," a woman said, stepping aside so she could leave as I entered. "Didn't see you. It's popping in there tonight."

"No worries," I said. *This is only a drink. This is only a drink.* My gun and badge were at home. I missed them.

Indoor smoking was banned in Minnesota in 2007, but the interior of the Spot reeked of ghost cigarettes, a geologic layer of smell that had settled into the carpeting, the wood-paneled walls, and the yellowed ceiling tiles. Kyle was perched on a stool at the end of a booth, waving at me.

"Van! Over here."

I saluted back and made my way to the bar. The Spot was busy, but it was an unhurried crowd. I was surprised to discover that I liked the place. That and the dusty Christmas lights strung over the bar, the bags of chips and nuts crammed in a corner, the way every surface was covered. It comforted me.

"Bulleit on the rocks, please," I told the bartender. "Make it a double."

He nodded approvingly. "First time here?" he asked, scooping cubes into a rocks glass. No fancy formed ice balls designed to melt slowly here. These were icy, sloppy chunks that would do their work as nature intended, melting quickly and thereby unlocking the bourbon's sweetness. Simple ice, smooth bourbon. Hard to beat after a long day.

The bartender slid me my drink.

I fished a twenty out of my back pocket, still ignoring his question. I was surprised when he handed me enough change to tip and put a ten back in my pocket. He rapped the bar with his knuckles, but I was already walking away, threading through the diverse crowd.

"Nice place," I told Kyle when I reached him. I nodded at Deepty, Johnna, and Harry, the two women sitting across the booth from Harry, who was perched like he wished he had coasters for his elbows. I swallowed my smile.

"Nice enough," Kyle said, indicating the open spot next to Harry. "We saved you a seat."

"I prefer standing." Once a cop. That, plus it was easier to leave if you weren't cornered in a booth.

"We have a couple pizzas coming if you're hungry," Deepty said. She was wearing a white mechanic's pullover, and I wondered if I'd ever seen her in any other style of clothing. I felt a burst of envy. How nice to pull on your outfit with one zip and get right to work. A onesie for grown-ups.

Johnna nodded in agreement, making her dangling gold earrings bounce. "There'll be plenty." She wore a pretty fuchsia blouse, her hair loose around her shoulders.

"I already ate, thanks." The crowd was so thick that I couldn't see the back of the bar. The Spot appeared to be made up of two conjoined common rooms—the main bar we sat in and a narrower room attached to it, that one holding dartboards, a digital jukebox currently playing "The Stroke" by Billy Squier, what looked like an ATM, plus pull-tab dispensers. A pinball machine—the Addams Family?—buzzed and hollered behind Kyle.

I took a sip of my bourbon. It tasted like caramel and a right hook. My shoulders immediately began unstitching themselves. We wouldn't talk about the case in public. This was colleagues being social, relaxed.

Colleagues who might one day be friends. I took a bigger swallow of the bourbon.

"Heard you're official lead," Johnna said, holding up her drink with a smile. "Congratulations."

"Hear, hear!" Kyle said. We clinked glasses.

It was pleasant and easy, and I was just about to ask Harry if I could drop by early tomorrow to ask some follow-ups about our victim's postmortem when I caught the heat of someone staring. My eyes zinged to the rear of the bar. A sea of heads, many of them wearing ball caps. Some profiles, men and women. Expressions bright and open in conversation.

And one pair of dark eyes trained on me.

Eyes with a knowing that I hadn't seen in over ten years.

Frank Roth's eyes.

My drink slipped from my hand. Kyle caught it before it hit the ground, bourbon sloshing over his arm.

"You okay?"

I shoved past him, split the crowd like I was saving someone's life. Part of my brain, the small sane section, told me it wasn't Frank. It couldn't possibly be. He'd disappeared after his jail time, our community disbanded, that part of my life forever in the past. It was only that I'd been thinking so much about him the last twenty-four hours. There was something similar in this man's eyes, that was all, a familiarly arrogant smile that he'd flashed before turning away.

Slow your roll, Van. That's what my sane voice was saying. *You're bugging out.*

The rest of me was charging toward the man who was slipping away. I needed to control myself, but I couldn't. Why was he running?

I thought I heard my name, but there was no calling me back. I plowed into someone, apologized, tried to make up my speed. The man was ten feet away, disappearing behind an unmarked door in the rear of the back room. I pushed forward, catching a familiar scent, one from my childhood. It was dirty, shameful fear, a stink I couldn't wash out even when I scrubbed my skin raw. I burst forward, grasped the knob of the door he'd entered, and stepped into the bar's storage room. The chaos I'd created behind me was muffled, like I was underwater. I slapped on the light, my chest heaving.

"Show yourself," I yelled. I'd have given my left foot for a gun and badge. "Now!"

The room was packed but neatly organized. One wall was lined with metal shelves stacked with straws, napkins, mixes. The other was invisible behind liquor boxes. The rear held a hot water heater. I shoved aside boxes, pulled napkin bundles off the shelves, searching, searching for Frank.

There was no one in there but me.

CHAPTER 17

Van

"Walk with me," Harry said. We stood in front of the Spot.

"There was someone back there. I *saw* him go in," I pleaded, feeling like I was right back at Frank's compound, standing naked to the world.

Harry nodded before removing his jacket and offering it to me. The night was warm, but I was shivering.

"Where do you think he went?" Harry asked.

I glared at him as I pulled on his blazer, trying to decide whether he was patronizing me. I couldn't tell, so I started walking. Kyle had tried to lead me out of the back room, but I'd pushed him away and marched out myself, tossing some money on a table whose drinks I'd spilled and throwing a couple twenties at the bartender.

Harry had followed.

"Did you know him?" Harry asked, trying again, his voice steady. "The man you saw?"

I shook my head, clutching his jacket tighter. I could smell his cologne on it. Clean, masculine.

"Is it the case?" he asked. We were walking down Randolph Avenue toward the Mississippi. It was a residential section of the city. Most homes were dark, but Harry kept his voice low as he continued. "The helplessness of those children?"

I didn't even bother to glare at him this time. "You researched me."

"Of course," he said. "Before we left for Costa Rica."

I felt myself floating away from my body. A trauma response. "What'd you find?"

To my everlasting surprise, he told me.

"You were one of Frank's Farmgirls, as the media dubbed you. Frank Roth was the father of most of the children there, but no child knew which woman was their mother. Ten of you were allowed to attend public school for a short time but were otherwise homeschooled. The FBI raided your compound in 2007 and charged Mr. Roth with tax evasion. It was a media circus. The women and children were led out, paraded in front of the cameras, everyone looking terrified."

He paused. "A photo of you staring at the camera made the cover of *Time*, headline 'Communes in Your Backyard.' The farm was confiscated to pay back taxes. Several of the children went into foster care, including one girl who'd been abused to the point of brain damage, but you were about to turn eighteen. You dropped out of sight for a year or two. Next time you appeared in the system was when you enrolled in the University of Minnesota criminology program. You were hired straight out of college by the Minneapolis Police Department. Some believed you were filling a quota. You worked your way up the ladder so fast that I expect they had to eat those doubts with a side of mustard. You landed in homicide, partnered with Detective Bart Lively. The two of you had an exemplary clearance rate. Others in the department must have been jealous. You were bullied when Bart died, and with it came the rumors that often follow successful women."

He knew a lot. Surprisingly, rather than make me feel exposed, it made me feel . . . worth his time. I risked a glance at him but couldn't stand the judgment-free sincerity in his eyes and looked away. "Go on."

"You quit. You were then hired by the BCA. Cold Case. You've mostly done desk work the last year and just today were assigned your first lead. On a case centered around children whose choices were stolen and who had to experience something unimaginably terrifying."

My mouth went dry. My last two nightmares featuring the trap-eyed woman in the red dress plus seeing abuse on those children at the shelter earlier today had me wondering: Might the Taken Ones case lead me down a path I couldn't come back from? Hearing Harry say my fears out loud was unsettling. "What else do you know about me?"

"That you're filthy."

He hadn't meant to say that. His accidental honesty followed by his stricken expression caught me off guard. I laughed out loud.

"I suppose I am," I said. "To someone like you."

I stopped and stared at him under the moonlight, standing near enough that I could count his eyelashes. "What rumors did you hear about me at the MPD? What specifically?"

He appeared shocked. "I refused to listen to them."

Now it was my turn to be surprised. "How do you pass on good gossip?"

"You tell people you're not interested," he said, like it was obvious. "Eventually, they stop trying."

I snorted. "Some of my best leads have come from rumors."

"Mine come from science," he said, rubbing the back of his neck and glancing up toward the moon. "From facts."

Another smile was bubbling up to my mouth. Could we be a real team? The odd couple of the BCA, his science to my instinct, joining our talents to bring home the Taken Ones, maybe even becoming friends in the process?

I would never know.

"I'm looking into the Sweet Tea case some more," he said, still staring skyward. "On my own time, that is. I'm wondering if you want to help."

I was falling inside my own body, *down down down*.

"I'm not trying to replace Detective Lively," he said, looking down and misreading my expression. "You don't need to think of me as your new partner."

"Sure," I said, my voice scraping along my throat. "I'll help."

What else could I say?

Then I tossed him his jacket, did an about-face, and walked back to my car.

He didn't follow.

hide
  in back
    hide
       she
      is
  losing
 her
  mind

It was only fair. He'd about lost *his* when she spotted him across the bar. They'd never met before. He was sure of it. And besides, he was wearing a feed cap and a fake beard and mustache; he hardly looked like himself.

But her eyes had bulged when they'd landed on him.

Then she'd barreled through the crowd toward him. He'd fled out of instinct and had been horrified to discover there was no exit at the far end of the bar. He'd tried the one unmarked door. Slammed it shut behind him. Launched himself toward the top of the shelves. Thanked all that was holy when he spotted the open vent.

Propelled himself up and through just as she smashed on the light.

He'd fought the urge to worm deeper in, just like when she'd seemed to spot him at the burial site. Instead, he forced his breathing to steady. Began the micro-movements that would rotate his body in the tight space. He was facing down, in the shadows, when the Black agent rushed inside the storage room and tried to lead her out by the shoulders.

He still couldn't believe that Comstock was the one who'd shown up at the burial last night. It'd made him terribly uneasy. Made him realize he needed to stay on top of what was happening. That's why he'd decided to follow home whoever was in charge of the scene. It had been between the fancy man—the one who'd shown up wearing a hat straight out of the '50s—and Comstock. The clothes made up his mind. Anyone dressed in a fedora and shoes that shiny must be the boss.

The fancy man led him to the Bureau of Criminal Apprehension.

He'd never heard of it before but looked them up on his phone while he sat outside the massive building. Turned out they were a cross between cops and the FBI, *and* they had a cold case division.

He'd followed the right person.

The BCA were the ones he'd need to worry about, that's what he'd thought sitting in his car. He'd left nothing at the burial the regular police could find. He was sure of that. He'd worn gloves, plus black sneakers he'd selected from a mountain of identical shoes at a Salvation Army. He would toss them in a gas station dumpster twenty miles east of Minneapolis, opposite to where he lived. He would drive another twenty miles north before disposing of the gloves. Even if he'd overlooked something at the burial, a flake of skin or a hair, he'd never been arrested so wasn't in the system.

Someone might have spotted him around the scene in the days leading up to it, but he really didn't think so. The cashier who took his money for the shoes might remember him, but it was unlikely.

No one ever did.

It had always been that way. He blended in wherever he went. He looked like anyone and no one. He was the guy your glance traveled right over.

But not her.

She'd *seen* him.

It terrified him. It also made his heart grow to ten times its natural size, like he was the Grinch or something. Her white-blonde hair, her petite size. She could be sisters with Lottie. And with the other girls, when they were younger.

So he'd been right to follow the fancy man to the BCA.

He'd been wrong about which agent was in charge, was all.

Which agent he needed to *pay attention* to.

CHAPTER 18

Van

I held myself, rocking gently, eyes squeezed shut. With each repetition of the mantra, my heartbeat settled a little more, and the sour bile receded from my throat.

It's better to forget. It's better to forget.

The last twenty-four hours had been a one-two-three punch. First, the woman buried alive leading to the activation of the Taken Ones cold case. Second, hallucinating Frank at the bar. Third, hearing Harry tell me he was going to keep looking into the Sweet Tea murders. *My* crimes.

Those three tornadoes? I was guaranteed a nightmare tonight.

I'd hoped it would have something to do with the Taken Ones case, some connection I could pull from my subconscious to help me with a solve, but I'd never been able to direct my dreams like that.

Instead, I was treated to my third lucid dream featuring the woman in the red pantsuit, only this time I could see her face, not just those terrible eyes. Her basement was clearer, too. Wall-to-wall gray carpeting. A beige hallway with three doors, weeping coming from behind two of them. Air thick with the stink of urine and fear.

I was forced to watch, suffocating with helpless rage, pulled along against my will, as she opened one of those doors. A small foot came into focus, a rope attached to the ankle. As my view panned upward and I saw the state of the child's body, I screamed. I always did, and it was always futile. Unheard.

But this time, for the first time since I'd begun having lucid dreams nearly twenty years ago, that cry did something.

It knocked me out of that vision and into a new one.

The jolt left me nauseous even in my dream state. I couldn't see my surroundings in the second vision, only a baby lying on a wood floor. The infant was swaddled in a white blanket covered in pink-and-yellow flower buds, fat tears rolling down her cheeks. A roll of duct tape lay alongside her. Muscled hands appeared near the baby. The knuckles were swollen, the hair dusting them silver in the moonlight. Those hands removed a floorboard.

The wood made a terrible warped shriek.

The noise woke me, sent me into the cold arms of a panic attack.

It's better to forget.

I jerked my head side to side, sending sleep-ratted hair into my face, trying to erase the image of the terrified infant. At least it hadn't been as bad as the nightmare it had displaced, I'd give it that. Of course, like Bart used to say, that was like winning the tallest leprechaun award.

Better bad is still bad, kid.

Thinking of Bart brought me back into my studio apartment. To safety. I wasn't watching a terrified infant or a monster with eyes like tar pits torture children.

I sucked in a few more shaky breaths.

Back-to-back nightmares was new territory, but I'd prepared for this. Taught myself how to ease back from the brink, slowly, gently, so my carefully constructed sanity didn't crumble below me.

Breathe in through the nose, out through the mouth.

I was just starting to relax when my cell phone shrieked from the table. Years of training was all that kept me from jumping out of my skin.

"Hello?"

Click.

The face of my phone told me it was a Leech Lake number. That was something the scammers did these days, assign nearby town names to a phone number and then pretend to call you from there. That's what this must be. A scammer.

Still.

I'd have Kyle check it out tomorrow.

CHAPTER 19

Van

I managed to calm myself after my double-feature nightmare and carve out six solid hours of sleep. As a result, I woke up with a new three-part attitude. First, I acknowledged that Comstock was never going to like me, no matter what I said or did, but I wouldn't let that stop me from finding out what happened to Amber and Lily. Second, I decided that sleep deprivation had caused me to hallucinate at the bar. Of course I hadn't seen Frank last night. Third, no way was Harry going to uncover anything new in the Sweet Tea Killer case—I'd been too careful. I'd play along, and he'd eventually lose interest.

Hell, I was feeling so fine I even gathered up two more bags of garbage and dropped them in the chute. You couldn't tell by looking at my apartment, but *I* knew.

The good feelings were why I decided it was my turn to stop by Magnolia's. Kyle had bought the last couple rounds. I ordered a mocha for myself and one of the syrupy iced lattes he loved and hoofed it over to the BCA, where I found him waiting outside my office. I handed him his drink. He wore the uniform of the young detective: dark-blue slacks, white button-down, navy-blue tie. On his face was an easy grin.

"Thanks," he said.

"Not a problem." I fished out my key card. "Why are you here so early?"

"You said to meet you at your office first thing. It's eight a.m."

I flicked my wrist to see the face of the watch I never removed except to shower. My colleagues thought I was a Luddite for wearing one or, worse, courting attention, but I had my reasons. Kyle was right about the time. "How about you do us both a favor," I said, "and after we get done with this meeting, you book us an incident room."

We needed a central location where we could hammer out this case, one with whiteboards, AV equipment, and maybe even a VCR. Not only would we need the technology, but it was also psychologically good for the case. Neutral ground, everyone an equal. People did their best work when they didn't need to establish pecking order. I should have put in the room request immediately after I'd been assigned lead.

My first mistake on the case. Hopefully my last.

"You got it," he said.

I dropped into my chair and invited Kyle to do the same. "Let's go over the plan before I hit the field."

Kyle sat, glancing at the legal pad balanced on his lap. He took most of his notes longhand and entered them into the system later. I approved. There was something solid about dropping down into the jungle of the words. "After I get us that incident room, I'll continue to flesh out the time line," he said. "You're good with starting it four weeks before Amber and Lily disappeared?"

"Yep." I turned on my computer and sipped my coffee. "Any more and we're going to wild-goose chase ourselves. Anything less, we might miss the catalyst."

He scribbled on his pad. "While I build out our time line, I'm checking financial and phone records and confirming our players' alibis. All the work that can be done from a phone or a computer I'll handle."

"Right." It was no small feat, his job. Back in 1980, reports were typed on a typewriter if we were lucky, handwritten when we weren't. Much of the data analyst's job was deciphering notes and deciding how the information should be handled. Yesterday, while skimming the files before my meeting with Chandler, I'd found what looked like "black into the beans," "father return," and "heart surgeon???" all crammed in the margin of a hand sketch of the crime scene, and that was only one example.

I knew from my experience as a homicide detective that it wasn't necessarily negligence that resulted in slipshod notes. Sometimes it was too many cooks in the kitchen, especially in a case that spanned decades. Each generation of officers brought in added their own two cents using whatever method they were accustomed to. Even in short-term cases, detectives would scribble down notes intending to type them later, and before later came, they'd be called to another crime scene more horrific than the last.

Of course, sometimes it was just bad police work.

"I'll also be researching the activities of the girls, their parents, all recorded witnesses, and all potential suspects," Kyle said. He sounded eager. It was a good sign.

His investigation would be a walk back through time. Hence the possible need for a VCR. Some of the interview tapes might not have been updated since 1980.

"Once you have all that organized, I'd like you to join me in the field," I said.

Kyle rewarded me with a grateful glance. A case worked better if each agent got to oversee their fiefdom, communicating with the rest of the team but managing their own corner. Some leads didn't like to cede control like that, though. They preferred to micromanage the second, tell them how to index, jump in here or there to put their stamp on the analyst's system. Kyle must have wondered if I was one of those.

"Sounds good," he said.

"Rue Larsen still hasn't returned my call," I said, skimming my phone log. "I'll try her again. She's priority one for an interview."

"Next are obviously the Kinds as well as Mrs. Larsen," Kyle said, reading off his notes. "Theresa Kind lives in a condo, Rita Larsen over a store, both of them still in Leech Lake. I'll track down the good doctor Charles Kind's home address as well as search for Rolf Larsen."

"Great," I said. I also planned to knock on doors up and down Elm Street, cross-referencing past interviewees, including Carol Johnson, the woman who'd discovered Rue, and talking to folks who'd moved in since to find out what they'd heard. We would add to the case file as we reinterviewed everyone we could locate and spoke with new people, including Detective Comstock, reporters who covered the original story, and nurses who cared for Rue in the hospital. We would call ahead when it was feasible, show up and hope for the best when it wasn't.

"I already reached out to the Leech Lake police station," Kyle said. "They said their records are at your disposal, though they didn't *expect* they had anything we haven't already seen. An officer from the original investigation still works there, though he didn't *expect* he had anything new to tell you."

That sounded about right, the local police department—and particularly an original officer—already distancing themselves from the case, giving Kyle some low-key pushback. I *expected* I'd see what they knew for myself.

"Good work," I said. "I want to talk to the parents and the local police before we revisit the other suspects. Catalog the ingredients before we bake the cake."

It's what Chandler had been getting at when he gave that weird little lecture yesterday about why cases fail. He'd referred to it as tunnel vision, but it was more accurately called inductive reasoning, and it was something good agents avoided: building a case thinking you knew who did it and working backward from there to prove it. In the rare cases this method drew results, it was luck more than skill at play. When it tanked, the wrong person—or no person at all—was charged. It was a disease of confidence, something every human was capable of. Who hasn't heard about a crime committed in their neighborhood or at their workplace and immediately pictured the guilty party based on their own biases?

Problem was, when cops did that, it cost people their lives.

It was always better to start with the evidence and build the case from there. It took discipline, though, quieting the part of your brain that wanted to toss everything into a neat container.

"I should also check back in with Comstock over at MPD," I said, trying not to let the unease at the thought catch hold. "Make sure the lines of communication stay open between the homicide investigation and Cold Case."

"Roger that," Kyle said, scribbling in his notepad. If he sensed my trepidation, he didn't let on.

I watched him writing busily, his face the picture of concentration. "Kyle?"

"Yeah," he said, still writing.

"What do you want to be when you grow up?"

His eyes shot to mine, a bemused expression on his face. "How's that?"

"You wanna be lead a year from now? Maybe you want to slide out of the BCA and into homicide? What's your long-term?" His ambitions hadn't been important when he was my mentee. They might be now that he was my number two.

"I want Chandler's job, and then I want to run the whole BCA," he said, no hesitation.

I snorted and shook my head. A life of paperwork and meetings, that's what he was gunning for. Well, at least he wasn't after my job.

"Let's get to it, then," I said. "I have to follow up with someone in Accounting, and then I want to be in either Rue Larsen's living room or in Leech Lake scoping out those woods by lunchtime."

❖

Erin Mason was in her mid to late fifties. Her hair was a dark brown streaked with enough gray that it gave her head a fuzzy appearance. She wore it in a low ponytail, a practical choice that went along with her wire-rimmed glasses and makeup-free face.

"Erin Mason?" I asked as I knocked on her open door. "I'm Agent Van Reed."

She swiveled from the computer she'd been facing. She didn't smile. I couldn't tell if she was annoyed I was there or was one of those naturally grim-faced people. She squinted at the badge clipped to my belt. "What can I do for you?"

I held up the yellow Post-it Note I'd found in the Taken Ones file, *Talk to Erin Mason/accounting* scribbled across its face. "Any idea who wrote this?"

She moved her glasses down her nose and peered at it. "Bring it closer."

I did. She pushed her glasses back up to read the note, her mouth quirked to one side like she was thinking. Then it formed an O. "You're from Cold Case."

We worked in opposite ends of the building, completely different departments. It was no surprise she didn't know me. "I do. We're reopening the Taken Ones case."

Something like relief passed across her face. "About time. Those poor babies."

"May I have a seat?"

She glanced at the chair across from her desk. I took it as an invitation.

"Who wrote the note and why?" I asked as I sat.

"Me." Erin placed the Post-it on her desk calendar and ran her finger along the top, sticking it in place. "And *when* might be a better question."

"When, then," I said, keeping my expression even.

"Thirty-three years ago."

I was surprised Post-its had been around that long. "Care to tell me why?"

"I graduated high school in 1982. From Leech Lake." She sniffed and sat up straighter. "Went to St. Cloud State for my accounting degree. I started at the BCA in 1989 and have been here since."

"You knew the two girls who were abducted?"

"I babysat for Amber."

I felt a sudden lightness. "What years?"

She thought about it. "Probably the first time was in '78, then off and on until she disappeared."

"Were you interviewed when Amber went missing?"

"No." She put her elbows on her desk and her fists to her cheeks, a surprisingly youthful gesture. "If I had been, I'd have told the police that the Kinds never let me watch Amber at their place. They always dropped her off at mine. My parents didn't mind. In fact, they liked it. Meant I could watch my little sisters at the same time. But I thought it was weird. No other family I babysat for did that, anyhow."

"That's why you wanted to be contacted if the cold case was reopened?"

She blinked rapidly, like I'd said something strange. "No. I mean, it was different, but plausible. Especially now that I've had my own kids. I get that parents would want the house to themselves sometimes. What I wanted to talk about was the Leech Lake police."

Erin glanced over my shoulder as a man and a woman walked past, chitchatting about a conference they were both attending next weekend. The accounting wing of the BCA was unfamiliar to me, but it resembled any other administrative office I'd been to. Cubbies and carpeting, the faint smell of burnt coffee, people wearing brown clothes and comfortable shoes.

When their voices faded, she continued. "They didn't interview me."

"You'd already mentioned that."

"It wasn't just me," she said impatiently. "My parents said the Leech Lake cops didn't really talk to *anyone* other than the parents of the girls."

"That struck you as odd?" It would have been if it were true, but I knew from the files that the police had interviewed six of the seven suspects as well as Carol Johnson, plus a Schwan's deliveryman whose route put him in the neighborhood when the girls went missing but who said he hadn't seen anything.

"I know what you're thinking," she said. "That just because the local police didn't tell a random teenage girl what they were up to doesn't mean they weren't investigating. But it was like they did just enough to look good on paper. I went to the same church as the Kind family. They were active members before Amber disappeared but stopped coming after. Not one person in that church was interviewed, not even the pastor. My mom worked for Mrs. Kind at her real estate office, and she was never asked a thing, either. Rue's mom worked at the school, and the police never talked to her coworkers. I know because some of us asked around. It's like the cops didn't want to find Amber and Lily. All us kids thought it."

I chewed on that. Not being thorough wasn't the same thing as being negligent. I'd need more information before I knew where the Leech Lake police landed on that spectrum. "Is this the first time you've talked about this?"

"It was *all* we talked about in high school. The two officers in charge—Bauman and . . . Schmidt? They weren't much older than us, graduated a few years ahead. They took great pleasure in busting our parties." Talking about this piece of her past made her tense, her words clipped. She made a visible effort to calm herself. "My point is, we knew both officers, and when they didn't dig deep when Amber and Lily went missing, it didn't sit well with any of us. We felt like they were maybe covering something up."

I raised my eyebrows. "Something like what?"

Her eyes slid to the side. "I don't know. Like they knew where the girls were but didn't want to tell?"

I needed to tread lightly. Erin could be a conspiracy theorist—there was comfort in believing in some great plan rather than acknowledging terrible things often happened for no good reason—or she could have relevant information. "That must have been stressful. Thinking that and having nowhere to go with it."

"It was before the internet," she said, nodding. "We couldn't just google 'who do you contact to investigate the local police.' I lost a lot of sleep about that in high school." She appeared momentarily disappointed in herself. "I suppose the urgency faded when I moved to Saint Cloud for college."

"New friends, new environment," I said mildly.

She didn't seem to hear me. She touched the Post-it again, tracing the edges with her pointer finger. "I didn't think about it again until the tenth anniversary of the girls' disappearance. I'd been here a year. We didn't have a cold case department yet, but we did have a copy of the files. I got permission to look at them, and it all came back. The way Bauman and Schmidt really only looked at one person for the abduction. Leech Lake's resident pervert, even though he had an alibi for the day Amber and Lily went missing. I didn't know what to do with my opinion, so I wrote the note and then I forgot about it, as much as a person can."

"Thank you for writing it," I said.

She looked up at me, clear-eyed. "You're not going to do anything with what I've told you, are you. I know how you all look out for one another."

"I'm looking out for those girls," I said firmly. "And that's why I appreciate you writing the note."

She leaned back, then nodded. It was hard, being certain an injustice had been done but having no more than your instincts to go on. I felt sympathy for her.

I offered her a card as I stood. "You'll call if you think of anything else?"

She nodded and stacked my card on top of the Post-it.

CHAPTER 20

Van

I thought the heat would ease up outside the city, but without the buildings to blunt the sun, it was all scorched earth on the drive to Leech Lake. The town lay eighteen miles west of Minneapolis, two miles east of the nearest lake. That's why the girls had been hiking to the secluded creek that day rather than splashing around on a beach out in the open.

Minneapolis bled for about ten miles before dropping off. There was no sign of the big city when I entered Leech Lake. No box stores, no factories on the perimeter. The population sign said 4,932 people lived here, and the only fast-food restaurant I spotted was a Subway. The billboards were all for small local businesses—a chiropractor, the Gold Kettle restaurant—rather than cell phone companies or resorts. People glared in my direction when I drove through, squinting at me through my windshield, and it wasn't just the heat.

Taken as a whole, it strongly suggested the community was insular. I knew the dangers of an isolated group better than most, and it had my hackles up. There were fewer people in the countryside but just as many reasons for violence, and all of it was personal.

It would add another layer to my job.

I drove to each end of Leech Lake to get a better sense of the place. It reminded me of the small Minnesota town near where I grew up. The bland storefronts offering hardware, dentistry, a five-and-dime. A high school long overdue for a renovation with a sign out front proclaiming LION PRIDE! A new build on the edge of town—a medical clinic—sticking out like a pyramid on the prairie. People who walked like they were pushing against the wind even though the day was still.

What had it been like for Rue to grow up here? Her mother had worked in the high school office, just like Erin Mason had said. Secretaries, they were called back then. She'd be referred to as an office manager now. If Leech Lake was like most other small towns, having a parent work at your school—unless they were the cool teacher—was a liability. It didn't pay well, either. Rue and her sister also wore secondhand clothes and got at-home haircuts, two more things that would have marked them as poor.

You didn't have to be a detective to wonder why Amber Kind was hanging out with the girls that day. No judgment against Rue and Lily. It just didn't happen. The small-town caste system was too ingrained. Rue was working class, Amber a queen. Rue must have felt like she'd won the lottery, getting the call to go swimming at Ghost Creek that day. It *had* been a phone conversation. The records were clear on that point. Had some after-school special on compassion brought Rue and Amber together? A few of their classmates still lived in Leech Lake. I hoped to speak with them.

Once I got the lay of the land, I headed to the police department. I would have stopped by first thing even without Erin's suggestion that they'd done a weak job investigating the case. It was best I introduce myself before they received word a stranger was poking around. The police station was a '90s-style brick box tucked in the shade of what had been a beautiful Carnegie library and was now a co-op of stores: Shannon's This-n-That, Calkins Accounting, Rainy Day Used Books.

Sweat began dripping down my neck the second I stepped out of my air-conditioned car. I had my hair gathered in a tight, low bun and was wearing a black T-shirt tucked into black cords, a black blazer over the top because it had pockets. Walking in, I considered how to play this and decided the direct route was best.

That was almost always what I decided.

The inside of the station was dingy, which wasn't necessarily bad. The wood paneling that kept the drop-tile ceiling from fighting with the green carpeting suggested that for the last couple decades, the Leech Lake Police Department had spent their budget on officers and equipment rather than interior design. At least that's what I hoped it suggested.

"Agent Evangeline Reed here to see Officer Bauman," I told the woman at the front desk, flashing my badge. "Agent Kaminski called ahead."

"That's right," she said, consulting her computer. Her Minnesota accent was thick. "We were told you'd be dropping by. I'm afraid Daniel isn't in at the moment, however."

She was in her sixties, gray hair hanging limp. Because she wore carefully applied makeup, I suspected she had also curled her hair before leaving home this morning. The humidity had taken it from there. Two framed photos sat on the edge of her desk, facing her. She wore a gold wedding ring with a speck of a diamond, so odds were the photos were of a husband and kids, maybe grandkids. The rest of her desk was neat: a large desk calendar with notes in blue ink, a pen-and-pencil cup, a stapler perpendicular to her computer. None of that told me if she was part of the pushback Kyle had received or the cover-up Erin Mason believed had happened or was simply telling the truth about Bauman's absence.

"Do you know when he'll be back?" I asked, introducing my own Minnesota accent. I slid it in gently, curving my mouth around the *o*, moving the *a* to the back of my jaw and sitting on it until it cried uncle.

She smiled and swiveled to face her computer. "Let me check. Oh, looks like it's his day off. He's scheduled the eight-to-four shift the next five days, starting tomorrow."

"With seniority comes a great schedule," I said, mirroring her smile. Daniel Bauman had been one of two responding officers back in 1980. The other, Alastair Schmidt, had died twenty years earlier. Both men had been young—early twenties—when the girls went missing, just like

Erin Mason had said. "I was told Matthew Clark would be available to speak to me if Officer Bauman wasn't."

"Oh darn," she said, her forehead furrowing. "He's out on patrol. I could call him back in."

I pretended to think about it. No way was I going to be at the mercy of his schedule for our first meeting. I needed to keep the power. "That's so kind of you," I said, my accent now nearly as thick as hers. "What he's doing now is too important. I know from my time as a patrol officer."

She looked relieved. "Oh. You sure? It'd just take a radio call."

I put up my hands, chuckling. "No, that's fine. I have plenty to do today without bothering Officer Clark. He said I could have a peek at the files, so I'll just do that real quick and be out of your hair."

Her mouth formed a circle, perfect for the sound that followed it. "Oh. I don't know about that. We keep our files pretty secure, you know."

"Of course." I kept my tone relaxed. "I believe we have a copy of everything back at the BCA. I just need to confirm it. But protocol is important, especially on a case like this one. Those poor girls."

She'd been leaning away from me but suddenly craned forward. "Isn't it awful? I was working here that day. Took the call from Carol Johnson. Do you know Carol?"

"She's expecting me today." That was the plan, anyhow.

"She's never recovered, I don't think. Never was her bubbly self again after those girls went missing. Imagine, seeing a lost child at the end of your driveway, cooking her feet on the blacktop." She shuddered.

"Cases like these can really tear apart a community." I was fishing.

"Not ours! Not Leech Lake. You should have seen this town when we got word. I bet a hundred people signed up for the search party, and this was well before the internet or cell phones, don't you know. We combed those woods looking for poor little Amber and the other girl."

I didn't offer her Lily's name. I wanted her to keep talking.

"We didn't find them, of course. Didn't find a thing. It was like those sweet girls were zapped up in a spaceship." She fluttered her hand at her neck. "Not that I believe in such a thing. I'm just saying."

I nodded.

"Well," she said, glancing behind her. A uniform was typing away at a desk in the rear, and another one was on the phone. "I don't suppose it could hurt anything to show you files you already have a copy of."

I flashed my teeth. "That'd be wonderful. The sooner I can check off that box, the sooner I can dig into the case."

"Wouldn't it be something if you found them, after all these years? My name's Jody Hutchinson, by the way. That's my married name. I was Jody Hemmesch back then. Why don't you follow me."

She kept talking all the way to the records room.

CHAPTER 21

Van

The files Jody showed me were identical to what we had at the BCA. Any new information would need to come from talking to Bauman, who, Jody assured me, hadn't worked patrol since 1996. Then she offered me a homemade lemon bar from the tray she'd brought into work.

Next stop, Carol Johnson.

I parked my unmarked car on the terminus of Elm Street, in the curve of the cul-de-sac. It was ninety-four degrees the day the girls had disappeared. That had been a record-breaking high for July 23, 1980. In the same month forty-two years later, the radio informed me it was currently ninety-seven degrees and predicted to top out over a hundred by 2:00 p.m.

The tar was spongy beneath my feet. The girls would have been uncomfortably hot so close to the pavement, all knobby knees and sharp elbows, their arms swinging in anticipation of the shaded woods and the blissful cool of the creek.

I held an envelope of neighborhood photos taken the day Lily and Amber disappeared. The street I was looking down—other than the hybrid SUV parked in front of a house, some paint colors, and the height of the trees—had not changed since. The homes on this end of Elm would have been considered high-end back then. To my modern eyes, they looked like aging televangelists: big, gaudy, and empty.

Whoever bought the Kind mansion had repainted it a butter yellow with pine-green window trim. It had been a stately white with black shutters the last day Amber Kind had walked out of it.

I toed the tar, and a great gooey chunk came up. They'd repaved since 1980—I'd checked—but apparently some things never changed.

I studied the Kind mansion and again chewed on the question that had been needling me: Why had Amber invited Rue out that day? Mrs. Larsen said she'd forced Rue to take her little sister along, but why had *Rue* been invited? Was it simply a matter of her living the closest out of all Amber's classmates? Would Rue be able to tell me once I spoke with her? According to multiple interviews, she eventually remembered everything before the three girls stepped into the woods, but the approximately twenty-three minutes spent in the forest were erased from her memory, a chunk of her life recording wiped clean.

I knew what a glassy thing memory was, how fragile. I also knew that victims were silently encouraged to feel shame for things that had been done to them, which sometimes led to memories being buried but not erased. Could Rue's recollection of that day still be accessed behind memory's curtain?

The flash of a window blind opening in the sprawling house two down from the Kinds' snagged my eye. Carol Johnson's home. She and her husband never sold the McMansion they'd been living in the day she discovered Rue. I'd planned to explore the woods before conducting door-to-doors, but I was not one to pass up an opportunity. The Johnson door opened as I stepped onto the sidewalk, sweat trickling down my neck. The smell of Lysol washed out on a cool wave of air-conditioning.

"Can I help you?" the woman asked. She was stooped, hair gray and thin, her eyes watery. She wore a bright-aqua tracksuit that made a swishing sound when she hid her body behind the door as I stepped onto her porch.

"Mrs. Carol Johnson?"

She blinked rapidly. "Yes."

"I'm Agent Van Reed with the Bureau of Criminal Apprehension here in Minnesota. I believe my colleague, Agent Kaminski, told you I might be stopping by?"

Her face lit up. She opened the door wide. "Of course! Come in. Wait, I should ask to see your identification, shouldn't I?"

I showed her my badge, letting her catch a glimpse of the gun beneath my blazer because she seemed like the type of person who'd like to add that detail to the story when she told it to her friends later.

Her reading glasses were looped around a chain at her neck. She perched them on her nose and leaned forward. "Very good," she said.

I let an easy smile stay on my lips. The BCA had approximately six hundred employees. Only a fraction of us carried what was considered a law enforcement badge, which meant very few people knew what they looked like. I suspected Mrs. Johnson was a fan of crime shows, and good for her.

"May I come in?" I asked.

"Please do. It's hotter than the devil out there. Can I get you something to drink?"

"I'd love some water, if it's no bother." I followed her into her foyer. The Lysol smell was overpowering. "Do you have cleaners?"

She appeared puzzled for a moment. "No. Well, yes, they come over every other week, but this is an off week." Her face cleared up. "The smell! I like to sanitize my washing machine once a month. Keeps my clothes bright, you know. But I spilled some, I'm afraid. Have a seat right in there while I grab your water."

The living room immediately off the foyer had windows on two sides. The furniture was high quality but faded, an enormous U-shaped couch across from matching stiff-backed leather chairs. A bar cart stood next to a gas fireplace. The sunlight through the bare upper windows made the dust on the bottles look furry. Her cleaning crew must not have been particularly thorough.

I walked over to the windows facing Elm Street, the ones Mrs. Johnson would have been able to see Rue out of if she'd looked that day. I pushed back the heavy drapes. The Kind house wasn't visible from here. Neither were the woods unless I craned my neck.

"Here you go."

I turned and accepted the glass of water. Warm. Took a sip. Tap. "Your house is lovely."

"Thank you," she said, doddering over to sit on the couch. "My son and daughter say I should sell it and move into one of those communities where you play cards all day with other widows, but then, where would my grandchildren stay when they visit, I ask?"

Her smile was forced. This room contained no photographs, grandchildren or otherwise. The sterile front yard didn't speak to afternoons on the Slip 'N Slide or kids shrieking in a water balloon fight. Maybe she had a rumpus room in the basement, but my guess was few children visited her.

"When did your husband pass?"

Her eyes brightened at this. I didn't know if it was the joy some elderly seemed to take in talking about illness or death, like it was an old friend come to visit, or if she hadn't cared for her husband. Maybe both. "Three years back. He always swore they'd never find those girls, that they'd quit looking for them. I told him that wasn't true, that the police would never give up. And who was right? Me, looks like."

I nodded noncommittally. She and her husband had owned a chain of car washes across the Midwest. They sold them at retirement and bought a condo in Phoenix, where they spent half their time until Mr. Johnson passed. Carol had lived alone in this empty echo of a house since, spending all her time in Minnesota. "Can I ask you what you witnessed that day?"

"Certainly."

She recited, nearly verbatim, what she'd told the responding officer, who happened to be Bauman. I wondered how many times she'd repeated that story in the intervening years. Wondered how much she'd built her identity around being the person who found the only girl to make it out of the woods that day, what Carol Johnson's life would have been like if the misfortune had never happened. If she hadn't witnessed the aftermath of a tragedy, would she have led a very different life, one where her home was filled with warmth and grandchildren and a husband she loved?

"Thank you for that," I said when she finished her recap, my notebook open in front of me. I'd written only *Carol Johnson confirms.* "How well did you know the Kinds?"

Her face had been relaxing into the comfort of a job well done, but her expression grew guarded at the question. "They don't live here anymore."

I angled my head. Was she being evasive, or had my question simply caught her by surprise? I pretended to page back in my notes and read from them, though I had the information committed to memory. "You and your husband were one of the first families to build in this development. Your home was constructed in 1974, I believe. The Kinds moved into the neighborhood in 1978. Did you know them well?"

She reached for a glass that wasn't there before recalling her hand to pat her hair. "They seemed like a nice couple."

"You didn't socialize with them?"

Those closest to us are the most dangerous to us. It's the risk of human relationships. If a wife vanishes, we look at the husband. If children go missing, we check out the parents. According to the file, Dr. Kind had been in surgery when the girls walked into the woods. His alibi had been easily corroborated. Mrs. Kind said she had spent the morning at work but that no one else had been in the office. Their demeanor at the initial interview fell down gender lines. She'd been distraught. He'd been reserved.

There was no record of neighbors being asked about their marriage.

Carol Johnson pursed her lips and shook her head.

My blood gave a little zing. Mrs. Johnson had been talking nonstop since I'd arrived, a soft chatter until she got to the story of finding Rue, when it picked up speed. This nonanswering was notable.

"Did they socialize with *others* in the neighborhood?"

This earned a tight nod.

"Mrs. Johnson, anything you can remember from that time would be helpful. Sometimes what seems like an unimportant piece of information breaks the case wide open. It's called being an unknowing witness."

"Why now?" she asked.

It was my turn to be caught off guard.

"Why is there sudden interest in the case, I mean," she clarified. "It's that woman who was buried alive in Minneapolis, wasn't it? I read about that."

Red flags were suddenly popping up all over the place. "What makes you ask that?"

"Reporters come around every few years on the anniversary of the day those poor girls disappeared to ask questions. I answer, hoping that having it back in the news might bring them home. But the police have never returned, not since that single interview the day it happened. Something else must be going on, something big, or you wouldn't be in Leech Lake. The only big thing I know about is that poor woman."

This one had good instincts. "I can't speak to an active case, Mrs. Johnson, but if you can tell me what you remember about the Kind family from the time right before and right after their daughter disappeared, it might be helpful in cracking the cold case. I'd like to see justice for those girls and their families, and I think you would, too."

She seemed to consider that, and then her face flushed scarlet as she made her mind up about something. "Edward and I didn't socialize with the Kinds. They had *parties*, do you understand? Parties that were very popular back then but that Edward and I had no interest in."

I kept my gaze steady. "Key parties?" If there was a more modern term for gatherings where everyone went home with someone different than who they'd arrived with, I didn't know it.

"I believe that's what they were called, but as I told you, Edward and I wanted no part of them."

I wondered if this was why Erin never babysat Amber at the Kinds. "Were other neighbors involved?"

"I recognized some cars out front of the Kind house."

"Could you tell me whose?"

I took down the names of those she remembered. She certainly wasn't describing anything illegal. The detail could be nothing.

Or it could be the thing that broke this case wide open.

"You've been very helpful, Mrs. Johnson. Is there anything else you can recall?"

She shook her head and stood, signaling the interview was over. "I'm sure I can't."

"Well, I really appreciate your time," I said, letting her lead me to the door.

She opened it, and the heat of summer rolled in like she'd cracked an oven. "I often wonder," she said absentmindedly, "about the kindness of girls."

"Excuse me?"

"If Amber hadn't invited Rue to swim that day, she never would have taken Lily, and the Larsen girls would have been fine," she said, a far-off smile on her face. "It can be a dangerous thing, the kindness of girls."

She closed the door behind me as I slid off her front stoop and into the past, landing on the edge of Frank's Farm.

CHAPTER 22

September 2001
Evangeline

"Such lovely jellies," the short-haired woman is saying.

I smile in her direction but don't take my eyes off her daughter. She's got dark hair and big brown eyes. She's maybe half my age, and she's clutching a candy bar. I can smell the chocolate, see the great golden strings of caramel stretching between her lips and the bar when she takes a bite. Frank's Farm is famous for its jelly, but he won't let us eat it. He won't let us have any sweets. He says they'll corrupt us.

"Why are you dressed like Laura Ingalls Wilder?" the girl asks me.

"Tiffany!" the woman says. "Be nice."

I don't know who Laura Ingalls Wilder is, but judging by the mother's reaction, she's not a respectable girl.

The mother turns her attention to me, her cheeks flushed with embarrassment. "I'll take six bottles of jelly. That'll help you, won't it?"

"Yes, ma'am," I say, though I don't know what she means. We fight over who gets to work the farm stand. It's the biggest treat. Not only do you escape the backbreaking labor of the Farm, you also get to play store clerk. Sometimes you even get to hear music as cars drive up.

I take her money and give her change. She's chosen six jars of the ground cherry jelly, which looks pretty but tastes like burps. I don't know if I should tell her she might want to trade out a couple of those jars, or if that'd be rude. Before I can make up my mind, she scoops up the jelly and begins walking toward her car.

I'm left staring at her daughter.

She blinks at me. Starts moving her candy bar to her mouth for a bite. I can't tear my eyes away. I maybe even make a little wistful noise. She giggles.

"You can have the rest," she says, dropping it on my red checked tablecloth and running to catch up with her mom.

I stare at the bar for a moment, unable to believe my luck. Veronica, my favorite Sister with her gap-toothed grin, claimed she got to try chocolate once. Got it from a customer when she was working the farm stand, just like I'm doing now. Said it tasted like heaven wrapped in love.

I snatch the half a candy bar and tuck it into my apron pocket before the little girl changes her mind and comes back. I think a woman digging through the summer squash sees me do it. I think she flashes me a look of pity, but I don't care.

I have a candy bar.

When Frank picks me up at the end of the day, he doesn't say a word. We load up the table and its cloth plus the three pumpkins and a handful of cornhusk dolls that hadn't sold. We drive back to the Farm. I think he must smell the candy, or my guilt, but somehow I get all the way back to the dormitory without him knowing. There, I slide the candy bar (it's called "Snickers," like secret laughter, and isn't that perfect?) under my pillow.

I somehow manage to make it through dinner, and then dishes, and then sleep preparation, and finally until after lights-out to solemnly and silently remove the candy bar from beneath my pillow to share it with my Sisters, giving each a nibble. I save the last nub for myself, letting it melt into my tongue.

It's sweeter than heaven.

But even better than the taste is the moonlit smiles on my Sisters' faces as they carry the flavor of chocolate into their sleep. I believe I will also have sweet dreams as I wad up the brown wrapper. I plan to get up early and toss it in the firepit, hide it beneath the logs so Frank will never know of my crime.

But I've made a terrible mistake.

I've been so excited about the Snickers, so curious if the taste will match the smell, so happy to share treasure with my Sisters, that I've forgotten one of Frank's dirtier tricks: spying on us. Since Cordelia tried to run away, sometimes he hides in our dormitory to hear if we talk about him, tucks himself behind the flour sacks in the pantry to catch us eating more food than we are allotted, lingers outside our bathroom window to listen for if we are spending too much time naked. The punishment, when he catches a child, is terrible.

And this night he's under my bed.

I watch in horror as his hand snakes out from beneath the edges of my long quilt the second I set the wrapper on the floor. Feel my bowels relax as he slides out, his face purple with rage.

"You dare to pollute the purity of this space?" he roars, drawing himself to his full height, a terrible giant. I might have gotten away with the naked punishment for littering, maybe with a shunning, but then he sniffs the wrapper, reads it. His eyes start sparking. He grabs me by the collar and drags me, kicking and screaming, out of the dormitory.

I'm making so much noise that the Mothers race out of their building, the Brothers out of theirs. I think I hear my Sisters yelling at him to stop.

I want to believe they are.

The more I fight, the tighter Frank holds me. I'm so wild that at first, I don't realize he is striding toward the horse pen, toward the water trough he uses to baptize us when he's furious. He holds kids and Mothers underwater until they're seconds from dead.

When I see the trough, I go limp.

Plead for my life. Swear I'll do anything.

I'll wear black for the rest of my life, I'll never step out of line again, just please don't baptize me.

Beneath the full moon, Frank stays silent, holding me by the neck of my shirt. His silence is more terrifying than anything he can say.

Finally, he drops me into the dirt, storming off into the woods.

I don't know what saved me, which means I can never be safe.

CHAPTER 23

Van

My lucid dreams started nearly a year to the day after my almost-baptism. I'd assumed they were nightmares. Awful, soul-crushing nightmares that were so gruesome, I'd considered ending myself to escape them. Then, one day several months after Frank had been arrested and we'd all been cut loose from the Farm, I was buying a pack of cigarettes, high or drunk—they ran together back then—when a face caught my eye on the overhead television.

It was a man I'd been having nightmares about for weeks.

He was being arrested for sex trafficking.

The things I'd seen him do in my nightmares had been *real*.

I began weeping in the middle of the gas station, great gasping sobs of relief as I watched him being led away in handcuffs. I hadn't been hallucinating. I'd witnessed *real* people committing *real* crimes while I slept.

That meant the monsters could be stopped.

I finished my GED in record time and applied to the University of Minnesota criminology program.

That's where I learned that environment was story. Story was investigation.

My Evidence Based Methods professor, Dr. McPherson, had drilled that into us. On the first day of class, she'd shared the example of a detective who'd taken notes on everything he witnessed the moment he'd pulled up to the crime scene. The smell of cherry blossoms. The sound of a dog barking. The unbroken dew on the front lawn of the bungalow that held two bodies, a man stabbed seventeen times, a woman twenty-four.

The detective did the same inside the house, writing down everything he experienced each step of the way. Keys hooked on a purple Vikings helmet key ring resting in the metal dish next to the front door. Glass-topped coffee table tipped over, magazines pinned beneath it. The sickly-sweet smell of blood and organs. An investigator new to a scene must enter as an observer, Dr. McPherson said. That was their sole job, and this man had been exemplary at it, noting everything—no matter how small, how potentially insignificant.

It was the detail about the dew that broke the case. The lead suspect, a meter reader, claimed he'd visited the bungalow in the early hours, traipsed through the grass to reach the meter, heard a commotion inside, and called the police.

But the detective had recorded no footprints in the dew.

That was enough to turn on the heat. The meter reader cracked. He'd been having an affair with the wife, and he'd killed her and her husband in a fit of jealousy.

Environment was story. Story was investigation.

As I stood on the edge of the gloomy woods that'd swallowed Amber Kind and Lily Larsen, I marveled at the towering trees and overgrown ferns, their depth and thickness so primeval yet so near to Minneapolis. A developer had yet to snatch up these lush woods, carving lots out of the six square miles of cool earth, advertising a creek-side view to urbanites who wanted to escape the city's bustle and crush.

But the longer I stood on the edge of the woods, the more I began to understand why they'd been left untouched. There was something off about them, an uneasiness that prickled my skin, exhaling a cool breath laced with rot across my naked neck. The scent of a dead animal? But the warning I was getting felt deeper than that, even more primal.

Jess Lourey

I swiveled to stare at the street behind me with its soulless homes, its shiny cars, the row of telephone poles disappearing into the distance. The wild woods lived too close to that manicured world. There was something uneasy here in the boundary. It reminded me of the North Loop spot where the recent homicide victim had been buried alive, an untamed tangle of weeds and gravel in the sleek city's shadow.

I used my phone's camera to snap photos of the street view and the forest view, and then I turned on my phone's distance reader and entered the woods.

The smell of loam was strong and ancient, cloying in the still forest. The scent opened a door to a room I'd forgotten about, one full of surprisingly happy childhood memories. We knew from books and trips to town and the two months we were allowed to go to school that those of us at Frank's Farm lived differently from other kids, that no one else slept in a bunk room with up to a dozen other children cared for by a rotating crew of women who were all called Mother. That no one else learned to sew their clothes at the same time they practiced the alphabet. That when we talked about Frank, it wasn't the same as when they spoke of their dads.

But we were kids, and we had games and giggles. When we finished our chores early, we were allowed to play hide-and-go-seek in the woods. We'd gather kindling or dig wild ramps and make up great grand stories of archers and princes.

This forest held something ominous in it, but it also had some of that fairy-tale magic I recognized from my childhood.

The path that ran through its center was overgrown. It suggested that all the children on this end of the cul-de-sac had left home and moved on. A creek will always call to kids, though, so there must have been another path coming in from somewhere. That would explain why there'd been enough seclusion on this end for an abduction to take place.

Rue Larsen's secondhand Adidas sneakers had been found fifty-seven yards into the woods, on the other side of a great oak tree.

116

They'd been tied and set next to the tree with the sort of care you'd take when removing your shoes in a stranger's home. Why Rue had taken off her tennies was one of the case's mysteries. Had she been commanded to? If so, why? Or had she removed them preparing to leap into the creek another two hundred yards beyond, then run as soon as she saw danger? Except Carol Johnson had been clear that Rue hadn't been running. She'd been stunned, motionless, as if she'd been transported from one spot to another by some alien beam.

My phone said I'd reached fifty-eight yards. I stood in a small clearing, more a wide spot on the old path. A garish bouquet of plastic flowers was stuffed into a hole in the base of a massive oak. It was shadowy here, so I skimmed my phone's flashlight across the forest floor before stepping over to the flowers. I crouched, shining the light inside. The heart of the tree had died a while ago, leaving a troll-size space at its core. The bouquet had no writing on it, no indication of why it'd been placed there or by whom.

The trees rustled overhead, a squirrel or a breeze, but the shushing awoke goose bumps along my arms. I took a photo of the plastic flowers and stood, my knees popping.

Other than Rue's tennies, the Leech Lake police hadn't discovered anything unusual at the scene, not broken branches or disturbed leaves, no clothing scraps caught by bark, no man-made weapon. This location had been first investigated by Bauman and Schmidt. They hadn't taken photos. At the time, they'd believed the situation wasn't serious despite Rue's cooked feet, her stricken face. They'd tromped into the forest, calling out for Amber and Lily, stopped when they spotted Rue's shoes, grabbed them, looked around, and then kept walking to the creek. It turned out there weren't any other kids swimming, despite the heat. Most of them were attending a local baseball game, planning to meet up at the water afterward.

Bauman and Schmidt had found a muddy towel and some garbage— candy wrappers, pop cans—at the creek but assumed they'd been left by past swimmers. No girls. Two hours later, a civilian search team was organized, the same one Jody Hutchinson had referred to. Their intentions had been good, but they'd marched through the forest, obliterating any evidence Bauman and Schmidt might have overlooked.

There'd been all sorts of theories about what happened to Amber and Lily, about why Rue was allowed to escape. Aliens who only needed two girls. A gang that chose the two blondes and let the brunette get away. That creepy guy—every small town has one—who parked his car near the grade school to watch the girls had chosen Amber and Lily and then tracked them here.

The most likely scenario was that one man had abducted two girls because he couldn't manage three. He'd either lived within the six-mile-square forest or had a car parked nearby. That he had a house in the woods was more likely on the face of it, because then he wouldn't have had to drag two crying children into public, but the three structures inside the forest had been thoroughly searched. One was little more than four walls and a roof left over from pioneer days. The other two were hunting cabins without electricity or water. All three had been found empty with no signs of a recent disturbance.

The owners of the hunting cabins had been tracked down. One of them resided in Florida and hadn't visited Minnesota in more than four years. The other was a Minneapolis resident, a physician who worked at the same hospital as Dr. Kind. He claimed he hadn't been to his cabin since Memorial Day weekend. His alibi for the day of the abduction was solid on the face of it.

Kyle was reverifying all that. Meanwhile, forensics was running tests on Rue's tennis shoes to see if anything had been missed. I was nearly to the creek, the sun glinting off the silver of the water and reflecting into my eyes, when my phone buzzed.

It was Rue Larsen, returning my call.

                                                why
                                  was
                          everything
                  going
          so
  wrong

Maybe it was because he'd been born on the wrong planet.

To a stupid mother who never saw how special he was. Not the kind of special where what people really meant was slow. *Special* special. When she learned what he was capable of, rather than give him the respect he deserved, she told him to hide it.

And when he didn't, she hid him.

> *hit him hid him hit him hid him hit him hid him hit*
> *him hid him*

She stuffed him into a narrow spot below the floorboards. Tight as a coffin. She'd break him and crack him and cram him in. Roll the sofa over on top. Stamp her foot when his terrified weeping annoyed her.

"That'll learn you," she'd say. "That'll learn you to bend those bones, won't it?"

It was *her* fault he was an outsider, unable to make friends. He'd had a girlfriend, though, or close to it, when he was eleven. Both of them were tender back then, hopeful. Her name was Lottie. She had pretty blonde hair and lips as red as cherries. She played house with him during recess. Let him carry her books home.

She even let him hold her hand one day. It was so sweet, so warm. But she screamed when his slid out of joint and rested at a ninety-degree angle from his wrist.

It doesn't hurt don't worry it's what I do I'm special

But she never talked to him again.

You never really forget your first love, though, do you? He'd read that somewhere. How you spend the rest of your life trying to fill the hole they left.

CHAPTER 24

Van

Harry's name lit up my phone seconds after I finished my call with Rue.

"I'm in Leech Lake," I said, by way of greeting.

"I ran the DNA collected from the burial scene," Harry said, straight to business in a way I liked. "As expected, the majority of it matched the victim. The brown hair recovered from her body did not belong to her, however. It also did not belong to Mr. Shaw, who had only his own DNA under his fingernails."

My pulse did a sideways dance. "Find a match?"

"No," he said. "Whoever's hair it is, they're not in CODIS. Deepty has volunteered to upload the profile to the genealogy sites that work with law enforcement to see if the person could be tracked down that way."

Not a breakthrough, but a start.

"There's more," Harry said. "I pulled the items taken from Rue Larsen in 1980. The catalog says we have her size four Adidas sneakers, white with blue stripes, small white T-shirt, small white shorts, medium orange swimsuit, and heart charm necklace. The Leech Lake Police Department obviously didn't have a lab, so it was all sent to BCA forensics to be checked for fingerprints and blood. The only fingerprints lifted at the time belonged to Rue Larsen. No blood was discovered. They've all sat in a preserving box since."

He'd have technology not available forty-two years ago. "You're running DNA on them?"

"Yes. Mitochondrial DNA, the preferred method when the perpetrator is likely male, but most of the DNA collected will be female. There's one thing, however. The necklace wasn't in the box."

I hitched my breath. "Cataloging error?"

"Possibly," he said.

Or possibly not.

"There's something else," he said. "The dental records matched."

There it was. I didn't know how I felt.

"Amber Kind's from 1980 and the Jane Doe from two nights ago," he finished, as if I didn't know who he was talking about. "I'll need DNA to make a definitive ID, but it appears that Ms. Kind has been alive all this time, until she was buried alive three nights ago."

"Holy hell."

Harry ignored that. "We need to proceed as if Lily Larsen is also alive and in real danger."

"The cold case heats up." My chest tightened. "Did you tell Comstock?"

"He's my next call. We need DNA from one of Amber Kind's parents to run against Jane Doe's before I'm comfortable calling it official. I'd like someone from your team and someone from mine to make the DNA request in person. You said previously that Mrs. Kind still lives in Leech Lake?"

"Yeah," I said. "I'm in. When?"

He didn't answer immediately. The ideal was to tell the family as soon as the information was available, but it was late afternoon, and he likely wanted to coordinate with Comstock. "Either tonight or tomorrow morning."

"That means we have time," I said.

"Time for what?" Harry asked.

"To talk to Rue Larsen. Have one of your team set up the meeting with whichever Kind is first available tomorrow so you can meet me at 5831 Forty-Third Avenue South, Minneapolis, in twenty minutes."

CHAPTER 25

Rue

She watched from her window as the silver sedan pulled up. Moments later, a nearly identical four-door parked behind it. An early-thirties woman with the blondest hair she'd ever seen stepped out of the first vehicle, and a sharp-dressed man maybe ten years older got out of the second.

Her throat felt greasy. There was hardly anyone on the planet more practical than Rue Elizabeth Larsen. But she'd wanted one more day. One more day of the small, safe life she'd built up before it was all yanked away again. Before she was dropped back onto square one.

That's why she'd waited until this afternoon to call the woman back.

Agent Van Reed.

Maybe it was for the best that her shadow life was ending. Maybe it was time. She was bone-tired, weary of carrying so many regrets and what-ifs. She was afraid in her own home and, worse, couldn't relax *in her own body*. It was probably good she hadn't had kids even though that'd been her one dream. It just wasn't in the cards for her. She was born to walk this earth like a scared, twitching rabbit.

They were coming up her sidewalk.

It'd be all over in a matter of minutes.

Rue knew it was either her sister or Amber they'd discovered two nights ago buried alive. *Knew it.* She didn't want to hear that it was

Amber, but it would be worse to learn that it was her baby sister, who she'd failed that day. She also didn't want confirmation that the monster she'd been hiding from for forty-two years was still alive. Didn't want to have to repeat *I don't know, I don't know* as parents wept and police shook their heads disapprovingly.

Didn't want her life made public once more.

When the rap came on her door, she was so wound up that she forgot how to put down her coffee mug. The million small motions she'd need to make were simply beyond her. She instead carried it, turning all the locks with her free hand.

"Rue Larsen?"

The female agent held up her badge, her face neutral. There was something in her eyes, though, something familiar. The man was so movie-star handsome that looking at him made an unhinged giggle bubble out of Rue's mouth.

"Sorry," she said, stepping aside. "Come in."

She closed the door behind them and started locking it out of habit. She stopped not because she felt safe with them but because it would be easier to escape if it were necessary. She didn't think it would be. She recognized these thoughts as trauma embedded in her neural pathways, tiny, nail-studded grenades that exploded on a whim, shredding what was left of her sanity.

"I'm Agent Van Reed," the female said. "We spoke on the phone. This is Agent Harry Steinbeck. Thank you for inviting us into your home."

"It's charming," Agent Steinbeck said.

Rue imagined it through his eyes—austere, almost military in its unbroken sight lines. She couldn't imagine how he'd consider that charming, but he sounded sincere.

"Please, have a seat." Rue indicated the kitchen table. She didn't own a couch. Too easy for someone to hide behind. "Can I get either of you anything?" It had been a while since she'd had visitors, but the dance was muscle memory. "I have water, iced black tea, coffee, and Diet Coke."

"We're fine," Agent Reed said, speaking for both. "As I said on the phone, we're hoping to ask you some questions about what happened in the summer of 1980."

"It's all in the file. It must be. I don't have anything new to add." She was still standing, still clutching the mug that she'd have to be buried with if she couldn't figure out how to put it down. The table was right there. If she could just place her mug on it. If she could simply rest in the chair.

Agent Reed nodded. "You were a good big sister. Dragging Lily along to the river would have been a hassle, might have cost you points with Amber. But you did it. You packed your lunches, even. And then a monster met you in the woods." She said "monster" like she knew what it meant. "These things shouldn't happen to children. But they do. All the blame is on that person. All the responsibility. Agent Steinbeck and I want to find him."

buried alive buried alive buried alive

Through the haunt of that memory phrase, Rue caught hold of Agent Reed's words. They were different from what she'd heard before. Only a little, just a click off what officers and her psychiatrist had said more than forty years ago. A person needed to have spent their life clutching a poisoned thorn to notice the difference, to feel the lighter touch. The way her worst fear had been acknowledged, then soothed, the blame placed elsewhere for one blissful second before it snaked its way back.

That's when Rue realized why Agent Reed had looked familiar. It was her bearing. Trauma recognized trauma. Rue fell into the chair. She set the mug on the table. Clumsily, like a puppet whose strings had been dropped, but she did it.

Neither agent batted an eye.

"I don't remember anything after we stepped into the woods," Rue said honestly, "except for Amber singing a line from 'Skip to My Lou.'"

"Do you recall which line?" Reed asked.

Rue shook her head, but then it came to her, clear and close, spoken in Amber's sweet, high voice. "I'll get another one prettier than you," she whispered.

Agent Steinbeck wrote it down while Agent Reed leaned forward, careful not to cross the invisible boundary Rue wore like armor.

"Thank you," she said. "What else do you remember?"

Like it was a fact that there'd be more.

"I don't know what happened to Amber and Lily," Rue said, a huff escaping her nose. "Last thing I remember is going in the woods, something pushing back, Amber saying that piece of the song, and then the hospital. My feet all bandaged."

"Something pushing back?" Agent Reed's eyes were bright.

Rue lifted a shoulder, dropped it. "Little-kid willies. I think we all felt it on the edge of those woods, or at least Amber and I did. Like it didn't want us to enter. That's how it is when you're a kid. You think you're at the center of everything. Like there's powerful forces at work, pushing and pulling you. Then you grow up and realize everyone is just trying to get through the day. There's no magic."

Reed's eyes still blazed. "I felt it, too."

Steinbeck's eyebrow twitched. There was something between the two of them. Some connection, some important shared experience. It further stirred Rue's melancholy, whispered of a normal life just out of reach.

"Felt what?" Rue asked.

"That darkness on the edge of the woods. I was there today."

Rue turned her hands palms up, studying the lines. "So they're haunted. Doesn't change anything. It certainly wasn't a ghost who kidnapped Amber and Lily."

"Who was it?" Reed asked.

"He—"

Both agents sat slightly taller, the smallest movement, but Rue was a master at noticing body language. *He*. This was the first time she'd thought of a gender. Everyone assumed a man had abducted Amber and Lily. Many people had used "he" when interrogating her about her experience. This was the first time she'd used it herself.

She continued, speaking quickly before the words slipped back into hiding. "He said something about 'buried alive.'"

The female agent's knuckles went momentarily white as she clenched her hands. "What else did he say?"

"You *know*, don't you?" Rue asked, the question escaping in a rush. "How this works, I mean. How when someone steals your center, you no longer know what's real. You cling too tight to a memory, and it breaks. Or you see danger in every corner, even when it's not there. Everywhere you go, you plan how to escape. *You know what it's like.*"

A great wave of pain rolled beneath the agent's skin. "I'm sorry for what happened to you," she said.

Rue's lips tipped up, but it wasn't a smile. "I don't remember anything else. I don't."

"Would you be willing to speak with a hypnotherapist?" Reed asked. "We have an exceptional therapist we use to help witnesses regain memories."

The male agent sat back. He didn't like that offer. His face was kind but too perfect. Its symmetry bothered Rue.

"I'll think about it," she said. Those four words, she'd found, were the only thing that stopped the questions. Paused the *need* people showed up with and laid at her feet. And she was suddenly exhausted.

"What were you like as a kid?" Agent Reed asked. She tipped her chin like she was genuinely curious. "Did you test boundaries?"

The question surprised Rue, washing her in a pink-edged sadness. "Not unless you count stealing a full-page photo of Richard Gere out of a *People* magazine in the dentist's office waiting room," she said. "Other than that, I was a rule follower. Average grades, average at sports, didn't stand out in any way. Amber, though? She was pure, like a fairy-tale princess. She had everything. She was popular. Pretty. Rich. She was nice, too. *Genuinely* nice. I'd won the keys to the kingdom that summer, her wanting to play with me."

Neither agent said anything. Rue continued.

"And Lily?" Her voice was a husk. "Lily was perfection. Smart with a streak of sass. She would have . . . she would have grown up to be something really special."

Rue closed her eyes. The image of Lily was always right there, waiting. Her messy ponytails, her gap-toothed smile, freckles sprinkled like cinnamon across her nose. An enormous cherry Ring Pop on her finger, a scraggly yellow Band-Aid on her knee.

"Ms. Larsen," the male agent asked, his voice gentle. "Do you know where the necklace you were wearing that day went? I looked for it in the box of effects the police took from you that day but didn't find it."

"I kept it," Rue said.

Both agents' mouths tightened.

"The police asked for my clothes, my shoes," she continued, feeling defensive. "At the hospital. They took the necklace, too, put it all in a box and then stepped out. I don't know why, but I grabbed the necklace back. I guess I needed something *solid* to pray over, you know? To beg for Lily to come home. It didn't hurt anyone, me keeping it."

"You're right," Steinbeck said quietly. "It didn't hurt anyone."

He might be lying to her. She chose to believe he wasn't. "I'll get it for you."

She stood, her legs liquid. Somehow, she made it to her bedroom. Because of the way her house was set up, they could see her open her jewelry box and take out the bauble. She hadn't prayed on it for years, but it gave her comfort, knowing it was there. She walked back into the living room, past them, and into the kitchen, where she grabbed a plastic baggie. She dropped the necklace in and brought it to the female agent.

"Here. I'm sorry I kept it."

The agent took the bag. "We'll return it to you."

Rue nodded. She was done. Her bones were heavy, her heart a cave. The agents had more questions, but she had no more answers. After consenting to a DNA swab, she walked them to the front door, turning all locks as soon as they were outside. She set her alarm system.

Then she leaned against the door and drew her first deep breath since they'd arrived.

They hadn't told her which one of them had been buried alive. That meant they either weren't sure yet, or they wanted to tell the parents first. It meant she had at least one more day. One more day before everything was ripped away from her all over again.

CHAPTER 26

Van

Harry and I had driven separately, so we couldn't immediately discuss the interview. The best we could do was agree to call a case meeting in the incident room, me bringing in Kyle and Harry inviting Deepty and Johnna.

I plugged the BCA address into my phone before pulling away from the curb. On a regular day, I could drive there with my eyes closed from any location in the Cities. But Rue had rattled me. Not her words, but her eyes. They weren't empty, as Carol Johnson had described them, or at least they weren't that way any longer. They were painfully wise.

She'd seen through me with those eyes. I felt exposed.

People assumed that Frank sexually abused the children. He didn't. He prided himself on only taking willing women, and there were dozens who sought out the structure of his farm. What had started out as a back-to-the-land enterprise in the late '70s began to shape itself as Frank's charisma grew, pushing out the other men, calling in women who sought security, or perceived value, or someone to make decisions for them. Single mothers with children in tow who'd heard that Frank would give them a home. Abused women who heard Frank would keep them safe. Curious women who wanted to live in harmony with the earth.

I didn't know which one my mother had been. Frank required children to be raised communally. By my best estimates, I'd been born in 1990. My early years were planting, weeding, watering, harvesting, broken up with games of tag and story circles. To a child, Frank was scary, but he also inspired awe.

I'd loved him. It was the love of an abused child for their tormentor, but it was still love.

Had Rue seen that in me? Could she feel the shame that still infected me like poison?

❖

The incident room Kyle booked was on the smaller side, but there was plenty of space for the five of us. He'd added notes and time lines to the walls, a computerized age-progression image of Lily, and 1980 photos of all the suspects next to recent ones where he could get them. The only open spot was the whiteboard, which I stood in front of. Having all eyes on me made me itchy, so I dived right in. I filled them in on my impression of Leech Lake, its police department, Carol Johnson, the crime scene, and finally, Rue.

Kyle whistled. "I can't believe she saved the necklace."

"I can," Harry said quietly. He was seated across from me at the rectangular table, both of us on the short ends. Kyle sat on his left, Deepty and Johnna on his right. "She was a traumatized eight-year-old."

His words brought a fierce warmth to my chest. People who'd grown up feeling safe in their homes often had a hard time comprehending the things the rest of us did, the routines or trinkets we needed to feel secure. Not Harry. He understood. The silver wristwatch I wore felt lighter for a moment.

"But it might have had the guy's prints or DNA on it," Kyle said, wording it as more of a question than a statement.

"Highly unlikely," Deepty said. "Measuring touch DNA wasn't a thing in 1980, but even if it had been, the perpetrator would have needed to hold the necklace for several seconds to potentially leave enough DNA for a profile. And he would have needed to place a finger dead center to leave even a partial print."

Deepty slid over the tray holding the bag Harry had requested she bring from the lab. It contained the heart charm necklace Comstock had found next to Amber Kind. She handed the bag to Harry, who held it next to the necklace Rue had given us. He joined the half hearts through the plastic.

It was a Cinderella fit.

"Those poor girls," Harry and I said at the same time.

"I coordinated with Comstock," Deepty said. A V burrowed between her eyes, like the task hadn't been easy. "You're all set to meet at Mrs. Kind's condo at nine a.m. tomorrow. She's expecting you."

The room went momentarily silent. Mrs. Kind would be hearing that her only child had likely been found. While there might be some relief in knowing Amber was no longer suffering, the idea of closure was a lie. The pain was never over for parents who lost their children. It changed over time, diminishing its stranglehold, but it never went away.

"What reason did you give her for the visit?" I asked.

"Potential cold case update," Deepty said. "Comstock asked me to set up an interview with Mrs. Larsen immediately following, so that's on the books, too."

Johnna snorted. "Secretary slide."

I grimaced. I was familiar with the act, not the term. Didn't matter how many degrees or years of experience you had, some men just automatically assumed you were their personal assistant. The older they were, the more common it was. I was unsurprised to learn it was part of Comstock's MO.

"Thanks," I said. "Are both women retired?"

"I've got that one," Kyle said, flipping open the folder in front of him and pulling out a white card. "Theresa Kind was born in 1949, making her . . ." He paused to do the mental math. "Seventy-three. She's still an active real estate agent, a very successful one by the number and price range of her Zillow listings, but she mainly works out of her condo."

He shuffled to the next card. "Rita Larsen is also seventy-three. She retired at age sixty-six, sold her house on Elm Street, and moved into an apartment in Leech Lake. She volunteers at the local nursing home and is active in her church."

"Well done," I said.

I didn't mean just that info. Kyle was knocking it out of the park as a second. He'd created an index card for every suspect and every witness. On the top left he'd written the person's full name or first name and LNU—last name unknown. It happened more often than we'd like when interviewing witnesses, and there wasn't a legal thing we could do about it. They weren't required to share their name. Same with address, phone number, and Social Security number. We recorded the information when we had it, but it was rare to snag everything from a single witness.

Next, he'd indicated the witness's role in the case—best friend of victim, pizza delivery kid, and so on—and any place they were mentioned, either in the Cold Case files or the original case files. We had a computer program called, cornily enough, Police Solutions that helped digitize this information, but Kyle preferred his method. I could see why. His way, you could hold the cards, add to them when you received more information. It felt *real*. Like you were making progress rather than simply typing. Longhand record-keeping was an odd quirk for a guy in his twenties, and I was here for it.

He was also creating two different time lines for each of the seven known suspects: parents, band teacher, classmate, pedophile. One time line laid out what the suspects claimed they'd been doing when the crime occurred. The second listed what witnesses said they'd *seen* the suspect doing. Often, the time lines matched up. When they didn't, we had something to check out.

"It's going well," Kyle agreed. "No real surprises. The list of suspects hasn't changed. I haven't tracked down Rolf Larsen yet, but I will."

"The Minneapolis PD will be proceeding as if Lily Larsen and possibly Amber's child or children are still alive," I said. I knew it was true because it was what I would've done. "And likely living within sixty miles of the area Amber Kind was buried."

Johnna appeared resigned. "Like Elizabeth Smart."

"Exactly," I said, nodding.

Elizabeth Smart's kidnapping was every parent's nightmare. A rosy-cheeked blonde of fourteen, she was taken at knifepoint from her bedroom in her family's Utah home. Her abductor chained her to a tree, raped her, starved her, and forced her to watch porn. The makeshift campsite where she was first held and underwent the nightmarish abuse was only three miles from her home.

She could hear search parties calling her name.

Her kidnapper, a married, self-proclaimed prophet who called himself Emmanuel, believed he was entitled to young wives. After traveling in the Southwest, eventually her abductor and his wife returned to Utah, where Elizabeth was spotted. After nine months of her ordeal, she was reunited with her family.

Some people were quick to judge Elizabeth when it was discovered that she'd gone out in public with her captors without trying to escape, but she was a terrified, abused child afraid to make things worse. There were hundreds of cases just like hers, cases of abducted children and sometimes even adults who cleaved to their captor for survival, who went so far as to quietly accompany their brutalizer in public and never tell a soul what they were suffering.

The rest of the world played its part, too. Statistics proved that most people who spotted a woman or child who appeared scared and miserable—at the mall or in a restaurant or airport—didn't say or do anything, even when they sensed something was off.

People tended to turn away from what made them uncomfortable.

Which meant we'd have to consider the very real possibility Lily and Amber had been living in plain sight since 1980.

"Kyle and I are going to revisit every angle of the cold case, but we also want to be on the lookout for any connections tying the original abduction to the recent murder," I said. "What linked the two locations, for example?"

"Isolated," Deepty said. "But *not* isolated. Near homes but also hidden."

I turned to write it on the whiteboard.

"Same time of year," Harry said.

"Close to a river," Johnna offered.

"There was a railroad track near the Minneapolis murder," Kyle said. "Was there one by the Leech Lake abduction site?"

I closed my eyes to picture the layout. "Not the Elm Street side where the girls lived, but on the other side, I think. Parallel to the main road. Confirm that, will you?"

Kyle nodded and wrote it down.

"I'm still running tests on the soil," Johnna said. "Deepty found the suspect's shoe."

Before any of us could get excited, Deepty clarified.

"I found the make and size. They're a StepSmooth size eleven. It's a knockoff extra-cushy orthopedic shoe made in China."

"Where are they sold?" I asked.

"Everywhere." Deepty wrinkled her nose. "But I got a lead on a big shipment coming into the Minnesota Salvation Army two months ago. I'll keep digging."

I paused to give space for Harry to tell his team member she'd done good work and realized he was letting me take charge. "Nice job, Deepty."

She nodded. "You got it."

I leaned against the table, studying the whiteboard. "Do we have anything else?"

I gave it a couple more beats. No one offered anything.

"All right. Kyle will continue to index and build out the time lines. Deepty and Johnna, you're both processing the crime scene evidence and continuing to look for connections to the cold case. Harry, you and I are going to Leech Lake tomorrow morning. I'll drive."

He nodded, and we all stood.

They walked out, but I stayed behind to erase the whiteboard before I remembered this was our room. I could leave it as is. It was a good feeling, having our own dedicated space. Being able to do our best work. Communicating. Working as a team. I needed that warmth against the darkness of the case. I held the comfort in my belly as I stepped out of the incident room, almost barreling into Chandler.

I had just started to apologize when I saw the woman from my most recent recurring vision standing five feet away.

CHAPTER 27

Van

She wore a crimson pantsuit and a bland smile. She was with Chandler as well as five others in similarly professional clothes and expressions. I gasped and blinked, the image of her standing in front of me superimposed on my memory of her walking down that hallway of horrors with her eyes as black as traps, pulling out her big brass key ring, unlocking a door that held a tortured, whimpering child.

"What the hell are you doing here?" I demanded.

She glanced to Chandler, then back to me, her face screwed up with concern. "Do I know you?"

"Reed!" Chandler barked.

I felt a tug at my arm, then heard Kyle's voice behind me. "Sorry, sir. We just had a bit of bad news in there. We both need to walk it off."

Kyle pulled me down the hall, and it wasn't gentle. He marched me all the way to my office before releasing me.

"What's going on with you?" he asked. "First that craziness at the bar, and now you're yelling at a tour group?"

Some hair had come loose from my bun. I curved it over my ear, trying to calm my rampaging heartbeat. This would not do, my dreams colliding with my ability to do my job. "Do you know who that was? That woman in the red pantsuit?"

"Hell yes," he said, rolling his eyes. "It's State Representative Marie Rodin. She's here with some other legislators. *They're considering upping our funding.*" He sharpened those words so they hit their target.

"Shit." I needed Bart. I needed to escape. I needed help.

"Exactly right." He nodded, agitated. "There was a memo about it. Said they'd be visiting today, said to be on our best."

Even when I had the luxury of time, I didn't read memos. They were almost always a waste of time. Focusing on that detail, on the absurdity of passing notes at work, grounded me just enough. The panic began receding. I could draw in a full breath. I'd had nightmares before. Plenty. I could navigate this.

"I met her earlier," Kyle said, taking my silence for reflection. "She's a nice lady. Why'd you call her out like that? She do something to you?"

"Being nice isn't a personality trait," I said, a tingling sensation returning to my fingers. "It's a strategy. Never trust someone just because they're acting nice."

"Jesus, Van. Back off. I'm on your side," he said. "You owe her an apology, doesn't matter whether she's nice or not. You just asked her what the hell she was doing here, when all she was doing was her job. We could expand Cold Case with more money."

"Yeah."

I must have sounded dazed, because his body language changed, relaxing, with his voice matching it. "This is hard, Van, cases like this, ones with children involved. It can get to a person; doesn't matter how long they've been doing it."

The anger was automatic. "This isn't about the case. I thought she was someone else. It happens."

He stepped back, holding up his hands. "Fine. You do you. Oh, and you're welcome for saving your ass back there."

I watched him storm away and then stepped into my office, relieved to find it exactly as I'd left it. Messy. Safe. I walked over to my desk and fired up my computer. Pulled up the Minnesota Criminal History System. With the correct paperwork, situation, or permission from the subject, a person could run a background check on anyone. I had none of those. If management searched, if they intentionally sought out my online history, they'd learn I'd done an invasive check without cause. I'd be in deep trouble, probably fired.

Yet I typed "Marie Rodin" into the search bar.

Took a breath.

Watched the cursor blink.

One click, and I could see what, if any, trouble she'd been in.

I pushed on my eyelids until I saw stars. Marie Rodin *was* the woman who'd been haunting my sleep. The basement of her house held three locked doors. I'd heard children weeping behind one of them, seen a battered body chained to a bed. I hadn't imagined any of it. Had I? Was my first field job in over a year—a nightmare of a cold case involving three little girls—getting to me, like both Harry and Kyle had said? Had the stress woven a vaguely familiar face into my nightmares, where I'd confused it for a lucid dream?

If Bart were still alive, he'd know what to do.

I steepled my fingers, blinking until my eyes cleared. Bart would tell me not to risk my career over a bad dream, that was for sure. Maybe an anonymous tip would work. I'd need a burner phone. But what would I say? That I thought Representative Rodin had two kids chained up in her basement? It'd be written off as a crank call.

Rue's words came back to me, about seeing danger in every corner even when it wasn't there.

Even if the Marie Rodin nightmares had been true visions, I wasn't required to act on them. I couldn't save everyone.

Last time I'd tried, three men had ended up dead.

A cold, heavy lead was replacing my bones. I needed to move before it reached my heart. I stood abruptly, so quick I clipped the soft flesh above my kneecap on the underside of my desk. I was desperate for a change of scenery. I'd drop by the shelter. I hadn't signed up for a shift, but they could always use an extra set of hands.

While there, I might look up the representative's home address on one of the computers.

Might.

CHAPTER 28

Van

Minnesota was woken up by a sloppy rain. My windshield wipers slapped as I steered toward Leech Lake, moving the hot soup falling from the sky from one end of the glass to the other. I cranked the air-conditioning to keep out the gummy humidity.

"You should drive slower," Harry said, his hand on the dashboard.

I'd checked out my usual car because it was my usual car, but also, it handled sweet in the weather. "Are you nervous because it's *filthy* outside?" I said, referencing his accidental comment outside the Spot the other night.

He managed to stop himself from glancing at the floor, where I'd tossed the fast-food bag and wrappers that had held the breakfast I'd chowed down before picking him up. I made a mental note to dispose of them next time I gassed up, in case someone checked out the car after me.

"I can't see three feet past the headlights," he said. "We won't be able to stop suddenly if something leaps out. It's best to slow down under these conditions."

I leaned forward to peer up through the sheeting water. "It's windy, too. Turn on the radio. I want to hear how long until this lousy weather clears."

He obliged. We waited seven minutes to learn there was currently a heavy rain with a potential thunderstorm warning this evening.

"Ever wonder why storms only happen at night?" I mused.

"That's largely a phenomenon of the plains region of the US," Harry said, donning his best teacher voice. "During the day, the heat rising from the earth is met by the sun's rays. However, at night—"

I held up a hand. "I was making conversation."

"It's knowledge."

"I prefer some mystery," I said, hiding my smile. I had to admit, there was comfort in Harry's consistency. If there was a fact to be discussed, he was there.

A great gale pushed the sedan a foot to the right, and then, just like that, the rain eased. I could suddenly see the fields and the woods behind them, the trees swaying like drunken men.

"Leech Lake is over that hill," I said. "We let Comstock take the lead?"

"Of course." Harry unpeeled his hands from the dashboard. "It's his case."

I nodded, cracking my window to let in the sweet incense of rain-soaked earth. "I'd like to ask Mrs. Kind some questions while we're there."

Harry glanced over at me. "You'll want to be on the same page as Comstock."

He was right. Theresa Kind would be learning about the possibility of her missing daughter's death today, a daughter who'd likely lived in the area for the past forty years. The more streamlined our questions were, the easier it would be on her. Unfortunately, I didn't think Comstock would be inclined to synchronize with me beforehand.

That was confirmed when we pulled up to Theresa Kind's condo and found him parked out front, sitting in his unmarked, windows down, cigarette smoke rolling out, his face all shades of pissed. He tossed out his butt, rolled up his window, and stepped out the same time as I did. Harry grabbed an umbrella. Comstock and I watched each other through the drizzle that had started, two gunfighters in a town with only room for one.

"You're late," he said.

141

"The weather," Harry offered genially, opening the car's back door to reach his traveling kit. "I'd like to be the one to tell Mrs. Kind about her daughter. It's crucial she understand we have a probable but not definitive ID until we run the DNA."

"You sure she'll give it to you?" Comstock asked.

"I don't see why not," Harry said.

"Do we need three?" Comstock asked, eyeballing me. "Seems like a crowd."

"A male-female team is protocol when available," I said. He wasn't going to let me ask a single question, that much was clear. "It's available."

Comstock turned to Harry. "You ready?"

Harry nodded.

"Then lead the way."

The pine trees that ringed the development were rain-smudged at the edges, their sharp, lean scent magnified. The development's four structures were identical: three condos to a building, each of them three stories with a balcony on the second floor, all painted taupe, all with white doors. Comstock positioned himself behind Harry, making me invisible from the front as we approached. The thought of kicking one of his feet behind the other was tempting. It would cost more than it paid, though.

Harry rang the doorbell. I stepped to the side so Mrs. Kind could see me when she answered. A shot of warmth hit my veins at the thought of her meeting Harry first. It was a terrible thing she was about to hear, but there was no better person to deliver the devastating news. Harry wore a dark-blue suit, immaculately cut, with deep-brown shoes and a somber tie. He looked like he was dressed for the most important thing in the world. Every mother deserved to see that level of respect when she heard tragic news. I'd donned my only pantsuit—black—for that very reason, my dress loafers tight around my toes.

The door opened. The woman on the other side was tall, maybe five ten, with thick silver hair to her shoulders. Her eyes were bright and blue, her lipstick a creamy coral. She wore a lilac tunic over matching pants, the fabric silky and flowing.

Her eyes traveled over us.

"You three look a little serious to be trick-or-treaters. Maybe because it's July." Her smile was light, but there was something rigid beneath it. She was bracing herself.

"Theresa Kind?"

"Standing before you."

"I'm Harry Steinbeck, an agent with the Minnesota Bureau of Criminal Apprehension. This is my colleague, Agent Evangeline Reed, and Minneapolis Police Detective David Comstock. I believe you've been told to expect us. May we come in?"

She tucked her lips into each other. The coral disappeared, leaving only a raw-edged line. "Tell me now."

My breath caught. Harry needed to go on instinct here, deciding on the spot whether to honor her request or follow protocol and get her seated first.

He didn't hesitate. "Preliminary dental testing indicates we may have found your daughter, Amber Kind."

A tightening of her hand on the doorjamb was the only indication she'd heard.

"Were they together?" she asked.

"Excuse me?" Harry said.

"The children. Lily and Amber. Did you find them together?"

My stomach plummeted. None of us had considered the natural assumption she would make: that we'd discovered her daughter's *bones*, forever eight years old. I silently railed against our stupidity.

"I'm so sorry," I said, stepping forward. "We should have been clearer. We believe Amber was alive until recently."

Her knees buckled, but Harry was quick. He grabbed her and held her upright. I moved in to help him.

"May we come into your home?" Harry asked.

She nodded.

Harry and I supported her through the tastefully decorated foyer to a den. I caught a glimpse of Comstock as we helped her to a wingback chair. He was looking away, toward the fireplace, his jaw clenched.

"Can I get you some water, Mrs. Kind?" I asked. "Or call someone for you?"

"Theresa. Haven't been a Mrs. for decades." She fanned herself, her eyes fluttering. "What did she die of?"

"We're not certain it's your daughter," Harry said.

"What did she die of?"

If it was her daughter, she had every right to know. If it wasn't, sharing the dreadful news of a woman buried alive, making her believe it was her child who had died so cruelly, would cause unnecessary pain. Harry'd been clear that we didn't yet have a definitive identification.

"What I can tell you," Harry said gently, circumventing her question, "is that we need your help. I'd like to do a mouth swab to gather DNA. You have my word that if the results are conclusive, I will drive out here personally with the information and stay as long as you need me to stay."

Theresa drew a shuddering breath. "You're a wily one, aren't you?"

He was. He was also being infinitely kind. My respect for him grew.

"I'm so sorry for what you've been through," Harry said. "I wish I could answer all your questions, but I can't, not without DNA."

His eyes were so sad I had to look away. Like I'd been spying on a private moment. Comstock must have felt the same, because he strode over to the mantel. It was all photos of Amber: one of her as a toddler waving at the camera with a fat little hand, her smile dimpled; another of her wearing a long white dress—her first Communion?—like a princess, her golden curls her crown; a third of her taking a big slurp from a garden hose, her sky-blue eyes staring straight at the camera; and on and on. Infant to eight-year-old, she was giggles and sunshine.

"Amber looked so joyful," I said truthfully.

Theresa followed my sight line, a wistful smile taking over. "She was that. Pliable, too. I know that's not a popular way to describe a girl

The Taken Ones

these days, but she was so docile. Would've followed Satan to hell if he'd asked. That's what I'd always figured happened to her, you know." She gave Harry a thoughtful look before indicating she'd accept the swab.

I turned toward the foyer to give them some privacy. Everything here matched, warm beiges and creams designed to soothe. Even the mail was stacked crisp and white in a pile. Made my skin itch. My eyes kept traveling, finally stopping on the cast-iron pan resting on an end table near the entrance.

"Did we interrupt you when you were cooking?" I asked.

"What?" she asked, sounding like she had a swab in her mouth.

"All done," Harry said.

I turned around, pointing at the ten-inch pan. "Were you cooking?"

Theresa leaned around Harry, her mouth twitching when she saw what I was referring to. "I carried it around with me after Amber disappeared. I went a little bit nuts. Became convinced the devil was coming for my husband and me, too. My husband said we should buy a gun, but I said, 'Charles, unlike a bullet, a cast-iron pan never misses.' Guess it became a habit to keep it near the door."

Comstock should have been asking the questions, but he wasn't. I didn't know what had his tongue, but no way was I letting this opportunity pass. "What made you think you and your husband were in danger?"

She rubbed her jaw. "I didn't at first. But then I went about three weeks without sleeping. Started to see ghosts."

I knew what that was like. "It makes sense you couldn't sleep back then."

She shook her head. "You don't know the half of it. I saw demons jumping out of the woodwork. Literally. Little lava-colored nasties with horns. My doctor prescribed a tranquilizer, and that took the edge off." Her voice grew distant. "Moving was the hardest thing. As long as I stayed in the Elm Street house, Amber would know where to run to if she got free. But then I decided that was foolish. My baby girl was

145

surely dead, and I needed to let her go. Needed to get on with my life."
Her chin quavered. "Now you tell me she was alive this whole time."

"We'll know tomorrow," Harry said. "I promise you that. Are you
sure there's no one we can call?"

Theresa's gaze slid to Comstock. "My sister, I suppose. Yes, I'll
text her."

She reached for her phone and typed a quick message. The response
was nearly instantaneous. "She's on her way."

"Are you still in contact with your ex-husband, Theresa?" I asked,
ignoring how my question made Comstock puff up like someone had
yanked his corset strings.

She made a breathy sound, one that suggested general annoyance.
"No, but I know where he lives. Perk of being a real estate agent. Would
you like his address?"

"Yes, thank you," I said, waiting while she scribbled it on a pad of
paper next to her chair. Kyle already had the information, but it can be
soothing to feel helpful.

"We've taken enough of your time, Mrs. Kind," Comstock said,
moving toward the door.

Harry didn't budge. "We can stay until your sister arrives. Longer,
if you need. It's no trouble at all."

She handed me the address and tipped her head toward the vial
containing the swab. "I'd prefer you take care of that. I need to know."

"Of course," Harry said. He reassembled his kit. The briefcase had
a pocket especially for the wrappers and his used latex gloves. "I'll be
back tomorrow."

She nodded. "If you don't mind, please show yourself out. I want
to sit for a bit."

"I'm going to leave my card here," Harry said. "If you need me to
return today, even if it's five minutes from now, please don't hesitate
to call."

She dragged in a sigh and offered him a soft smile. "You're a good
man. I'll be fine. I've lived through worse."

Comstock showed impressive restraint by waiting until we reached our cars to rip me a new one, gripping my arm and twisting it just enough to sting. "That was *my* room," he said, his voice a low snarl. "You were supposed to be seen and not heard."

I stared down at my arm, then up at his face. "I'm sorry if I overstepped," I said through gritted teeth. I was dying for a crack at him, but there was too much riding on this investigation. "I was trying to support my partner."

Comstock dropped my arm but was still towering over me, sneering. This close, I could smell his ashtray breath and see the pores on his nose, but I refused to step back. Harry stood nearby. He didn't offer anything. Not agreement or disagreement. I didn't know if he was letting me fight my own battle or if he wanted at least one of us to stay on Comstock's good side. I appreciated the play either way.

"You're off the case," Comstock said. "I don't need you."

"You can't end my investigation of the Taken Ones," I said, unable to stop the words from tumbling out. Best I could do was file down their edges. "But you've got to know I don't want to get in your way. I *always* let Bart take the lead. I prefer to run support."

It was how our partnership appeared from the outside, at least.

Comstock considered his options. It didn't take him long to land on the truth of things, which was that he could shut me out from the homicide investigation but had no jurisdiction over my cold case. "You say anything besides 'hello' and 'goodbye' at the Larsen place, I call your DS and tell him you're impeding an active investigation. Clear?"

"As a creek," I said.

He gave me one last scowl before stepping out of my space. The relief was immediate, but I kept my fighting posture until he turned away.

CHAPTER 29

Van

The drizzle had stopped completely by the time we pulled in front of Setzland Corner Drug. The way the sun was grinding through the haze, I worried anyone caught outside might be steamed like a dumpling by noon. I set my sunglasses on the dashboard and slammed my door as I exited the car.

"Gonna be a hot one," I said to Harry as he joined me next to the sedan. The street smelled like worms and wet asphalt.

"I thought you liked this weather." He'd kept his aviators on. Did he have sensitive eyes? They were a pale blue, almost gray. Maybe the sun hurt them.

"What makes you think that?" I asked, surprised he'd noticed.

"You told me in Costa Rica." His eyebrows lifted. "Said it made you feel clean."

I looked away so he didn't see me grin. It wasn't that he'd noticed. It was that he'd remembered.

"Comstock is gunning for you," he said, an invitation to talk as we both waited for the detective. From my tour of Leech Lake yesterday, I knew a shorter route than the GPS offered. I'd taken it knowing it would cheese off Comstock if I beat him here. Annoying him in a way he couldn't call out would take a little off the top, enough to ensure I could hold my tongue inside.

"Yeah," I said. "He is."

"Me, I wouldn't say anything in there." Harry tipped his chin toward the drugstore's second story. Rita Larsen lived upstairs.

"You're a better man than me, Harry Steinbeck," I said, watching Comstock pull up, "but I'll do my best."

Comstock climbed out of his Lincoln Town Car—a vehicle that screamed "cop"—and marched toward the tucked-to-the-side door leading to the second level without so much as a "ready, Freddy." Harry fell in behind, removing his sunglasses as he walked, with me taking up the rear. The street-level door was unlocked. The stairwell beyond it was dusty, the stairs paint-chipped wood with black rubber treads stapled to their center. The steps creaked loudly, a different note for each of our six legs. We sounded like a gang of furious seesawers approaching Rita Larsen's door, so it was no surprise she had it open before we reached it.

"Mrs. Rita Larsen?" Comstock asked.

"Yes, thank you," she said.

I couldn't see her, but her odd word choice and tone—breathy, mildly desperate—stirred something in my memories, something I couldn't quite grasp.

When I reached the top of the stairs, she looked all of her seventy-three years: sooty gray hair coiled from curlers she likely slept in, lonely eyes tired behind her glasses, her nose drooping over her mouth like a rain-soaked awning. Beneath the dust of age, there was a clear resemblance to Rue. It was in the wide jaw, the cheekbones still high and sharp. She held the door as we entered, indicating we should sit in her kitchen. Exactly as her daughter had done when Harry and I interviewed her yesterday.

"We won't take up too much of your time," Comstock said. "We're reopening the cold case of your daughter's 1980 abduction, and we were hoping to ask you a few questions."

It was a good move, laying this on the shoulders of the cold case rather than getting her unnecessarily worked up. I couldn't fault him for it.

"Oh," she said, patting her hair. "Oh. Well, I suspect I don't have much new to offer."

"We understand. It was a long time ago." Comstock pulled out a worn leather-bound notebook with a pen hooked to it. "If you could walk us through everything you remember, that would lock down what we have on file."

"Oh." Her chin bobbed. "Well."

She was slow to start, her voice quavering, but she was a good storyteller. She stuck to chronological order, left out the offshoots. It killed me, not being able to scribble notes, but Comstock might have taken offense at that, so I instead cleared my head and listened with everything I had.

"That's about all I remember," she said, tying it up after a steady ten-minute stream of talking. She'd run through exactly what we had on file. Her daughters had gone to the creek with Amber that day. Mrs. Larsen had visited that end of the cul-de-sac herself many times when she was out walking the dog. It was different times back then. It was safe. She didn't remember what she'd been doing when she got that call about Rue, but she'd rushed straight to the hospital to be with her daughter. Rue hadn't remembered a thing, not then and not now.

"My girl was happy as an egg before that," she said. "Rue. But I lost both my children that day, don't you know? Lily in body, Rue in spirit. We do our best, though. Our best to get by. To be happy."

She nodded briskly, like she was trying to convince herself. I understood the impulse. You want to believe that you can block out the worst of it. That even in the face of horror, you'll manage. In the brief period we Farm kids had been allowed to attend public school, my history teacher had been obsessed with the Kennedy assassination. He called it a beautiful day gone raw. He'd show us the sprocket-hole Zapruder film—minus frame 313, he always pointed out, like we had any idea what that meant—on repeat, Kennedy clutching his throat, then jerking as his skull exploded, Jackie in bright pink jumping onto the rear of the convertible to scoop it up, to put it back into place and paper over it as if to make everything okay.

That's the part that stuck with me, Jackie Kennedy's response. Even as a child I understood her. I knew what it was like to fight to make things appear normal day after day.

"You didn't spot any strangers around the neighborhood?" Comstock asked. "Anyone who set off your alarm bells the week or so before the girls disappeared?"

Her eyes cleared at that, chin coming up like she wanted to study Comstock from a new angle. She was quiet for a moment. "No alarm bells."

"No workers around who you'd recently hired to mow your lawn or wash your windows?"

Her mouth curled. "Riled-up students deciding whether or not to toilet paper the house, maybe. I worked in the high school front office back then. I was the first face they saw when they were called in for detention. But workers? No, I couldn't have afforded that. We mowed our own lawn and washed our own windows."

Comstock scratched something into his notebook. "How often have you seen your husband since the day the girls went missing?"

"Goodness, not once." She leaned toward Comstock, like she wanted to share a secret. Someone raised their voice below us, in the drugstore. I tensed, but it melted into muffled laughter. "I used to have a phone number I could reach him at. About a year after Lily went missing, I called him up. Told him I wanted to hold a funeral for our girl. He said no, absolutely not, because our Lily was still alive. I wanted him to be right, of course."

Her head drooped. "Most days I wanted to picture her alive, anyways. Other days, it was easier to think of her as being with the Lord than to imagine what she must be suffering."

I would have blown it, sent Comstock past the point of no return by comforting Rita, if Harry hadn't set his hand on the table, near hers, and said, "Of course it was. Any mother would have felt the same way.

It's a measure of your love, preferring you be in pain rather than your daughter."

She gripped his hand, squeezed it tight. "I told Rolf even a hamster gets a funeral when it dies. Tried to explain that I needed to give Rue a starting point in her life. All of that had been stolen from her, you see? Her childhood. Her security. And as long as she believed her sister might still be alive, she was going to live in the past rather than step into her own life. A funeral would give her some sort of permission. But Rolf wouldn't have it."

"Do you know where he is now?" Harry asked.

She shook her head. "I don't. He's always been good at running away. I don't believe the police ever interviewed him, either. It wasn't him that took our Lily and Amber. I know that in my heart."

Between a person's heart and their loins, it was hard to gauge which was the poorer judge of character. It was worth noting that Mrs. Larsen spoke kindly of a man who'd walked out on her, though.

"That's all we need, Mrs. Larsen," Comstock said. "Thank you for your time."

Harry and I exchanged a glance across the table. There were so many more questions to be answered. Did Mrs. Larsen have any new information? How often did she see Rue? Was she still in contact with Mrs. Kind? They would all go unasked as we stood to follow Comstock out. I pushed in my chair and straightened the table runner I'd disrupted, which earned me raised eyebrows from Harry.

I shot him a "I wasn't raised by *wolves*" look and nodded at Mrs. Larsen as I passed her. I'd managed the whole visit without uttering a word, a fact Comstock couldn't possibly ignore. We made it all the way to the sidewalk, the air close as a punch, when I patted my back pocket. My jaw fell in what I hoped was a believable fashion. Comstock was turning to, I assume, dismiss Harry and me.

"What?" he said.

"My phone must have fallen out. Be right back."

I swiveled and was up the stairs lickety-split, taking them two at a time. I knocked, the sound echoing down the stairwell. "Mrs. Larsen? This is Agent Reed. I think I may have left my cell in your kitchen."

She opened the door, appearing mildly flustered. I stepped in quickly and closed it behind me. "It must be on the chair where I was sitting," I said, stepping over to it, talking as I did. "Can I ask you something? Were there any rumors about those woods when you lived on Elm Street?"

She looked confused before her face smoothed. "The hauntings, you mean? Never believed those stories."

I nodded. I'd been fishing, stalling until I had my phone. "Yes, the hauntings."

Her face tensed as she leaned back in time, and then she chuckled. "If I remember correctly, the story was an old homesteader walked the forest in search of the child he lost to cholera. They called him Bendy Man because his bones were all loose at the joints. He was supposed to shamble toward little kids, falling apart and collecting himself again at every step. Like a thumb-push puppet. Does that sound right? Or was it that the new houses by the woods had been built on an Indian burial ground?" She shook her head, releasing the recollection. "Nonsense, either way. I'm sure every town has their version of that story. Superstition, all of it."

I pulled back my chair, spotting my phone exactly where I'd placed it. "Found it. Thanks so much, Mrs. Larsen."

She nodded. "Not at all."

"One last question," I said, as if it had just occurred to me. "Have you and Detective Comstock met before?"

"Not that I recall," she said, her smile pleasant.

I unlocked my phone and pulled up the photo of 1980 Comstock that I'd taken from the First Precinct wall. "Do you know this man?"

She fluttered her hand to her chest. "Oh yes. I think so. Maybe." She squinted. Laughed. "Him! Mr. Black."

"What?"

"Oh, that's what I called him. He was a regular visitor at the Kind home."

My mouth went desert dry as Rita kept talking. "I saw him leaving two or three times, back when I walked Benji. I thought he was so handsome. I imagined an entire relationship with the poor man, as only a foolish single mom will do. He'd sweep me off my feet, all the while being the father my girls never had." She laughed at her own extravagance. "Called him Mr. Black because of his beautiful hair. I believe I made up my mind that once he noticed me, he'd fall immediately in love and whisk us away to a better place."

I hoped my face stayed calm, because her revelation was scrambling me inside. "What do you think he was doing at the Kind house?" I asked.

She tapped her chin. "He was dressed informally, I remember that. Carpentry? Pest control? I don't recall a work truck out front. Made a fool of myself the whole two weeks he was around, I can tell you that for sure. Put on a face full of makeup just to walk the dog."

It was a fight to keep my voice even. "When were those two weeks?"

The genial expression on her face began to crumple at the edges, unpleasant awareness working its way in. "I believe it was early July. Right before the girls disappeared. You don't think . . . ?"

I closed the image on my phone, my heartbeat thundering in my ears. "We're just trying to account for everyone, Rita. You've been more helpful than you know. Do you mind if I stop back again this week?"

"I . . . I suppose I don't."

"Thank you," I said, hurrying toward the door. I opened it to see Comstock halfway up the stairs. I held up my phone.

"Success," I said to him before brushing past.

oatmeal

bananas

juice

basket

beautiful

blonde

hair

she is so pretty

Small, one-of-everything stores used to be the heart of a town. Not any longer. Most of the neighborhood shops had dried up and disappeared, replaced with great, impersonal box stores or, even worse, grocery delivery where you didn't need to exchange so much as a glance with the person who brought you the food you needed to survive.

He thought that disconnect might be at the root of what was wrong with the world.

The box stores had been a good development for him, of course. Once they arrived, it meant he didn't have to drive so far to shop anonymously for female supplies. But on the rare occasions when he found himself in a local market, he felt a stab of righteous grief for an imagined better time.

He watched Setzland drugstore across the street as he shopped. Comstock and the two BCA agents had gone upstairs to Rita Larsen's apartment. He congratulated himself on placing the tracker on Van's car, both her blue Toyota RAV4 and the silver Impala she checked out from work. It was shockingly easy to order the tiny black GPS with the magnetic strip, park next to someone, drop your keys, stick the tracker in a wheel well, grab your keys, and be on your way.

He knew her first name because the Black agent had hollered it at her by the gravesite. He had yet to discover her last name. The BCA website listed only the upper administration. No agents. Made sense, but it meant he didn't know her position or her experience level.

He *did* know where she worked, where she lived, and where she was every moment of the day.

He returned the metallic blue canister of Ajax to the shelf and selected a gold tube of Bar Keepers Friend. He pretended to read the label. The old lady at the till had smiled at him when he'd walked in. Wished him a good morning. When she asked if he needed help finding anything, he'd said, "No, thank you." That would buy him five or ten minutes until she would start nosing around. She reminded him of his mother. They were the same age, but that wasn't it. In the attitude—that's where they were twins. Criticizing, disrupting your ability to think, a presence that couldn't sit still and had nothing to contribute.

The trio had stopped by a townhome before visiting Rita Larsen. There'd been no cover at the first stop, so he'd kept driving past when they parked. He'd recorded the address and done a reverse search on his phone once he was out of sight. The townhome belonged to Theresa Kind.

They'd identified the body.

He didn't like the way that made him feel, like he'd swallowed something not quite dead. He'd known they'd figure out who she was. He just hadn't known they'd do it so *fast*. Not that it changed anything. He'd left no evidence behind. Nothing they could trace to him. Still, he found himself gripping the basket's plastic handle so tightly that it cut into his palms. When he felt hot like this, like everything had sharp edges, it was Iris who often calmed him down. She'd stand right in front of Violet and say soothing words, taking the hits until he was able to think straight again.

But now Iris was gone. Forever.

He realized his fingers had left indents in the cardboard canister of Bar Keepers Friend. He needed to focus. He was sure the girl agent was the reason he felt so unsettled. Exposed. The way she'd looked at him at the bar . . . He would need to do something about her. It'd be risky, taking a law enforcement agent, but she'd learn to love him, like Iris and Violet had.

He was setting the second bottle of cleanser back on the shelf when the door across the street opened and the two men walked out. He watched them. Waited for the girl. But she didn't follow.

"Do you need any help?"

He recoiled.

"I didn't mean to frighten you," the ratty old clerk said, laughing. She was chewing gum, a great pink gob that blistered between her teeth. It was disgusting for a woman of her age to chew gum. "Just wondering if I could help."

"I don't need help," he said. It came out too harsh. He softened it. "But thank you."

She cocked her head like a curious chicken. "I know you, don't I?"

He glanced into his empty basket. "Do you carry gluten-free bread?"

She rested her pointer finger on her cheek, ignoring his question. "Do you live here? In Leech Lake?"

"Up the road," he mumbled.

"I never forget a face." She squinted. "You haven't been by in a while, though, have you?"

He suddenly wished for a gun. He'd spray bullets across her face, make her body dance. Instead, he pushed past her, toward the produce, grabbing items as he went, dropping them in his basket. He reached the counter before she did. He glanced to his right, just in time to see the female agent walk out the door followed by Comstock, who looked furious. They all three got into their cars, the BCA agents in one,

Comstock in the other, slamming their doors so loud he could hear it through the grocery store window.

The cashier or owner, he didn't know which, slid behind the counter. Her penciled-in eyebrows flew up as she saw what was in his basket. A sponge. Dish soap. Birthday candles. A decorative lightbulb. An orange.

"Need anything else?"

Both cars pulled away. "No," he said, avoiding her gaze.

The box of Ring Pops on the counter caught his eye. "Wait, I'll take one of these."

It would keep Violet happy until he made up his mind about when to bury her.

Not

    much

        longer

CHAPTER 30

Van

"What did you go back in to say to Mrs. Kind?" Harry asked.

I'd driven us out of Leech Lake coiled as tight as a spring. Harry hadn't said a word until the population sign was in our rearview mirror. Rather than answer him, I flicked my eyes over my left shoulder, checking my blind spot. "Slow day on the road," I said.

Harry smoothed the front of his slacks. He knew my response wasn't an answer.

Comstock had raced away while I'd managed to drive a surprisingly steady speed, holding exactly the limit. Two other cars had passed me, one of them honking. We were now the only vehicle visible on the stretch of county road connecting Leech Lake to Minneapolis. It shimmered from the earlier rain.

"She said she remembered him," I said after a few beats, still unsettled from what I'd learned. "Rita. Said Comstock was in the neighborhood during the time that the girls disappeared. He was a patrolman back then in Crowville, a town just up the road."

"Was he in uniform when she saw him?"

My cheek twitched. "No."

Harry was quiet, like he was turning that information over in his mind, testing the angles. "What do you think?"

I glanced at him, holding his gaze longer than safe driving allowed. "I think it's worth looking into."

Harry closed his eyes. "I agree."

The relief I felt over those two words caught me off guard. Bart used to talk like that. Simple and supportive. I put my elbow on the inside of the window ledge and leaned my head into it, driving with one hand. Rita could have misremembered, but the way her face lit up when I showed her that photo, I didn't think so. But why hadn't Mrs. Kind said anything when we showed up? It was a stretch, the idea that she'd forget the face of a man who'd visited her home "several times," according to Rita Larsen.

"I'm staying in the lab until I get the DNA results," Harry offered, nudging the medical kit at his feet. "They'll need to be verified and reported before I can inform Mrs. Kind of the results, but with luck, it may happen tonight."

I gave my head a quick affirmative shake, returning to my Comstock train of thought. Mrs. Kind had said she was understandably out of her mind the approximate time Rita believed Comstock had visited, and it had been over forty years ago. Maybe she *had* forgotten. Or maybe Comstock had been a visitor at one of the key parties, and she'd wanted to protect his identity. Another option: Comstock had been visiting her husband when she was out.

I squeezed the bridge of my nose. Was I really placing him at the scene of the crime, considering him for a suspect in Amber and Lily's abduction? It'd explain why the case had gone unsolved.

"My sister disappeared."

I pulled over so fast that the wheels screeched. I parked the car on the shoulder, the smell of burning rubber acrid in the humid air. I turned to stare at Harry, every nerve singing. "What?"

His expression was resigned, a little sad. "You didn't research me."

"What happened?" I said, grateful that my voice sounded gentle.

Harry stared at his hands, which were fanned out on his thighs. "Her name is Caroline. She disappeared in 1998. At first, we thought she would be ransomed. My parents are quite wealthy. But we received no note. No contact at all. She just vanished."

Heat pushed at the back of my eyes. All this time I'd been thinking about how this case had sparked my old pain, I hadn't given a thought that it might also be affecting Harry. I felt a bleaching shame for not being a better friend. "How old was she?"

"Nine. She's ten years younger than me."

Harry was speaking as if she were alive. My heart ached—what was that costing him? "No leads?"

He shook his head. "You know the statistics on missing children."

"Is it a cold case?" I was desperate to do something, to help. "At the BCA?"

His hands clenched into fists. "Yes. And if you look it up, you'll see the thinnest wisp of a document, nearly tissue paper for how inconsequential it is. Caroline had been walking to a friend's house. She never made it. I was away at college at the time. My mother was hosting a tea party. My father was overseas. No one saw anything."

"Well," I said, staring out across the car's hood. "I'm sorry." It was a stupid thing to say. It was also the only thing that made sense.

Harry nodded.

"Do you want me to look into it?" I asked. Pleaded.

His shoulders relaxed, but there was no hope in his words. "No, thank you. It won't make any difference."

I tried that on for size. I didn't like how it fit, but Harry clearly wanted me to get back on the road. I glanced over my shoulder. Pulled out. We were still the only visible car. We drove in silence for a while.

"You think you could have done something?" I asked. "Saved her?"

Harry rubbed his hands together. They'd left prints on his pants. "No," he said. "I don't. That doesn't soften the loss, however."

"No, it wouldn't."

The spires of Minneapolis appeared on the horizon. The skyscrapers weren't there, and then they were. Harry and I reached for the radio at the same time, our knuckles brushing. We both yanked our hands back.

"I might have information on criminal behavior involving a state representative," I said. "Marie Rodin." The words surprised me. *Terrified* me, actually. Harry had opened up, and the only way I could see to demonstrate that his pain mattered was to return the favor. It could cost me my career. "It's out of my jurisdiction."

He was quiet for a moment. Then: "Can I help?"

It felt like a house was sitting on my chest. How much more could I tell him? Could I let him in a little bit, like I had Bart? "Maybe," I said.

We both sat in the silence of that for a few beats. And then Harry broke my heart.

"I've been meaning to tell you that there might be a new witness on the Sweet Tea Killer case," he said, his voice casual. "I got an email from a delivery driver who believes he saw a woman coming out of Lester Dunne's the day he died. I was going to follow up on it. If it's got legs, we might be able to reopen that case. Do you want to join me?"

A grip tightened around my throat.

Lester Dunne had owned a small Minneapolis publishing house that specialized in sports books. He was twice divorced and single at the time of his death. In addition to cheering on the Vikings in the fall and playing volleyball in the summer, he visited Thailand every year, where he paid to abuse underage boys. My visions started when he brought his crimes back to Minneapolis. They came right after Bart died, and they wouldn't stop.

Dunne was the first man I'd forced at gunpoint to drink poison.

The second was John Wilson. He was a salesman at a Kinko's knock-off at the time I started having lucid dreams featuring him assaulting preteen girls he'd befriended in jailbait chat rooms.

Randall Devries was the third and final man. He was a successful girls soccer coach credibly accused of assaulting more than a dozen of his underage team players, girls who had trusted him. I started having lucid nightmares about him when he began visiting his daughter's bedroom. Had Bart been alive, together we would have caught all three, but I'd been out of my mind with grief. It wasn't an excuse, just a fact.

By the time Harry and I were sent to Costa Rica to keep an eye on Devries's wife, who I *knew* hadn't killed any of those men, I was back on more solid footing.

But I was always waiting to be caught.

How long had Harry been sitting on news of the email tip about the case? I was sure he'd only brought it up now as a courtesy, to buy me some time to decide how much more I wanted to tell him about the representative. He couldn't have known how devastating it was.

"Sure," I said, amazed I could speak. "We can interview him when we close this case."

"Of course the Taken Ones case is the priority," Harry said.

"Of course," I said.

It was settled, then. Once I found what had happened to Lily and Amber—and hopefully found Lily alive—I would go to jail for murdering three pedophiles because, with Bart gone, I hadn't known how to catch them, and I couldn't have survived another night of watching what they did to children.

CHAPTER 31

Van

Magnolia's coffee shop had a dinosaur of a PC shoved against the far wall. It was for public use, but I'd never seen anyone on it. Most patrons packed their own top-of-the-line high-speed Macs, sleek and glossy, earbuds popped in as they took for granted their access to every bit of information gathered since the dawn of time. I eyed the old beast as I waited in line. I'd dropped Harry off at the BCA and was grabbing a quick road lunch before my next interview.

Our conversation still buzzed in my chest. Harry'd had a sister, and she was missing. I didn't know what to do with that information, but I wasn't going to do nothing, I knew that much. My time was limited, though. The idea of a witness who'd seen a *woman* leaving Lester Dunne's? When Harry asked the delivery driver to describe the killer, they'd simply point at me. There was nothing to do with this new information except compartmentalize it and get on with my job until I ran out of rope.

I was at the head of the line. I started to ask for my drink when the barista said, "Mocha. I know."

"Thanks," I said, blinking. "And a ham and cheese to go."

She was brunette, brown-eyed, maybe two years younger than me and pretty in a midwestern way. She hadn't started making my drink. Had I missed a social cue?

"Weather, am I right?" I said.

She chuckled. "You don't remember me."

"Sure," I said. "You're working here about half the time I come in. You do a great job."

"I was volunteering at Minneapolis Animal Haven the other night. First time getting trained. I thought you saw me, but you were pretty busy dealing with that bossy volunteer who was trying to tell you what to do." She grinned. "I liked how you handled her."

I nodded, but my mind had taken a different track, thinking about all the unseen folks whose paths we crossed every day. Repair people were allowed into our homes without a second thought. Baristas who could slip any manner of poison into our drinks. Cleaners who entered our homes and offices. And children were the most invisible of all. Was something like that at play in the case of the Taken Ones? What unseen folks had known those three girls would be heading to the creek that hot summer day in 1980?

"You were taking care of that big dog," the barista continued. "MacGuffin?"

"Oh, yeah," I said, drawn back into the moment. I smiled thinking of him. "What a sweetheart. I hope he gets adopted soon."

"Me too." She took my money, gave me change, then turned to start on my order. "Do you do yoga?" she asked over her shoulder.

I shook my head. "I should. The stretch would feel good." I was just making small talk. My brain had already moved on to setting up a meeting with Kyle, brainstorming the below-the-radar people we needed to look at.

"I teach a class on Tuesdays. You should stop by sometime."

I glanced behind me. The lunch line was long. I didn't know if she was flirting with me, recruiting clients, or working for a bigger tip. I took out the dollar I'd dropped in and replaced it with a five. "Where?"

She handed me my mocha and pointed at a flyer taped to the counter. It had a picture of her smiling face beneath an Om symbol. "It's over in Minneapolis."

I scanned the sheet. The class was being held at the YWCA a mile from my apartment.

"Your sandwich will be another few minutes," she said. She smiled. "I'll call your name when it's ready?"

"Evangeline," I said. "Van."

"All right, Van." She kept her smile on as I turned away to walk over to the clunky computer, taking a deep draw on my sweet coffee. I sat in the plastic chair, set my cup next to the keyboard, and opened Chrome, switching it to Incognito mode. I typed "Marie Rodin" into the search bar. Her Wikipedia page came up first. It featured what I assumed was her official headshot. She was forty-one but appeared much older. It was the stiff-looking hairstyle, the pantsuit, the pearls. Kyle had been off about her elected office—she was a state senator, not a representative, and she represented District 56, which was just south of Minneapolis.

She was also the *chair* of the Judiciary and Public Safety Finance and Policy Committee.

A sandwich wrapped in brown paper appeared near the mousepad.

"Figured I'd bring it right to you," the barista said, her eyes dancing. "My name's Alexis, by the way."

"Thanks, Alexis." The sandwich smelled like heaven. Warm bread, creamy cheese, and salty ham. I considered eating while I finished my search. I'd have chowed down at home, not worrying about where the crumbs fell. What the hell. I crinkled the paper back and jammed a dripping corner into my mouth. Flakes of croissant rained onto my dress pants. I'd changed out of my stiff shoes in the car, opting for a pair of black Converse low-tops I'd packed. It was too hot and humid for boots. Holding the sandwich with my left hand while I chewed, I clicked "Personal life" on the senator's Wikipedia page.

Her politics didn't matter to me. Who might be behind those doors in her basement did.

The page told me she was married to Michael Rodin and that they had two children, Madeline and Marcus. I had to drop down to the gossip blogs to discover that Michael Rodin had been a well site supervisor in the oil and gas industry before being diagnosed with Lou Gehrig's disease, now in the advanced stages. He was thirty-six, disturbingly young for the diagnosis.

The two children were adopted. When I found photos of them, I had to put down my sandwich, unable to swallow what I had in my mouth.

They were the two scared kids I'd seen at the shelter.

The woman in the gray ombré, her back to me, the one MacGuffin had growled at? It must have been Marie Rodin. I spit the ball of chewed ham and cheese into a napkin. The internet told me the girl, Madeline, was nine. Marcus, the boy, was seven. A recent *Pioneer Press* interview with Senator Rodin said she had a full-time nurse during the day for her husband but cared for all three at night on her own.

I considered what a toll that would take. I knew very little about Lou Gehrig's, but I imagined it would be a challenge caring for a spouse who'd been diagnosed with it. I grabbed my phone and dialed Kyle. He picked up on the second ring.

"Yeah?"

He sounded crabby. I didn't have time for it. I was about to kill two birds with one stone. "What hospital was Dr. Kind working at in 1980?"

The shuffle of index cards came through my ear. "Ridgeline."

A couple had just walked into the coffee shop. They were stupid in love, their hands all over each other. "The same hospital where Rue Larsen works now."

"Yep." The clicking sounds of typing. "Consider it a treasure chest, because the guy who owns the cabin near the abduction site is still employed there. Craig Carlson."

"Small world." The couple had reached the front of the line. They kept their hands tucked in one another's back pockets as they ordered. "Any crossover between Rue and Dr. Kind?"

More click-clack sounds. "Naw. Kind lasted another four years after his daughter disappeared before he quit. My notes say his final day was in 1984. Rue Larsen didn't start until 1996, by which time it had converted from a private hospital to a public medical center."

"Hmm. Remind me what we have for his alibi the day the girls disappeared."

"He was in surgery."

That's right. "Who confirmed it?"

"Looks like his wife, him, and a call to the hospital by Leech Lake police."

"Pretty thorough."

Kyle grunted.

"I'm still gonna pop over and check," I said.

"Fine by me," Kyle said.

"I also want you to look into any invisibles who might have been in the girls' path that summer. Painters, house cleaners, that sort of thing." I didn't add "off-duty cops" to the list, though I knew from firsthand experience that law enforcement was its own kind of invisible when it came to committing a crime. It wouldn't be good to air my suspicions about Comstock this early, though. They could be written off as me swinging for him because of how he'd treated me back at the MPD.

"I'll add it to the list," Kyle said. "Hey, how did it—"

"Go with Mrs. Kind and Mrs. Larsen? I'll fill you in when I get back to the BCA. I've got an old hospital to visit." I hung up, tossed what was left of my sandwich, erased my search history, and for good measure restarted the computer. Then I grabbed my coffee and hoofed it to my car.

❖

The Ridgeline Medical Center was located in Edina, a tony suburb south of Minneapolis. It resembled a beige 1970s-era Las Vegas hotel with a futuristic, glass-fronted swoosh of a parking ramp out front. I drove in and parked before pulling up the layout on my phone. Cardiology was third floor, East Wing. Psychiatric Health was fifth floor, West Wing.

Neurology was immediately below Cardiology, but I was betting any doctor here could give me the broad strokes of Lou Gehrig's disease; I wouldn't need to consult a specialist.

The smell of modern medicine greeted me inside the center, a blend of cleaning products, hand sanitizer, and something papery and unidentifiable.

"May I help you?" asked a woman behind a plexiglass shield marked Information. Her desk was near the automatic doors. Behind her, a vast, upscale lobby featured comfortable-looking chairs, live plants, and walls dripping with abstract art in soothing pastels. A bank of elevators dinged musically in the background.

"I'm here to see Dr. Kind," I said, starting a ways back from my goal.

She was young, early twenties, with square, black-framed glasses and blonde hair streaked pink and purple, though it was cut in a conservative bob. She turned her attention to her computer, fingers pressing the keyboard, her rainbow-hued nails so long it looked like she was searching for a pulse rather than typing. "He hasn't worked here for years," she said. Worry lines creased her smooth cheeks. "I'm so sorry."

One piece confirmed. "That's okay. I was told Dr. Carlson could also help me."

She consulted her three-ring binder labeled Office Numbers. "Take the elevator to the third floor," she said, pointing. "Follow the signs to Cardiology. That's where you'll want to check in."

"Thanks," I said, aiming toward the elevators. The smells, the hushed conversations, the palpable presence of illness, it all made me uneasy. Other than for police work, I'd managed to avoid medical facilities. Frank Roth didn't believe in such extravagance. He taught us to heal ourselves with herbs and tinctures. Thanks to that or the whole-food-before-whole-food-was-a-thing diet I'd been raised on, I'd never been sick enough to pay someone to check me out. The bright, sterile lights set my teeth on edge, and the medical staff rushing past all looked like they were tending to patients with some terrible disease I was about to contract.

When I reached the cardiology waiting room, a mini version of the massive lobby but with a burbling water feature, I flashed my badge. "I was hoping to speak with Dr. Carlson about an urgent matter. Is he in today?"

I was rewarded with another bland smile, another face reflecting the green of a computer screen, though this woman was in her fifties, and her hair wasn't streaked. She wore scrubs patterned in Keith Haring hearts. "I'll check."

I rapped my knuckles on the desk and glanced around the waiting room. Eight people who appeared to be patients—faces drawn, clutching their phones like lifelines—sat in padded yellow chairs. Two of them had someone with them. Six were alone.

"He's in, but I'm afraid he's booked solid."

I turned. "Only need five minutes."

"I'm sorry," she said. I mirrored her tight mouth until she sighed. "If you have a seat, I'll see what I can do."

"Thanks." I dropped in the chair immediately across from her. The receptionist disappeared into the back, then returned to signal I join her. I should have given her more credit.

"He really only has a minute," she said as I approached, her smile brittle.

"Perfect."

She led me in back and knocked on a door marked Dr. Carlson, Cardiac Electrophysiologist.

"Come in."

She opened the door for me and disappeared down the hallway.

The office was large, with a view of County Highway 62. The wall was papered with diplomas and posters of cartoon bodies sliced open. The doctor behind the desk had a great shock of white hair, his brown eyes sharp behind bifocals. "Natalie tells me you're a BCA agent here on an urgent matter."

"I am." I stepped into his office and stood next to the chair across from his desk. "I won't take much of your time. I'm looking into the 1980s disappearance of—"

"Amber Kind and Lily Larsen."

I nodded. Waited.

He rested his bifocals atop his head. "I don't have anything new to offer, but I'm happy to answer your questions."

I sat. "I appreciate it. I just need to verify a few points of information from the file."

"May I ask why?"

He didn't sound defensive, so I didn't feel defensive. "I'm an agent in the cold case division. Our job is to work the unsolved cases."

"I see."

"You own one of the cabins near where the girls were last seen?"

"I do, and I'd give my left leg to have sold it the second I inherited it. Before all this happened." He returned his glasses to his face. "It was originally my father's hunting cabin. I joined him out there when I was young, early teens maybe. I never took to the sport, but the cabin reminded me of spending time with him. So I kept it."

"You still own it?"

"Yes. Or, I should say it's in a trust. It'll pass to my children when my wife and I die."

"Where were you on July 23, 1980?"

His mouth cramped. I took it for empathy. "My wife and I were in Duluth. She was accepting an award for a grant she'd written. There are photographs of us in the newspaper from that day and evening."

"You spent the night in Duluth?"

"We did. We ate brunch in Canal Park the next morning."

I would ask Kyle to verify those details. "Did you ever attend swinging parties at the Kind residence?"

He sat up straighter, his cheeks pinking. "Excuse me?"

"A witness reported adult parties taking place at the Kinds' home. Did you ever attend any?"

He made a delicate sound. It took me a moment to realize he was laughing. "A few. They weren't particularly swinging, though. More fumbling, as I recall. I promise you they only took place among consenting adults."

I angled my head. "With a child in the house?"

"Absolutely not." His voice was firm. "Not when I was there, and I'd be willing to bet my practice that nothing inappropriate happened in Amber's presence. Theresa and Charles loved that girl. They were good parents. *Exceptional* parents. She was at a babysitter's house the few nights we had our fun."

He maintained eye contact, but even without that, I would have believed him. If he were going to lie, he would have told me he remembered nothing about the parties. "Could I look inside your cabin?"

He tented his fingers. "Certainly. The key is in the knot of the oak tree on the west side of the building. Shoulder height. Stick your hand in, and you can't miss it."

"Is it safe leaving a key out there?"

"Doesn't matter. There's nothing to steal inside. Haven't been there in years."

I hesitated before asking my next question. It seemed silly to say out loud in the harsh light of a doctor's office. "I don't suppose you've heard rumors of those woods being haunted. Indian burial ground, or someone called the Bendy Man bringing bad luck?"

"The *Bendy* Man?" He drew the words out as if he wanted to taste their absurdity from every angle.

"Yep," I said.

"I'm afraid I can't help you," he said.

It was worth a shot. All myths started somewhere, and I knew firsthand that monsters were real. "Can I ask you an unrelated question? It's about Lou Gehrig's disease."

"Amyotrophic lateral sclerosis." He seemed relieved to be on more clinical ground. "ALS."

"Do you know much about it?"

"I'm a doctor," he said by way of answer, before continuing. "In essence, your nerves stop listening to your brain, which means your muscles stop working. Your arms. Your legs. Your lungs. You keep your mental capacity, you can see and hear, but you lose the ability to move or breathe. It's an incredibly cruel disease. It's like slowly being buried alive in your own body."

A coolness washed over me, and I suddenly wanted to be anywhere else. "Thanks," I said. I stood, pointing at a framed poster of the anatomy of heart disease. "What's it like?"

He raised his eyebrows.

"Knowing all the ways the human body could fail and still going about your regular life?" I said. "I'd feel hunted."

"That's an ironic comparison, in your line of work," he said. "Surely you see myriad ways that people can die."

I shrugged. "But I try to make it so they live."

"Me too."

He sounded impatient. Time to wind this up. "Thank you for your time, Dr. Carlson. Is it all right if I call you if I need anything more?"

"Please do," he said, in a way that made clear he hoped I didn't.

I mulled over what I'd learned—next to nothing—as I walked to the elevators. I considered riding one up to Psychiatric Health. I wanted to see where Rue worked to get a better feel for who she was. If she happened to be on shift, though, I'd make her unnecessarily uncomfortable by showing up. Besides, I felt unbearably hemmed in. The fresh air of the outdoors was calling me. I grabbed the elevator to the main floor and was beelining toward the exit when a "Ma'am!" caught my attention. It was the receptionist with the pretty streaks in her hair. She waved me over.

"I wanted to tell you," she said when I made it back to her desk, "that I was wrong about Dr. Kind."

"Excuse me?"

"Well, not really *wrong*. He hasn't worked here for years, just like I told you. Dr. Charles Kind, that is. He retired in 1984. His dad, though, Dr. Quincy Kind, worked here until 1998."

My heartbeat did a rumba. "His father worked here?"

"Yep. Surgery. It was still a hospital then."

According to the file, Dr. Kind had been in surgery when the girls walked into the woods. But *which* Dr. Kind?

"Can you point me toward HR?"

It took an hour to have my suspicions validated. Dr. Quincy Kind had been performing a coronary artery bypass on July 23, 1980, during the window of time when Amber and Lily disappeared.

His son, Dr. Charles Kind, had not reported to work that day.

I reached for my phone, pulse thick. Harry answered immediately. "I want to search one of the cabins in the Leech Lake woods, and I need forensics. You free?"

"I have a meeting with the ME today. Tomorrow?"

I appreciated that he didn't ask questions. "I'll drive."

CHAPTER 32

Van

I had Kind's address down as a sixth-floor apartment in the brutalist-looking Cedar Riverside apartment complex on Minneapolis's West Bank. Anyone who'd watched *The Mary Tyler Moore Show* would recognize the building. Blocks of primary colors broke up the unrelenting poured concrete of the thirty-nine-story structure. While it had initially been planned as a blend of subsidized housing, middle income, and luxury, its current population was largely new Americans.

Dr. Kind had lived in the complex since 1996. Before that but after he and Theresa had divorced and he'd quit his job, he'd rented a condo in southwest Minneapolis. He'd worked in sales for the same insurance company since then, but at what cost? Honest work was just that, but a man who'd invested the time and money to become a cardiologist certainly couldn't have transitioned easily to a career of shilling life insurance.

Or maybe he was perfectly suited to it.

What mattered to me was whether it was grief or guilt that had driven him to forsake a medical career and a marriage for a solo life in sales. When I'd called Kyle on my way over to the complex to tell him that Kind's 1980 alibi was as weak as a be-right-back promise, he'd said "Ho-lee cats" and then gotten to work researching what other properties the Kinds owned.

"Nothing showing up under their names," he'd said, talking to me as I drove. "But I'll do a deep dive for a trust or any other properties in their family."

"Land, too," I said. "And dig around for phone and flight records for that week. I want to find out where he was."

"You could ask him," Kyle said, his tone light.

"Because that worked so well in 1980."

"Anything else you need?" he asked.

"I'll let you know."

The Cedar Riverside complex had good parking, I'd give it that. It was another plus that the hallways smelled like roasting meats and warm spices and that bright-cheeked, preschool-aged kids were playing on the sixth floor when I stepped off the elevator, rolling what looked like a leather ball from one end to the other. They broke into giggles and disappeared into the apartment next to Kind's when I appeared. It was a long shot he'd be home during the workday, but I wanted to speak with him, and his office had said he was on the road. Maybe I'd fall into some luck and discover he was playing hooky. If nothing else, I was interested in seeing where he lived.

Specifically, checking out whether it would be possible for him to hide two women there.

I knocked on his door. No response. I knocked again, then jammed my ear against it.

"He's not home."

I glanced back toward the apartment the children had run into. A woman in her thirties, hair wrapped in a colorful turban, watched me from the doorway. She looked more curious than suspicious.

"Is he a good neighbor?"

She shrugged. "He's quiet. You're a police officer?"

"I was. Not anymore." I didn't offer her my current role. I didn't know if it'd make her more or less forthcoming, and I liked where we were at. "Does he have a lot of company?"

Her nose twitched. "Ahh, not women. Not pretty ones like you."

"Ugly ones, then?"

This earned me a chuckle. "None at all, at least what I've seen. He's a man with no joy. Sometimes at night, I hear noises through the walls. Scratching sounds. Like a squirrel or a rat lives between us. But I see no droppings."

"How about children?" I asked. "Does he have any?"

"Again, not that I've seen." The two kids who'd dashed into her apartment peeked around the door. "I've even offered him mine."

"Nooo!" the oldest child said, giggling. "I will not live with that man. He's too sad."

This started the other one laughing.

I crouched so I was at their level. Both children had dimpled cheeks. They wore soccer shorts and T-shirts with cartoon faces on them. "Why do you think he's sad?"

"Because he has no children of his own," the youngest said. He was four by my best guess.

"Did he tell you that?"

"Not with his mouth," the older child, a girl, said. "With his eyes."

I stood. "You've got smart children."

"Only one of them is mine," she said. "But you'll give them both big heads."

"Thanks for your time."

I turned toward the elevator.

"Your eyes are sad, too," the older child called to my back. "Have you forgotten how to play?"

Her words were innocent, gentle even, but they thrust me back to Frank's Farm nonetheless.

CHAPTER 33

"Olly, olly, oxen free!" Veronica calls out as loud as she can without
drawing attention.

"Here I am!" I tumble out of the chicken coop, giggling, hay stuck
in my hair. One of the Brothers has broken apart a clean bale and left
it just inside the door. It provides a perfect hiding place.

"You weasel!" Veronica says. She's laughing, the tip of her tongue
poking through the gap in her teeth, but she's also glancing over her
shoulder. We're supposed to be digging up thistles, not playing hide-
and-go-seek. We've gathered a pile as high as our knees, though, and
the day is hot. No way can we sneak to the swimming pond, but at least
we can play for a bit.

"Your turn," I say, tugging spokes of hay out of my braids.

Veronica's perfect pink mouth pinches in worry. "I think we should
get back to work."

"Just one more round?" I wheedle. "Everyone else is out in the field
or in the kitchen. No one will—"

"No one will what?" Frank asks, coming around the corner. He's
shirtless, drenched in sweat that makes him smell like bitter soup. He
carries a pitchfork in one hand, the same hand that bears the silver
wristwatch he never removes. He's wearing the straw sun hat made

famous on our jelly jars, but he does not look like the same man in those pictures. He looks like an angry bear.

"No one will mind if we leave the thistles to run water out into the field for our Family," Veronica says, without pause.

My jaw drops. Veronica is the smartest of us, the prettiest, but I now see she is also the bravest. She's gambling Frank only heard the last words I said, that he won't notice the hay in my hair or the relaxed look of play on either of our faces. If he's not only caught us shirking chores but also her lying, she'll get baptized for sure.

Our heads should be bowed in respect, but I risk a peek at Frank. He's studying Veronica beneath his straw hat. Her head is tipped downward, her eyes closed.

"You're a kind little star, Miss Veronica," he finally says. His voice is as soft as cotton. "Thinking of your Family like that. Well, get on with it. Both of you. Bring buckets and a ladle, and when everyone has had their thirst slaked, return to your own work."

He places his hand on her bent head, the highest form of approval for children, and then strides toward the barn.

Veronica swivels her head and winks at me. "We better hurry on the water."

"I can't believe you did that," I whisper, my eyes wide. "You're as brave as a bull."

She glances in Frank's direction to make sure he's out of earshot, then takes my hand and pulls me toward the well.

"I'm going to be a leader, too, someday," she says. "Just like Frank. Only I'm going to give kids more time to play, and let them have sweets for dessert, and never punish them! I'll wear a silver watch, too, just like Frank's, to let people know I'm the big boss. I'll make sure everyone feels safe then." She squeezed my hand tighter. "Everything is going to be all right, Evangeline."

I smile. It is the most magical thing I've ever heard, so sweet that I want to taste the words on my own lips.

"Everything's going to be all right, Veronica," I say.

She laughs as we skip to the well.

CHAPTER 34

Van

I sat in front of the First Precinct station, "Cat's in the Cradle" playing on the radio. It was the perfect melodramatic dirge to prep me for talking to Comstock. He needed to hear what I'd learned about Kind's alibi. It had direct bearing on his active investigation. I could have called, but I was hoping it'd earn me points to show up in person, even if he wasn't inside and I ended up passing along the info to his second.

Actually, the latter option was the best-case scenario.

I held on to that possibility as I waded through the humid air to the precinct's front door. Now that I knew where Comstock's office was, I didn't bother checking in, just hoofed it up the stairs, where I was dismayed to find him behind his desk.

Bart's desk.

A sneaker wave of renewed fury knocked me sideways. I clenched my jaw and got right to it. "Comstock? I have news."

He stared at me over the top of his glasses. "Unless you've come to tell me what the hell stunt that was back at Rita Larsen's, I haven't got time for it."

"Forgot my phone, like I said."

His lips twisted into a treble clef. "Bullshit."

I didn't have time for his pettiness. "Amber Kind's dad's alibi is dead in the water. It was his own father who was in surgery that day. A Dr. Quincy Kind."

Comstock's spine snapped straight, an emotion I couldn't name glinting in his eyes. "You sure?"

I nodded. "I stopped by the hospital where he was working at the time. Their HR confirmed it. Agent Kaminski is looking into where else Kind could have been when Amber went missing. Can we coordinate?"

Comstock scowled. It was neither a yes or a no, and that rage wave returned. He and I both hated each other. So what? That was playtime stuff. We had a job to do. I'd suddenly had enough of tiptoeing around him.

"By the way, what's *your* alibi for that day?" I asked.

"Excuse me?" He managed to make the question sound like a threat.

"July 23, 1980." I took a step forward. "Where were *you?*"

A swamp of rage backfilled his face. "Get. The. Hell. Out."

I stayed put for just long enough to let him know that my power resided with me.

CHAPTER 35

Van

Kyle brought coffee the next morning. It was the natural order of things.

"Thanks," I said when he offered me my mocha. I about had it to my mouth when I saw the smiley face drawn on the side of the paper cup next to my name. I pointed it toward him. "You?"

He was drinking one of those syrupy iced drinks. He shook his head. "Your biggest fan. Dark hair, dark eyes. Said to remind you to come to yoga." He eyeballed the empty chip bag lying next to me on the table. "You do yoga?"

"Not if I can help it. Fill me in on what you found out yesterday."

I'd gone to the animal shelter to cool off after talking to Comstock. Probably not fair to the animals, off-gassing my stress into their lives, but I figured my cleaning up their poop covered at least part of my emotional tab. The place closed to volunteers at eight, but I had special dispensation to stay until midnight. I spent a good two hours with MacGuffin. He'd been so excited to see me he about turned himself inside out with all his wagging. I scrubbed his pen and then him before walking him around the yard until his muscles warmed and his stiff hips relaxed. He snuffled my hand when I left him, a big, gloopy thank-you.

It was enough, somehow.

I'd slept through the night and made it to work before seven. My office had felt strangely dark, so I'd grabbed the information I needed and headed to the incident room, which was where Kyle found me.

He tugged a rubber band–bound packet of index cards from his blazer pocket and scanned the top one. "No property for Charles Kind, other than the house he and Theresa owned, the one they were living in when Amber went missing. Their divorce settlement was straight down the middle, with Theresa buying out his half in 1984 and staying there until the early '90s."

"His parents don't own any property? Any place he could hide his daughter and a friend?"

"That's just it," Kyle said, tossing me a doubtful look. "If he wanted to get funny with his own kid, why kidnap her? He *lived* with her."

I glanced over at the whiteboard. It took up the east wall of the small room. The only thing on it was the list of potential connections between the two crime scenes that I'd written the other day in purple marker. "Because he wanted two girls and only had one? Or he wanted her away from his wife?"

Kyle flipped to the second index card. "His parents still own the house they raised Charles in. Out in Minnetonka. Other than that, no land, no condos, no overseas second homes for the family. If the father is good for the crime, he disappeared those girls."

I swallowed the mocha and felt it flow into my spirit. Alexis made a mean coffee. "You figure out where he was that day?"

"No place that required him to buy a plane ticket."

"Leech Lake," I said, more to myself than Kyle. Somehow, it had lost two of its children.

"Yeah, and there's not even a lake there." He was scanning another card.

I turned. He suddenly had my full attention. "You've been?"

"Yeah. My grandparents are from there."

I placed my hands flat on the table. "What?"

"Gran and Gramp. My mom's folks. They lived out in Leech Lake."

I leaned forward. "When?"

He still wasn't looking at me. "Dunno. They moved after I was adopted, I think. They were living in Richfield when they sold everything and headed to Leech Lake to 'get away from it all.' I visited a few times in the summer, and there wasn't a GD thing to do."

"You didn't think to mention that?"

My tone finally earned his attention. He shrugged, a bemused smile on his face. "Sorry. What's to tell? I was a kid. It was the early 2000s."

"Your mom or dad ever live there?"

"Naw. They visited same time I did, but it wasn't anyone's childhood home or anything. They moved my grandparents to an assisted living place nearer to them a few years back. All I remember about Leech Lake was it was hot in the summer and boring in the winter. Not to mention everyone stared at me like I was a zoo creature. Only Black kid in sight."

I studied him, looking for reasons to be suspicious. For someone with a lot of secrets, I didn't care for them in others. He really should have mentioned his link to the town, as tenuous as it was. "Any other connection to Leech Lake or the case I should know about?"

He grinned broadly. "That's it."

I rolled my eyes. "Good to know. Harry and I are driving out there today. To search that cabin in the woods."

"Enjoy yourselves," Kyle said sarcastically. "I'll keep working the files."

I stood. "Let me know what you find."

"You too," he said.

❖

The afternoon drive to Leech Lake started out with a flurry of words—I told Harry about Kind's false alibi plus the swinging parties confirmed by the cabin owner, and he told me how Theresa Kind had received this morning's confirmation of her daughter's death.

"Her sister was there," he said. "They were both devastated when they realized how she'd died. Mrs. Kind displayed some relief, as well. I gave them contact information for counseling services. I'll check back in tomorrow."

It made sense that Mrs. Kind exhibited some relief, and I suspected it did to Harry, too. The truth was no match for imagination. Whatever Amber had been suffering, it was over. "I want to drop by the Leech Lake Police Department while we're in town," I said. "See if Bauman is in. Plus, I want to ask Mrs. Larsen if she knew about the swinging parties going on over at the Kind house. Do you have time for that?"

Harry thought on it for a moment. "I do."

"Good," I said. Something occurred to me. "Did you tell Mrs. Kind that Amber had been pregnant?"

His cheek jumped. "I did. It was her right to know."

I nodded. It must have made the hard news impossibly more difficult to swallow. We couldn't tell her if that child was alive or dead, or how old. I sat for a moment in the pain I imagined Theresa must have felt. Then I filled Harry in on Comstock's reaction to me last night.

He stared at the road for a while. "You'll want to tread lightly on that."

"I know." I pointed at his shining shoes. "Speaking of treading lightly, you're not wearing those into the woods, are you? The cabin is a hike."

"Don't be silly," he said. "I packed shoe covers."

"Smart," I said, swallowing my laughter. Harry Steinbeck was definitely one of a kind. I drove him down Elm Street, pointing out the house Rue and Lily had lived in, then Carol Johnson's home as well as the Kinds' old place, and finally, as I parked, the woods. We both stepped out of the car and walked silently toward the forest's mouth.

He stared into the snaking, overgrown path for a few beats. "It's heavy, isn't it?"

I thought I knew what he meant, but I waited. The air smelled mostly fresh, with only undertones of decay today.

"We had a forest near where I grew up, a big city park, really," he said. "Those woods were full of kids playing. These?"

"I know," I said. The trees at the edge were all colors of green, from a vibrant emerald to chartreuse to lime, but just beyond, toward the center of the forest, everything was cloaked in black, shadows spreading like oil. "Not a place where you'd imagine children frolicking. Rita said there were rumors about it being haunted. Indian burial grounds plus some old prospector floating around that the kids called the Bendy Man."

Harry coughed, a dry sound, similar to the one that Dr. Carlson had made when I mentioned the tales.

"Those stories start somewhere," I said, a little defensive on the town's behalf.

"Then let's keep our eyes peeled for ghosts," Harry said before reaching into his kit to pull out mesh foot covers. "Shall we?"

The ground in the ditch squished beneath us. It was another hot day, but it was early. Yesterday's gully washer hadn't cooked off yet, not in the shade of the woods. If I hadn't worn sneakers, I would have borrowed a pair of those covers for myself.

We entered the heavy silence of the forest, our eyes adjusting to the gloom.

"The abduction site is up here," I said, fighting the urge to whisper.

We walked until we reached the clearing, our isolation growing so complete that we could no longer hear the modern world—no car horns, no passing trains—only an earthy deep. The plastic flowers were still stuffed inside the tree. Harry bent over to inspect them, then walked the perimeter of the clearing.

"Why this side?" he asked, glancing back toward the path we'd walked down. The bright world of the cul-de-sac was invisible in the thick, tree-covered murk. "Why would someone wait for the girls to enter here?"

I'd wondered the same thing. "He knew them. He didn't want just any girls. He wanted *those* girls."

Harry rubbed the back of his neck. He was wearing what I'd come to think of as his Safari Lite outfit—linen shirt, pressed khakis, leather loafers. "Which lends credence to the possibility it was Charles Kind. But if it was him, why take them?"

"Kyle had the same question," I said. "Maybe one of the children had seen something he didn't want them to testify to?"

"Something that would cost him more than his marriage and his career?"

Harry had a point. But we both knew that most criminals didn't operate from logic. They reacted, striking out like surprised animals.

"Let me know when you're ready for the cabin."

"I'm ready," Harry said.

The path was nonexistent, but I trusted Kyle's coordinates and my phone's compass to lead us to Dr. Carlson's hunting shed. Still, we'd have walked right past it if Harry hadn't tripped over a fallen branch.

"There," he said, on his way down.

He was pointing at a forest-colored shape, a hobbit lodge of sprouting roof and water-soaked logs. I shoved away branches to reach it, surprised at how rustic it must have been even in its heyday. Maybe thirty by thirty feet, it couldn't have housed much more than a stove and a bucket to pee in.

"Key's supposed to be over here," I said, walking around the rear. The ancient oaks and elms were thick and twisting, doing their best to shield the cabin from wandering eyes. On the west side of the cabin, I found the largest oak tree I'd ever seen, soaring so high through the thick canopy that I couldn't spot where it ended. An infected-looking knot beckoned to me from its trunk at shoulder level.

Exactly where Carlson had said it would be.

Harry appeared next to me, brushing forest floor off his knees.

"You want to stick your hand in there?" I asked him.

He raised an eyebrow. "I do not."

I shoved my own in before I could change my mind. My fingertips brushed against something cold and hard. I clutched it, praying I wasn't holding an enormous beetle.

"Key box," I said, relieved, once I had the small black case in what passed for sunlight in these woods.

Harry was holding himself gingerly.

"Is your hand bleeding?" I asked.

He held them, palms up. "Both. I fell hard."

Without thinking, I uttered one of the phrases the Mothers used to say when we got hurt. "Don't worry. Most everything clears up."

"Nonetheless," Harry said. "I'd like to visit the pharmacy after this."

A pang of shame flicked me. I wished I could rewind my previous words and offer some kindness in their place, but that wasn't an option, so I stepped toward the cabin and unlocked the front door. It screamed in protest as I pushed it open. The scent of mushrooms and animal pee was strong. I tugged out my phone and flashed its light around the interior. I stood inside a one-room cabin. No evidence of running water or electricity.

Harry appeared beside me and clicked on his flashlight. His beam was significantly brighter than mine. "When was the last time Dr. Carlson was here?"

"It's been years, he said."

Harry's light snagged on an energy drink can crumpled in the corner. "Others might be visiting."

"Secluded cabin near a swimming hole," I said. "Makes sense kids would be curious. They were very neat if they were here, though. I see no signs of breaking in."

I walked over to the nearest window. It was unlatched and slid open easily. "Scratch that."

Harry was scanning the floor. "I'll search low, you look high," he said.

I appreciated that he hadn't at any point asked what we were looking for. I hoped it was because he knew the answer—anything that might have been left forty-two years ago—and making me say it out loud would have underscored what an impossible task it was. I had a mental tally of the things I liked about Harry. I added inhuman patience to the list.

He crouched to the right of the door. I began with the only items in the room: a bed shoved against the far wall and, next to it, a potbellied stove. The gray-striped mattress was thin with brownish stains. They didn't smell like anything, which suggested they were old. The spring holding the mattress was just crisscrossed wires. A person would have to be exhausted to get a good night's sleep on it. The inside of the stove was full of ashes with the crispy edges of a newspaper still visible, one with a date. March 3, 2019.

"Come here, please," Harry said.

I'd nearly forgotten he was there. He'd made it two feet from the door. "You find something?"

"Maybe. I need you to hold my light."

I strode over and aimed my phone into a crack running parallel with the seam of the barnwood floor. It was half an inch wide at the wall and narrowed to a quarter inch before disappearing a foot out.

"Shine it nearer the wall," he directed, pulling on his gloves before he extracted a long, curved-end tweezer from his kit.

I obliged, peeking down. I caught a glimpse of bright yellow. "What is it?"

He leaned forward and inserted the instrument into the crack. He pulled out a raggedy bandage the color of artificial sunshine. One end had a design. When he held it toward my light, I saw it was the black outline of an elephant.

"Band-Aid," he said, tugging an evidence bag out of his kit. He dropped it in. "Similar to the one Lily Larsen was reported to be wearing the day she disappeared."

It

       was

             all

                   his

                         mother's

                               fault.

She punished him until he learned to conceal the best part of himself.

He hid it so well, he wondered if she forgot about it.

He made it through middle school and then high school with only a few extra visits to the hospital. Straight out of high school, he landed a good job. He wanted more, though, things he couldn't acquire where people knew him. So he changed his name and bought the house where he kept his family.

The family he'd made.

That gave him two lives, and there wasn't a person in either who knew who he really was, what he could do. What he *had done.* He looked regular to all those folks. All that practicing when he was young paid off. He blended right in.

Well, mostly blended in. Sometimes he slipped, showed his true colors, but people liked to look away then. Talked themselves right out of the ugliness they'd seen.

Maybe his mom had done him a favor, teaching him how to hide in plain sight. That's what he decided as he drove past Elm Street.

CHAPTER 36

Van

I waited outside the drugstore while Harry bought antiseptic spray. The forest scrapes on his palms were already looking better, but he'd mentioned that an untended cut could introduce a staph infection. I studied him when he came out, watched him remove the spray's seal right there on the street and irrigate his palms.

"All done?" I asked when he returned the packaging to the drugstore bag and then tossed it all into a nearby garbage can.

"Yes," Harry said. "Ready to speak with Mrs. Larsen?"

By way of answer, I entered the door to the stairwell leading to her apartment. This was a necessary stop, but I was anxious to return to the BCA. Harry said he didn't know if he could run DNA on the bandage he'd found. Forty-two years in the elements was a long time. It was unlikely there'd be anything left for him to analyze. If the physical description matched, though, this was a significant development. It put the girls in the cabin after they disappeared. That, combined with Amber's father's missing alibi as well as his connection to the cabin's owner, was information that could change the course of the investigation.

Mrs. Larsen had her door open before we reached the top of the stairs.

"Hello," she said. There was a papery quality to the skin around her eyes that hadn't been there yesterday.

"Hello, Rita," I said. "May we come in?"

"Sure." She stepped aside and let us pass.

Her kitchen looked the same, not so much as a mug on the counter. We both waited for her to indicate if she wanted us to sit at the table or move into the living room.

"Can I get you anything to drink?" she asked.

She hadn't asked the same yesterday. I didn't know if she was becoming more familiar with us, if Detective Comstock had made her uncomfortable, or if it was a third thing.

"You're nice to offer," I said, "but we're fine. Did Mrs. Kind call you?"

Mrs. Larsen looked startled but quickly recovered. "She did. She said Amber's gone."

I nodded. Waited.

"That poor woman. But at least she gets to know where her baby is." Rita wrung her hands. "When do *I* get to know?"

"We're doing our very best, Rita." I put a comforting hand on her arm. "That's why we're here. We'd like to ask you a few more questions. Do you mind if we have a seat?"

She took a chair at the kitchen table, her movements stiff. We followed suit.

"I blame myself," she said, repeating her litany from our last visit. "I shouldn't have let them go into the woods that day. It was a different time, you know. Kids ran wild all summer back then, but I shouldn't have let mine."

"It *was* a different time," Harry said.

I wondered if he was thinking of his own missing sister.

"I wanted to ask you more about the Kinds," I said, "and specifically Dr. Kind. What do you know about him?"

"Wonderful man," Rita said, her face softening. "So generous, both he and his wife. It was hardest on him, I think." Her mouth tipped downward as she leaned forward empathetically. "When the girls disappeared. Broke him in two, even worse than it did his wife."

"Why do you think that was?" I asked.

Mrs. Larsen thought on that. "I suppose because he was head of the family. It was his job to protect them, you understand."

"When was the last time you saw Dr. Kind?"

She put a finger to her lips. "Let me see. I suppose it was a year or so after the girls disappeared. Both he and Theresa stopped coming to church. I heard they divorced not long after that, and then he moved. People think tragedy should have made the three of us close, but it doesn't work that way. I didn't really know them, but I always admired them."

The next question was more difficult to ask. "Were you aware of the Kinds hosting adult parties?" I asked. "Swinging parties?"

She appeared genuinely shocked. "I can't imagine they would have."

"The picture I showed you last time we were here, the photo of the man you called Mr. Black. Do you remember seeing him at the Kind house during the evening as well as during the day?"

She shook her head. "I only walked Benji during the day."

"You didn't spot him anywhere else? Around town? In one of the search parties?"

"Not that I recall."

She was growing agitated. I was reaching the end of my questioning, and I'd learned nothing that would help the investigation. "How often do you see Rue?" I asked.

Mrs. Larsen ducked her chin, causing the delicate folds across her neck to multiply. "Not nearly as often as I would like. I tried to call her about Amber, but she didn't pick up. It's not something you want to leave in a message, do you understand?"

"I do."

The refrigerator kicked in. It held no magnets, no hand turkey or broccoli tree drawings created by beloved grandchildren. It reminded me of the bleakness of Carol Johnson's home. The walls here were white, the owl cookie jar free of smears and likely empty. The furniture outside the kitchen looked nearly unused. It was impossible to know what

Mrs. Larsen's life would have been like had one of her girls not been abducted, but it was safe to assume it would be very, very different.

"That's all we needed to know for now, Rita," I said. "Is it all right if we stop by if we have more questions?"

"Oh yes, oh yes," she said.

❖

"They don't like me at this place, sight unseen," I said.

Harry and I sat in the BCA sedan outside the Leech Lake Police Department. Mrs. Kind had been unreachable by phone. Her office said she was on the road today but that they'd pass on the message that the BCA had further questions.

"Do you want me to wait in the car?" Harry asked.

"No," I said, sighing deeply. "I can always use an extra set of ears."

Harry followed me inside. I was pleased to see Jody Hutchinson of the lemon bars at the counter, and even happier when her face lit up at the sight of me.

"Your timing is great!" she said, offering Harry an admiring, too-long glance. "Daniel's in his office. Let me go tell him you're here. Be right back."

"Her name's Jody," I told Harry while we waited. "She was working dispatch the day the girls disappeared."

The precinct was largely one open room, but some offices lined the left. A uniform in his late sixties by the look of him emerged from the middle one, following Jody. That he had a private office spoke to his tenure, but the way he carried himself—thumbs parked in his belt loops, a slight smile on glossy lips—suggested an arrogance that didn't bode well for this interview.

"Van, is it?" The officer removed his left hand from waist level and offered it to me. A southpaw, no wedding ring. "I'm Officer Bauman."

"Nice to meet you," I said, turning toward Harry. "This is Agent Steinbeck. Could we talk to you in your office?"

"No secrets here." He indicated the open room behind him. Jody returned to her desk and immediately began typing with such alacrity that I suspected she was producing strings of nonsense so she could give this conversation her full attention. One other uniformed officer was seated at a desk ten feet away, his back to us.

I would have liked to have this conversation in private, but you play the hand you're dealt. "Can you give me a rundown on July 23, 1980?"

"Good day for the stock market," Officer Bauman said, glancing behind him.

"Specific to the abduction of Amber Kind and Lily Larsen," I said. My tone sent a signal he'd have to be intentionally ignorant not to notice.

"I can't offer anything not in the files." Bauman stared down his nose at me. "I double-checked them myself, and recently. Everything we got is in there."

"You revisited the files recently?" I asked. "What day?"

"Right after Agent Kaminski first called," he said. "I had Jody here pull them."

She smiled in the affirmative before returning to her typing.

"Such *thorough* files," I said.

I waited for Bauman to hear the sarcasm. His bulldog face didn't twitch.

"But I still have a couple questions," I continued, deciding to make this quick. "First, who do you think did it?"

Harry's throat-clearing surprised everyone, including, apparently, him.

Bauman recovered first. "It's the worst-kept secret in Leech Lake that Donald Tucker took those girls. He's a convicted pedophile. We could never pin it on him, but there you go."

I nodded. The original police files didn't come right out and say Tucker was the only one they'd seriously looked at, but it was there, between the lines. Too bad his alibi was as solid as a cement truck: he was at work when the girls were abducted and for three hours on each side of that. There were more than a dozen witnesses. "He's currently at the assisted living facility downtown?"

"That's right. Harmless now. More power to you if you can get him to tell you where he hid the bodies."

"You also investigated a Schwan's delivery driver," I said, pulling out a notepad, flipping it open, and staring at it. It was a blank page. "Didn't find anything?"

"Nope," Bauman said, leaning into the nearby counter. "Nothing on nobody because it was Tucker who did it."

I scribbled *Bauman = Tucker did it.* "Who called in the Schwan's guy?"

"What's that?" Bauman asked.

"Who reported him as a possible suspect? I couldn't locate that information in the file."

He scratched his chin. "Hard to say after all these years. We got a lot of tips come in."

"Maybe it's written down somewhere?"

"Like I said, doubt it." He sucked on his teeth before grinning at me.

"Jody, would you mind looking?" I asked, lightly layering on my Minnesota accent.

Jody glanced to Bauman, who gave her a curt nod before she disappeared into the back. Bauman wouldn't like me ordering his employees, but he also couldn't override my request without a good reason, not with everyone watching.

"While we're waiting," I said, "what can you tell me about other officers who helped the investigation?"

"Nothing. It was Alastair and me."

"I was told this officer was on the scene," I said, pulling up my phone.

Bauman bent in to look. The softness at his jawline tightened, and he shoved both thumbs back into his belt loops as he stood up straight, pulling all his height. "Doesn't look familiar. What'd you say his name was?"

"I didn't." I was buzzing. Bauman had immediately recognized Comstock, and he'd just as quickly covered it up. What was he hiding?

The Taken Ones

Bauman flicked his eyes to my feet and then back up. "Yeah, don't know him. We had so many volunteers. He might have been one of 'em. If he was even here, that is. Everyone in town wanted to find those little girls, wanted it as bad as if they were their own babies."

I made no response, not even a nod. Silently, internally, I added another line to the "Comstock" column. He was about to get himself promoted to a full-blown suspect.

"Nothing," Jody said, appearing from the back. "Nothing that I didn't already show you, anyhow." Her eyes bounced from me to Bauman. She was caught between the two of us, not sure who to orient to. I felt bad for her.

"Well, I appreciate your looking," I said, offering her a warm smile. "Please let me know if you think of anything after we leave."

Bauman made a grumbling noise.

"I'll stop back," I told him. I kept my voice free of intonation. There were many ways he could take it.

Harry and I left the cop shop and piled into the car. We were quiet as we rode out of town, the sun dropping toward the horizon.

"They sound like rain," I said when we were free of the city limits, my thoughts still on Comstock and what he must be hiding.

"What does?" Harry asked.

"The bugs hitting the windshield," I said. "They sound like rain. I'd forgotten that about driving in the country."

197

CHAPTER 37

October 2001
Evangeline

"Veronica, I'd like you to read the summer vacation essay you wrote about me. To everyone."

Frank has just finished his four-hour Sunday sermon. We girls think we are going to the kitchen to prepare the afternoon feast, but Frank has different plans. It takes me a moment to remember Veronica's essay, to recall school. It was only three weeks ago, but we've returned to the rhythm of our life so quickly, so thoroughly, that it feels like a dream.

We don't know who put the bug in Frank's ear to send us to school in the first place, who convinced him that his "human garden" needed to spread beyond its current acreage, that we would become the seeds carrying his message of patriarchal communal living into the world. Maybe it was one of the Mothers. Maybe God had spoken to Frank, like he said. All we knew for sure was that our time at school lasted only two months, and we'd loved every second of it. School lunches with *dessert*. A whole library full of books. Music, gym, teachers who smiled at us.

"Sir?" Veronica asks, the word whistling between the gap in her teeth. Her body is in the appropriate submissive posture, her eyes on the ground.

"Your essay." He takes a paper from his lectern, steps off the altar, and walks it over to her. His face is pleasant. Serious, but not angry.

"Your teacher called me about it right before I pulled you all out of public school. You don't remember?"

His tone is so inviting, but his eyes don't match it. The Mothers are shuffling in the pews. One of them has a wet face. Do they know what's about to happen? I feel the sudden urge to grab Veronica's hand and run. She's so close to me I wouldn't even have to lean over to do it.

But I think of the naked punishment, and almost being baptized, and I stay still.

Veronica takes the paper Frank is offering her. It flutters like a wounded bird in her shaking hands. "I love living on Frank's Farm," she reads, her voice high and clear. "It is my favorite place. But I do not like the naked punishment—"

"Aha!" Frank booms. We all jump. "You *did* tell them our secrets."

Her eyes widen. I know what she is thinking, because it is what all of us who went to school are thinking: Frank *told us* to share with the world the wonder of his Farm. I remember because on the day he informed us we'd be going to school to evangelize, I thought, *God made me for this. It's in my name. Evangeline.*

I open my mouth because there must be a mistake. I know it will cost me dearly to speak out of turn, but Frank has to be reminded that Veronica was just doing what he asked of us. But before I can get out the words, he has her by the neck. Not the neck of her long dress—her *neck.*

We gasp.

Frank is quick. He drags her toward the door by her tender skin. "Follow, my children!" he bellows. "See the fate that awaits those who speak out against their Father. Bear witness as I share grace with her and wash away her sins."

We freeze for a moment, all of us. A *baptism.* We've whispered about it after dark in the girls' dormitory. How the best thing to do is to fight a little to make it seem real and then play dead because Frank holds you under until you stop moving.

Does Veronica remember? She's my Sister, but also my best friend. She's the one I gave the first bite of that candy bar to, the one who sneaked me honey when I had a sore throat.

Everything is going to be all right, Evangeline, she'd told me that day after Frank almost caught us playing when we were supposed to be thistle hunting.

Everything's going to be all right, Veronica, I told her right back.

I can't let that be a lie.

I rush to the front of Frank's Flock, trying to catch her eye, to somehow signal to her to remember what to do, to play dead so Frank doesn't kill her, but I'm only eleven and have always been small. I can't reach her. We spill out of the church and toward the center of the compound. It's fall, the air cool. I'm behind the others, struggling to push through, but I'm too late because we're at the trough.

Frank holds Veronica high, still by her neck, like she's a newborn kitten. Our eyes meet. Hers are the size of eggs. She doesn't seem to recognize me. My mouth goes dry.

He shakes her, and she whimpers. The sun catches on his silver wristwatch, blinding me for a moment. "Does anyone have anything to say on behalf of this evil child?"

I want to speak, but I feel small, smaller than I am, and more naked than I was that day I stood in front of my Family, my shame on display for everyone to see. But I have to say something. I think the words—*stop, you told us to share our lives, don't hurt her*—but only a grunt escapes. I look to the Mothers, but they're watching their feet. Something cold and wet touches my hand. I look down to see Honeybear, just a puppy but still taller than my waist. He's snuffling his nose into my palm, his eyes sad.

"You are all party to this grace," Frank says, turning to the trough. I expect a speech, but instead, he brings Veronica's body down with such speed that some part of her hits the side with a clang. I'm able to shove forward. I reach the trough and see no movement underwater, no thrashing.

Veronica is a girl, and Frank is a man, his arms corded from farmwork.

My body begins screaming for air like it's me underwater, not Veronica. Can she see him poised above her, holding her down? Is she crying? Letting the water rush in, cold and thick, filling every crevice?

The seconds tick past, and then the minutes, but my voice won't come to me. I'm unable to speak out, unable to move. We are her family, and we are watching her die.

When Frank finally pulls Veronica out, her body drapes like a rag doll. She doesn't look human any longer, the blood pouring from a gash in her forehead too bright for her gray skin. The Mothers rush her to the infirmary. We are not allowed to ask questions, even after she's carried into the dining hall and strapped to a chair two hours later, mouth open, eyes half-lidded, her forehead swathed in bandages. A Mother tries to feed her, but the porridge dribbles down her chin.

I let Frank do that to my Sister.

That night, with my brain and heart cracked wide open, my first lucid dream creeps inside.

CHAPTER 38

Van

I dropped Harry off feeling both tweaked and exhausted. I was missing something right in front of my nose with the Taken Ones case, and I couldn't get at it because memories of Frank were breaking out of their neat little compartment and stealing my focus. When I got home, I tried cleaning, tried reading, tried sketching out notes, but none of it worked. Finally, I decided I might as well try sleep.

It was a terrible idea.

As soon as my head hit the pillow, there they were, a string of nightmares. I'm in Marie Rodin's basement. Wall-to-wall carpeting. Weeping behind the doors. Marie in her crimson suit pulling out her brass key ring. I can't survive seeing what's behind those doors, so I run and find myself in the wood-floor bedroom. The infant is swaddled at my feet, whimpering next to a roll of duct tape. Silver-haired hands are ripping up the floorboard.

I run again.

I'm back in Marie Rodin's basement.

The horrible loop takes me through the night until I wake, panting, hot yellow sun cutting across my blanket.

It's the Taken Ones case. I need to let it go, but I can't.

I didn't save Cordelia or Veronica. I *can* save Lily.

Harry had promised he'd soon have the DNA results from the shoes as well as the bandage, if any were available. I just needed a break in the case, that was all, and the visions would ease off. I dragged myself out of bed, showered, tugged on clean clothes, grabbed a Coke from my fridge, and headed to work.

I rolled in punchy and strung out from the nightmare marathon. There I discovered that Dr. Kind hadn't yet returned my call, but Kyle had gotten ahold of Theresa. She said that as far as she knew, her husband really had been in surgery that day, just like he'd told the police, and in any case, what did it matter? She had to know parents were always the main suspect when a kid went missing, but it would be difficult to imagine the man you slept next to murdering your child. It wasn't that you couldn't picture him doing it. It was that you couldn't accept that you'd missed the signs.

Kyle would keep trying to reach the former doctor as well as digging even deeper into any other land or buildings he might own. There was no way Kind had hidden Amber and possibly Lily in that apartment for the past ten years, but with an ex-wife who was a real estate agent, he'd know the ins and outs of buying property under shell corporations.

The more I looked, the more it seemed like Dr. Kind was good for this. The false alibi was big. I needed to talk to him. The hardest call would be to Comstock. If I brought Kind in for questioning, it would need to be at the First Precinct. Comstock would take over. It wouldn't be my first choice, but if it solved the case, my feelings didn't matter. I had the phone in my hand and was about to dial when someone rapped on my office door.

"Yeah?" My eyes felt gritty, my head thick. I'd need to steal some real sleep soon.

Chandler stepped in. His dark-gray suit was pristine, his bald head reflecting the overhead lights. I felt a sudden pressure on my throat. I returned the handset to the cradle and stood.

"Have a minute?" he said.

I nodded. Indicated the chair in front of my desk. He shook his head and closed the door behind him.

"That was quite the scene the other day," he said. "With the senator."

I'd hoped he'd moved on from that. "Sorry, sir."

His gaze bounced off the black blazers piled over the back of the office couch, the stacks of papers on top of a filing cabinet, an empty chip bag balanced like a cherry on the very top. He'd never visited my office before; management didn't slum down here. "I told Rodin it won't happen again."

The threat was so clear that I didn't think it required a response.

His eyes came back to me, and I wasn't surprised by their clarity. Chandler was a political animal. He was also an intelligent man. Some people assumed one negated the other. Not me. When he played easy, it was only because he was after something.

"Detective Comstock called me," he said.

How about that. I willed my hands to remain unclenched, soft on the desk. Two colleagues talking.

"He requested another agent on the Taken Ones case."

I made two fists and opened my mouth, but Chandler's hand shot up before I could speak. "I know, I know. He has no jurisdiction over a cold case. The way this one overlaps with his homicide, though, has me twitchy. I'm stopping by to give you a warning. Keep your nose clean, yeah? Lotsa fingers in this pot."

"Understood, sir," I said.

❖

Harry's text lit up my phone. Please meet me in the lab, it said.

I wondered, as I walked there, what Harry was like on a date. Without a doubt, he brought flowers and opened doors. Did he also throw his jacket down over a puddle so his lover could cross without getting their feet wet? Did he ask permission before he kissed you? I was trying to cheer myself up, I realized. I was feeling unraveled. On top of everything else, being forced to work with Comstock was getting to me. My joints weren't matching up.

I didn't knock this time before I entered the lab. Seeing Harry leaning over a microscope made me feel a little bit more grounded. His immaculate suit jacket was draped over the back of a nearby lab chair. His probably-name-brand white button-down shirt was rolled up to the elbows, a lavender tie fastened to his shirt with a gold tie clip.

His face was so smooth and so handsome he reminded me of a statue.

"You have something for me?" I asked.

His nose crinkled. "Not as much as I would like. We're lucky the shoes have been so well preserved all these years. I was able to collect nuclear DNA off them." He tapped a printout lying on the table next to him. "As expected, Rue is all over it." He paused. "I also discovered Kind DNA on it."

Hope knocked at my chest. "Amber's?"

He shook his head. "No, but it was a 50 percent match to her, meaning it came from one of her parents. Because I have Theresa's DNA, I was able to rule her out." He paused. "The evidence I gathered belongs to Amber's father. Charles Kind."

I wanted to run over and hug him. "That's enough to bring him in!"

Harry strode over to the sink to wash his hands. He didn't seem at all pleased by the news. His lack of excitement was jarring.

"What about the yellow bandage?" I asked.

Harry finished washing his hands, then dried them more thoroughly than I would have thought possible. When he finished, he tossed the used paper towels in the trash before turning to lean against the counter, still keeping considerable distance between us. "Too much degradation. No identifiable DNA, though the description matches exactly the bandage Lily Larsen was wearing that day; it was from the Band-Aid brand Strips and Spots Charmers line. They discontinued that design in the early '80s."

He must have seen my face light up again, because he held out a warning hand. "There are a lot of reasons Charles Kind's DNA could be on Rue Larsen's shoes."

"Really," I said drily. "In your experience, how often does a grown man touch an eight-year-old's sneakers? She was plenty old enough to tie them herself. Not to mention that—given how much exposure to the elements the average middle schooler's shoes experience—he had to have touched them *that day* or close to it for the DNA to remain at measurable levels, which leads to one obvious conclusion: Charles Kind set Rue Larsen's tennies next to that tree right before he left with Lily Larsen and Amber Kind."

Harry clenched his jaw, highlighting his cheekbones. "The unidentified hair taken off Amber Kind's body does *not* match Dr. Kind. Deepty still hasn't been able to track down its owner on the genealogy sites."

"That doesn't mean anything! That hair could have come from a million places." Why did it feel like we were suddenly fighting? "Kind's DNA on those shoes is enough to warrant a search of his apartment. Are you coming with?"

"You don't need me." Harry's voice was strained. "Be sure to call Comstock. An active murder investigation takes priority over a cold case."

"I'll follow protocol," I said, whetting each word as it passed over my teeth. Then I turned on my heel and marched out of his lab, letting the anger roll off me in waves. There was a lot that Harry hadn't said, but he'd still managed to make clear that he didn't approve of giving Kind the starring role in this one. I wouldn't let his fears cost me the case.

Because . . . false alibi, connection to the cabin, DNA evidence? I was going in.

I yanked my phone from my coat as I stomped down the hall. I punched in Comstock's number.

He answered on the second ring. "Yeah?"

"We have Charles Kind's DNA on Rue Larsen's shoes. The ones discovered at the abduction site." I was talking too fast and unable to slow down. "I'm getting a search warrant to check his Cedar Riverside apartment. Agent Kaminski is still working on finding other property Kind might own, but that's what we have for now. Would you like to join us?"

A snort came down the line. "I sure as hell would. Let me know the time."

There was something dangerous in Comstock's voice. "You want lead on this one?"

It was a courtesy question. I was offering to do the work and give him the glory.

Another pause. "This one's all yours."

If Harry's reaction hadn't been a red flag, Comstock's would have been. A red flag set ablaze. But all I was after was an apartment search. It was a reasonable request given the evidence.

That's what I kept telling myself, over and over.

CHAPTER 39

Van

My skin felt like a sheet drawn tight as I strode toward Cedar Riverside, Kyle alongside me. He'd been on board with getting the search warrant. Even Chandler, after asking me if I was sure, had given it his stamp of approval. That, along with the DNA evidence and proof of Kind's falsified alibi, had been enough to get the warrant within an hour. Still, it felt like a sniper dot on my neck the way Comstock kept a respectful distance behind me as we entered the building.

The odds of Lily being in Kind's apartment were next to zero. The chance of finding evidence that Kind had kidnapped her and Amber? I'd take that bet. As the three of us rode the elevator, I considered what it would mean if we cracked this case. If Lily Larsen was alive, we would rescue her—and potentially Amber Kind's child—from whatever nightmare they'd been living in. Introduce Lily to her mom and her sister. Give her the tools to reenter the world. And we'd put Charles Kind in prison. He would serve time for what he'd done to those girls.

He would pay in ways Frank Roth had never had to pay.

I was inflating even bigger, engorged on my own certainty, which should've told me everything I needed to know. A feeling of invincibility should be a signal to any good agent that they are done. But I couldn't stop thinking about Rue's roasted feet, that terrified final expression stamped on Amber's face as she suffocated to death belowground, the possibility that Lily Larsen was still alive and frantic for her nightmare to end.

I would see this through.

Rap rap rap on Kind's door.

The neighboring family didn't come out this time. The halls were quiet. You grew up poor or on the margins, you developed a second sense about hiding yourself when the law was hungry for someone to arrest. I'd done it myself before I'd stepped onto the other side of the equation.

My blood tumbled when Kind's door opened. It had always been a possibility that he'd be home, but I was still surprised. "Dr. Charles Kind?"

The man who answered was the right age. Early seventies, wispy white hair, a bushy Sam Elliott mustache covering most of his lower face. His passive posture—he held himself like he expected to be hit—pissed me off.

"Retired doctor," he said. "What's this about?"

The search warrant was burning in my pocket. It would look better for him if I didn't have to use it. "I'm Agent Reed, and this is Agent Kaminski, both with the BCA. That's Detective Comstock of the Minneapolis PD. We'd like to speak with you about the 1980 disappearance of your daughter and Lily Larsen."

Kind shrank even further, like someone had peeled out his backbone. "My ex-wife called to tell me you found Amber."

"You've been a difficult man to get ahold of," I said, spicy with defensiveness for Harry. He and I might not see eye to eye on Kind's guilt, but he'd worked very hard to report to both parents in person.

Charles slid backward more than invited us in. It was enough for me. I pushed past him and took an immediate read of his apartment. It looked like he'd built an indoor nest, boxes piled high. The only visible wall was plastered with photos of Amber, pictures that I hadn't spotted at Theresa's. Amber as a baby in his arms. Riding a Ferris wheel. Birthday cake smeared across her face, four candles teetering on the edge of the frosted devil's food.

My feeling of unease grew.

"Will you have a seat?" Kind asked, indicating the only visible chair.

Kyle and Comstock stood at my back, feeling too large in this crowded space. "Dr. Kind, where were you on the day your daughter disappeared?"

He reached out for support, but poor luck found him standing in the only open area in the entire room. His hand kept moving, trying to find purchase. He looked like he was swimming in air. "I was in surgery."

"No, you were not."

He had the decency to blanch, but he didn't offer anything.

"Your DNA was found on Rue Larsen's shoes."

He collapsed onto a waist-high stack of boxes. The top one bent open, revealing newspapers. "I might have moved her shoes when she visited," he said, his voice weak.

"Dr. Kind," I repeated, "where were you when Amber Kind and Lily Larsen disappeared?"

He made a noise like a tree groaning. "I was in surgery."

My nerves began zinging, telling me he wasn't our guy, but he'd limited my options by holding firm to his lie. If Comstock weren't here, I could use some tricks to get Kind to talk, some lies that Comstock would assuredly call me out on. That left me with only one choice. "We'd like to take you in for some questioning while we verify that."

Out of the corner of my eye, I saw Kyle stiffen.

"You don't need to take me in. I'm not going anywhere." Kind's voice was lonely. "I *can't* go anywhere. I'm here until I die, making one mistake after another. It's my curse."

If he wanted to evoke pity, he'd missed his mark. "Detective Comstock can take you," I said.

A subtle rustling came from behind me, like Comstock was adjusting his stance, but he didn't otherwise protest.

"Am I under arrest?" Kind asked.

There was still time to nuance this, to use the threat of arrest to get Kind to come clean without the weight of actually arresting him, but

Comstock was too quick. He stepped forward. "At Agent Reed's request, I'm arresting you for the abduction of Amber Kind and Lily Larsen, as well as the murder of Amber Kind."

And there was Comstock's play.

He'd taken my hunger for Kind and used it to force my hand. There was a slice of a second where I could have said something, eaten crow on the spot, but I'd lose any momentum with Kind if he saw Comstock and me bickering. Comstock knew I wouldn't risk the case like that.

He put his hand on Kind's shoulder and guided him toward the door, reading him his Miranda rights as they walked. The sudden despair I felt made me light-headed. I glanced around the living room. Kyle and I would be here cataloging this for the rest of the day. If we didn't find anything, at best, I'd look like an idiot. At worst, I'd be taken off the case.

Kyle tossed me a look once Comstock and Kind were out of the apartment. It was eagerness mixed with something else.

"You think that was a mistake," I said. It was a statement of fact, one I was inclined to agree with. I'd let Comstock sucker punch me and had only myself to blame.

Kyle shrugged as he pulled on his gloves. "Comstock cornered you just now, and you made the only call you could. That aside, I don't think we needed a search warrant. Charles Kind is a good man." He snapped a glove for effect. "He volunteers in his spare time. He's never been arrested."

I wanted the room to stop tipping. I wanted to feel confident again, sure of my choices, like someone who hadn't just been. I settled for petty bickering with Kyle. "Tell me you're not so green as to think that makes a difference. Good people do awful things all day long."

Kyle shrugged. "I'm not saying he was a saint. I'm saying he shows up on paper as a stand-up guy, and those kind of dudes don't abduct and kill their daughters. That's all. But if there's something here to find, better damn well believe I'm going to help you find it."

CHAPTER 40

Van

Kyle and I didn't find anything other than the detritus of a man who'd spent the past four decades hoping to die. The state of Minnesota allowed us to keep Kind for forty-eight hours before we filed formal charges. The sick feeling in my belly confirmed that Comstock had let me take lead so he could make it look like I'd exercised poor judgment; the kicker was that he couldn't have done it without me. I'd walked into Kind's blindly confident the former doctor was guilty, and I'd gotten what I deserved. My only way out of this hole was to retroactively uncover something to justify arresting him. Out of more desperation than I cared to admit, I drove to Rue's house.

The press was camped outside.

I swore, using every bad word I knew and a few that I made up on the spot. Comstock must have leaked either that we'd identified Amber or had arrested the former doctor. Maybe both. That meant the lizard was no longer only working against me, he was working against his own case. It had to be inspired by more than hatred for me alone. If he was connected to the girls' disappearance, it would be a double dunk for him that I'd set up Kind to be arrested and me to be discredited.

Dammit.

I popped on my aviators and shut down my ears against the press as I walked to Rue's front door. At least they were respecting her driveway and lawn. The snap of photos being taken sliced through the air, even louder than the questions being lobbed. I peeked inside Rue's front window as I knocked. Her curtains were open, and she was nowhere in sight, which meant that if she was home, she was hiding in her bedroom or her bathroom. I moved my face near the camera mounted to her front door and spoke softly.

"Rue, it's Agent Reed. I need to speak with you."

I was answered by the sound of locks clicking.

The woman who opened the door was almost unrecognizable. She was gray. Her skin, the roots of her hair, the whites of her eyes, all of it gone ashen.

"The sooner you let me in, the fewer pictures taken," I said, shielding her with my body as much as possible.

She stepped aside and indicated I should enter. She didn't bother closing the locks behind me.

"How are you?"

She ran a hand through her limp hair. "A little bit worse than I look."

"That bad?"

She offered me a wan smile. It was something.

"I want you out of the sight lines," I said. "Do you prefer your basement or your bedroom? Because I think the bathroom is too small for both of us."

Her eyebrow lifted. "You knew how I'd set up the place?"

"It's how I'd arrange my home if I'd been through what you have."

She nodded and walked toward her bedroom. I followed. Once we were both in, she closed the door behind us. Her bedroom was dark and as austere as the rest of the house. She didn't even have a book on her bedside table. What had she been doing in here with all that press outside?

"I want to show you something Agent Steinbeck and I found in the woods near where Lily and Amber disappeared."

"It's funny, you know," she said as I tugged out my phone.

I scrolled, searching for the photo I'd taken of the yellow bandage with the black elephant on it. "What is?"

"Steinbeck. Reed. Some people love to read Steinbeck. Do you get it?"

My forehead furrowed. I hadn't thought of it, actually. "I suppose it is funny. Can I show you the picture?" I held my phone toward her. "Do you recognize this?"

Her face tightened, and then almost immediately, it relaxed as if she were looking at the photograph of a long-lost friend. She reached out to touch the edge of my phone.

"I stuck that on Lily's knee that day," she said. "She kept skinning them. Her knees, I mean. You said you found it in the woods? After all this time?"

"Agent Steinbeck did," I said. "In a nearby cabin. Rue, is there any reason Charles Kind's DNA would be on your tennis shoes that were found in the woods that day?"

She withdrew her hand from my phone. It floated between us for a moment, trembling, before she ran it through her hair. I didn't know if it was a self-soothing gesture or a general response to awkwardness. "I was over at their house, you know, a lot that summer. Dr. Kind liked to keep things neat, I remember that. Him being a doctor and all. Maybe he moved them."

Not a single twitch or a sliding glance told me she was lying. Her body language was serene, dreamy almost. She was not afraid of Dr. Kind.

The sand was running out of my hourglass.

"Have you thought any more about seeing our hypnotherapist? We have a specialist at accessing childhood memories. It's far from an exact science, but she's very good."

Rue suddenly focused on me intently, all the mistiness gone from her face. "What is it you're not seeing?"

For a confusing moment, I thought she was referring to the case. It was the exact same question I'd been asking myself. But the way my blood pressed at my wrists told me she was asking for something deeper, something more vulnerable. She was asking me about myself. Could she see in my eyes what I'd allowed to happen to Veronica, my Sister with the gap-toothed smile? "Nothing as bad as what you experienced. I grew up in an unusual situation. I had to escape it. A story as old as time."

That wasn't going to be enough for her, not today. "But you know what it costs to remember, don't you? To be forced to relive the worst of it like it's a movie you can't look away from?"

Everything's going to be all right, Veronica.

I sighed raggedly. "I do."

She frowned. "And you still want me to see a hypnotherapist? You want me to crack open what's left of my egg?"

That reminded me of how her mother had described her as a child. Happy as an egg. "There could be freedom on the other side," I said. "It could help us find out what happened to Lily and Amber."

I almost believed it myself.

She hugged herself. "I'll think about it."

CHAPTER 41

Van

Kyle had called three times while I was visiting Rue. I waited until I was in my car and around the block—away from the eyes and ears of the press—to call him back hands-free. He didn't bother with greetings.

"Kind came clean. He was at the downtown Minneapolis Hilton with a nurse the day his daughter got abducted. We tracked down the nurse. She confirmed. Said he was a wreck afterward, felt like if he'd been home rather than with her it never would have happened. She saved the receipts. Literally. She has the hotel receipts."

The world outside was summery and bright, so open and free, so in opposition to the reality of two children imprisoned for decades, one of them cruelly murdered. "You've seen them?"

"I called you as soon as I hung up the phone with her. She said she's going to track them down and email them to me."

"You believe her?"

A pause. "I do."

"I'll call Comstock."

"Van—"

Like the devil hearing his name, Comstock's incoming call lit up my screen. "He's on the other line right now," I said before I hung up on Kyle and answered.

"You're in deep on this one, aren't you, Reed?" Comstock taunted. "I don't believe our old friend would like this at all. No, he definitely would not approve."

My gut twisted. I hadn't thought Comstock would go low enough to say it.

I was wrong.

"Our friend Bart, that is," he said. "I think you made stink, Reed. Kind has an alibi for that day, just not the one he told us. He was banging a nurse. Should have done a little more research before you went in guns blazing, eh?"

I was grateful I'd heard the news from Kyle first, so I'd had a hot second to prepare. "The DNA on the shoe was a good-enough reason to talk to him, or I never would have gotten the search warrant," I said. "*You* were the one who took him in."

"You were lead," Comstock said. "Paperwork proves it. Besides, that DNA doesn't even live in the same neighborhood as circumstantial, considering how much the kid was at Kind's place that summer. And the alibi and the DNA were all you had. Your man called to confirm we should release Kind."

A needle of betrayal pierced me. "Kaminski?"

"Steinbeck," he said.

What had been a sting exploded like a land mine, sending venom through my veins. Kyle must have called Harry after he couldn't reach me. Or maybe he'd started with Harry. I had only Kyle's word that he'd tried me first. The BCA guys were turning against me just like the MPD had. I rubbed the bridge of my nose, my joints aching, my stomach sour.

"Looks like you banked your blow on the wrong guy, kid," Comstock said.

He couldn't have known "kid" was what Bart used to call me. Or maybe he did. "Looks like I did," I said, fighting for calmness. I couldn't let Comstock know he'd scored a direct hit. "Let him go."

"Already did."

Comstock's delighted cackle was the last thing I heard as I hung up.

CHAPTER 42

Van

Marie Rodin stood outside the first basement door. Her scarlet fingernails were almond-shaped blades. She slid the key into the lock. She opened the door. I couldn't look away, not to save my soul. I was drawn to what was inside, to the chained ankle, painfully thin. Up that ankle to a girl—the same one who'd been at the shelter with Rodin—wearing soiled underwear and a VeggieTales T-shirt, her eyes closed, her eyeballs racing beneath them. She was either having a nightmare or doing a child's impersonation of sleep.

"You've been very bad tonight, I see," the senator said.

As I opened my mouth to yell, I was jerked backward out of the room, down the hall, and out the front door like a giant string in my back had been pulled. Before I could breathe in the relief of it, I heard the screaming infant. I was back again in the other house, a floorboard removed, revealing a gaping hole. Except the baby couldn't be screaming, because she had silver duct tape pressed tight over her mouth. With that realization, I shot awake, grabbing my gun from my nightstand out of instinct.

I was in my bed. In my apartment. Still, my heart was hammering so hard it was making me nauseous. This getting dragged from one horrible nightmare scene to another was unbearable. I didn't know if it was my imagination or a vision, but I couldn't just let it happen again. *I couldn't.*

I scrambled out of bed, yanked jeans and a T-shirt on over the sports bra and underwear I'd been sleeping in, and buckled on my holster. I tucked my gun inside but left my badge where it lay. Then I grabbed my phone and keys, ran my fingers through my hair, and headed outside. The cooler night air should have brought me back to my senses, but I didn't want it to. *A child, chained to her bed. Her legs covered in burn marks, bruises peeking through where her shirt rode up. Nobody helping her.* I hurried to my car and drove to the senator's house.

I had to know.

And if I knew, I had to act.

It had been like this with those three men, the visions driving me to the brink. Without Bart there to help me build a case against them, I'd had to stop them all by myself. Would I need to stop the senator to save those kids? A prick of clarity whispered to me that I was strung out by the case, from Comstock's fuckery, from the Farm flashbacks, from messed-up sleep since before we'd discovered Amber Kind's body. That same lucidity told me that I had the tools to calm myself. That I was stronger now than I'd been in the weeks after I lost Bart. Grounded. Separate from the visions.

But the obscene nightmares lived in my head, and the only way to escape them was to stop the monsters perpetuating them.

I realized I was panting, my system on high alert as I sat in my Toyota three houses down from the Rodin rambler. I was parked as far from the streetlights as possible while still in view of the house. I felt no relief keeping watch. What was going on in that house? Was Rodin torturing her children? I could break a window, charge down to the basement, and check for the three doors I'd seen in my vision. I'd be in and out before the senator could get to a phone. If I discovered her husband or kids in danger, I could figure out what to do next. If they were all fine, if what I'd been experiencing were nightmares rather than actual visions, I could trust sleep.

I'd bungled the interview with Kind. I no longer trusted Kyle or Harry. My nerves were razor wire rubbing against tendon and bone, and I was starving for deep rest.

I opened my car door, its interior light cutting an alarming brightness through the dark night. I stepped out and closed it quickly, cursing myself; under normal circumstances, I would have remembered to turn the light off first. I padded soft as a cat down the sidewalk. The signs at the edge of the senator's landscaping told me she had a security system installed.

That wouldn't matter if I was quick.

I had to know.

I trod lightly through the grass, the mercury dewdrops like tiny lanterns reflecting the nearest streetlight. I thought of the case Dr. McPherson had discussed with the class, the one where the murderer had been caught because of the lack of tracks in the dew, but that story had been about a criminal. *I was a law enforcement agent.* Was I even awake? I glided toward the side of the house and found myself wedged between thorny bushes and a double-paned window. I stuck my face up to the glass, hands pressed on each side of my cheeks so I could peer in.

On the other side was a floor-model living room. Brown couch, tan carpeting, photos over the fireplace. So sterile, like it was begging for a family that never visited. But the senator had two children, both under eleven. Where were the toys? The books? The science project splayed out on the floor?

I heard a rattling at the window and realized it was me at the same time a police siren keened through the night. An upstairs light clicked on overhead, spilling a cracked-yolk glow across the lawn. Awareness slapped me, hard. *She knows I'm out here.* Heart in throat, I raced to my car.

The red lights were pulsing like blood across the underbelly of the night clouds as I pulled away from the curb.

CHAPTER 43

Van

It felt like everyone stared at me the next day at work. Gawked as if I'd grown an appendage out of my forehead. I glared and snapped, startling Kyle as he offered me a coffee in the hall. He turned on his heel, probably going straight to complain about me to his new best friend, Harry Steinbeck. They were likely trying to figure out how to push me out of the BCA, just like I'd been elbowed out of the MPD.

I marched straight to my office, head down. I wished it had *more* garbage in it. Prove to them I couldn't care less what they thought of me. I plunked down at my computer and wrote a report delineating exactly what had happened with Charles Kind and then added a summary of my interview with Rue.

If nothing else, my paperwork would be flawless.

My exhausted brain swirled as I typed. What was I missing? A gnawing told me the key to the cold case was dangling right in front of my face. Rue, Lily, and Amber had entered the woods that day. They had encountered something terrifying, something so shocking it knocked Rue's memory right out of her head, yet she'd been inexplicably allowed to go free. Lily and Amber were brought directly to the cabin. Had the person or people who'd kidnapped the girls planned to assault them there, or had the plan always been to ferry them out of the woods, and if so, why stop at the cabin at all? Was the abductor some-body familiar or an outsider? Nothing about this case was lining up.

A knock at the door made me jump.

Chandler thrust his head in. He looked like an angry thumb. "I heard about Kind. What the hell, Reed."

I blinked, my eyes grainy, my thoughts slow. It was the second time in as many days that Chandler had visited my office. The guillotine blade was being drawn up.

"I thought he was good for it," I said. "He wasn't."

If Chandler thought he was owed an apology, he'd need to look elsewhere.

He grimaced. "I want you to take a day off. Get your head on straight."

I was on my feet before I knew it. "I'm close to a solve," I said, my voice too loud. "I feel it."

"I wasn't asking." His head disappeared from my doorway. The door clicked shut.

I'd never been ordered to take a time-out before. I was furious.

I raced through a mental list of people I could report Chandler to even as part of me realized he was making the right call. I considered following through on the interviews I had planned for today, low-key, but if that got back to Chandler, I was done at the BCA. In the end, the only option that wouldn't sink my career further down the tank was to spend the morning at the shelter. I sighed. *Fine.* I'd stay long enough to leave a paper trail of where I'd been, but I'd bring all the case files home so that I could scour them until I was allowed to return to work.

Find what I missed.

I punched off my computer, stuffed my backpack full of the Taken Ones files, and stormed out my door. I nearly ran into Harry, who stood just outside, hand raised like he'd been about to knock. I shoul-der-checked him on the way to my car.

The animal shelter's smells, as pungent as they were, relaxed me.

"Hey, Van!" someone called from behind the front desk. I glanced over. My plan had been to get to work without talking to another human, but there was the barista slash yoga teacher looking like sunshine and wanting to talk.

"Hey yourself, Alexis," I said, thinking again of the invisible people, those who watched us, clocking our moves as we obliviously went about our day. I'd need to pick that thread back up. "How are you?"

She smiled. She was cute. I bet she'd been popular in high school. Not cheerleader popular, but farmgirl-who-was-everyone's-friend popular.

"Good," she said, still smiling.

What must that be like, to be so open and happy? It was a foreign life, that's all I knew. I nodded instead of answering, tightened my emotional belt, and strode through the swinging doors. MacGuffin's tail thumped like a bass drum when he spotted me. He had two poop piles in his pen, and his water dish had big runners of snot across the top. They did a decent job caring for animals at the shelter, but it wasn't the same as a dog having its own loving home.

"Who wants the cleanest pen in all the land?" I asked in a voice I reserved for four-legged creatures. I let myself into MacGuffin's kennel and knelt to scratch the sweet spot behind his ears. His tail thumping reached a dangerous velocity. His acceptance made me want to weep. "Mark that spot, am I right?"

After I gave him the good pets, I led him outside into the sunshiny day and walked him around the enclosure so he could relieve himself. We even played a little ball until a limp indicated he was getting tired. I guided him back inside and secured him outside his pen while I scrubbed it cleaner than any bathroom I'd ever touched in my life. After, I selected a knotted rope and a chew bone I thought he'd like from the bin of donated dog toys and placed them next to his clean bedding for later tonight. Then I led him back outside to give him a bath. The shelter had a dedicated bathing section indoors, but on hot days like today, we were allowed to bring the animals outside. That warm, clean sun would feel so good on his wet fur. I soaped him up, rinsed him, and then brushed a Chihuahua-size pile of loose hair off him. Finally, I clipped his nails, made sure his eyes were clean, and hugged him tight, his steady heart beating near mine.

I'd reek of wet dog later.

It was truly the least of my problems.

"You're a really good boy, MacGuffin," I whispered into his wet fur. "The best dog in the whole world. You know I love you, don't you?"

We stayed like that until he groaned and nudged me. I think he wanted to get at the toys I'd placed in his pen. I was leading him inside when out popped the woman who'd tried bossing me around the night Amber Kind had been discovered.

She glanced down at MacGuffin. "He sure looks happy," she said brightly. She was wearing shelter-appropriate clothes this time—ratty sweatpants, a faded Johnny Cash T-shirt.

I might have judged her too quickly the other day. Job hazard. "He sure does," I said.

She put her hand out for him to sniff. "I hope he gets adopted soon. You know that poodle I was showing that woman and her kids a couple days ago? Got adopted."

I felt a zing like someone had pinched me. I absolutely *did* remember Rodin and her children visiting the shelter. "By that woman you were showing him to?" I hadn't heard a dog at the senator's last night.

"No." She smiled as MacGuffin gave her palm a big, slobbery lick. "Someone else. A guy. That woman came back, though. Did you know she's a state senator?"

I stayed as still as stone.

"I didn't," she said. "Not the night she and her kids checked out the poodle, anyhow. But she returned today. Marie Rodin is her name. Adopted one of the pitties. Said she needed a guard dog. Makes sense, I suppose. Someone with a job like hers probably gets stalkers all the time."

"Probably," I said. Rodin had known someone was outside her house last night, had called the cops. I was lucky I hadn't been busted.

"Hey, what line of work are you in?"

I suddenly couldn't stand to be there a moment longer. I handed her MacGuffin's leash and walked straight out of the shelter.

CHAPTER 44

Van

Kyle popped his head into my office. "Rue and Lily Larsen's dad is in town."

I jerked to attention. No small feat given I'd slept only in fits and bursts last night. That made it officially too long since I'd had good sleep, but the only way I could keep hooked in reality was by making sure I didn't dip back into those nightmares.

"Where?" I asked.

Kyle looked like he hadn't slept much, either. He was also watching me like I was a bomb about to go off. I felt a surge of guilt, but I couldn't navigate one more thing, not if I wanted to hold myself together.

"A hotel down by the Saint Paul Depot. Trackside Inn. He called into the hotline. Said he saw the news and wanted to talk."

I'd set up the hotline after I'd left the shelter yesterday, after my eight-hour "cool-off" had ended. I figured since Comstock had spilled the beans, we might as well harvest them, even though collecting useful information through a hotline was like looking for a freckle in a sandstorm. In the twelve hours since the hotline had been created, we'd fielded more than a hundred leads. People who'd recently spotted Amber and Lily at the grocery store or a local day care but insisted that they were still children. A man who was sure his daughter's kindergarten teacher was Lily Larsen, all grown up. Several men claiming to have been the one who murdered Amber.

A broad subsection of the population was weirdly eager to be associated with tragedy. Maybe that was the only way they knew how to connect. In any case, we had to follow up on every tip. We'd brought in some floaters for exactly that purpose, and if they discovered anything of merit, it went through Kyle. Anything he believed was legit, he passed on to me.

"I'll stop by and see Mr. Larsen today," I said. "What's the word on the others on the interview list?"

Kyle had arranged for me to talk with Donald Tucker, the registered sex offender who resided at the Village Lake Nursing Home. He was the one the Leech Lake police—or at least Bauman—were certain had abducted the girls. Last I'd heard, Kyle was still trying to track down Bruce Anthony, the hinky band teacher who in the 1980s had been questioned every which way but Wednesday and found clean. He was also reaching out to Jacob Peters, a long shot by anybody's measure. Rue's classmate and purported crush had been an eight-year-old at the time of the abduction. There was also the Schwan's man, who as far as we could tell had no connection to the case other than having been in the wrong place at the wrong time, doing his job.

"Bruce Anthony is dead," Kyle said matter-of-factly. "Heart attack a decade ago. The Schwan's man, a.k.a. Bill Briston, is a greeter at a Walmart halfway between here and Leech Lake. He said you're welcome to drop by anytime." Kyle's mouth curved. "I don't think he understood the importance of what I was asking. Sounded pretty old."

"Thanks," I said. "I'm heading out in ten. Anything you want to say to me?"

The strain between us was palpable, but Kyle shook his head. "I'll let you know if anything turns up."

My throat tightened. Had I been hoping for an apology, an "I'm sorry I told Steinbeck about your face-plant"? Or maybe I was desperate for him to show me how to repair what I'd cost us.

I'd never know.

As soon as he left, I drove over to the Trackside Inn.

✦

The motel lived up to its name, situated as it was next to the train tracks in a run-down part of town. It was a dilapidated structure, just a strip of rooms and an office. If it were a smell, it'd be cigarettes and dry skin.

Rolf Larsen, father to Rue and Lily and ex-husband to Rita, answered his door looking like he'd been plucked straight out of a casting call for an Old West gold prospector. He was as small and white-haired as a dandelion gone to seed, with a liquor-swollen nose that clung precariously to his face. He had a nervous gesture of rubbing his hands together like he was dry washing them.

I held up my badge. "Agent Reed. Mr. Rolf Larsen?"

"Yep, that's me. Might as well talk out there, 'cause my room ain't much to write home about."

I glanced behind him. Two queen beds, one unmade and the other neat as a pin, with the bedspread and the walls seemingly made from the same thin cardboard. The unslept-in bed held a simple black duffel bag. Inside was probably everything he owned. By all accounts, Rolf Larsen lived his life on the road.

"After you," I said, stepping aside so he could exit.

He locked the door behind him. The motel was so old that it took an actual metal key. We made our way to the two fraying webbed lawn chairs nearby. He claimed the one farthest, a beer bottle stuffed full of cigarette butts next to it. He tugged a pack of Camel straights out of his shirt pocket, then selected one and lit it, all in a single fluid move.

I took the other chair. We faced a parking lot with a dozen cars of various vintages, most of them held together by rust. The groans and shrieks of the nearby rail yard offered an irregular symphony. I wondered whether a railroad man like him even heard the noises anymore, or if he did, if he found them soothing.

Larsen took a deep, crackling drag off his cigarette. "I saw it on the news," he said. "About them finding Amber Kind. It was Amber, wasn't it?"

While she had not yet been officially named, "someone" had leaked Dr. Kind's arrest, and the press had done the rest. That meant that— although the Minneapolis PD had yet to go on the record about it— Amber's identity and her gruesome manner of death were currently the worst-kept secrets in Minnesota. In other words, I wouldn't get in trouble for confirming, and I needed this man to trust me.

"It was Amber Kind."

He sucked on his cigarette, creating an inch of ash in a breath, his face looking pained. "And my Lily?"

Those words had cost him. And the use of "my" surprised me. Other than the garnished wages he'd paid until Rue turned eighteen, Rolf Larsen had earned a gold medal in the Deadbeat Dad category. "We haven't heard anything," I said.

His eyes shot to me, shiny with hope. "So she might be alive? Still to this day?"

I watched a sputtering, fish-colored Honda Civic pull into the far end of the lot. Its driver studied me over his sunglasses before pulling straight back out. "Where were you when the girls disappeared?"

Rolf took another drag. "Working on the railroad," he said. "There's a million songs about a ramblin' man, but there's never been one as dedicated as me. Can't stay still for nothin'."

I gave him time to answer.

It took several seconds, and then: "I can't rightly say where I was that day, but I know I wasn't in Minnesota."

I took out my notebook. "Do you have witnesses?"

He dropped his cigarette into the brown beer bottle and immediately lit another with the same flowing gesture. "Can't say for sure."

I hadn't yet written anything down. "You have to know how that sounds."

The crisp crackle of paper burning filled the empty space between us. "Can't do nothin' but tell the truth," he said.

We both sat with that for a minute. I believed he was being honest. I also believed it was going to take a hell of a lot of legwork to prove.

"You see Rue?" he asked, his voice raspy.

A beetle crawled across the sidewalk, forging a drunken path. We both watched it. "I have," I said.

"How she look?"

I chewed on that for a minute. "Not good," I said finally. If he wanted more, he'd have to ask her himself.

"I'll be here for a week," he said. "My skin will just about itch off staying still that long, but I figure that's time enough for you to find out what you need to know about me."

I stood. "I'll hold you to that."

He shaded his eyes to peer up at me. "You're a runner, too. I can see it on you. You might be staying in one place, but you're running away inside."

Everyone wants to tell you something about yourself, but no one wants to see themselves, not really. "Your daughter said something similar," I said.

I texted Kyle an update as I walked to my car.

◈

The Village Lake Nursing Home had an assisted living wing that housed residents who needed minimal care. Donald Tucker was one of those residents, a man who relied on a wheelchair because of a bum leg but was otherwise in moderately good health. When I asked which room he was in, the distaste showed on the receptionist's face, though she was professional enough to cover it by rubbing her nose.

"He's down in 311. He's expecting you."

I nodded. "Does he ever leave?"

She shrugged. "He could if he wants. This isn't a jail. The wheelchair means he can't get far, though."

"Could a friend take him out?"

"If he had any," she said, before returning to her paperwork.

When I walked into Tucker's room, the first thing I noticed was the odor. The entire building had so far smelled like industrial cleaners and baby powder, a queasy combination, but Tucker's room stank of meat just about to turn. I kept my mouth open so I didn't have to breathe through my nose.

"Donald Tucker?" He sat in a wheelchair next to his bed watching TV, in profile. "I'm Agent Reed. I'm here to ask you a few questions. I understand you've been expecting me."

The side of his face twitched, but he waited until the commercial to turn toward me. A power move. Good, I thought, my blood boiling. I craved a fight.

Even though he was sitting, it was obvious he'd been a tall man. Age had melted him, transforming his height into loose rolls that steadily cascaded, growing wider and wider until they reached his lap. There was something piggy about his face, too, with his snubbed nose and tiny black eyes that darted to my chest as he put the TV on mute. He turned his wheelchair to face me. Kyle had been clear that Tucker could walk, but the staff said it was easier to move him with the chair.

"I heard they found one of 'em taken girls," he said as he rolled toward me. "I'm so glad." His yellow teeth showed in what he must have believed was a smile.

I would not engage on that level. "Where were you on July 23, 1980?"

He took his own sweet time answering, stopping his chair a yard away. "You either know that or you're dumb, and in neither case does it make sense for me to answer. That certainly is pretty hair you have, baby girl. You bleach it that color?"

"You were driving the bus for Leech Lake's special education kids' summer camp," I said, my voice low and even, ignoring his question and the heebie-jeebies it gave me. "From nine a.m. until five p.m., you were in sight of either the parents, the faculty, or your boss."

Must have gone sideways for Officers Bauman and Schmidt once they'd realized Tucker's alibi was unassailable. Still, they'd watched him for weeks after the abduction. He never strayed from his regular routine. If Tucker had taken those girls and then hidden them, which the abductor had done with at least Amber, he was a wizard, capable of being in two places at once.

Yet even after all these years, Bauman hadn't been able to drop Tucker's scent. I wondered what actual leads it'd cost him. Law enforcement was like any other job. Some of the employees were great, most were fine, and a bunch were terrible. The big difference was a bad or even mediocre cop could hurt a lot more people than, say, a subpar cashier at the local Dairy Queen.

I continued my rundown of Tucker's whereabouts. "On July 23, you'd either already chosen your victim from the students you were driving, or you were on the verge of picking her out. Took you another six weeks to molest her." I leaned forward to be sure he was hearing every word, though the stink of him made me want to gag. "But you did a piss-poor job choosing your target, because that brave little girl told on you the first chance she got. You served a year in Stillwater."

Tucker's mouth turned ugly. "I did my time. I got nothing to hide." He tipped his chin to look at me from beneath his eyelids, suddenly sly. "But I can help you, pretty girl. Might even be able to save that other one. I know how a kiddynapper's mind works. I got *secrets* I can tell you."

I stepped back but he rolled his chair forward, no more than a foot separating us. It took every ounce of control I had not to recoil from his cadaverous smell. "I can tell you how he picked those two and why," he continued. "I can tell you what he *did* to them." Tucker adjusted his body in the chair, popping his shoulders up around his ears, and the reek grew impossibly worse. I hoped the aides changed him irregularly.

He was bluffing, that much was clear, trying to get his slice of the trauma pie, hoping it would win him fame or redemption. I was confident he had no insider information. Still, I had to ask. "Where did he take them?"

He cackled. "For starters, he would've had his hidey-hole all scouted. No one takes two girls without a strategy. One you can keep quiet. Two needs a plan."

Ants crawled across my scalp. This monster had been out in the world, had been *paid* to interact with children. "Who took them?"

He sat up straight, his beady eyes glittering. "Well, now, it'll take a few visits to get that out of me. You might even want to bring a camera crew. I ain't gonna be remembered as no kiddynapper. I'm gonna be remembered as the man who brought that last girl home. You just wait. People will finally see me for who I really am."

I bent down to his level, fury pushing aside the rest of my senses. I jabbed each of my thumbs into the tender spot just above his elbows and shoved my face right up next to his slobbering, unshaven piehole. "I see you perfectly well right now," I snarled. "You're a useless piece of shit, so weak that you prey on children. There is no redemption for you." I twisted my thumbs deeper. "The sooner you leave this earth, the better for all of us."

His chin wobbled. "But I know who did it!"

"No, you don't," I said. I'd never been more certain of anything in my life. "You have no friends. You have no family. All you know is your own dark jail of a mind."

I released my thumbs. The white spots they left quickly turned a satisfying red. I suspected they'd be bruising a deep purple before I walked out the front door. I pulled a business card from the inside pocket of my blazer, ensuring he saw my pistol. I snapped the card onto his lap. "But if you think of anything helpful, give a ring. Know that I'll be the one who shows up. Every time."

CHAPTER 45

Van

When I called Kyle with the latest update, he responded by saying he still hadn't been able to get ahold of Jacob Peters. It was a strange thing in this day and age to fly under the radar, but before I could point that out, Kyle clarified that Jacob was on a Canadian fishing trip with friends. They had no cell reception. His family had been told that it was urgent we speak with him, and they assured Kyle that they'd call the moment Jacob was in contact. It was the best that could be done.

My next stop was the Eden Prairie Walmart, but first I drove past Leech Lake Elementary, a 1960s, single-story brick bunker of a building. It looked like it hadn't been updated since it'd been built. Amber, Rue, and Lily had walked through those doors, as had thousands of other kids over the years. What had set Amber and Lily apart from the crowd? Who'd been watching? When the building didn't give up any secrets, I motored past the cop shop, the drugstore, and a string of alleyways until I reached the Elm Street cul-de-sac.

The *why those girls* was connected to the *why this place*. By all accounts, their decision to swim at Ghost Creek that day had been a spontaneous one. Nobody but their parents would have known about it. Of course, on a hot summer day before central air-conditioning was common, it would have been a safe guess that the girls would be playing outside. Yet there had to have been something about those three and that day.

The woods. The town.

What makes evil haunt a specific place in time?

I turned the question over in my head as I drove to the Walmart. It wasn't an ideal place to interview somebody, but I didn't think this would take long. Bill Briston had followed his regular Schwan's delivery route that day, hitting all his stops—before and after the girls disappeared—on time. Other than the phoned-in tip, there would have been no reason to suspect him. The notes had been unclear, though, about who called him in and when, and so he was a "t" that needed crossing.

I parked in the enormous lot beneath an oppressively clear sky and walked through a wall of heat toward the wide doors.

"Welcome to Walmart, may I point you toward a cart?"

The smiling greeter had perfect teeth. Dentures, surely. His glasses were the square ones favored by shop teachers in the '80s, and his gray hair was combed over an age-spotted skull. His name tag said BILL.

"Mr. Briston?" I asked. "I'm BCA agent Van Reed. My colleague said that you'd be expecting me?"

"Yes, ma'am." He bobbed his head and then peered over my shoulder. "Welcome to Walmart! Can I help you find a cart?"

The pair of black-clad teenagers who were entering snickered and ignored him.

I waited until they were past. "Mr. Briston, I'm wondering if I could ask you about July 23, 1980."

"Oh yah." His Minnesota accent was as thick as hotdish. "That was an awful day. Those poor girls. I delivered right down that street every Wednesday. Elm Street. The nicest folks lived there. They didn't deserve what came to them." His face picked up as he stared past me. "Welcome to Walmart! Can I help you find a cart?"

This time his services were needed. He returned short of breath and said, "I wish I had something to add. It was just a regular day. Sun was shining like nothing bad could happen."

"Do you know why the police questioned you?"

He scratched at his sparse hair. "Not that I recollect." He peered over my shoulder and smiled broadly. It must be exhausting to turn yourself on and off like a windup toy. I rested a hand on his arm before he could offer a greeting.

"This is important," I said.

It clearly pained him to ignore his duties, but he stuck with me. "Well, I suppose someone turned me in. Said it was suspicious I was down there. I remember having a meeting with my manager about it. We both agreed there was nothing out of the ordinary at all about a man doing his job. But better safe than sorry, I suppose, when it comes to children. Have to check out everything. I hold no ill will toward whoever called in."

"Any idea who it was?"

He rubbed his nose. "I did have a bit of a rivalry with a man named Larry Olsen back in those days. Seems he thought I was looking at his wife a little bit too long. He confronted me about it. I told him she was a beautiful woman, but I would certainly stop looking if he wanted." Bill smiled at this memory as if it were a good one. Gave me the creeps, two guys talking about a woman like she was a show pony.

"Where's Larry Olsen now?"

"Saint Mary's Cemetery," Bill said, smiling. "Six feet under. Guess who won that round?"

I thanked him for his time. I'd add all this to my report, but it didn't seem like there was much here.

The first thing I did upon returning to the BCA was drop by Harry's lab. I told myself it wasn't that I wanted him to explain why he'd called Comstock before speaking to me; it was that we had to work together. The air needed to be clear between us. Still, I slammed his door a little more forcefully than necessary. At least I tried to. The damn pneumatic systems prevented the dramatic effect I was after.

Harry glanced up from the blue QIAgility machine he was running. Reminded me of a space incubator. He wore reading glasses. He squinted over them at me, then back at his computer screen. I stayed put.

It hurt how kindhearted and capable he looked, yet so distant. *Please, Harry Steinbeck, be on my team,* I thought desperately. *I can't do this alone, not anymore.*

"Donald Tucker is a dead end," I said instead. "Same story, I believe, with the Schwan's man and Rolf Larsen. Still waiting to talk to Jacob Peters. Not much rope left on this one."

"Johnna completed the soil work," Harry said, writing something on the notebook alongside his laptop before staring at the robot again. "All of it is from on-site. Nothing brought in from a second location."

"Another dead end," I said.

"Another fact confirmed," he corrected.

Something in his tone coaxed out the words. "Harry, did you go around me to tell Comstock he should let Kind go?"

This time he gave me his full attention. "Yes." His expression was troubled. "Because the sooner Kind was released, the better for everyone. Especially you. He never should have been brought in." His voice was mellow, deep. "I'm worried about you, Evangeline. You look like you haven't slept well in days."

I almost corrected him from days to years but thought better of it.

"Something is eating at you," he continued. His expression was so sympathetic. "You can tell me about it, and I'll do my best to help, but I won't put you before the case. You made a mistake arresting Charles Kind. I stepped in to make sure it didn't get any worse."

My body cocked itself to argue, to say that I never planned on arresting Kind, but the truth was, I wasn't so sure I wouldn't have, even without Comstock there pushing it. I'd been in the deep end. Plus, Harry looked so steady—in a way I was coming to rely on—that this spilled out instead: "I think Senator Marie Rodin is abusing her kids and possibly her husband. I can't sleep knowing it. I have no jurisdiction, no proof, nothing but a hunch."

Could he hear my heartbeat? It was pounding between my ears as loud as thunder. This was how I'd opened the door with Bart, driven by desperation and exhaustion. Bart had walked up to the entrance of my secret and then stayed there during our ten-year partnership. It'd been enough. It had been *more* than enough, and I missed it every single day. What would Harry do? Tell other people what I'd said? Slam that door? Walk to the edge, like Bart had, and keep me from falling too far down the other side? Or maybe he'd step all the way through, and I could finally tell another person the whole story.

I'd tried at the Farm, tried talking to my Sisters and even a handful of my Brothers about my nightmares.

One of them told Frank.

I don't think he believed that I was having true visions, but he hated for any of his children to stand out. He'd immediately trotted out his third punishment. Frank called it "shunning." It was the mildest reprimand on the face of it: you traded in your soft-colored, hand-dyed shift for all black. As long as you wore the color, you were considered invisible, and anyone who acknowledged your presence would be punished.

At the end of your shunning—which could last from a day to several weeks, depending on Frank's mood—he gathered the entire Family into a circle, and everyone had to tell you something they disliked about you. When they were done, only then were you allowed to put regular clothes back on.

Because of my visions, I'd been shunned for three weeks.

I felt paralyzed, waiting for Harry to respond.

"I see," he finally said. Then, ironically, he took off his glasses. Rubbed an eyelid. "I looked into Senator Rodin after you first mentioned her on the drive back from Leech Lake. I found that her reputation is above reproach. She's active in her community, her church, not to mention making a career of public service."

The sudden wave of melancholy almost drowned me.

Harry returned his glasses to his face, then walked to the sink to wash his hands. I wondered how many times a day he did that. He turned off the water. Dried his hands. "I'm holding a science workshop tomorrow for the children of the legislators in charge of our funding," he said, his voice casual, like we were talking about two separate things. "It'll be in the show lab. Marie Rodin's children will be in attendance."

My eyes felt suddenly hot. "How long has this been in the works?"

"It was a bit of a last-minute thing."

He believes me.

Or, he'd at least considered the possibility that I might know something, enough to bring the kids in so he could see them with his own eyes. That was worth something, wasn't it? It had to be. Because it was all I had if we were going to save Rodin's children.

"Thank you," I said, my voice cracking.

His gaze softened. He opened his mouth, then closed it. Looked away. He seemed to be struggling to say something. Finally, he shook his head, his tone businesslike. "While you're here, can I show you the email from the witness who claims to have seen the Sweet Tea Killer?"

So this was how it would be for Harry and me: every time we began to let down our guards, my past crimes would come between us. It was only fair, I supposed. I certainly didn't deserve any better. Still, it twisted my guts.

"Sure," I said.

He nodded. Walked over to his computer desk. Came back with a sheet of printer paper that he handed to me. I scanned it.

> Dear Agent Steinbeck:
> I'm writing about Lester Dunne, that guy who committed suicide a year and a half ago. I delivered coffee and a breakfast sandwich to him the morning I guess he was found dead. I didn't know he was dead. I figured he just wasn't answering the door. I saw the

story online later and didn't think anything of it, but a friend of mine who's into true crime said there's a wiki about the case. It says Lester Dunne and some other guys were actually murdered but no one can prove it. That's when I remembered I saw someone leaving his house when I pulled up with his order. A woman. Figured I should report it in case it's true that he really was murdered. This is from my school email account. You can email me back at this address if you want to talk.

It wasn't signed. The email address was horst009@umn.edu.

My head was swimming, and for a moment I feared I would pass out. "Good," I said, keeping my eyes pinned on the paper. "We'll go talk to him as soon as we close the Taken Ones case. Deal?"

"Van?" Harry said, his voice tender.

I looked up. Whatever he'd wanted to say before was back, right on the edge of his lips. If it was something kind, I couldn't have borne it, so I handed him back his sheet of paper.

"Save it for later," I said, trying to smile and failing. "I've got a meeting I need to get to."

CHAPTER 46

Van

Despite my body longing for sleep, I felt strangely light as I left Harry's lab.

That the witness had seen me was confirmed. My time was running out. But the email had nudged something, making me think again of all the invisible people. The baristas, volunteers, delivery people, construction workers. Those we didn't see but who saw everything. I wondered if Erin Mason, the woman who'd left the Post-it Note in the Taken Ones file, would have any insight on that front. I carried that thought into the incident room.

Kyle was there with Johnna and Deepty.

"Thanks for your soil work, Johnna," I said.

"Not a problem," she said. "Wish I'd found something more helpful."

I turned to Kyle. "I'm sorry for being so short with you lately. You're doing great research, and I need you to do some more. I'm still trying to get a bead on why the two spots—abduction and burial—were chosen. I need you to look for any work done at or near both locations. Any ditches newly dug, buildings built, poles put up, anything constructed right before the crimes were committed. Also, any housecleaning or plumbing companies, those sorts of businesses, that would be used by the folks on Elm Street in Leech Lake as well as by the people living or working in the part of North Loop abutting the second crime scene. I'm after witnesses as well as suspects, anyone who would have been doing a job at both locations."

"You got it," Kyle said. His face loosened, and he flashed me his thousand-dollar smile. I realized it had been a couple days since I'd seen it. I'd do better.

"Anything good come through the hotline?" I asked.

Deeply stopped herself from rolling her eyes, just. "Not unless you're writing an article for the *National Enquirer*," she said. "But we'll keep on it."

"I know you will. I know all three of you will. You're a good crew."

They were already back to work. My team. I would enjoy it while I had it. I kept that warmth as I popped down into Accounting. Erin Mason's door was open, so I knocked on the doorframe. "Have a minute?"

She paused typing to look over at me. She wore the same wire-rimmed glasses, low ponytail, and grim expression. In her black turtle-neck, she reminded me of Steve Jobs.

"Agent Reed," she said, swiveling her chair to face me. "What can I do for you?"

"I was hoping you could answer a couple follow-up questions about Leech Lake."

She indicated the chair in front of her, then laced her fingers together. "Of course."

She was one person, one perspective, and time would have colored or dimmed her memories, but at this point in the case, I needed anything I could get.

I took the chair, pulled out my notepad, and flipped it open. "Do you know if the Kinds or the Larsens had a housekeeper?"

"The Larsens for sure wouldn't have, and the Kinds for sure would, but I have no idea who it would've been. I was never at their place, remember."

"So I suppose you wouldn't know any other workers the Kinds would have had in their house, or any construction done on that end of Elm Street?"

She turned her hands palms up. "Sorry."

"Do you know Carol Johnson? The woman who found Rue that day?" Kyle had checked Johnson out. She was squeaky clean, but sometimes that was its own warning.

Erin tapped her chin for a moment. "Lived by the Kinds? Uptight lady?"

I let that lie. "Did you hear any rumors about her?" Harry would be turning himself inside out right now.

"Naw," she said. "The only rumor over there was about the Bendy Man."

My throat tightened.

"Supposedly," she continued, "he haunted the woods on that side of town. Tried to lure the kids with candy, then would wrap them up in his arms and legs like Stretch Armstrong. Strangle them to death before he sucked their blood."

It was broad daylight, I was in one of the most secure buildings in the state, and still the way she said that made goose bumps erupt along my arms. "You believe the rumors?"

"At the time? I believed them enough to avoid that part of town. One more reason I was glad the Kinds brought Amber to me." She shuddered. "You grow up and you know better, but those old stories stay under your skin."

"They can," I said, nodding. "Anything else unusual from that time period you can remember?"

She rested her cheeks on her fists, the same youthful gesture she'd made last time I was there. I bet she didn't even know she was doing it. "Nothing comes to mind."

"You know anything about Jacob Peters?" He was the only living suspect I'd yet to talk to. There was no urgency to my question, which was why her response caught me off guard.

"The Freak?" she said.

My heart skipped a beat, then returned with twice the force. "Freak?"

She had the good grace to blush. "Sorry. It's not a kind word. It isn't mine, not really. He called *himself* that back then. He was fearless, unbreakable. He'd jump off the school for money. Charged a quarter to everyone who wanted to watch. 'See the Freak fly'—that's what he said. Probably some of us older kids should have stopped him. He was only a middle schooler. He never got hurt, though, not that I know of. Why do you ask about him?"

"Just crossing my t's and dotting my i's," I said, my face calm and my blood cold.

CHAPTER 47

Rue

Rue watched her father limp back to his car. The news ghouls who'd returned this morning were lapping that up like starved dogs, yelling out questions and snapping photos. She didn't care. Let them have the pictures they needed to sell ad space on their blogs.

After living a lifetime splintered, she'd just regained a little bit of herself.

Her dad had apologized, but that wasn't it. She'd made it her whole life without him. In fact, she hadn't laid eyes on the man in thirty years. So it wasn't a stranger saying he was sorry that had made her feel better than she had in forty-two years. She suspected he didn't even know what he'd been apologizing for. It was that he'd shown up and *she could see Lily in him.* In his face, the slant of his eyes, the way he rubbed his hands together like Lily always had, even when she was wearing that cherry Ring Pop.

Seeing her dad had given Rue a piece of Lily back.

For the first time, she considered her baby sister might still be alive.

It was a terrifying thought.

She knew what hope would cost her if she was wrong. It would send her spinning off the deep end, never to return. But what did she have now that was so great? Fear. Routine. The certainty of nothing.

At least the hope was something different, a new flavor after all her empty days.

She locked the door behind her father before picking up her phone.

She'd memorized the number. When Van answered, she said, "I'll try the hypnotherapy. I'm off from work the day after tomorrow."

messy

shame

disgusting

wrappers

clothes

dirty girl

Her apartment was even worse than her car had been. Somebody should call the health officials on Evangeline Reed. He was glad her mail hadn't been sorted, though. He dropped down and pawed through it. Got her full name. Peeked inside her fridge, her cupboards and closets, her bathroom—which was clean—before returning to his hidey spot.

His heartbeat picked up pleasantly when she stumbled home later and beelined straight to her bed, pausing only long enough to remove her firearm and phone before dropping onto her mattress. He watched her sleep. She twitched and moaned like someone was poking her with hot irons. His mother had said people pay their dues in their dreams, and if that was true, Agent Van Reed owed the devil.

It was only fair that he'd come to collect.

The dimensions of the spot he was tucked inside meant his shoulder blades were overlapped behind his rib cage, but even in that position he could feel himself relax. All his problems were about to disappear.

Her gun lay next to her. He could spill out of his confined space, expand outward with cracks and pops until he was reassembled, grab her gun, and shoot her dead with her own weapon. When her colleagues showed up and saw the state of this place, they'd probably assume it was a suicide. That would be precious, wouldn't it? Killing her with her own weapon. Or maybe he could strangle her until she passed out and bring her unconscious body home. He knew how to break a girl. It took time and it took patience, but he believed he still had both.

He'd make up his mind when he laid hands on her.

Her warmth would be his guide.

He was reaching toward her, pleasantly juiced on what was coming next, when his phone dinged.

His nerves screamed.

He'd sworn he turned it off. *Sworn.*

CHAPTER 48

Van

The ding of a text reached through the misty layers of sleep and yanked me awake. I swung a heavy arm over and nabbed my phone, bringing it close to my face. I rubbed my eyes. Blinked.

No messages.

I was on my feet with gun in hand in the space it took my heart to skip a beat.

I'd heard a phone. It hadn't been mine.

I kneaded my eyes again, willing them to adjust to the darkness, to tell me which shapes and mounds meant danger. My blood pumped hot, clearing the last of the sleep from my brain, bringing with it a clear memory of the dream I'd been having when the noise woke me. It had been about Frank Roth. *Father.* He had been walking toward me, his face blurred and watery but growing clearer.

Careful to keep my back to the wall and my gun pointed forward, I leaned over to pick up my phone from where I'd dropped it. I commanded it to call Harry as I eased toward the light switch. I flicked it on as the phone rang.

A groggy voice answered. "Van?"

"Someone's in my apartment," I said.

"On my way," he said, his voice immediately alert. I dropped the phone and began to clear the room. I kicked at every pile, swinging my gun at imagined noises.

The main room was empty.

Next, I cleared my closets. He wasn't in there, either.

He must be hiding in the bathroom.

I stepped gingerly forward, heart thundering, and yanked open the bathroom door. The room was pristine and empty. I twitched at an imagined noise overhead and peered up through the vent cover. I thought of the space between the two buildings at last week's crime scene. I recalled the man at the bar, the one with the hat and the mustache and beard who'd disappeared into thin air. Remembering them cued the same crawling across my flesh as I felt in this moment. I climbed onto the sink and tried to peek inside the vent. The angles were all wrong. I couldn't see in.

I returned to the main room and found my phone. I rang Harry.

"Never mind," I said, fighting waves of nausea. Had my lucid dreams finally cracked my reality? Was I now hallucinating in real time? "It was a nightmare. My apartment's clear."

"You sure?" he asked. He sounded worried.

"I'm sure. Thanks for being willing to come over." I hung up.

CHAPTER 49

Van

The next day, I jumped at every noise—a branch against the window, footsteps in the hall, the kick of the fridge humming—as I got ready. I drove a different route to the BCA, studying the faces inside the other cars, jerking my eyes to the rearview mirror. Was I being followed? I'd already told Harry about Marie Rodin. I couldn't drop this on him, too. Couldn't tell him that either I was losing what was left of my mind or a freaky, boneless creature—the Bendy Man?—had abducted Amber and Lily back in 1980 and was now following me, lurking in my vents. Because they'd both take me to the same place: straight ticket to a padded cell, don't pass Go.

Marie Rodin's children would be touring the BCA today. I'd deal with that problem first. I pulled into work, parked, grabbed two cups of good black coffee from the cafeteria, and slammed one on the way to my office. There, I fired up my computer and gulped the second cup, wiping the back of my hand across my mouth before I marched straight to the biggest, brightest lab in the building.

The show lab.

Harry was there, Deepty and Johnna flanking him, the three of them the only adults in the room. Eleven children were hanging on Harry's every word, not even glancing my way when I entered. Their parents the legislators either hadn't been invited or were in another wing so that Chandler could do more of his schmoozing.

The kids were, I guessed, between the ages of six and fifteen, varying heights and races. Marie Rodin's children looked exactly like they had at the shelter, tiny for their ages, wearing turtlenecks and long pants even though it was already a hot morning. They had dark circles under their sunken eyes. The younger child, a boy, clung to his sister.

Looking at them, rage bloomed in me. Harry, likely reading my expression, held up his hand. "We have a special guest here, an actual cold case officer. Agent Reed, do you mind telling our audience what you do?"

Stepping forward, I spoke directly to the Rodin children, their faces reminding me of bleak Victorian dolls. "I help bring bad people to justice. Sometimes they're strangers, and sometimes they're neighbors or even family. In all cases, it's my job to make sure they stop hurting other people."

Deepty and Johnna both raised their eyebrows. I'd spoken with the passion of a street preacher. I was about to say more when Harry cleared his throat.

"Thank you," he said.

"I'm not done," I said. "I—"

Chandler stepped into the lab before I could get out my next sentence. "Reed, there you are. Come with me."

This couldn't be good. I tossed Harry a look that I hoped signaled "follow up on these kids" and then let Chandler lead me out. He smelled like Old Spice and meetings.

"Your office?" I asked.

"Not necessary. We'll talk and walk."

My chest squeezed. The man loved showing off his office. I clamped my mouth shut, walking alongside Chandler.

When we reached an empty hall, he said quietly as he walked, "You have twenty-four hours."

He didn't slow down, so neither did I. "Twenty-four hours for what?"

"To solve this case, goddamn it," he said, throwing up his hands like it should have been obvious. "If you can't crack it by then, you're off."

"The hell, Chandler?" I was too pissed off to worry about my tone. "It's been unsolved for forty-two years and you want me to blow it open in less than a week?"

He stopped dead in his tracks. If we were in a cartoon, steam would have been billowing out of his ears.

"That's not the shape of this, and you know it. You shit the bed with Charles Kind." His eyes darted down the hall as he spoke, and I realized he hadn't called me into his office because he hadn't wanted a scene. Out in public, he figured I'd keep my cool. "I can carve out space for you for another day. Anything more than that and I risk losing the good graces of the Minneapolis PD. I don't have to tell you that's a price we cannot pay."

"So it's Comstock running your show? And you're gonna let him get away with it?"

Chandler rolled his eyes. "Tell me you're not that naive, Reed. We don't have rapport with the PD, we got nothing. Me, I don't care whose name is on the solve, as long as they follow the rules and don't get us in trouble. Twenty-four hours."

He marched away.

I wanted to pull my hair out. I couldn't wrestle this case in twenty-four hours, not without some good news. I jogged to the incident room. Kyle was the only one in it, surrounded by files.

"What do you have for me?"

"Good morning to you, too." He shook his head and stared down at the sheet of paper he'd been reading when I came in. "Not much. Not unless you think Jacob Peters arriving back in town this morning is a positive, that is. Oh, and me getting the best hypnotherapist in town to make time to meet with Rue first thing tomorrow."

A grin split my face. "You know, you're not half-bad at this job."

"You either," he said, matching my smile.

"Thanks," I said. Then: "You hear Comstock talked Chandler into giving me twenty-four hours?"

His eyes shuttered. Made me wonder for a moment what role he'd played in the decision. It would be a good career move, him slipping into lead this early in his BCA tenure. Nowhere to go but up after that.

"Yeah, I heard," he said. "That's why I'm busting my hump right now."

CHAPTER 50

Van

Jacob Peters was still an hour out from Leech Lake, so I drove past Carol Johnson's home. She stood out front, watering her yard. It was so uniformly green that she must have had an underground sprinkler system, but I wasn't going to judge her for wanting to pull out a hose. It was her time to spend how she liked.

"Mrs. Johnson," I said as I stepped out of my car. "What a lovely day for gardening."

It really was. Back on Frank's Farm, we'd have been harvesting the first early tomatoes, plucking the lush oregano and basil, turning them into sauces that we'd eat throughout the winter.

She smiled vaguely and patted her hair. Then she glanced up at the sky like she'd just noticed she was outdoors. "It is, isn't it. What can I do for you?"

I walked steadily toward her, my hands out where she could see them. Something about her stance suggested an animal about to bolt. "I have a question, if you have the time."

I stopped five feet away, stared down the road to give her a chance to orient to my request. "Do you remember any work being done in the neighborhood back in the '80s? I know it was a long time ago, but anything you remember could be useful. New houses going up. Sewer pipes being installed or replaced. Anything at all."

She released the handle of the sprayer, her face relaxing into relieved folds. "Well now, that's an easy one. You see those poles behind you? They were so fresh they still ran with creosote back then. The whole neighborhood was torn up for months putting them in. You wouldn't think it was that much work to dig holes and stick some wood in the ground, but you'd be wrong."

A jolt of electricity shot from my spine to my fingertips. I shaded my eyes so I could gaze at the poles, gone a greasy brown-black with age, staples from missing-dog posters or a local teenager's lawn-mowing service tearaway visible on the nearest one. I could picture Carol Johnson ripping those flyers down as soon as they went up. "That's helpful, Mrs. Johnson."

"Not at all, dear," she said. She was still standing there with her sprayer turned off when I slid back into my car. I cranked my AC as I called Kyle.

"Got a new lead," I said. "Carol Johnson said poles went up in 1980. They might be electric or telephone. Verify that, and then see if there's been any recent similar construction at our downtown site. You got that?"

"Got it," he said. "You still in Leech Lake?"

"On my way to talk to Jacob Peters."

"Good," he said. "When you're done, we got a tip come down the line. A woman in New Berlin—twenty minutes past Leech Lake—says her neighbor used to have two women living with him, one of them matching a general description of Amber Kind. Early fifties, gray-blonde hair, medium build. The neighbor hasn't seen her in over a week. Jack Davis is the man's name. The neighbor said he and the women always kept to themselves, so it might be that the missing woman isn't missing at all, or that we have an unrelated case."

Or it might be the golden ticket.

"On it."

CHAPTER 51

Van

Jacob Peters was a mild-looking man. He was the same age as Rue, but the years sat easier on him. His body still held the suggestion of the high school quarterback he'd been, and his smiling, tanned face spoke of a life of relative ease. He'd never been married, no kids, but his eyes crinkled kindly when he greeted me and led me into his air-conditioned living room. He already had two ice waters out for us.

"I apologize for how I look," he said. "I haven't had a chance to shower and shave since I got back from my fishing trip. I was told this was urgent."

I nodded. "I appreciate your making time for me."

His glance flicked to my hair—I wore it in a ponytail, but maybe some had escaped?—before he dived in. "I understand you can't confirm that it was Amber Kind who was . . . murdered recently," he said. "However, let's begin this interview with you knowing that I believe it to have been her. If there's anything you could share with me, I'd be grateful."

I smoothed my hair and took a sip of the water. He'd added a lemon slice. Fancy. "You live alone?" I asked. Thanks to Kyle, I knew the answer.

"My job keeps me busy." He opened his hands, indicating that he'd made a choice he was fine with. "Never had time to date, let alone marry."

"I see." I supposed the same could be said of me. "What can you tell me about July 23, 1980?"

There was an air of calm about the man. According to Kyle, he worked in some sort of construction.

"It was the day innocence died in Leech Lake," he said. He stretched his fingers, bending them uncomfortably far back. Were they stiff from driving? "These things happened before, I'm sure of it. Hell, Donald Tucker was busy that whole time. But nothing that felt so personal. Cracked us awake like a gunshot."

I stayed silent. Most people want to fill that space. Jacob Peters was no exception.

"We had a baseball game that day, or all of us boys would have been at the creek. We would have heard those girls cry for help. Maybe saved them." He stretched his fingers again. Maybe not so calm after all.

"I heard a rumor about you," I said, my tone mild.

His eyes flicked to me, then he reached for his water.

I continued as he drank. "Something about you being fearless in school, getting paid to jump off buildings."

He made a snuffling sound in the water and set it down, coughing. "Who told you that?" he said, wiping his mouth.

"A few people, actually," I lied. "From back in the day."

"Yeah," he said, chuckling. "Called myself the Freak. Probably a name like Evel Knievel would've been cooler. It wasn't build*ings*, though. Just the one. The school. There was a patch of marsh grass off the back. It's not too hard to jump off a one-story building if you know where and how to land. Mind you, if I had kids, I'd forbid them from being so stupid, but I made good money at it. Charged a quarter to watch."

I nodded. It all made sense, and yet it all sounded off.

"Is she still alive?" he asked, interrupting my train of thought. "Rue Larsen, I mean."

I tilted my head. "An online search would provide the answer."

He rubbed the back of his neck. "I ignored her when she finally returned to school. Avoided her like she was contagious. That poor kid.

Do you know I'd asked her to square-dance once? Had a whole proper crush going, and then this happened. It's my biggest regret, the way I treated her."

Fifty years' worth of mistakes, and his number-one regret was how he'd treated a childhood friend who'd been traumatized. Was the guy auditioning for sainthood? "You were a kid, too."

"A kid who knew better," he said vehemently. When he looked at me, his eyes were clear. "I'd like to apologize to her. Do you think she'd accept it?"

I thought it over. I did think she'd accept it. I also thought he could grow his own pair. Rue deserved at least that much from someone claiming to care about her. "Only one way to find out," I said.

I left him with my card and a request to call if he remembered anything else from those days.

❖

Jack Davis lived at the end of one of those two-mile driveways common to rural Minnesota. Wild lilacs grew on each side, their purple flowers gone, leaving only brown spikes among the velvety green leaves. I drove up to a white farmhouse with blue trim, neatly painted. Potentilla bushes lined the porch, and I spotted a decent-size vegetable garden in back next to a large shed.

My farmgirl instincts kicked in. Whoever tended that plot should have planted marigolds next to those tomatoes to repel cabbage worms and attract aphid eaters. The beans were neatly tied up, but they'd been planted on the wrong side of the garden, where they were blocking a row of stilted onions from the sun's nourishment.

I missed having my hands in the dirt. It would have been simpler if everything about my past was dark, but it wasn't.

A man stepped onto the porch as I pulled in front of the farmhouse. His face was shadowed. *Frank.* Automatically, I checked for my gun. Then he stepped into the sunshine, and my stomach dropped back into place. Early to midsixties. Thin but strong looking, tan and wiry in a way that suggested he worked outside. I got out of my car.

"Mr. Davis?"

He remained on his porch. "Can I help you?"

"I'm Agent Van Reed, sir. With the BCA. We received a call that something might have happened to one of the women who lives here."

He drew his head back like I'd just told him he was the Prince of Wales. "*One* of the women who lives here?" He chuckled. "I don't think my wife'd allow that for a second."

"Is she here now, sir?"

"My wife?" His face crinkled. "Naw. Gone to see her sister. Who'd you say you're with again?"

"The Bureau of Criminal Apprehension."

He seemed to be considering whether I was legitimate. Or, given his age, it might be my gender making him uncomfortable. I pulled out my badge and opened it, offering it as I strode toward him. "Only you and your wife live here?"

He smiled easily. "Unless you count chickens."

I was now standing at the foot of the veranda that followed the length of the house. Jack Davis was a tall man, maybe six foot two, and the height of the porch gave him an extra three feet. I didn't much care. I wanted to get in and out of there quick.

He squinted at my badge. "How do I know if that's official?"

I snapped it shut. "When did your wife leave?"

He looked like he was gearing up to argue, and then his face relaxed. "This morning. You better come inside. I can tell you're not going to believe me without a look around." He turned and walked into the house.

A rooster crowed. The coop must have been on the other side of the farmhouse. That would mean there were three buildings total on the property—house, garden shed, coop. No barn, so not a working farm, yet there was something so familiar about this place. Made me feel almost wistful, like I was visiting the good part of my childhood. I shook myself, texted Kyle my location, and followed Davis inside.

The kitchen stood right off the front door. A four-top table was covered with a red-and-white checked cloth that matched the curtains. The avocado refrigerator and matching stove looked like they could have voted for Nixon, and I didn't see a microwave or a dishwasher. The room was dated but clean. Davis, or more likely his wife, liked to keep a neat home. Davis took a chair at the table and indicated I should do the same. Sitting across from him would require I put my back to the open living room door. It was dark in there, curtains drawn. I stayed standing.

"Where does your wife's sister live?"

"The one she visited is over in Moorhead. She's got another in Fergus Falls. Can I get you something to drink? Sweet tea, maybe?"

My cue to leave couldn't have been plainer. "I should be going. I'm sorry I bothered you." I scanned the kitchen again, taking in the smaller details. A metal bread box. A salt and pepper shaker near the stove. A folded rectangle of flowered cloth lay next to the drying rack. It was well made but had the telltale signs of being hand sewn that I would've recognized a mile away, given that I'd made all my own clothes until age eighteen.

"You or your wife sews?"

He turned to look. "The wife."

I leaned back to peer in the living room. In the shadow of a rust-colored sofa, I spotted a pile of magazines stacked on a TV tray. The house was dead quiet.

"You want to go in there?" he asked. "You're free to look around."

He was staring at me, his expression serene. The twenty-four-hour clock Chandler had given me was winding down. "I'm good. I hope you have a nice day, Mr. Davis."

CHAPTER 52

Van

Twenty minutes on winding country roads took me to Theresa Kind's condo. She opened the door as I walked up and stood on the other side of it, arms crossed. "Agent Kaminski called me," she said.

I'd asked him to after updating him on the Davis nothing burger that made a matched set with the Jacob Peters dead end. Theresa was as well put together as last time I'd seen her, but she seemed hollowed out. The shock of her daughter being alive and so close, of the wasted years when they could have known each other, must have slammed into her, and I couldn't begin to imagine how learning you might have a grandchild out there added to the pain. I had to look away for a moment to collect myself. Theresa Kind did not strike me as the kind of woman who appreciated pity, no matter how much pain she was in.

"Thanks for seeing me," I said when she stepped aside. I followed her past the cast-iron pan and into her living room. She perched herself on the edge of the couch and left one of the stiff-backed chairs for me. I took it, tugging my notebook out of my blazer. I needed to at least acknowledge what she'd experienced, though words were not nearly enough. "I'm so sorry for your loss."

A spasm of pain squeezed her face. Even with the grief, she was a polished woman, her blue eyeliner and coral lipstick subtle but striking, her hair styled loosely. She had an approachable glamour. I bet Amber had adored her.

"Thank you," she said.

I clicked my pen. "We spoke with your husband."

She snorted. "*Spoke* with him? You arrested him."

I let that roll off me. "Did you know he lied about his alibi for the day your daughter went missing?"

She stared off toward nothing. "I did."

I let the silence settle between us. I had time for what came next. It took nearly three minutes, at the end of which Theresa startled like she'd forgotten I was there.

"I regret those days," she said. "Agreeing to an open marriage. I played a part because I didn't want to lose him, but I would have much preferred a traditional relationship." She shrugged. "I was young. He was a doctor."

She put her hand to her chest and studied me. "Most Minnesota men are tough little seeds that aren't ever going to grow. Did you know that? My mother did. She told me never to marry a seed. Marry a gardener instead, she said. But did I listen? No." She laughed. For the first time, I noticed her subtle overbite. It gave her face character.

"So all along, you knew your husband had been with his mistress that day?"

She shoved her hair behind her ears. "I suppose I did. And I suppose, like him, I knew it didn't matter where he was. He didn't take Amber. For his many faults, he was no predator."

I asked the question that had been scratching at me since I'd first read the case. "Theresa, why was Amber playing with Rue?"

She shrugged. "It was a hot day. Rue was a neighborhood girl. They wanted to swim. What more do you want?"

"Your daughter and Rue were in different social strata," I said. "Strikes me as unusual that they would've played together at all, not just that day."

She bit her bottom lip, but her coral lipstick stayed put. "If you must know, it was a charity project through church. I never told Rita Larsen or Rue, of course, but we were all assigned a poor family. Our priest took us . . . what did you imply? Higher-strata folks? He took us higher-strata folks aside and asked us to each pick a struggling family in the church. See if we could bring them into the fold and lift them up to our heights." She chuckled darkly. "It's horrible, isn't it? The things we do in the name of religion. For what it's worth, I never told Amber. She was a sweet girl, and as far as I could tell, Rue was, too. They were oblivious, just two kids who enjoyed playing together. Maybe it wasn't such a bad idea after all."

She stared at a faraway spot.

"Do you still attend that church?" Erin in Accounting had said they were regular attendees before dropping out. Rita Larsen had also mentioned Mr. and Mrs. Kind stopped going after Amber disappeared.

She made a scoffing noise, like a rusty engine starting. "Haven't been back since Amber was abducted. Not interested in a God that plays dirty. And it wasn't only that. I was told Charles and I couldn't divorce. That church cost me my girl and my love."

Now we were closing in on what I'd come to find out. "Your husband?"

Her eyebrow arched. "No, not my husband. A police officer, of all the things. We were together that morning, he and I. Charles didn't mind. He was off with his nurse. I had no intention of being intimate with another man with Amber in the house, but my lover surprised me. Brought me yellow roses, if I remember correctly. He sneaked in the back, said he couldn't stay away. I insisted he leave. He was about to when Amber walked in on us." Her voice was steeped in regret.

"We were fully clothed, holding each other," she continued. "I saw the horror in Amber's eyes, nonetheless. The realization who her mother was." She shook her head. "I shot out of that bedroom, slammed the door behind me. Told Amber to call Rue and find something fun to do. Can you believe I thought I could erase what she'd seen by pretending she hadn't? I even made her lunch while Dave hid out in the bedroom. Packed it in her little Strawberry Shortcake lunch box before sending her into the world to be snatched because I was ashamed she'd seen me in another man's arms. How's that for serving your daughter up to the devil on a silver platter?"

The pain in her eyes was suffocating. I wouldn't look away. I could give her that much at least. But it wasn't her confession about her sending her daughter out that morning that had my pulse blowing up my veins. "Dave? Dave Comstock?"

Her mouth curled. "None other. We tried to hang on for a couple weeks after Amber and Lily went missing, but my life had become a circus. He left one morning and didn't come back. I never saw him again until you showed up with him a few days ago. He pretended like he didn't know me, so I returned the favor." She looked like she wished she had a cigarette. "I swear to God, when it comes to men, I've always been the worst picker."

❖

At the time of the girls' abduction, Comstock had been an officer in Crowville, one town over from Leech Lake, which he'd confessed that night at Amber's grave.

He'd left out the part about being the reason Amber had gone into the woods that day.

I drove a hundred miles an hour to reach Crowville, damn the speed limits. I screeched to a stop in front of the police station at the center of town. Sat in my car long enough to compose myself before walking inside.

The Crowville Police Department was more modern than Leech Lake's but smaller. A silver-haired, buzz-cut, giant-size officer in his sixties was leaning against the front counter. I pulled out my badge.

"Agent Van Reed of the BCA," I said. "Is your commanding officer around?"

The man smiled. "You're looking at him. Sergeant Schroeder." He offered me a meaty hand. I shook it.

"I'm working on the Taken Ones cold case. I'm hoping you can pull your work logs for the two weeks preceding and the two weeks following July 23, 1980."

Sergeant Schroeder leaned even farther forward on the counter, outwardly casual. "Now why would you want that? The crime happened out of our jurisdiction."

"I understand." I kept my voice calm despite the warning bells that had begun to go off in my head. Something here was wrong. "However, some of your officers were on scene."

He tilted his head like he was ready to dispute but kept that wide, almost robotic grin stapled to his face. "Not officially," he said. "They went as volunteers."

A sensation like cold oil began dripping down my spine. "You were on the department back then?"

He nodded.

The oil began coursing. I believed I was learning why the Leech Lake police had seemed so apathetic to Erin Mason and her friends. They *had* been looking out for one of their own. But had they been covering up an indiscretion or something more? "I'd still like to see those logs."

He steepled his fingers on the counter like humongous spider legs. "I gave all that information to my good friend Dave Comstock," he said. He blinked slowly, like a marionette, one corner of his smile rising so high it about split his cheek. "Anything you want to see, you can ask him. In fact, I'll save you the trouble and call him right now."

He tugged a phone out of his back pocket. I watched him begin to dial as I turned and walked out.

Comstock had potential witnesses sewn up, had my evidence boxed in, and had Chandler watching my every move as my twenty-four hours ticked down. Heck, he probably had someone on his team tailing me right now. He'd known it wasn't Kind all along, probably even known that Kind had been with his mistress that day, and he'd let me walk into it mouth-deep. On top of all that, I had not a single suspect front and center, and it was only a matter of days until Harry found out I was the Sweet Tea Killer.

I was balanced at the edge of a razor, and below was the river of my job, being flushed away.

There was only one outcome left that I had any control over.

CHAPTER 53

Van

It was dark when I pulled up in front of the Rodin house.

I couldn't save Lily before my twenty-four hours were up. Me thinking some creature had been in my apartment last night meant that the walls separating my waking life from sleep had degraded to the point that I could no longer keep the nightmares at bay, and the flashbacks to Frank's Farm were exploding everywhere I stepped. I couldn't any longer pretend to forget how Veronica went from being the sweetest, smartest among us to being unable to feed herself after Frank baptized her. How I hadn't spoken up for her, for any of us.

The only worthwhile thing I could accomplish before I lost everything was to save the children in Marie Rodin's basement.

I had to believe that the visions I'd experienced were true.

I had to.

I charged through the steamy night and made it halfway up the sidewalk before a missile struck me from the right. I hit the ground with a *humph*, certain I was fighting off a mugger. I got off one good kick before I realized it was Harry.

"What are you doing here?" I hissed, having the presence of mind to keep my voice low.

He opened and closed his mouth like a landed fish, unable to draw air. I must have kneed him in the diaphragm. I shot to my feet and helped him up, staring at the house and then back at him like a worried terrier.

"I'll call it in," he wheezed when he could speak. He clutched his stomach.

"Call what in?" I asked suspiciously.

He nodded toward the house. "What's going on inside. I'll call it in."

My knees buckled, but I managed to stay on my feet. "You've seen it?"

Whatever he saw on my face—naked hope?—was too much. He looked away. "No," he said. "But I believe you. Go home."

I remained frozen, staring at him. I'd been operating alone for so long that I didn't know how to accept help. Given enough time, your cage becomes your home.

He met my gaze. "You can't be seen here. Trust me."

I wanted to, more than anything. Besides, I didn't know if I could save those kids without him, so I limped toward my car. I must have skinned my knees when he tackled me. Realizing that, I walked normally despite the pain. I didn't want Harry to see me hurt. He'd feel bad, and he was already accepting a burden that wasn't his.

One that might end his career.

CHAPTER 54

Van

The next morning, my wing of the BCA was buzzing like a kicked hive.

"Did you hear the news?" Kyle called out when I passed his office.

I'd spent the night huddled in a corner of my apartment. I'd vowed not to close my eyes. Still, I must have dozed off. When I startled awake, it was daylight. I'd brushed my teeth and hair, cleaned up knees raw from Harry's tackle, and rushed to work. I'd deliberately avoided listening to the radio. I'd trusted Harry to make that phone call last night. I also knew what it would cost him. Thinking about it hurt so bad it made my teeth ache.

"Senator Marie Rodin," Kyle said, leaving his office to walk me to mine. "They found her husband and two kids tied up in the basement. Covered in bruises and burn marks, stewing in their own waste."

I felt myself float outside my body. It'd been true. My visions. And Harry had believed me enough to save those children.

"I was called in to search," Kyle said, studying me like he was questioning why I hadn't also been called in.

I shrugged, surprised I could make my shoulders work. "I turned my phone off."

He nodded. "Be glad you weren't on scene. Top floor was pristine. It was the basement that was a horror show. Smelled like raw sewage." He shook his head. "Why bother adopting if you're going to do something like that to the kids?"

"What else did you find?" I was desperate to know where Harry was but couldn't ask directly in case Kyle didn't know Harry had made the call.

"Not much, other than those three chained up and a pit bull that looked as scared as them. It's going to take a lot of counseling to get Rodin's husband and children back on track. I need to finish this report and then I'll hop back on the Taken Ones case." He was turning away when he stopped like he'd remembered something, shaking his head in disbelief. "We did find evidence that she was adopting another child, though. You know what that means? It means Harry Steinbeck saved *three* kids last night. He was the one who called it in, you know. Crazy. Said he was just driving by when he spotted a kid in the window. Said the kid was pounding and begging for help. Don't know how that was possible when they were all chained up." Kyle lowered his voice. "Chandler is livid, but it looks like he's not gonna fire Harry."

I leaped up and threw my arms around Kyle's neck.

"Hey, now," he said, chuckling uncomfortably, holding his hands away from me.

I released him. "I'm sorry," I said, trembling. "I shouldn't have done that."

"S'okay," he said. "This week's been hard on all of us. We can use some good news."

"Yeah," I said, fighting back tears. Something had gone right.

He craned his head back, looking at me. "You're all right," he said, his tone comforting. "I'll catch you in a minute. Just have to finish up some paperwork real quick." He turned and strode back toward his office.

Those kids are safe.

Harry trusted me.

"Rue Larsen is coming in ten minutes to meet with the hypno-therapist," Kyle called over his shoulder. "I've got them booked in the incident room. You're welcome."

"You're the best," I said, hurrying down the hallway. What were the odds that Chandler was so frazzled by last night's discovery that he'd forget that my twenty-four hours on the case were up?

❖

Rue appeared composed when she walked in. Peaceful almost, her brown eyes clear, her body relaxed. She'd been advised to wear comfortable clothing, and her lavender sweatshirt and matching sweatpants above black New Balance sneakers fit the bill. Her clothes hung loosely on her, but she otherwise looked healthy. In fact, her appearance and energy had done a complete one-eighty since I'd last seen her. She seemed to have reached some new understanding with the disappearance of her sister and Amber. I didn't know what it was, but I was grateful she was here.

Rue sat across the table from Lana Decker, the hypnotherapist, and me, her fingers interlaced on the table as Lana explained the process. Lana was a woman nearly as round as she was tall, with gorgeous gray hair she wore straight down her back and glasses that usually hung off her neck on a beaded chain. Her voice was as warm and comforting as cocoa.

"There should be no pain," she was saying, "and very little stress. Think of it as a mental clearing."

For someone who had visions, I was surprisingly distrustful of woo-woo things like hypnotherapy, but I'd seen Lana work before. I knew she would at least do no harm, and she might dislodge something. I'd certainly witnessed stranger things.

Lana guided Rue to the reclined chair and began with basic questions. Rue's name. Date of birth. Where she'd gone to school. If she'd had any pets. When Rue started showing signs of deep relaxation, Lana began playing soft music, counting backward. Her words were suggestive, soothing, leading Rue to an even profounder relaxed state.

"I want you to take me through that morning," Lana said. "The morning of July 23, 1980. It was a hot day. You were walking down Elm Street with your sister, Lily, who had a yellow bandage on her knee and wore a red Ring Pop on her finger. Amber Kind was along. What else can you tell me?"

I was impressed that Lana knew the specifics of the case. These sensory details would set the scene, ease Rue into the day. I wondered what Lana would find if she hypnotized me. A chest full of screaming nightmares?

"It *was* a hot day," Rue said. "So hot. I wore a T-shirt but had rolled up my sleeves to turn it into a tank top. I was worried my shoulders were going to blister." Her voice didn't sound faraway and drifting, like how a hypnotized person was often portrayed on television. Rue sounded very present. Sure of herself. "It was a surprise when Amber called to invite me to the creek that morning. It was always a surprise when she called. She was so popular. So pretty. I was excited to maybe see Jacob. He'd asked me to square-dance the last day of school. I thought he might be swimming, too."

"Tell me about the woods," Lana said. "What were they like?"

Rue fidgeted but kept her eyes shut tight. "The three of us didn't want to cross over into the forest. We were hot, and the woods looked so cool and shady. I thought I could even hear the water, but something was pushing back at me. I didn't want to go in."

She swallowed. "I remember looking back at Amber's end of the street. It looked like something out of a movie. Lines of big houses, cars. Those fresh telephone poles."

Rue had noticed the new poles. Of course she had. Her neighborhood would have been disrupted all summer with their installation. Would she remember more?

"I should have listened to my instincts. I could smell the danger. Amber felt it, too, I know she did. If Lily hadn't—" Rue hooked her breath, then continued. "If Lily hadn't pulled us in, I think we would've gone home and run through the daisy sprinkler. Lily was just a little kid, though. She wanted to swim in the creek, and who could blame her? So we went in. The path was narrow. I tried to stay alongside those two, but it wasn't always wide enough for that."

Her voice was growing deeper, husky. "One of those times I was behind a tree, Amber and Lily came to a dead stop. They were staring at something. I couldn't see what it was, not at first."

She paused, her chest rising and falling, her body twitching with agitation.

Lana prodded gently. "When you looked around to see what Amber was looking at, what did you see?"

"Him." She was trembling all over now, her skin gone white, as if her blood had drained onto the floor below. *"He* lived in the tree. *He* poured out like water. *He* grabbed Lily and Amber. I couldn't fight. I couldn't moooove!"

Lana leaned forward, her face tight. "Who grabbed them, Rue?"

"The Bendy Man, the Bendy Man, if he can't get you, no one can!" she shrieked, shooting straight up and out of the chair, her face a mask of terror.

Lana rushed to comfort her.

"What did he look like, Rue?" I asked. "What did the Bendy Man look like?"

Rue was shuddering.

"He had no face," she whispered. "He was the Bendy Man."

CHAPTER 55

Van

When I was certain Rue was calmed, I found Harry in his lab. He looked like he hadn't slept any better than me.

"I heard about the arrest," I said. My knees were sore from my fall, and my skin was still crawling from Rue's revelation, but standing near Harry made me feel . . . better. *Capable.* I didn't know if it was his steadiness, or what he'd done for me last night, or just something inherent to him, but it was a nice change from how I regularly felt. "You saved a dog, three people, and maybe an infant. Kyle told me Rodin was trying to adopt another child."

"How did you know what was happening in that house?" Harry asked. His clothes were sharp, but his expression was bewildered, pleading.

I turned away from it. "A hunch," I said to the countertop.

When he didn't respond, I looked back at him. His face said he wanted to know more, but he wouldn't push me.

"Thank you," I said simply. I'd said those two words more in the past week than I had in the last ten years. I squared my shoulders. "I need your help again."

To his credit, his flinch was barely noticeable.

"I just came from Rue's hypnotherapy session. She remembered the Bendy Man." My skin grew tight remembering the animal fear in her eyes when she'd said his name. "She claims he poured out of a tree in the clearing and took Amber and Lily." Harry seemed to be following along so far, hadn't yet filed this conversation away in the Ridiculous folder. "You and I have both seen that tree. Its opening is small, maybe twelve inches in diameter. A man would have to be boneless to fit inside."

Rue's description, as terrible and bizarre as it was, lined up with my paranoia that someone had been watching me from the six-inch crack between buildings near Amber Kind's grave, had disappeared within a sealed storage room at the Spot, and had hidden in my apartment. Her description had also given me a bananapants theory, one that didn't involve me being completely nuts. "Is there some sort of genetic mutation that allows a person to shrink their size?"

Harry's body relaxed as he leaned into the science. "Not *shrink*," he said. "The law of conservation says mass can change shape, but it's always conserved, not created or destroyed. But . . . hold on." He strode over to the nearest computer and began typing. "You're familiar with people who are double-jointed?"

"Sure. One of my bro—" I swallowed. I never talked about my family, but we'd come to a place where I owed Harry at least that much. "One of my brothers could bend his fingers all the way to touch the back of his hand."

Harry nodded, grabbed his reading glasses, and studied his screen as he typed. "Exactly. In some cases, people who are hypermobile have something called Ehlers-Danlos syndrome. There are thirteen types; those with the hypermobile version are able to, in extreme cases, completely change the shape of their body. Daniel Browning Smith is a famous example. He makes his living as a contortionist. Calls himself Rubberboy."

Harry indicated I should look at his computer screen. I walked over and leaned in, momentarily distracted by his scent, clean like cinnamon and sandalwood. Then the gallery of photos on his computer drew my complete attention, both fascinating and repelling me. A grown man folded inside a small box, smiling at the camera. The same man with his legs tucked backward and under his shoulders, his head resting on his rear. Another with him looking as if he'd been dropped from an airplane, his torso flat on the ground and his legs completely bent over his back.

"Here's a video of another famous contortionist, Wanglei, fitting through a tennis racket."

Harry clicked the button to start the clip. The video was mesmerizing. Wanglei was thin and striking, wearing a black tunic and pants, his long black hair pulled back in a partial ponytail. He began by rotating his arm 360 degrees, a demonstration of what his body could do. Then he stood, picked up the unstrung tennis racket, and stepped into it, guiding it up to his knees. What came next took less than a minute. He leaned over to thread his head through, followed by his right arm and then his left, shoulders popping to fit. Bent over, with the racket circling his lower back and upper thighs, he gave one final dramatic flourish before gliding it off his butt.

I was astonished. He'd spilled through it like he was made of water. It seemed to take no effort at all.

"How narrow can someone with Ehlers-Danlos make themselves?"

"In extreme cases, any joint can be bent up to 360 degrees. So conceivably, the only barrier is the skull, which remains the same size. Every other body part can be disconnected and realigned."

It made my blood run cold, the idea of seeing someone unexpectedly pour out of a small hole. "Could the facial structure be changed? Rue said the Bendy Man didn't have a face."

Harry glanced upward in thought. "Not that I know of. Possibly, her trauma is still shielding that detail from her."

I nodded. "How common is Ehlers-Danlos?"

"Hard to know." He clicked back to the previous screen. "Estimates range between one in 2,500 to one in 5,000 people having it. It's usually identified in children. Those afflicted often have velvety, loose skin. Trouble healing from wounds. Sometimes, they dislocate bones just walking."

"Can you test for it?"

"There are genetic tests for the rarer forms. Nothing for hypermobile Ehlers-Danlos. It's diagnosed based on symptoms."

"Is there any treatment?"

"Only management, for now. You're thinking the person who abducted Amber and Lily had Ehlers-Danlos?"

I nodded, suppressing a shiver. If Rue truly had seen a grown man burst out of a hole in a tree, it would make sense her brain wiped the memory to protect her. "It's a possibility I want to explore. Would someone with Ehlers-Danlos have more hospital visits than the average person?"

"It's likely," Harry said, immediately understanding what I was getting at. "Their diagnosis might be in their chart, but if it was a smaller hospital, you'd look for someone admitted with an unusual number of sprains, dislocations, bruising, scoliosis."

"What's the life span for someone with Ehlers-Danlos?"

"With the exception of those with vascular EDS, individuals with the disorder can live to a ripe old age."

CHAPTER 56

Van

Harry and I requested our team join us for an emergency meeting in the incident room. The plan was to call hospitals and clinics in a hundred-mile radius of Leech Lake to search for patients who'd been treated for symptoms of Ehlers-Danlos.

By the time we reached the room, Kyle, Deepty, and Johnna had done us one better.

"We've been following up on your invisible-people theory," Kyle said, not even bothering with a greeting.

"Yep," Deepty said. "I pulled the city building permits to find out which companies have done work within sight of the most recent crime scene in the last year. Turns out, the majority of the work was done by a single company. Koehler Construction."

"Which is the same company that laid the telephone poles in Leech Lake in 1980," Johnna jumped in. "The corporation was passed down from father to son to daughter."

Back to Kyle, who looked so pleased he was about to split his shirt. "The Koehlers were kind enough to share their employee records. They have one employee who worked both sites."

I'd stopped breathing.

"Garrick McCormick," Kyle said. "Born in 1958. Grew up in Crowville. He graduated and moved away in 1976. Fell off the grid after that, but his mom's still in town."

"You have an address?" I asked.

"Do bees have knees?" Kyle responded as he slid a piece of paper over to me.

My pulse was racing, but I'd learned from prematurely arresting Kind. I couldn't put all our eggs in this one basket. "I'm going to check the mother out. Everyone keep digging. There might be more. Another company, another connection on the invisible-people angle, or something on the hospitalization angle."

Harry had begun setting up his laptop.

The other three were already so busy on their computers that I got only nods. Good enough. I checked the charge on my phone and hurried toward the nearest exit. I'd almost made it out of the building when Chandler caught me.

"Reed!" he barked.

I wondered what would happen if I just kept walking. I decided to find out, because what did I have to lose? I strode confidently through the exit and toward the car lot to check out my usual sedan. Chandler had to jog to catch up to me. He grabbed me sharply by the elbow, huffing in his navy-blue suit. The sun reflected off the top of his peach-colored dome.

"I'm sorry, Reed," he said, and to his credit, he looked like he was, beneath a veneer of annoyance. "You're off the Taken Ones case. Your twenty-four hours are up."

I'd been expecting it, but hearing it said out loud still made my throat burn. "Was Comstock happy when he called to check that your leash was still on tight?"

Chandler's eyes slid away from my face, telling me everything I needed to know.

"Put Kyle in charge," I said. "He's an exceptional agent."

CHAPTER 57

Van

The first and only consequence of Comstock's most recent malice was that I needed to drive my own car to Nadya McCormick's place in Crowville's exhausted-looking north side. The houses in the neighborhood were small and faded, the lawns sparse, not a playground or even a tree-lined sidewalk in sight. When I pulled up to Mrs. McCormick's, it reminded me of Rue's place in Minneapolis. A 1950s box. Simple, almost lonely in its plainness.

I knew from the phone call that I'd just ended with Kyle that Mrs. McCormick was in her nineties, living off Social Security, and a regular volunteer at her church. A friend picked her up every Sunday because her sight was too limited to drive herself.

I knocked at her door. While I waited, I studied the ramp leading up. Her only landscaping was rocks over black fabric creating a three-foot perimeter around the house. It was weed-free, which meant someone tended to it.

I was going to lose my job for being here. I no longer cared, not if there was a chance Lily Larsen was still alive.

The door opened. A smiling, raisin-faced woman in a wheelchair sat on the other side, her snow-colored hair cut short and curled tightly to her scalp. "May I help you?"

"Hello, Mrs. McCormick. I'm a police officer." In for a penny. "I have a few questions about your son, Garrick. Do you mind if I come in?"

Her milky eyes widened. "Is my boy all right?"

"He is, ma'am. May I come in?"

She reversed her wheelchair to make room for me to enter. "You surely may. I just baked some cookies. I can brew up a pot of coffee."

The smell of warm chocolate chip cookies washed over me. "Thank you, Mrs. McCormick, but I'm good."

"Nonsense," she said. "I insist you try one. Been baking them for decades. Could do it in my sleep."

It seemed easier to accept than to argue. She demanded I wait on the too-firm couch in her front room while she disappeared through a door that I assumed led to the kitchen. The front room held an older-model TV, two uncomfortable-looking chairs, a coffee table, and the couch on which I sat. The walls were covered in velvet paintings of cherub-faced girls on their knees, hands clasped in prayer. Knitting supplies rested on the coffee table.

Mrs. McCormick returned moments later. I accepted a perfect round cookie off the platter she offered. I took a bite. The sweetness melted across my tongue. The cookie was still warm and chewy, dripping with gooey chocolate and accented with a flavor I couldn't identify. Clove? Almond?

"These are delicious," I said. "Were you expecting someone?"

She smiled a perfect dentured smile. "I enjoy visitors, so I make sure I'm always ready for them. Now what is this about my boy? He's gone through a hard time as of late, you know. But he's a good man. Always has been."

I finished my cookie and reached for a napkin. "What else can you tell me about him?"

"His dad disappeared when I was pregnant." Her eyes shot to me to see if I would judge her. "So he didn't have a father around, but I think he turned out just fine."

Mrs. McCormick still hadn't asked me why I was inquiring about her son. She either didn't have a suspicious bone in her body or she was a simple woman. I wasn't so sure they were that different.

"Poor Garry had some medical trouble back when he was a boy," she continued. "Broken bones, mostly. It's how boys are, you know. Roughhousers."

My pulse picked up. "Did he have a lot of friends?"

Her smile faltered. "Well, he had to study, you know. So smart, my boy. He worked for a construction company right out of school, kept the same job this whole time. It hasn't been easy. He specialized in putting in telephone poles, but of course there's not much need for those anymore, not with all the kids and their smartphones." She nodded at my blazer, where my cell phone was tucked in an inside pocket, though she couldn't possibly see the outline. Yet was that something sharp-toothed swimming up through her cloudy gaze?

"My Garry is Steady Eddy, though, no matter the surprises life throws at him. First the job retraining they forced on him, and now the *big* one." She reached into a bag attached to her wheelchair and brought out a white blanket with pink-and-yellow rosebuds. "I was hemming this for him and his wife. They just had a baby, you know. Garrick said he's too old for that, but if he's too old, what does that make *me*?" She cackled and slapped her leg. "I cannot possibly get over to New Berlin to see the little one, not with these stems."

Her laughter turned hysterical.

I was feeling a complex brew of emotions, with panic foaming to the top. I heard a distant rumble, like a train coming toward me. I had to connect the pieces before it arrived. I had met Garrick McCormick already, hadn't I? But that hadn't been his name. Part of me was aware that it was too late to step out of the train's way. It was going to slice me in two, leave bloodied parts of me quivering on each side of the track. I suddenly, desperately did not want that to happen inside this house, beneath the terrifying corpse gaze of Garrick McCormick's mother.

"Mrs. McCormick, what does Garrick's wife look like?" I asked, even though I knew the answer. I just needed to keep her talking before I lost my mind.

"When she was younger—oh, just a baby when she married my boy!—she was as blonde as a Swede. Now it's gone to gray. Heavens, everything about her has changed over the years, which'll happen to the best of us. The only constants were how quiet she was, and that half-a-heart necklace she always wore. Wouldn't take it off to save her soul. That and her love for her little sister. She was a shy one, too. They used to come twice a year, but I haven't seen either of them in a while. I need to ask Garrick for a visit."

The flowered blanket on her lap. It was the same one in Jack Davis's kitchen.

The same one in my vision.

Jack Davis is Garrick McCormick. He abducted Amber and Lily. The baby in my nightmares is his.

It occurred to me that Mrs. McCormick might be as mad as a hatter. I hoped to hell she hadn't poisoned the cookie. "Thank you for your time," I told her, standing. "But I have to go."

"You sure you can't stay?" She slid out her dentures and rested them on the platter alongside the cookies. "I hate to eat alone." Her mouth became a gaping hole, widening past human possibility, unlocking like a snake's jaw.

I didn't bother to close her door as I stumbled to my car. My head began to clear the moment I hit fresh air. I ordered my phone to call Kyle. He picked up immediately.

"Chandler's looking for you, Van." His voice was taut. "It isn't good."

"No time. Jack Davis is our guy. I'm on my way over there. Tell Harry. Tell Comstock."

"The man whose neighbor called in about one of his ladies gone missing?" Kyle's voice was disbelieving. "He's good for the cold case?"

"Yes!"

"But Van, Chandler said you're off it."

"Call Comstock. Tell Harry," I repeated.

Then I hung up and drove like a bat out of hell.

Should
      be
            deeper but
            it'll
            have
        to
    do

He'd placed the hole two hundred yards from the house, just on the edge of the woods. It was a good spot, relatively concealed by the trees without being clogged with their roots. He'd only dug it three feet down, but he no longer had the luxury of waiting until he was ready. Not since *she'd* come to his farmhouse.

He had no paper trail, he knew that. At least Jack Davis didn't. It was what he'd changed his name to when he graduated high school and moved to New Berlin. Jack Davis was a homeowner. He'd worked the same job for years. He never even visited the doctor, and he stayed out of trouble.

Until his terrible neighbor called the BCA tip line two days ago. He'd actually considered calling it himself. Nobody looked closely at the guy who stepped into the spotlight. That's why he'd gone into the police station back in July of 1980 and told them he'd seen the Schwan's delivery guy watching those girls. He became invisible to the cops after that.

But this time, he'd discarded the idea almost immediately. He needed to lie low, stay out of sight of the law. But the opposite had happened. By allowing Violet and Iris—when she was alive—to take walks down the road, he'd exposed himself to questions once Iris disappeared. The only good news was that Van Reed hadn't recognized him when she'd stopped by. Still, it'd made him cold all over when she pulled up.

That's why he had no choice but to get rid of Violet before he was ready.

He'd let her live so she could take care of the baby. The senator was scheduled to pick up her new child today. But then he'd heard on the radio this morning that Rodin had been arrested, some sort of raid on her house. *Everything* was going bugnuts on him. All that he could do was eliminate Violet before it got worse, before they showed up and asked questions. She was good in public, just like Iris. They kept their heads down and their mouths shut, even when they could've run. It proved how much they loved him. But Violet was only a woman. Weak. She wouldn't be able to withstand questioning from the police.

Yet it wouldn't be easy to kill her. Oh, no.

She was his favorite. He'd watched those two blonde angels for weeks while he put in those phone lines. They looked so much like Lottie, his first girlfriend. In his head, he began calling the oldest Iris, after Jodie Foster's character in his favorite movie of all time, *Taxi Driver,* and the littler one Violet, after the girl Brooke Shields played in *Pretty Baby,* his second favorite film.

He dreamed of them at night and went to work the next morning to discover they were even prettier than he remembered. Day after day, his need ratcheted higher, his plan for abducting them solidifying. He waited in those woods every morning he didn't work, tugging a nylon over his head so they couldn't identify him, then tucked himself into the tree. The path leading past it was narrow and rarely used. Most kids came to the creek from the other side. But if the angels decided to swim, they'd need to walk this way. The fifth time he hid, he got lucky.

He didn't want the brown-haired girl. He didn't need to hurt her, either. He wasn't that kind of man. He demanded she remove her shoes—he knew how hot that tar was—to slow her down, told her he'd bury her little sister alive if she told on him, then made her close her eyes and count to one hundred. He'd taken the two blondes to the cabin he'd found when checking out the woods, planning for that to be the end.

But then he'd fallen in love.

He had no choice but to bring them home.

They stayed in a locked room in the basement for the first while, sharing a single bed, crying constantly. It was months before they learned to sleep through the night. It took a few more years until they'd look excited when he'd unlock the door and bring them food and sometimes presents. Eventually, he let them out when he was home, locking them up when he left for work.

By the time they were old enough for him to start treating them like women, he trusted them to roam free on the property. He threatened them, sure—telling them he'd bury them alive, beating them when they talked back, withholding food if he believed they were getting too comfortable—but only as necessary to keep the peace.

Iris had been old enough to know how to read when he brought them home, and she taught Violet. He'd buy them books on canning, tanning hides, gardening, sewing. The two of them became regular pioneer women. It even got to the point where he could bring them to visit his mother, and boy had that made her proud.

But then, three months ago, the unexpected had happened: after decades of peace, Iris gave birth. She said her pregnancy was an act of God, and he almost believed her. In any case, the baby turned them into different women. Insufferable ones, ones who might finally leave him. He'd had no choice but to take out Iris to save Violet.

He'd scouted locations, landing on the one in the North Loop while at work. It was relatively secluded for a city but far enough from his home that if some animal dug up the body, there'd be no way to tie it back to him. After he'd watched to confirm that no one came back there except the occasional druggie or bum, he'd shoveled out the hole.

He'd brought along his metal detector so if anyone stopped by to ask him what he was up to, he'd tell them he'd thought he found treasure and plead ignorance if it turned out to be private property.

But no one stopped by to ask. He'd never crossed paths with another soul back there.

He let that hole sit out there for two entire weeks to see if it'd draw anyone's attention. It hadn't. Even when it rained, the hole remained unaffected. So last week, he'd driven her out there. Even brought along a chair and set it right alongside the grave. She'd looked scared, but she didn't believe he'd really bury her alive, that was clear. After all, he'd been threatening it for decades. He had her sit in that chair while he hopped into her grave and showed her how deep it was, lectured her on her poor behavior, made her promise to do better.

And then he'd duct-taped her and tossed her in it, putting the boards on that special lip he'd made so she'd have time to get right with the Lord before she passed.

And now, he was going to have to do the same with Violet. It might have been easier if he could just put a bullet through her head like he would for an old farm dog, but he'd promised he'd bury her alive, and he was a man of his word.

He hadn't yet decided what to do with the baby. He'd been expecting $10,000 for it. If the senator couldn't pay up, maybe someone else would. He'd figure it out after he got rid of V. He stepped into the living room, too sad to even remove his muddy shoes. He was surprised to feel the tears on his cheeks.

"It's time," he told her. "Put the baby in the crib. Let's go, now."

"No!" she screamed, her face a ghastly white. It made her blue eyes look huge. She never used to raise her voice to him before, but Iris's post-baby sassiness had infected her, too. It wasn't only time, it was *past* time.

He struck her across the face, snatching the infant from her arms as she fell. He tossed the now squalling baby into the crib he'd had to hide along with Violet when Van Reed pulled up. Lucky for all of them, the baby had stayed quiet.

He reached for the roll of duct tape, winding it around Violet's arms until she stopped struggling. She was yelling, pleading for him to leave the baby alone, *please please please*, right up until he slapped the tape across her mouth.

Then he threw her over his shoulder and carried her outside.

CHAPTER 58

Van

Jack Davis's two-mile driveway felt like two hundred miles.

I braked the car to a skidding stop in front of the house. I charged inside.

"Lily!" I screamed. The muddy tracks on the floor caught my attention. I followed them through the kitchen to the back door. Twenty feet behind the house stood a windowless garden shed, its door open and still swinging as if someone had just stepped inside. I raced to it. The inside was shadowed. I groped for the light switch and flicked it on. A dirty shovel rested just inside, mucky boots next to it. I touched the dirt. Still wet. The shed was maybe twenty by twenty feet, tools hung neatly on hooks. A garden tiller and a snowblower were parked near one wall. A potbellied stove sat in the corner next to a workbench, opposite the front door.

I pulled out my gun, whirling. He could be in any corner, angled into any shape. "Jack Davis. You are under arrest for the abduction of Amber Kind and Lily Larsen as well as the murder of Amber Kind." I kept turning, pointing my gun in every direction, my heart battering my chest. All my senses were amplified, the scent of gasoline and dirt overpowering, the sound of my feet scraping the cement floor deafening. I felt myself slipping off the lip of sanity, but sometimes that's what it was like when you were right, and you were the only one who knew it.

Jack Davis could be anywhere, but I was banking he was still in there with me, that I'd caught him just after he'd buried Lily. I couldn't save her until I stopped him or I'd risk a bullet to my back. Could he be twisted inside the snowblower like a giant snail? Squeezed beneath the floorboards? An overhead vent caught my eye. The shed was wired for heat even though there was a woodstove, not uncommon in the Midwest. I dragged a stepladder over and climbed up, snapping my phone into flashlight mode.

If Jack Davis was up there hiding, I would find that creepy bastard.

The vent came open easily. I shined my light into the space, my hairs standing on end. I felt dangerously exposed, like a clawed hand could grab my ankle at any time. It was every childhood nightmare come to life.

"Show yourself, you sick son of a bitch!" I yelled.

I craned my neck to peer down the shadowy duct. My throat filled with acid at the thought of a contorted no-face staring back at me, but I'd fight it. I'd do whatever I had to do to save Lily.

It was empty.

I drew a shaky breath, turning to look in the other direction down the duct, when I heard a creak. A wash of terror hit me with such force that I lost my balance, my phone clattering to the ground. I landed on my feet just as the front of the stove began opening. First a hand slunk out, and then another, that one holding a claw hammer. Between the hands, the grinning ghoul face of Jack Davis appeared.

I moaned.

"Drop the hammer," I said, my voice sounding like it was coming from a deep well. "Now."

Davis had a face, the same face I'd seen when I'd checked on the missing woman the neighbor had called in, but his body was a horror show, a series of clicks and pops as he reassembled himself in front of my eyes, mutating to his full height in less than a second. The speed and distorted movements turned my stomach. I was unprepared when his shoulder released, giving his arm extra inches, enough to swing his hammer into my hand.

My gun clattered to the ground. I dived for it, taking a hammer crack to the side of my head. I tasted metal as a burst of hot fireworks exploded in my temple. I collapsed, my gun closer to Davis than to me. He kicked it away.

"Sassy girl," he hissed. "You have no right to be here."

My eyes crawled up his body, landing on his face. It was *not* the face of Frank Roth, but I saw the same evil light in his eyes, the same obsession that made a man believe his needs were scripture.

Jack Davis was a monster.

My brain had gone white with terror, but something was building behind my teeth, growing, pushing. I drew in the deepest breath I'd ever taken, and I *howled*. It started out throaty and wordless, a child's yell that had been stuck inside me since Frank had baptized Veronica. It grew to something more, something with words.

"I grew up on nightmares, you bastard," I screamed. "I know how to fight them. You will *not* get Lily!"

I leaned to one side and swept my leg around, knocking Davis's legs out from under him. I shot to my feet, battling dizziness, and snatched the hammer from his hand as he dropped. He instinctively put up his arms to cover his face, but I aimed for the side, going for his ear.

I swung so hard that I twisted his torso as he fell, his eyes rolling back in his head.

It wasn't a cast-iron pan, but it did the trick.

Blood was coursing down my cheek as I felt for his pulse. It was erratic but there. He was still alive. There would be no witnesses if I killed him now, no one to argue if I said it'd been self-defense. He'd abducted two girls, abused them, murdered at least one in the most horrific fashion. He was certainly irredeemable. The world would be better off without him. I raised the hammer over my head, but as I prepared to swing, I thought of Harry.

Enough.

I heard the word in my head. It didn't come in Harry's voice, or even Bart's. It was mine. I dropped the hammer. I picked up my firearm and holstered it, swaying, my head throbbing. I considered handcuffing Davis but immediately saw that for the foolishness it was. There was no tying up this man.

I thought I heard sirens as I raced outside, fighting nausea, but I didn't know what was real anymore. I stared back at the white farmhouse with its blue trim. Lily wasn't in there. I knew that, but still, I shouted for her.

"Lily!"

Sunlight sparked off something in the woods a couple hundred yards away. I squinted. A wheelbarrow sat just inside the tree line. I raced toward it, panic and pain making me stumble. Behind the wheelbarrow I spotted a fresh mound of dirt.

"Lily!" I yelled. "Lily Larsen, are you in there?"

I dropped to my knees and started digging with my hands. It would take too long. I raced to the shed, grabbed the dirty shovel Davis had used to bury her, and galloped as fast as I could back to the hole, fighting light-headedness. My chest and throat were hot, and I realized I was crying. I pushed on, flew at the mound, moving dirt furiously until my heart was about to explode. Lily was in there. Was she still alive? Could she hear me?

"Lily!" I screamed. "Hang on!"

The keen of the police sirens reached me, yet I kept digging. When I felt hands on me, I fought them.

"Van, let us help!"

It was Kyle and Comstock and a uniform. All three carried folding shovels. They were digging. Digging like it was their own daughter down there.

CHAPTER 59

Van

Harry appeared and pulled me away from the dirt. I tried to push him off until I realized there was only so much space to dig. It was best for Lily that I step back.

"An ambulance is on the way," he said, examining my head and then my hands. Two vehicles—one a Minneapolis PD cruiser, the other Harry's—had pulled in behind mine, their doors still open. Kyle had called in the troops. They'd raced here.

"I didn't dig with them long enough to hurt them," I said. The words sounded fuzzy. I was slipping into shock. There wasn't much time. "Can you trust me on one more thing?"

Harry was still holding my hands, palms up. They were caked with dirt.

"All right," he said.

I tugged him toward the shed, talking as we jogged. "Jack Davis is in there. I knocked him out with a hammer."

Harry held his tongue.

"He could be the poster child for Ehlers-Danlos syndrome," I said, my voice reedy. It felt like I was running through marshmallow. "He's going to slip out of any cuffs. When he comes to, he needs a padded transport plus constant supervision, or he'll escape. That's for later. For right now, we need a crowbar from the shed."

"Got it," Harry said, unclipping the walkie-talkie from his belt as he ran alongside me. It crackled and buzzed as he relayed my instructions. He finished the message just as we entered the shed.

Davis was still splayed out on the floor, his legs facing down and his torso facing up, blood pooling beneath his head. He looked like a mannequin, his body bent and deformed, but his chest was rising and falling with breath. I fought the urge to kick him as I grabbed two crowbars off the wall and tossed one to Harry.

He caught it and followed me into the farmhouse and up the stairs. I charged into the first bedroom off the landing, stared at the floor, and felt my guts twist. It was the room from my nightmares. I fell to my knees and gently inserted the end of my crowbar into a floorboard.

"Help me," I said, "but be careful. It's under one of these."

Harry dropped down and got to work. "Are we looking for a weapon, or a diary, or something to connect Jack Davis to the Taken Ones?" he asked, wincing as a floorboard screamed when he removed it.

"No," I said. "It's a—"

"Holy shit," Harry whispered.

I'd never heard him swear before. I looked over to see him staring, pancake-eyed, into the space below the floorboard he'd removed. Beneath was a baby bundled in a flowered blanket, her mouth covered with a silver strip of duct tape, her long-lashed eyes wet and quivering. He released the crowbar as if all the strength had gone out of his arms. It landed with a clang.

I rushed to his side, reaching for the infant, cradling her to my chest, not entirely sure she was real. I began crooning to her and rocking as I delicately removed the tape one tiny corner at a time.

"They're connecting," I said, my voice laced with reverence. "The visions are connecting to the cases."

My tears flowed freely, matching Harry's.

CHAPTER 60

Van

Lily was unconscious but breathing when Kyle and Comstock pulled her out of her grave. That she was alive was a miracle for many reasons, most notably because Jack Davis a.k.a. Garrick McCormick hadn't bothered with the breathing chamber. Nothing so fancy for Lily. It was Amber refusing to give up her baby and Lily standing up for her that had set McCormick off. Until that point, they'd both been docile, Lily reported, sounding as bewildered by her story as the world would surely be.

She explained as much as she could.

"He told us no one wanted us but him," she said, her hospital bed angled so she could sit up. She still carried traces of the girl she'd been around the edges of her face, the set of her chin. The nurses said she'd refused to release the infant since she'd been wheeled out of the examination room, where they'd both had their bruises looked over and their vitals taken before being pronounced healthy, all things considered. "We were so little. I guess we grew up in the shape of what he told us."

"You survived," I said, her words reaching down to my bones. Your captor abuses and brainwashes you until your own fears ultimately imprison you; he doesn't even need to be around for his evil to do its work. That's why I'd stayed at Frank's Farm until they took us away. Why Lily and Amber had never been able to escape. "That's what's important."

Lily dropped her eyes. She knew Amber hadn't made it. It was the first thing she'd asked when she regained consciousness.

With Lily's permission, her mother and sister had been called. Theresa and Charles Kind had also been informed of their grandchild and were on their way. I hoped they wouldn't take her from Lily right away.

Rue fell to her knees sobbing when she realized her sister was holding a baby. She and Rita kept patting Lily and the infant like they couldn't believe they were real, Rue's hand finding Lily's and gripping it tightly. The three of them were strangers to each other, but their ache for more was palpable. I hoped they could find their way back to family.

Harry and I recorded the broad strokes of Lily's story before leaving the three of them to their reunion. We would collect the rest of the information tomorrow. Garrick McCormick was in protective custody in the same hospital. He'd be under 24-7 surveillance. Agents were combing his property at this very moment.

Harry and I had a mountain of paperwork to do, if I still had a job. But first, I needed rest.

We had to wade through a huge presser outside the hospital, one Comstock was leading. He was just finishing up. I didn't care that he was getting the glory—well, I hardly cared—but I didn't want to talk to him. I thought I spotted Jacob Peters, Rue's elementary school classmate, in the dispersing crowd. I hoped so. Rue was going to need all the friends she could get.

"Reed!" Comstock yelled as he jogged over to us.

I would have kept walking, but Harry's expression stopped me.

"He might have something useful," he said.

I scowled, which tugged at the healing skin beneath the bandage on my forehead.

"Fine," I said.

"I need to talk to you," Comstock said when he reached us. He was wearing his best gray suit, sharp tie surely chosen by his wife, his slicked hair particularly shiny. "Just you," he said to me, flashing Harry a look.

"I'll meet you at the car," Harry said.

Comstock waited until Harry was out of earshot. "I know you know about me and Theresa," he said quietly, his back to the press corps, who were starting to leave. "She was the one who sold my wife and me our house. That's how we met. I want you to know that my wife and I didn't partake in those parties, though. We had a bad marriage, not an open one. I regret the affair, but it happened. There you go."

He made a face like that was the end of it. The sun shone hot and bright overhead. Upstairs, Lily, Rue, and Rita were likely trying to assemble the thousand-piece puzzle of their shattered lives.

"You were in Theresa's house the day the girls disappeared?" I asked, not bothering to lower my voice. My head throbbed, I was rubber-bone tired, and no way was I going to let this slide.

Comstock rubbed his chin. Nodded. "Yeah," he said. "Amber walked in on us hugging. Theresa kicked me out. I came back later. Saw what a terrible job the cops were doing."

"And you didn't intervene?"

He puffed himself up. "A man is responsible for his own actions. Not the actions of others."

"Saying it doesn't make it true," I said.

Comstock glanced over his shoulder, at the uniform who'd helped dig out Lily and who was getting his photo taken. "I called Chandler. Told him I'm fine sharing this collar with you. Said I'd be happy to work with you again."

I laughed out loud. "Just like you talked to the Leech Lake and Crowville cops and told them to cover up the fact that you were the reason Amber went into the woods that day? Taking your boot off someone's neck doesn't make you a hero, Comstock."

He frowned. He looked like he wanted to say more, but instead he turned and marched away. I was willing to bet it was the smartest thing he'd done all week. I hoped not to see him for a while, but Minneapolis was a small town.

CHAPTER 61

Van

Harry wouldn't let me drive myself home because of the head injury. I could tell he wanted to come up to my apartment when he pulled in front of the building.

"I'll be fine," I said. "I just need a shower, aspirin, and about a million hours of sleep."

He leaned in close. It took me a moment to realize he was studying my pupils.

"How's it look?" I asked.

The first wrinkle I'd ever seen on his face appeared between his eyebrows. I fought the urge to touch it. "No signs of a concussion yet," he said, "but it can take up to forty-eight hours. I can stay with you."

"Un-unh," I said, sliding out of his car. "The doctor checked me out at the hospital. Said I was probably fine and told me what to look for."

"Van?"

I turned so quickly I almost gave myself whiplash. Had uptight Harry Steinbeck just called me the informal version of my name? "What did you say?"

Something like a smile played across his lips. "Pick up the phone if you need me, okay?"

The sudden warmth in my chest made me uncomfortable. "My car's still at Davis's farm. It's either you or a Lyft who's my next call."

He nodded. "I'll pick you up tomorrow. Eight a.m."

"Thanks," I said.

I meant for everything. I think he knew that.

❖

Sleep, like hunger, has a point where if you go too long without, your body no longer wants it. I was miles past that point, so rather than lie down, I stripped off my clothes and took a long, hot shower. The water ran red with blood and black with dirt before turning muddy, then eventually running clear. I stepped out and toweled off. Then I put salve and bandages on my knees and the cut on my forehead, which was already looking better.

Wrapping a towel around my body, I stepped into my living room.

Harry had been correct: I was filthy.

And for the first time in my life, the clutter felt suffocating. I pulled on a sports bra and boxer shorts and dug in, falling into the soothing rhythm of physical work. I began by gathering all my dirty clothes into a pile, stripping my sheets, and hauling it all to the basement laundry. It took three trips and filled six washing machines. While the clothes and bedding swirled, I returned to my apartment and began hauling out garbage. Stacks of pizza boxes. Piles of chip bags. Tossed napkins. I paused only to move my clothes into the dryer before returning to garbage removal. Things that were neither trash nor dirty clothes, like my winter gear or a sentimental gift from Bart, went into a box and then into my storage closet in the apartment's underground garage.

Once I could see my floor, I went in, wiping out the fridge and the cupboards and the closets, emptying the dishwasher and filling it with a new load as I worked. After I'd scrubbed every visible and interior surface, I tied towels to my knees and dropped to the floor to scrub, using a toothbrush to get into the cracks.

The sun was coming up as I finished, the cut on my head only an uncomfortable ache.

I turned to look at my apartment. It was clean. It felt safe.

It was mine.

I couldn't tell if it was the beginning of something, or the end.

CHAPTER 62

Van

Harry was on time, of course, and so handsome he took my breath away.

"You didn't sleep at all, did you?" he asked as I slid into his car.

"Hey," I said, mock offended. I pointed at my hair. "It's still wet from my second shower in twelve hours. I think I'm doing pretty well."

He didn't respond, instead pulling out into traffic. We were on our way to check in on Lily and the infant, but I sensed something else was on his mind.

"What is it?" I asked, not sure that I wanted the answer.

He drove in silence for several more seconds. Finally: "That potential Sweet Tea Killer witness I told you about? The fellow who saw a woman coming out of Lester Dunne's? He's agreed to meet with us today. After we check in on the Larsens."

So it had been an ending, me cleaning my apartment.

Something like peace settled over me.

Guilt had been hunting me for months. Maybe there'd be relief in getting caught, the same reprieve I'd seen on Devries's face when I made him drink the poison. The worst part was that once I was in prison, I wouldn't be able to repay Harry for his friendship by helping him search for his sister, not unless they let me use the computers.

Seemed unlikely.

"All right," I said.

Harry glanced over at me and then smiled a sad smile.

❖

Two uniformed police officers stood outside Lily's door. She would likely be sent home today, either to her mother's or her sister's. The MPD would protect her from the press and any disturbed individuals who liked to follow violent crime, at least until she was settled.

Harry and I showed the officers our badges and entered Lily's room. It was full of balloons, flowers, and cards, the hospital's sterile scent no match for the smell of roses and sunflowers.

"It's a lot, I know." Lily lay in her bed, the infant in her arms. She appeared drawn, her skin ashen, yellowing bruises along her arms indicating the struggle she'd put up. She'd suffered immeasurable trauma. But she had a fire in her eyes.

"People care about you and the baby," I said. Harry and I were the only other people in the room. "Where's your mom and sister?"

The baby made a whimpering sound. Lily gently rocked her. "The cafeteria, I think. It was hard for them to leave, but . . ." Her eyes flicked up, then back at the infant.

"You're not used to so many people," I offered.

"That's it," she said, smiling gratefully. The expression wiped ten years off her face.

I was again reminded of the child she had been, with her two blonde pigtails and a freckled nose. The freckles had faded, and her cheeks had hollowed, but against all odds, there was something *hopeful* about her. Johnna had brought up Elizabeth Smart when the team was discussing how a person could be held captive close to their home without trying to escape. What hadn't been mentioned was that Elizabeth Smart claimed her story in a book and advocated for victim rights, including in front of Congress. It was early, but I could see a similar path for Lily.

"The Kinds are letting me keep Daisy," she said, staring lovingly at the child in her arms. "Until they decide what to do. It might not be forever, I know that. Don't worry."

Somebody must have already cautioned her on that front. I threaded my way through the plants and flowers, pushing aside balloons, until I was by her side. "May I touch your shoulder?" I asked her.

She appeared startled, then nodded.

I laid my hand on her as gently as I could. Her eyes, when they met mine, were both fierce and sorrowful. Lily was a survivor. "You've taken wonderful care of Daisy. I talked to the doctor. He said she's completely healthy."

Lily nodded, her chin quivering.

"You're going to have a lot of information coming at you, a lot of new experiences, and I want you to know you can call"—I hesitated here; I didn't want to make a promise I couldn't keep, and what happened in a few hours would decide whether I'd have the freedom to accept calls—"us at the BCA if we can do anything."

"It's true," Harry said, striding to the other side of the bed, his pen already out. "I'm going to write my personal cell on the back of this card. You can call anytime, day or night. I mean that."

Steady Harry, with the sincerest blue eyes I'd ever seen.

"Thanks," Lily said, taking the card with her free hand. She was being polite. I could see she was already retreating. This was a world she did not know, peopled with strangers who she thought had no idea what it was like to grow up in terror.

"I was raised on a commune," I said. "Frank's Farm."

I was hyperaware of Harry's presence in the room. Every inch of me wanted to run and hide, but I fought it. I wanted him to have a piece of the real me.

"Frank was a psychopath who regularly abused all of us. He destroyed my sister Veronica, holding her underwater until she was brain-dead. I stood by and watched it happen, and I never left to get her help even though I could have." I tasted the salt of my own tears.

"But I'm out now," I said, my hand still on her shoulder and my eyes pinned on it because if I looked at Lily or Harry I'd lose my courage. "And I get to make different choices, my *own* choices. I make some really, really bad ones, but I keep trying to figure out how to be in this world. So will you, Lily. You've got the strength. It's in your eyes, in the fight you had that kept you alive all these years, in the way you're going to keep doing whatever it takes to protect Daisy."

I heard a sob and thought for a moment it was me, but it wasn't. It was Lily.

"You see me," she said, her voice barely a whisper.

"I do. You're strong and you're beautiful," I said, and it was true. "It's not going to be easy, but everything's going to be all right, Lily."

Everything's going to be all right, Veronica.

Lily put out her arm for me, and I gently leaned into her. Together, she and I held the baby and each other.

CHAPTER 63

Van

"What'd Chandler decide he's going to do to you?" I asked Harry as he drove us away from the hospital. Lily would be discharged later today. It had been decided she would live with Rue. I couldn't think of a better person to care for Lily and Daisy.

"About Rodin, I mean," I continued. "He couldn't possibly have bought that drive-by story."

Harry exited off Interstate 94. The supposed Sweet Tea Killer witness we were going to interview, Eric Lund, lived in Dinkytown, a neighborhood near the University of Minnesota that skewed young.

"Nothing," he said. "Except watch me more closely until he loses interest. The call was clean, as far as Chandler is willing to admit."

He kept his eyes on the road. "You saved them," he said. "You know that, don't you? Marie Rodin's children and husband. Lily and Daisy. You saved them all."

"But you can't ever save them all, can you?" I asked.

I felt dreamy, detached from myself. It was weird, being driven to my unmasking by Harry. That would be the hardest part, the disappointment on his face when he realized I was a murderer. But Lily and the rest were safe. Frank Roth was still out there somewhere, but Garrick McCormick and Marie Rodin were off the streets. Those were the things that I'd hang on to.

"You're trembling," Harry said, reaching over the seat to grab a yellow cashmere cardigan. It was the softest thing I'd ever felt, and it smelled pure and clean, just like him.

"Thanks," I said, snuggling into it. "You think this Lund kid really saw the killer?"

"It's possible," Harry said.

"You know . . ." I began. "I'm grateful for everything you've done. You've been a good . . . a good partner."

"You too," he said matter-of-factly. "You're an excellent agent. But you're talking like we'll never work together again. It's your injury and fatigue. Some rest is going to do you wonders."

My sigh was pure melancholy.

"This is it," Harry said.

He parked in front of a Dinkytown duplex that looked like it'd been built by Dr. Seuss, all veering angles and bright colors. A young man I assumed was Lund waited for us on the front porch of the ground-floor unit. He was white with locs, wearing a tie-dyed V-neck shirt and matching sweatpants, their colors blurry.

He stood when we approached. He looked nervous. I'd seen it before. The law in theory—at least when they weren't after you—seemed reasonable. When they were marching up to your doorstep, though, with the authority vested in the job, your perspective tended to change abruptly.

"Mr. Lund?" Harry asked.

"Yeah, man, that's me." Lund scratched at his scalp. "Harry Steinbeck?"

"Yes. This is Agent Reed. Thank you for emailing us."

"It's like, no problem," Lund said. "Just doing my part. When I read about that murder, I couldn't sit on what I knew, dig? I saw the killer plain as day. Plain as these two hands." He held them out for Harry and me to see.

I cleared my throat. "What did she look like?" I asked, stepping forward, my shoulders set. I tipped my face up so he could see it clearly. "The woman you saw leaving?"

Lund aggressively nodded. "Right on. Let's get to it. She was *old*, man. So old. An old, old lady."

The laugh came up my throat so loudly and so quickly that it sounded like a bark. "What else?" I asked, wheezing.

The kid smiled in response. "It's weird, right? An old lady murdering people. That's about it. Just that she was old. Hair was all tucked under a hat. Sunglasses on. Not really short, but not super tall, either. I don't remember much more, but if you showed me a lineup, I know I could pick her out. She chilled me, man. Made me wish I had a dog. I had a good pup when I was a kid. Saint Bernard. He was my best friend. Walked him every day. Can't afford a dog like that these days, you know? It's an expensive breed. But man would I love him if I had him. He could go on deliveries with me!"

I almost hugged the kid but caught myself just in time. So this was what it felt like to land in the net of grace. I would not waste this. I stepped forward and offered Lund two cards. "One's my phone number," I said. "Call if you think of anything else about the woman you saw. Second is the number to the Minneapolis Animal Haven. They have a brilliant dog there named MacGuffin. He's half–Saint Bernard. His adoption costs will be covered, and there'll be a big bag of dog food waiting for you. He's old, but he's got a lotta love left to give."

"Right on!" Lund said, bobbing with joy as he took both cards. "Really appreciate it."

Harry was quiet as we made our way back to the car.

"People see what they want to see, don't they?" I asked as I buckled myself in. I felt like I could fly.

"What's that?" he asked.

"We all see the world through our own lens. Who knows what's old to that kid, or if he even saw someone? I'm glad we checked this out, though. Thanks for asking me along."

"Yeah," Harry said.

On impulse, I squeezed his arm. The electric jolt caught me off guard. I never touched him. I never used to touch anyone.

"I'm thinking about taking a yoga class," I said. "Want to join me?"

EPILOGUE

Harry

Harry Steinbeck glanced to his left to hide his smile.

This was the first time Evangeline had asked him to accompany her outside of work.

She'd been vulnerable at the hospital, too, letting down her guard for Lily's benefit. He felt honored to have witnessed it. She was a puzzle, Evangeline Reed. He recognized many of her behaviors as trauma responses, but her brilliance? Her warmth, when she allowed it to shine through? Those were all her. And then there was her otherworldly insight. He was still shaken by her knowing about Marie Rodin, and then the infant beneath the floorboards. There had to be a logical explanation for both, and he looked forward to learning what it was.

Once she was ready to tell him.

But first, he needed to tell her something about himself.

"There's something you need to know," he said. He pulled back onto 94, focusing on the traffic. "It has direct bearing on our job."

When he'd successfully merged, he looked over at Evangeline. She was fast asleep, her neck at an awkward angle, her mouth open wide enough to catch flies. Harry read his gas gauge. The tank was nearly full, enough to drive for four hours if he kept the braking to a minimum. He mentally mapped out the route with the fewest stops.

He'd tell her his secret another time.

He liked things as they were right now, with the two of them friends, her thinking of him as a good man.

ACKNOWLEDGMENTS

Big thanks to Jessica Tribble Wells at Thomas & Mercer, who is my literal partner in crime. She makes all my books better, but she straight up midwifed this one. Charlotte Herscher, thank you for your brilliant combination of guidance and support; please always be my developmental editor. Jon, my writer friends are jealous I have such a magnificent copyeditor, one who cheers when I (correctly) write *Dr Pepper* without a period. Thank you for your service. And if Jon isn't gift enough, I also had Kellie as the final eyes on this manuscript. Her attention to detail and familiarity with the *Chicago Manual of Style* are unsurpassed. All remaining errors are mine alone, left because I "like how it sounds" (sorry, Kellie).

Jill Marsal, how do you manage to be an agent, editor, business partner, and cheerleader all at once? No one is happier for my successes, and no one has been more instrumental in making them happen; thank you. Jessica Morrell, not one of my books has gone out into the world without you taking a pass at it; I'm grateful for your time and talent.

I owe a debt of gratitude to Ann Marie Gross, BCA forensic scientist extraordinaire, for being generous with her vast knowledge (and for having great taste in breweries). All errors are my own, made either in service of the story or because I was too clueless to know better. While it's true that the BCA has a cold case division, and while the history of the BCA as presented here is accurate, the day-to-day operations of

Cold Case and general workings of the BCA in this book are a product of my imagination.

If you have information on a Minnesota cold case or any case, you are encouraged to call the BCA tip line at 1-877-996-6222 or email bca.coldcase@state.mn.us. You may also submit an anonymous tip via their online web form.

To my dear friends Cindy and Christine: thanks for keeping me solid. Shannon, Erica Ruth, Susie, and Lori, you're the best squad a writer could ask for. Shannon, your emails and texts are like candy along the trail; thank you for being hilarious and huge-hearted. Carolyn, our writing time is one of my favorite parts of the job.

Last but not least, Zoë and Xander: I love you, babies. You'll always be my best work.

ABOUT THE AUTHOR

Photo © 2018 CK Photography

Jess Lourey is the Amazon Charts bestselling author of *The Quarry Girls*, *Litani*, *Bloodline*, *Unspeakable Things*, *The Catalain Book of Secrets*, the Salem's Cipher thrillers, and the Mira James mysteries, among many other works, including short stories, young adult fiction, and nonfiction. Winner of the Anthony and Thriller Awards, Jess is also an Edgar, Agatha, and Lefty Award–nominated author; TEDx presenter; *Psychology Today* blogger; and recipient of The Loft's Excellence in Teaching fellowship. Check out her TEDx Talk for the true story behind her debut novel, *May Day*. She lives in Minneapolis with a rotating batch of foster kittens (and occasional foster puppies, but those goobers are a lot of work). For more information, visit www.jessicalourey.com.